About the Author

Patricia Scanlan was born in Dublin, where she still lives. Her books have sold worldwide and have been translated into many languages. Patricia is the series editor and a contributing author to the *Open Door* series. She also teaches creative writing to second-level students and is involved in Adult Literacy.

Find out more by visiting Patricia Scanlan on Facebook.

D1150535

Also by Patricia Scanlan

Apartment 3B
Finishing Touches
Foreign Affairs
Promises, Promises
Mirror Mirror
Francesca's Party
Two for Joy
Double Wedding
Divided Loyalties
Coming Home

Trilogies

City Girl
City Lives
City Woman

Forgive and Forget
Happy Ever After

Love and Marriage

Patricia
SCANLAN

With All My Love

SIMON &
SCHUSTER

London · New York · Sydney · Toronto · New Delhi

A CBS COMPANY

First published in Great Britain by Simon & Schuster UK Ltd, 2013
A CBS Company
This paperback edition published 2014

Sailor
Words & Music by Fini Busch, David West & Werner Scharfenberger
© Copyright 1961 Universal/MCA Music Limited.
All Rights Reserved. International Copyright Secured.
Used by permission of Music Sales Limited.

Seeman
Words & Music by Werner Scharfenberger & Fini Busch
© 1959 Hermann Schneider Buehnen-Musikalienverlags (AUME)
All Rights Reserved

1 3 5 7 9 10 8 6 4 2

Simon & Schuster UK Ltd
1st Floor
222 Gray's Inn Road
London WC1X 8HB

www.simonandschuster.co.uk

Simon & Schuster Australia, Sydney
Simon & Schuster India, New Delhi
A CIP catalogue record for this book is available from the British Library

PB ISBN: 978-1-47116-323-4
EBOOK ISBN: 978-1-47111-079-5

Typeset by Hewer Text UK Ltd, Edinburgh
Printed and bound in Great Britain by CPI Group (UK) Ltd, Croydon, CR0 4YY

I dedicate this book with huge gratitude to the following men who have enhanced my house and my life. Their professionalism and good-humoured kindness was much appreciated. So to Mark Kennedy and Dara Mulhern for the lovely plans and to Philip Halton and James Igoe (the apostles) of Halton Construction, and their terrific team, Doril, Tomas, Robbie, Mark, Bruce, Rupert, Eddie and the gang, you did a fantastic job and I'm very grateful to all of you. XXX

Dublin

November 12th, 2012

Dear readers,

It's been more than twenty-two years since *City Girl*, my first novel, was published and I wanted to thank you for all your support down the years. You have been such loyal readers and I'm so grateful to all of you.

To my new readers, a warm welcome also. I hope you enjoy *With All My Love* as much as I enjoyed writing it and that you will like my other books.

I am now on Facebook and to all of my readers who have contacted me there, a big thank you. I love being able to interact with you and keep you updated about events and signings and the progress of my novels as I'm writing them. And it's great getting your feedback and hearing your news.

So, dear readers, Enjoy! Enjoy! Enjoy!

With all my love,
Patricia xxx

When the heart weeps for what is lost. The spirit laughs for what it has found.

Sufi saying

PROLOGUE

He could feel the heat of the sun streaming over him, and had a flash of vibrant memory of lying with his brother in a field of prickly golden stubble, the scent of new-cut straw filling his nostrils, the drone of the tractor fading as it drove away, towing its bounty of neat bales to the nearby farm.

As adrenalin surged through him he raised his face to the blue immensity of sky, reaching higher, higher, every muscle, ligament and fibre protesting as he strained to reach his target. His hands curved around the hard leather of the ball and Jeff felt a rush of emotions, triumph, joy, and deep satisfaction that nothing else in life could equal. Every aching bone, every second of weary exhaustion from the punishing training regime he followed was worth it for this moment.

The roar of the crowd lifted him higher. The shiny red faces of the men he soared over, a blur in the bright sunlight. If only Valerie were here to see this, he thought with a brief pang of regret as his hands tightened around his prize and he plotted the optimum trajectory towards the goalmouth. But Valerie didn't like football. She resented the time he spent training. He should be spending it with her and their young daughter, she'd say. He hated how she made him feel guilty about his passion. It took the good out of moments like this. He twisted on the downward descent, elbowing his marker in the shoulder as he tried to grab the ball from him, clearing his way to prepare his onslaught on the box.

The pain hit, gripping him like a vice, forcing the breath out of his lungs, and bringing him to his knees. The roar of the crowd faded. Surprise and shock staggered him. He crumpled to the ground and saw the blue of the sky briefly before the darkness enveloped him.

And then it seemed that only a moment had passed and brightness bathed him in a soft light as he opened his eyes and felt a wondrous sense of wellbeing. Thank God for that, Jeff thought, relieved. He felt so well, so fit, so . . . so . . . *perfect*. Perhaps he'd imagined that brief, shocking jolt of pain. Or maybe he was in hospital and they had injected him. That must be it. He had no memory of getting there, no memory of being in an ambulance. He must have been out like a light.

Had they won the match? He'd liked to have scored that goal; it would have been a beauty, one of his best, he mused, feeling utterly relaxed. Whatever they'd given him was working a treat. The light drew closer and his eyes widened . . .

Everything was going to be absolutely fine, Jeff knew as he recognized his beloved grandmother coming towards him, smiling at him as he took her outstretched hand.

CHAPTER ONE

Briony McAllister felt the glorious heat of the Mediterranean sun on her upturned face as she contemplated the cobalt sky above her and felt the tension ease out of her body, dissipating into the soft green tartan rug she was lying on. Little cotton puffs of clouds drifted over the sharp-ridged peaks of the sierras to the north, and the breeze whispered through the pine trees.

Beside her, her 4-year-old daughter, Katie, was engrossed in plaiting her Moxie Girl's hair. It was a Sunday afternoon in September and a somnolent, peaceful air pervaded the Parque Princessa Diana, a pretty park on the Costa del Sol. Katie had wanted to go there instead of the beach, the swings and modest playground being a big attraction. Thankfully, she was now happy to play with her dolls after twenty minutes of blissful soaring back and forth on the swings, and Briony was content to lie drowsily in the late afternoon sun, her novel unopened beside her.

Riviera, a small town on Spain's southern coast, was empty of tourists, who had long gone back to their jobs and mundane lives, their Costa holiday a faded summer's dream. Where once older couples and retired ex-pats would have filled the many restaurants and coffee shops,

the recession had ensured that the Costa del Sol was deci-
mated after many years of lavish boom. Briony knew full
well the effects of economic collapse. She, too, should
have been back behind her desk, dealing with the thousand and one queries that came with being an adminis-
trator in a busy private hospital. But life as she knew it
had changed completely the day, two months previously,
when the owners of the Olympus Sports clinic had called
staff together and told them that due to the current
economic climate and falling patient numbers, redun-
dancies would have to be made.

Briony knew, even before it was her turn to meet with
HR, that she would be one of the staff to be 'let go'. She
had been last into the department, having left a similar
position in a big teaching hospital the previous year to
work nearer home and closer to her daughter's crèche.

Briony sighed and brushed away a mosquito that had
taken a fancy to her lightly tanned flesh. The truth was
that with all the cuts in her salary in the last couple of
years, the prohibitive crèche fees had taken most of what
was left, and now that she was redundant she and her
husband, Finn, were almost no worse off with her dole
money, especially without having to pay for child-
minding. They had decided after much discussion that
for the next year, before Katie started school, Briony
would be a stay-at-home mother.

It was disconcerting adjusting to her new circumstances. Strange not having to get up at the crack of dawn
and wake her daughter from sleep to feed and dress her
before dropping her off at the crèche, greeting the other
equally stressed, bleary-eyed parents she had got to
know. And then making the bumper-to-bumper commute

to work, hoping that she would get a parking place and not be last in, keeping her head down like a naughty schoolgirl and not a thirty-something, self-confident, career woman and working mother. She was still a 'working' mother, she thought defensively, realizing in these last few weeks how irritating the term was to mothers who could choose to stay at home and rear their children themselves.

Why *did* she feel guilty every morning, though, when she and Katie shared cuddles in bed when Finn had left for work? It was such a treat having a leisurely breakfast and fascinating conversations with her 4-year-old. She had already missed so much of her child's development. When she'd worked in the clinic, the time they'd had together after Briony collected her from the crèche in the evenings was often ruined by teary tantrums and squabbles over bath-time and bedtime, both of them exhausted after their early start. It was all so different now, so much *fun*! But no doubt this, too, would change. It was still very new and different. She felt like she was playing truant from real life.

She was going to make the most of this unexpected blessing. It would be her gap year, Briony decided. This unemployment that had been foisted upon her would not diminish her. She would not allow herself to feel guilty that she wasn't contributing to the family income, or that she was taking money from the state. She had paid her hard-earned money week after week, in social insurance, for just this eventuality.

How she and her colleagues had complained bitterly about the previous government's atrocious handling of the economy and the 'brown envelope' mentality that pervaded every level of society from the top down, the avarice of bankers, politicians, developers and the so-called 'golden circle'. The negligence and incompetence of the so-called regulatory authorities, too, had led to the country being bankrupted and Briony and Katie's generation, and generations to come, would carry a huge burden of debt. For all the good their complaining did. Ordinary folk like them were being hammered while the people responsible were still living in their big houses, holidaying in the sun and paying outrageous sums for lavish weddings, at the expense of tax payers. Every tea-break there would be heated discussion of some new revelation of chicanery, or some new pay cut proposed, that would leave Briony and her friends despairing of how they were going to manage in the future and worry about what lay ahead for their children.

She hadn't wanted to be made redundant from her job. She had been perfectly willing to work, albeit, she conceded with hindsight, at the expense of her relationship with her daughter. But the old saying 'When one door closes another one opens' was true. Everything depended on the way you looked at things.

This time had been given to her and Katie to strengthen their bond and that was how she would view it. She no longer had money for life's luxuries; eating out was a thing of the past for them, where once they had dined out three or four times a week and not given it a second thought. Even buying books, glossy mags and make-up now required a 'Do I really need this?' debate, whereas before they would have been tossed willy-nilly into her supermarket trolley. She'd sold her Ford Focus reluctantly, trying not to cry when she'd seen it disappear down her street, and with it, the privileged life she'd taken for granted.

The upside now, thought Briony, was that she was no longer time poor. The speed on her life's treadmill had decelerated and she felt she was slowly exhaling years of stress and tension that juggling her life as a wife and mother, combined with holding down a job, had entailed.

Briony felt the knot that had been in her stomach since she had walked out of her office for the last time loosen another little bit as she lay in the sunshine, and the feelings of failure, guilt, helplessness and fear wafted away on the balmy breeze blowing across the sea from Africa, as the scent of jasmine and the chorus of birdsong sent her drifting off into drowsy slumber.

'Mom . . . Mom . . . I is hungry.' An indignant poke brought Briony back to wakefulness and she squinted up to see her daughter's indignant face hovering over hers. 'Can we have our picnic now?'

'Can we have our picnic now, *please*?'

'Can we have our picnic now, *pleeeease*?' Katie echoed exasperatedly and Briony managed to hide a grin as she struggled up into a sitting position and wrapped her little girl in a joyous hug.

'Let's have our feast then. I'm hungry too,' Briony smiled, nuzzling into Katie's neck. Her daughter smelled of suntan lotion and talc, and as Briony inhaled the scent of her she wished Finn was here to share their lazy Sunday afternoon.

They had spoken earlier. He was up to his eyes doing a last edit on a report he had written for his MD. He headed the export department of a large food producing company who were constantly looking for new foreign markets. He was good at his job and in the last year the company's revenue had bucked the trend as new markets in China and Brazil opened up. Ireland's booming export market was the one bright shining star on the gloomy economic horizon and Finn had never been busier.

Briony hated that he had to work so hard, but he was driven and enjoyed it. He had *urged* her to take the few weeks to help her mother settle into her new villa, despite Briony's protests that she didn't want to be away from him for too long. Had she still been working in the clinic, they would have been like ships that pass in the night. Funny how life had balanced out for them as a result of her redundancy, she mused, as she opened the picnic basket she'd brought with them and spread out the egg, and tuna salad sandwiches, and their absolute favourites, the pear and custard tartlets she'd bought from the bakery in the big Super Sol supermarket across the road. She and her mother, Valerie, had done a shop on the way from the airport the previous day and Briony still found the difference in food prices hard to believe. They had bought two huge fillets of salmon and a big bag of prawns for half the price she would have paid at home, and a bottle of Faustino was almost a third less than what she was used to paying.

The two weeks she was going to spend with her mother, helping her settle into the small beachside villa she had recently purchased, would not cost her a fortune; in fact she'd live far cheaper here than in Dublin. She watched as Katie busied herself putting sandwiches on two bright green plastic plates, revelling in this great new adventure. 'One for you, one for me,' she sang in a singsong voice, putting her juice bottle beside her Moxie Girl. Her Lalaloopsy doll, Jenny, had been left back at the villa as a punishment for some naughty deed. Katie was a very stern mother, and the dolls lived under a much stricter regime than Katie herself did, Briony thought, grinning as her daughter admonished her doll to 'sit up and eat properly and say thank you'.

Mother and daughter munched companionably on their sandwiches, Katie chattering away to her doll, sometimes singing, oblivious to all around her as she immersed herself in a scenario with her dolly that mimicked what was happening in her life right now. She had a vivid imagination and was a self-sufficient little girl who could entertain herself for hours on end. Even so, Briony longed to get pregnant again, to give her daughter a sibling. She didn't want there to be too big an age gap between her children should she be blessed with another baby.

Briony savoured the creamy egg sandwich, a hazy memory of picnics she'd had in her own childhood floating into her mind. Picnics on a golden beach under the cliff at the end of her grandparents' house. She could remember the gritty grains of sand mixing with the egg as the breeze whipped the sand around them. Sadness pricked like an unexpected wasp sting as she remembered her grandmother, Tessa. She had loved her father's mother with all the love her child's heart could muster, and she had been greatly loved in return. And then the indescribable shock of separation, of being told by Valerie that Gramma Tessa didn't want to see them any more. The grief of that bereavement equalled the pain of the loss of her dad. Briony's eyes darkened at the memory and she brushed it away, annoyed that it still had the power to wound, even after all these years. It was a long, long time ago. Looking back only brought unhappiness and pain, and what was the point of that? For all she knew, the woman could be dead. She knew nothing of her father's family now.

And yet, she had been curious when, earlier, she'd unpacked a box of photo albums and tatty brown A4 envelopes full of old photos curling at the edges. Black-and-white ones, faded Kodak colour prints, and memory cards of long-dead relatives she didn't know. Now that she had a child of her own she had become more inter-ested in her family history; the time would come when Katie would want to know more of her family back-ground. Valerie had always hated talking about the past and wasn't very forthcoming when Briony quizzed her, but the photos would give her an excuse to bring up the subject.

She was looking forward to sitting out on the patio over a glass of chilled wine, the comforting shushing of the sea as it feathered the beach below them in the background, and studying this tapestry of her and Valerie's lives.

She'd not been able to resist bringing one of the old-fashioned albums with her to the park. A photo of her father and mother had caught her eye. Snuggled close together, laughing, her father squinting into the camera as the sun caught him, looking so handsome and vital next to Valerie, petite and tanned, in a pretty blue sundress and making a face at whoever was taking the photo. Probably Lizzie, Valerie's best friend, and Briony's godmother.

Idly, she finished off her sandwich, took a slug of fresh orange juice and reached into her beach bag to pull out the album with its garish plastic cover of pink daisies and splashes of yellow. A torn brown A4 envelope fell out from the back flap and a pale blue envelope slid half-way out of it. She was about to put it back when she saw that it was addressed to her: *Miss Briony Harris, 12 Eldertree Road, Dublin 9.*

Eldertree Road, she noted, surprised. That was where Valerie and she had lived all those years ago when they had first moved back to Dublin before her mother had bought her own house. Who would have been writing to her there, and why had her mother never given her the letter? And why was the address written in a different pen and by a different hand from that of her name? The fine elegant cursive, written in blue ink, was neat, precise, the letters beautifully formed – script from a bygone era, she thought, studying it intently. No one wrote like that now. Why on earth were they writing to her, this person with the graceful old-fashioned writing? The address, however, was scripted in a rather untidy, less meticulous style.

She opened the thin envelope and eased out the two pages of closely written script, and for a surreal moment was sure she caught a hint of a long-remembered scent. Gramma Tessa had always worn perfume, and face cream. Briony could remember playing with the cosmetic jars on her grandmother's dressing table and Tessa daubing her face with Nivea and spraying her wrists with scent. Even to this day she could remember cuddling into her grandmother's shoulder, as Tessa sang *'Sugar and Spice and all things nice, that's what little girls are made of.'* That sweet distinctive smell that would forever remind her of a time when life was good and she was safe and happy.

'My Darling Briony,' she read as Katie hummed happily beside her, completely oblivious to her mother's mounting shock.

Slowly, shaking her head, Briony read and reread her grandmother's letter, so engrossed she hardly heard the 'Yoo-hoo!' that a slender blond-haired woman was hollering as she ran up the steps of the park.

Almost in a daze, Briony studied her mother, willowy and tanned, looking ten years younger than her fifty years as she waved at them.

'Hello, my darlings, are you enjoying your picnic?' she asked breezily, bending to kiss Katie and tracing a tender finger along her cheek.

'Valwee,' squealed Katie, throwing her arms around her.

The rush of bitterness that surged through Briony almost made her gag as she stood up.

'Having fun?' Valerie raised laughing eyes to her. The smile faded from her lips when she saw Briony's expression. 'What's wrong? Are you OK?' She straightened up and reached a hand out to touch her daughter.

'How *could* you, Mum?' Briony's voice was shaking, as was the hand that held the letter, the letter that revealed that her mother had betrayed her in the most cruelly grievous way. A letter that revealed a litany of lies, lies and more lies. A letter that showed that Valerie Harris was a heartless, selfish, cruel bitch, who was now standing in front of her pretending to be concerned.

'You make me sick,' Briony hissed, not wishing Katie to know that there was anything amiss.

Aghast at the venom in her daughter's voice, Valerie glanced at the letter in Briony's hand. Comprehension dawned. She paled under her tan.

'I can explain,' she said urgently, running her fingers through her blond bob. 'I did it for you, Briony. You must believe me. I can explain.'

CHAPTER TWO

She stands on the uneven cobblestones watching the small green and white tug nudge the enormous cargo ship up the wide mouth of the river towards its berth. The steady thrum of the engines, rhythmic, insistent, blends with the raucous shrieks of the gulls as they circle then swoop and dive into the choppy sea on some tasty titbit. The wind is getting up and she wishes she had brought her scarf. Behind her, down on the beach, the sand is whipping across the rocks, and shells and small bits of driftwood skitter along the strand, taking on a life of their own. The ship is looming closer and she turns to observe the action on deck as it passes before her, blocking out the view of the opposite shore.

She likes to come and watch the activity in the port: the toing and froing of ships and liners, the big ferries, regular as clockwork, the arrow-swift little pilot boats that race towards the open sea, always an indication that a ship is coming. And then, as the new arrival appears on the horizon, the sturdy dependable tugs chugging down the river, preparing to take charge, reassuring, she imagines, for a weary captain and crew at the end of a voyage.

This is her favourite place now. The place she comes to be peaceful and still. The place that she comes to escape.

The wind whips her grey hair around her face and she inhales deeply, enjoying the salty, bracing air. Great banks of leaden black clouds loom up over the trees and rooftops of Clontarf and Sutton across the bay. Howth is shadowed and grey. It will be raining soon. The ship ploughs past, churning up the water, almost home. The white caps of the wash slapping hard against the seawall and, as the ship heads up the river, soon to disappear from view, she turns and makes her way, with some difficulty, down the rocks and sand to the shelter of the beach that faces the Southside.

'Blackie!' She calls the black Labrador who has his nose stuck in a cleft trying to get at some buried treasure, a dead crab or fish head or some such. Tessa smiles as he lopes towards her, tail wagging furiously. 'Good boy, good boy,' she says, leaning down to stroke his dear face as he gazes at her with brown-eyed adoration. 'What would I do without you?' she murmurs, grateful beyond measure for his unconditional love, especially today of all days.

Even after all these years the memory of that warm September day is still clear and present whenever she resurrects it. Time has dulled the sharp edges of the pain, but it is always there in the background. She glances at her watch. It was around this time . . . She gazes unseeingly towards the mountains and Dun Laoghaire, lost to her memories.

The wind's keening and Blackie's bark at a plastic bag flying past him brings her back to reality and she pulls her parka around her. 'Come on, Blackie, come on, boy.' She hurries across the sand to where she has parked the car. Once she would have been able to run, she thinks ruefully. Her left knee aches and stiffens and she is glad when her dog is plonked on his rug on the back seat, chewing on a treat before settling for a snooze. He knows the routine; knows that she will pour herself a cup of tea from a flask and take out her pen and pad, and for a while his beloved mistress will be immersed, her pen flying over white paper, interspersed with mouthfuls of hot sweet tea and gingernut biscuits.

Tessa pours the tea into a plastic cup, looking forward to that first taste of the warming golden liquid. What is it about tea from a flask? she wonders as she screws on the white top and lays the flask on the passenger seat. She savours that first sip, holding the cup between her hands, the steaming heat a comfort as she stares across the sea to where rain has blotted out Sandymount and Dun Laoghaire, a sombre impressionist painting that does not have the glorious light of a Manet or Monet.

Tessa sighs and nibbles on her biscuit. She should go home, she has spent longer that normal walking Blackie. Lorcan will be querulous on her return, annoyed with her for being gone so long, especially today of all days. But she needs this break from him. She is the only one he can take his frustrations out on now. Chronic arthritic pain has turned him into an angry, frustrated old man. He was so vibrant and vigorous, even into his late sixties, and then came the grinding pain – like ivy strangling a tree, he'd once told her – and the slow, unremitting descent into decrepitude. Old age was the cruellest stage of all, the real test of 'for better, for worse'. She still loves her husband, and understands his frustration, but there are times now when she sometimes doesn't like him. She has pleaded with him for months to see a shoulder specialist and he has finally let her make an appointment. He could have saved himself a year of pain, and made her life much easier if he had not been so stubborn. Men can be so *irritating*, she thinks.

She finishes her tea, wipes the crumbs from her lap and hesitates, hand poised over the key in the ignition. The rain has reached her little haven and spitter-spatters blur the windscreen. Tessa glances at the clock on the dash. She really should be going; she doesn't want to get stuck in traffic. People out for a Sunday afternoon spin, dog walkers like herself, parents with kids who still have homework to do, will head for home now that the rain has come. She can see mothers on the beach, urging children to hurry as the rain grows heavier. It is dancing in fury on the roof of her car, a steady tattoo that increases her sense of being in her own safe little world.

Her notepad is sticking out of her bag; she pulls it out and roots for her pen. She settles herself more comfortably, shifting her weight to ease her knee and flips over the cover to a blank page.

'*My Darling Briony*,' she writes, yielding to her reluctance to go home, oblivious to the rain battering the car.

'*Today I think of you more than ever . . .*'

CHAPTER THREE

'Briony, there is so much you don't understand. We'll sit down and talk about it when we get home. Let's not upset Katie.' Valerie Harris laid a placatory hand on her daughter's arm, trying not to panic at the realization that one of her greatest fears had come to pass.

Briony shrugged it away. 'I'm booking a flight home,' she said coldly, busying herself with packing up the picnic things.

'Are you cross, Mom?' Katie paused from feeding her doll and glanced up at them, a little frown furrowing her brow.

'No, no. How about a last swing before we go back to the villa?' Briony suggested brightly.

'Yesssssssss! Valwee, will you mind Millie?' She thrust her doll into her grandmother's hand. Valerie looked down at her granddaughter and her heart contorted with love and pain at the sight of the innocent little face raised trustingly, with its cornflower-blue eyes and an adorable smattering of freckles across her nose.

'Of course I will, darling.' Valerie stroked Katie's flushed cheek.

Katie danced gaily over to the swing. 'Come on, Mom,' she called over her shoulder.

'We have to talk, Briony, on our own. At least let me—'

'Are Gramma and Granddad still alive?' Briony was stony-faced. Valerie felt she was being punched in the stomach when she saw the contempt in her eyes. '*Are they?*' her daughter persisted.

'Yes,' Valerie sighed. 'As far as I know both of them are still alive, yes.'

'And Dad, did you lie about *him*, too?' Briony fixed her with a hard, cold stare.

'*No!* No, of course *not*, Briony!' Valerie's voice shook. She struggled not to cry, appalled that her daughter would think that she would ever lie about Jeff.

'I will never forgive you for this, Mum, *ever*. And I won't be coming out here again with Katie. Let's see how *you* feel, knowing you'll never see *your* granddaughter again!' She marched across the grass, bristling, and Valerie watched her go with a sickening lurch to her stomach, and had to sit down on the rug. Her heart had begun to pound and she felt faint. She adored Katie. Katie had given her more joy than any other relationship in her life had. Even her relationship with Briony could not compete with the absolute, unconditional love she felt for her only grandchild.

For years she'd worried about this moment of reckoning. There had been a few close shaves, notably when Briony was getting married and had wanted to try to reconnect with Jeff's family, but Valerie had managed to put her off, and Briony, caught up in the wedding preparations, had accepted all she'd told her at face value.

Over time Valerie's anxiety had eased, and she didn't give the past too much thought. Today, of course, was different, she thought sadly. What an irony that Briony would discover her grandmother's letter on this, the anniversary of her father's death. It was so long ago, she thought distractedly. Twenty-six years today. Briony had been almost four and a half when her mother's life had been shattered.

She couldn't think straight. Valerie's mouth quivered and she had to stifle the sob that escaped as the memories of that dreadful day came roaring at her like a tsunami, enveloping her in wave after wave of grief and regret. Just when she'd finally thought life was good, and she could relax, the past had come back to confront her with a crushing intensity. The decisions she'd made, the lies she'd told, had returned to confront her and this time there was no avoiding them. Briony was so hurt and angry she would never listen to her mother's side of the story. And she *had* a side, Valerie thought sorrowfully. Everyone would think she was the worst mother in the world when it all came out, but she had her reasons, no matter what Tessa would say. And Tessa would have a lot to say, Valerie thought bitterly, remembering Jeff's mother.

Tessa had despised her. Behind the façade of motherly concern, Jeff's mother had only been nice to her because of Briony, not because she'd cared anything for Valerie. She had always known that Tessa had felt that she'd trapped Jeff by falling pregnant. Tessa had never felt that Valerie was good enough for her precious son.

It was partly thanks to Tessa that she had had to leave home with her young daughter and make a life for them far away from all that she had grown up with, Valerie thought bitterly. What would her life have been like if she had been able to stay in her home village with Briony? But Tessa had put paid to that, and when fate had intervened that glorious September day when Jeff had been taken from her so cruelly, and the future she had planned had been snatched away, all her dreams had been left in tatters.

CHAPTER FOUR

'You're very late,' Lorcan says crossly, lifting his head from his crossword. 'Lisa phoned. She'll be up tomorrow.'

'The traffic was heavy. The rain . . .' she sighs, stifling a rush of irritation. She's seventy-five, for God's sake, and she has to account for her time like some schoolgirl!

'How is Lisa?' she asks, wishing she could sit in her favourite chair and read the paper, but Lorcan's tea has to be got before she can relax.

'She's fine. She got a Mass said for Jeff. She said she'd ring later.'

'Did she put flowers on the grave?' Lisa, their eldest, is a loving, caring daughter who tries hard to support them as best she can, despite having three children in college and running her own crèche.

'I'm sure she did.' Lorcan lowers his glasses. 'You should have gone down to the grave yourself today. I know it gives you comfort. I just didn't feel up to going.'

'We'll go together one of the days.' Tessa pats his hand, and feels a pang of sympathy as she sees how mottled red, stained with liver spots, and knotted, twisted and swollen they are. Before arthritis distorted them, her husband's hands were firm, his long fingers capable of surprising tenderness. Those fingers had brought her much pleasure, she remembers, as a distant memory of joyous, abandoned lovemaking one stolen afternoon suddenly surfaces. Where did that come from? she wonders as she fills the kettle and takes the remains of the Sunday roast beef from the fridge to cut thin slices for a sandwich for her husband's tea.

Once, she and Lorcan had lived full, busy lives. They had been young, confident, resilient, and the future held no fears for them. They'd embraced parenthood enthusiastically and enjoyed their children until fate had taken their youngest son from them. Now there's always fear lurking, fear that Lorcan will be taken from her, fear that something will happen to her remaining children and grandchildren. Death has taught her that peace of mind is a myth.

Tessa holds out a cut of beef for Blackie and he scoffs it with relish before easing himself down into his basket beside Lorcan, to rest his head on his paws and observe proceedings.

'Where did you go?' Lorcan asks.

'The usual, the South Wall and the Shelley Banks.'

'Many there?'

'A few. I saw a ship arriving. It's a pity you didn't come, you would have enjoyed it.'

'Ah, I wasn't up to it today.'

They have this conversation every time. She tries not to get irritated with him. She thinks he has given in too easily and made an invalid of himself. There is no equality in their relationship now that she has become the minder. She cannot help her resentment.

She needs minding, too, she thinks mournfully, imagining how nice it would be to have her meals handed up to her day in, day out. She's fed up of cooking, after all these years: the sameness of it, the wondering what to have, the preparing of meat and vegetables, the dishing out and serving up – she could *scream* with the monotony of it. Lorcan won't even come out and have lunch at a pub or restaurant any more. It's all about him, now, Tessa thinks resentfully as she slathers mustard on the beef and lays the buttered slice of bread on top.

'Aren't you having any?' he asks when she calls him to the table.

'I'm not hungry.'

'Is it the day that's in it?' He lowers himself onto the chair, grimacing as pain shoots through him.

'I suppose.' She pours his tea.

'It's hard to believe he'd be in his fifties if he was alive,' Lorcan reflects, reaching out to squeeze her hand. That small gesture of unexpected tenderness is her undoing and the tears she has managed to suppress all day overflow. Her husband continues to hold her hand as she weeps. 'Better out than in, Tess,' he says gruffly. 'Sit down here beside me.'

'I can't stop thinking of Briony.' She hiccups, wiping her cheeks with the back of her hands as she sits down at the table. 'She's been on my mind all day.'

'Mine too,' Lorcan admits.

'I hope that Valerie can live with herself,' Tessa says bitterly. 'It was the sorry day she set her sights on Jeff. May God forgive her for what she's done to us.'

'She might say differently. She might say may God forgive *us* for what we did to *her*,' Lorcan says quietly.

'Lorcan! How can you say that?' Tessa pulls her hand away. She wants to pummel him.

'It wasn't all one-sided, Tessa, you know that; we played our part too.'

'Don't say that!' She jumps up from the table and marches into the hall and climbs the stairs. Lorcan has overstepped the mark this time, she fumes. How *dare* he suggest they are to blame for being separated from Briony? It is that horrible girl's fault that their grandchild has grown up not knowing them. Tessa might have told Valerie a few home truths when Jeff died but that was no reason to take Briony away from them in a fit of spite and malice that had left them doubly devastated after their son's death. Lorcan had no business to say that to her, no business at all, Tessa rages as she bangs the door of the bedroom and sits on the bed. It was cruel, mean and unkind after all the goodness and kindness she has shown him over the past few years.

She opens the top drawer of her bedside locker and takes out an envelope containing an old colour photo curling at the edges. A young man with warm brown eyes and a wide grin is cuddling a little girl, who is squinting and smiling straight into the camera, pointing a chubby finger. Tessa smiles in spite of herself. She remembers as though it was yesterday that warm sunny Sunday and the Indian summer they were enjoying.

'Gramma, Gramma, you didn't tell us to say "cheese",' Briony had chided, and they had all laughed.

It's the last photo she has of them. A few hours later her son is dead, and less than two months after that, Valerie Harris took Briony up to Dublin to live and she never saw her grandchild again.

Maybe she *was* a bit harsh when she'd spoken her mind to Valerie the day of Jeff's death, but she was utterly distraught, and it was Valerie who had started the row, accusing her of terrible things. Tessa's lips tighten as she remembers the vicious attack Valerie had launched on her as Jeff lay cold as marble in that hospital room. Some things could never be forgiven. Never. And Lorcan can say what he likes, it was Valerie who had taken Briony away, and Valerie who had made the decision never to allow them to see her again. And nothing would change that.

As dusk settles around the room, etching the treetops outside against a gunmetal sky, Tessa holds the photo to her heart and feels the jagged shards of grief that this day always brings.

Lorcan pours himself another cup of tea and stirs in an extra spoonful of sugar. He needs it today. The kitchen has grown dark and only Blackie's snores break the silence. Tessa is upstairs, angry and resentful. She will never accept her part in what has happened to their family; she will never accept that what she said to Valerie started the chain of events that has brought them even more sadness than they should have endured. He has held his tongue all these years because he loves his wife.

But sometimes it's been hard listening to her rant and rave and today he has finally said what has to be said. Living in denial for so long has warped his wife's memory of events. She'd read an article some time back, about the Family Justice Review in the UK, ruling against giving grandparents automatic access to their grandchildren in the event of the parents separating, and that had set her off again, worse than ever: 'One million grandchildren in Britain, and how many here, that have little or no access to their grandparents? It shouldn't be allowed, Lorcan, something has to be done!' For weeks she'd nearly driven him mad. He had wanted to say that Briony could have come looking for them once she'd turned eighteen, but that would have hurt her even more and given her another excuse to go off on a tirade against Valerie for poisoning their granddaughter's mind against them.

He has tried, down the years, to tell his wife that the bitterness that consumes her helps no one, least of all herself, but she has never wanted to hear it. She has wrapped her grief and anger around her like a blanket, and found a strange comfort in it, until it now defines her. *Poor Tessa, the woman who has lost her son and her granddaughter. The woman against whom a grave injustice has been done.*

He decided, after giving it much thought, that he would not visit their son's grave on this, the anniversary of his passing. He knows from experience that the grave visits are an excuse for Tessa to stoke up the bitterness again, to immerse herself into that darkness that she will not let go. He said that he wasn't up to it, but that was an excuse; he would have gone if things were different. He has lost as much as Tessa has but he has dealt with it.

They are in the departure lounge of their lives now, and she needs to make her peace with the past. It has gone on too long, this war of attrition. It is time to bring it to an end. He is her husband and he loves her, he always has, although she has doubted that this is true sometimes. Since their son's death he has been pushed aside from time to time because of her great sadness and he has had to live with that too. But he can see what she cannot and this is why he has said what he has said.

He has tried to soften the blow by saying 'what *we* did' instead of 'what *you* did'. That would have been far too accusatory. That would have smacked of laying blame and he wouldn't do that to her. But Lorcan wonders, as he sips the hot sweet tea and gazes unseeingly out at the dripping damson tree, if his wife will ever forgive him for what he has just said.

CHAPTER FIVE

Briony pulled the sheet gently up over Katie's shoulders, bent down and gave her a butterfly kiss. Her daughter lay with her hand tucked under her cheek, her lashes a dark fan against the honey glow of her skin, her rosebud mouth curved upwards, even in sleep her sunny nature asserting itself. She looked almost angelic, Briony smiled. She had been asleep before Briony had read two pages of her bedtime story, deliciously exhausted after a day of play and sun and fresh air.

Briony sighed wearily. How wonderful to be so innocent and free, with no concerns other than would they be going to the toyshop in El Zoco and could she spend her pocket money that her daddy had given her on *anything* she wanted.

Briony wanted to cry. She wanted to lay her head down on her arms and howl. This wasn't the way it was supposed to be. This was meant to have been the most relaxing few weeks she had spent in years. A time of renewed closeness with her mother, a time devoted to Katie, and, an added bonus, time for her. Time to read. Time to sit and stare out to sea. It had been so long since she had had such a luxury. No following some mad timetable, squeezing in a few minutes here and there for herself. Now she had, in a strange sort of way, been gifted with time to *live* her life rather than racing through it at a mad gallop. This was to have been *her* silver lining. Now the discovery of her grandmother's letter had blown her plans to pieces like one of those stealth bombs that come unseen and unheard, and suddenly life is changed for ever.

The sound of the sea brought back memories of another time, another place, of Rockland's Bay, where she had spent the first four years of her life, so much of it in her grandmother Tessa's house. The memory of her grandmother was stronger than her memories of her dad. Even to this day she could still remember them baking fairy cakes. They'd probably be called cup cakes now. She could remember Tessa singing nursery rhymes with her and reading fairy tales to her. 'Rapunzel', 'Thumbelina' and 'The Snow Queen' had fascinated her. Briony had pleaded with Valerie to let her grow her hair long just in case she got locked in a tower and needed rescuing. She recalled rainy days sitting at her grandmother's kitchen table, a blazing fire crackling in the grate throwing dancing shadows on the walls, while she made houses from a deck of cards, groaning when they would inevitably come tumbling down. She remembered going out to the garden with her granddad to pick peas and dig carrots and potatoes, and plunder the raspberry and strawberry beds of their juicy offerings. The sweet taste of the peas fresh from the pod, and the luscious ripe berries that her grandfather would hand her as they filled the basket were as much a treat as the pocket money he would give her every week. She remembered her grandmother's currant loaf, her steak and kidney pie, and – Briony's absolute favourite – the crispy Yorkshire pudding that Tessa served with the Sunday roast. She still loved it now.

She remembered sticking her hands over her ears when she would go shopping with Tessa to the local butcher's. Billy Kearney would bang and chop with his big cleaver, loud fearsome noises echoing around the shop. Sawdust would stick to her shoes as she hid behind her grandmother, terrified yet fascinated at the sight of the big carcasses hanging on massive steel hooks.

The memories kept flooding back. Unstoppable now, wave after wave of them. She could almost feel the comfort of her grandmother's arms around her, remembering how frightened she had been of thunder and lightning, and Tessa telling her that it was just God moving his furniture around in heaven, as sheets of lightning rippled across the sea and the sky seemed to crash and crumple above them. That sea could be so benign on a balmy summer's day, yet so treacherous when the weather turned. The fishermen's wives would pray fervently and watch the entrance to the harbour for their menfolk's safe return. Her granddad had been a fisherman, and her dad had often worked on his trawler, the *Lady Tess*. Briony had a sudden memory of her dad jumping onto the quay after a fishing trip and lifting her up in his arms, saying to her, 'How is my best girl?' as he nuzzled his nose into her neck, making her laugh.

She hadn't thought about Rockland's or her dad or grandparents in such a long time, but in her mind's eye now, as clear as day, she could see the blue and white house with the wisteria growing over the front door and downstairs windows, and the big clumps of rhododendron and hydrangea shrubs that filled the front and back gardens with vibrant colour. She could remember the small wooden gate that led to the vegetable patch, protected by a neat evergreen hedge, and then beyond that the red swing gate that led out to the top of the bank, below which was a sandy crescent beach separated by rocks from the pier, which curved out protectively around the harbour.

The sound of creaking masts, the jangles of rigging, the thrum of the trawler engines and fishing boats as they made their way in and out of the harbour were so much a part of her life back then that she never noticed it, and now, it was only on the rare occasion when she took a trip to the Sunday market in Howth that the sounds and smells evoked memories of her idyllic childhood. A blissful childhood that had been sundered with brutal abruptness the day her father died.

She had been too young to absorb it all. Her recollections of the event and the following days were mostly of her mother weeping inconsolably and the terror she felt when she saw her grandmother and grandfather crying. She had never seen an adult cry until then. She'd only been a little older than Katie when her life had been turned upside down and all the security she had known, which had been such a safety net for her, had been destroyed.

Life was so arbitrary, she thought with a sudden dart of fear. What if anything happened to her or Finn? Katie's life would be irrevocably changed just as her own had. 'Stop that!' Briony said aloud, banishing the notion from her mind. It was too terrifying to think dark thoughts like those. Sitting on the side of the bed, she took the letter from her tote bag and smoothed out the pages again. Her grandmother's script was so elegant, so neat and clear, unlike her own untidy scrawl. She read:

My Darling Briony,

I am giving this letter to your Granny Harris to send to you as I don't have your new address in Dublin. I hope that you like your new house and that you make lots of friends when you start school. Your granddad and I miss you very, very much and wish you could come and visit. We are very lonely for you. Maybe when your mammy has settled down in Dublin she will be able to bring you down to Rockland's some day. I will cook your favourite dinner for you with loads of Yorkshire pudding, and a cream sponge with raspberries and strawberries from the garden for dessert.

I have a great book to read to you. I found it in your dad's bedroom when I was tidying it up. I used to read it to him when he was small. It's called The Grey Goose of Kilnevin *and it's about a little girl called Sheila who has a little goose for a pet called Betsy, and a little boy called Fergus. They have great adventures getting away from a horrid woman called Fat Maggie! You will love it so much, we will have a great time reading it together some day.*

When you learn to write I will look forward to getting a letter from you telling me all your news.

You know I love you very much and so does Granddad. I say a prayer for you every night before I go to sleep. You are my beautiful girl.

With all my love,
Gramma XXXXXXXXXXXXXXXXXXXXXXXXXXX

Tears prickled Briony's eyes. What must it have been like for her grandmother, waiting for a response to her letter?

Waiting for a phone call that never came. A visit to or from Dublin would have taken only an hour and a half on the train, an hour by car. What bitter history had Valerie and Jeff's parents that Valerie would deprive them of the comfort of their grandchild, and Briony the comfort and love of her paternal grandparents? Valerie had told her after they had moved to Dublin, when she had pestered her day in, day out about going to see Gramma, that her grandmother didn't want to see them any more because she was too sad about Jeff going to heaven.

'But why, Mom? Why does she not want to see us? We're sad *too*,' she'd protested. 'Please can we go home? Please! Please! *Please!*'

'No, Briony, this is home now and we're not going back there. Don't ask me again!' Valerie had said sharply. Her mother rarely used that tone with her. She'd never asked to go back to Rockland's again. Soon her life had filled up with playschool and then she had started school and made friends with other children and gradually the memories of those early years had slipped away to the back of her mind.

Briony stood up, slid open the doors to the terrace and stepped out into the clement evening, upset at the painful recollections that she had buried deep for all these years. The more she thought about it the more devastated she felt. How could a mother do that to a child? She could never do something like that to Katie. Even the beauty of the scene that she gazed out on could not soothe her. Flamboyant orange and purple slashes streaked the sky and she looked over to the west to where the sun was sinking behind the high sierras, their jagged outlines silhouetted sharply against the multihued firmament. Venus glimmered in the indigo sky south towards Gibraltar, and out on the inky sea, small lights were beginning to flicker in the deepening dusk from the fishing boats that had sailed earlier from various villages along the coast. Cicadas chattered, breaking the stillness of the night, and the perfume of the flowering shrubs scented the air around her. Africa materialized, enigmatic and alluring on the horizon, the high Atlas Mountains darkly engraved against the dusky sky. It was the best time to see the coast of that neighbouring continent and the sight usually thrilled her, but tonight Briony could see nothing of the beauty laid out before her.

She had sat on the terrace the previous evening and felt she was in heaven as she'd sipped chilled wine and nibbled on olives and cheeses and a selection of crackers, while catching up with all her mother's news. Tonight, though, she felt she was in hell knowing that she was going to have to confront Valerie and hear things that would grieve her sorely. She couldn't stay after today's events. Her mother's betrayal was unforgivable. She'd have to book a flight home. If Valerie's internet had been set up she would have gone online immediately and booked a flight. She'd deal with it tomorrow, she thought wearily, making her way along the terrace to the wide open doors that led to Valerie's elegantly designed lounge. Her mother was seated on one of the pastel-covered sofas, flicking through a photo album.

'Is Katie asleep?' Valerie raised her head and Briony could see she had been crying.

'Yes!' she replied curtly. 'Why, Mum? Why did you lie to me? I want to know. I want to know how you could have done that to Gramma and me? Because there is *nothing* in my mind that could justify such cruelty and I will never forgive you for it,' she added heatedly, her anger overflowing.

Valerie raised her hand as if to ward off an attack. 'Please, Briony, not tonight. I just can't deal with it right now. You don't know because I've never told you, but today is your dad's anniversary. If you want to rake up the past and hear the story I'll tell you my side, because there are always two sides to any story. *Then* you can judge me! But tonight is not the night for it. So please, let me be.'

'Another thing you never told me: the date of my dad's anniversary. Did you never think I would have liked to mark it? It wasn't all about *you*, Mother, no matter what you think,' Briony retorted. 'I'm going for a walk. And don't worry, we'll be gone as soon as I can get a flight home and that will give you all the peace and quiet you want.' She turned on her heel and left the room, then slipped into Katie's bedroom to retrieve her tote bag. She let herself out of the villa and walked down the back garden to the steps that led to a wrought-iron gate and through it, a narrow path. She walked briskly, fuelled by rage, along the winding track that led to the beach. The lights of the coast shimmered and twinkled on either side of her. To her left, along the beach, she could hear the faint sound of the music playing in Max's, the waterside restaurant they had often dined in on previous visits. To her right, the lights of the apartments that lined the resort of Calahonda.

She pulled her phone out of her bag, She needed to talk to Finn, to tell him what had happened, to pour out her fury and frustration, to have him comfort and console her, but just as she was scrolling down her contacts it beeped and the battery died and she cursed herself for not charging it earlier. She flung it back into her bag and turned right, head down, finding her stride along the damp, hard sand near the water's edge. There were a few people out walking their dogs but mostly she had the beach to herself. But neither the welcome breeze that blew her hair away from her flushed angry face, nor the moon preparing to shine silver on the sea, nor the lullaby of sounds from the waves and the sighing pine trees that fringed the beach could act as an unguent to her aching spirit.

CHAPTER SIX

'Oh God! God! God! Could you not give me a break? Just when things were going well. Why do you *always* pick on me?' Valerie berated the Almighty as from the end of the garden she watched Briony rummaging for her phone before throwing it back into her bag and striding off along the beach, disappearing around a bend into the dusk. She'll walk to Marbella, the humour she's in, Valerie thought glumly, making her way back up the garden to the terracotta terrace.

She would have liked to pour herself a big glass of fruity red wine and get smashed but she wouldn't drink knowing that her granddaughter was asleep inside, and Briony was scorching along the beach in a temper, having given Valerie no indication as to what time she'd be back.

That damn letter. She'd forgotten all about it. Tessa had given it to Valerie's mother, Carmel, some time after Valerie had moved to Dublin, and Carmel had asked her if she wanted her to forward it on.

'Absolutely not!' Valerie had declared emphatically. 'Don't post that to me.'

Carmel had shoved it into one of Valerie's photo albums where it had lain forgotten about for years. It was only when Valerie was clearing out her parents' house in

Rockland's that she'd found the albums. She'd thrown them in a cardboard box and put them under the stairs at home in Dublin, along with some other personal effects she'd taken from her mother's bedroom, and forgotten all about them.

Valerie had sold her own house at the height of the boom, soon after Briony had got married, and had bought a smaller town house for herself. When the banks had gone belly up a few years later and she'd been worried about her nest egg, she had decided that she could take advantage of the property crash in Spain and buy a small villa on the southern coast, a place where she had spent many happy holidays.

When she'd bought the villa in Riviera, she'd taken six months' unpaid leave from her job as a senior staff officer at Dublin City Council to move in and get the place sorted. She'd packed up some belongings in cardboard boxes, taken the Cork–Roscoff ferry, and driven down through France and Spain. Briony had flown out a week later.

There were boxes everywhere, some from Valerie's own home, others from her mother's house in Rockland's. She had been glad Briony had arrived to help sort the place out. It had been a nightmare clearing out her childhood home, she remembered with a pang. When Terence had phoned her to tell her that her mother was 'going doolally', as he'd put it, Valerie had finally accepted what she'd being doing her best to disregard. Her mother's increasing forgetfulness and bizarre behaviour could no longer be ignored. Carmel had been diagnosed with Alzheimer's, and, as her condition rapidly deteriorated, father and daughter were in agreement for once: Carmel needed to be in a nursing home.

The house had got shabby and untidy after Carmel had gone into the home some years back. Terence had been too mean to get in a cleaner once a week, even though he could well afford it. And then he'd gone and died and she'd had to deal with everything whether she liked it or not.

Typical of Terence to piss off and leave her with the responsibility of her mother, Valerie thought, heading for the kitchen to make a spritzer for herself. She'd cried no tears at *his* funeral. In fact, she couldn't get away from the grave quick enough after the priest had said the last prayer and the soil had been thrown on the inexpensive wooden coffin she'd selected for him. She was damned if she was going to spend any of her mother's money on an extravagant coffin just to impress the neighbours.

Valerie threw a couple of ice cubes into a long glass, poured a measure of Chardonnay and topped it up with a can of slimline tonic. Her father would have been furious with the send-off she'd given him because if there was one thing Terence Harris liked to do, it was to impress his neighbours. She hadn't paid a singer to sing at his funeral Mass, she'd used taped music. She hadn't paid a fortune for an expensive wreath, just a basic red and white carnation cross. There had been no book of condolence. There had been no eulogy, something that her father would have very much aspired to, especially for all his good deeds in Rockland's. She had left it to the priest to do the readings, determined not to do one herself and be a hypocrite. She certainly hadn't paid for a black car to follow the hearse. She'd driven her mother's old banger behind it. Chitty-Chitty-Bang-Bang, her friend Lizzie had called it. Lizzie had been by her side throughout. Secretly aghast, Valerie felt, but like the true friend she was, she had said nothing, a witness to the long years of antipathy between father and daughter.

Valerie hadn't let Briony come to the funeral despite her daughter's heated protests. 'I don't want you standing at his grave, Briony. He had no time for you when you were alive; you aren't going to waste one second of your life on him now that he's dead.' She'd been unequivocal. Briony was not to know that Valerie had no wish for her daughter to be anywhere near Rockland's for fear that she would encounter Tessa and Lorcan, and the past would rear its ugly head.

'But I want to support you, I want to be with you,' Briony had argued.

'Believe me, it won't be a hardship for me, Briony,' Valerie said grimly. 'As soon as Terence has been prayed over I'll be off. I'm not playing the part of a grieving daughter and the neighbours won't be getting soup and sandwiches for their trouble. I've never been a hypocrite and I'm not going to start now.'

'But what about Granny? Would you not do it properly for her?' Briony couldn't hide her dismay. 'Are you not going to have a removal?'

'He can go straight to the church. Lots of people are doing that now. Granny doesn't know what day it is, let alone who's going to be at Da's funeral. There's no point in taking her out of the nursing home to go. She'd only get agitated and confused. She's better off where she is. Don't you miss a day's work going to the funeral of someone who couldn't care less about us. Don't worry about me, I'll be fine,' Valerie had insisted.

'Are Dad's parents still living in Rockland's? Should we try and make contact with them and—'

'Briony, let's leave them in the past where they belong. We've managed very well without them. I have no desire whatsoever to make contact with them now or in the future, and besides, I don't even know if they still live in Rockland's,' Valerie had interrupted sternly. Briony had said no more, knowing from experience that it was pointless arguing with her mother when she got a bee in her bonnet about something.

Now Valerie frowned as she carried her glass out to the terrace, kicked off her espadrilles and sat on a thick-cushioned lounger. That had been a close shave. For one awful moment she'd thought her daughter was going to insist on trying to find her paternal grandparents. Briony knew that Terence hadn't wanted her in his life and that was just the way he was. Because she was used to the situation it didn't bother her unduly. But Valerie could never forgive him for it. She would love to have told all the old dears in the parish who were under the impression that he was a kind person just how mistaken they were.

He had always been involved in the Meals on Wheels, and the bingo, in Rockland's, but Valerie knew that Terence hadn't done it out of the goodness of his heart. Her father had always had an ulterior motive for doing any perceived act of kindness. The old dears were always slipping him a twenty here and a twenty there for doing their shopping and weeding their gardens. And Terence always took it.

He'd slipped on ice putting a bag of rubbish into a neighbour's bin under cover of darkness, because he was too mean to pay the bin charges. He'd hit his head on the footpath and had lain in the freezing cold, unconscious, unmissed by his befuddled wife in her nursing home, until he'd been found suffering from hypothermia, early the following morning when a neighbour had been going to work. Valerie had been visiting Lizzie in London, when she'd got the phone call from a neighbour telling her to go to the hospital immediately if she wanted to see her father to say goodbye. She said it would be later in the week before she got home, weather permitting. Flights had been cancelled because of the Big Freeze, as everyone was calling it. Typical of Terence to pick the worst time of the year to die and make life awkward for everyone. She earnestly hoped that she wouldn't end up doing a death vigil at her father's bedside and that he would do them all a favour and not drag it out, that he'd shuffle off this mortal coil a.s.a.p so she could get things sorted. Carmel's future was her priority. Valerie wanted to do the best for her. She'd told the nursing home staff to say nothing to her mother about Terence's imminent demise. There was no point in agitating her.

Terence had, for once in his life, obliged his daughter and had died the following morning. She'd made the arrangements, by phone and email, and had flown into Dublin the next day when flight restrictions had been lifted, and driven to Rockland's. After spending time with Carmel, who hadn't recognized her on this visit, though she sometimes did, Valerie had driven to the funeral parlour in Wicklow. She had told the undertakers she didn't want to see her father in his coffin and to have it closed when she got there. She had no intention of kissing his corpse.

'Some people prefer to have their last memory to be of the loved one alive,' the undertaker said understandingly.

As if Terence would even get a kiss from her when he was alive, *or* a prayer even, she thought with dark humour.

She was petrified that Tessa or Lorcan would appear at the funeral and had been on edge from the minute she'd driven into the car park of St Anthony's, behind the hearse. 'Can you see the Egans?' she'd asked Lizzie, doing a quick scan herself of the various clusters of people waiting to follow the coffin into the church.

'I don't think they're here. I'm sure they'd know you wouldn't welcome their attendance,' Lizzie assured her, taking a good look around to see if she could see Jeff's parents.

Valerie had hardly heard a word the priest said. All she wanted was to get the hell out of Rockland's as fast as she could. Knowing Tessa of old, she wouldn't put it past her to cause a scene.

There'd been a good turnout at her father's funeral, although she had no idea why. Nosiness probably, she'd thought crossly as she'd stood shivering outside the church, receiving the neighbours' condolence, wishing the whole charade was over.

'A terrible tragedy – what was he doing out on a night like that?' Jonny Carroll, a nosy little git who liked to know everyone's business, had asked her.

'I've no idea,' she'd said crisply.

'Was he putting out rubbish or something?' Jonny asked slyly, hoping to discommode her. She'd long got past the stage of being mortified by her father's behaviour – not like when she was young – and she was damned if she was going to let that sly little turd of an accountant get to her.

'How would I know, Jonny, and I hundreds of miles away in London? But one thing I do know, I hope Da didn't take any of *your* advice about tax dodges. I don't want the tax man after me.'

'Ye were always a little madam,' Jonny muttered, melting away into the crowd gathered at the church gates.

And you were always an obnoxious little bollox, she thought, remembering his hard groping fingers when he and Terence would come lurching home after doing the rounds of their elderly neighbours at Christmas.

Valerie had only spoken to a few more people. It had been bitterly cold with snow still on the ground, and she'd told the undertaker she wanted to go straight to the graveyard in case it snowed.

She had caught a glance of Jeff's headstone as she followed Terence's coffin up the cemetery path. The grave looked so fresh and well tended, with pots of red and yellow winter bedding. She felt, for the first time that day, like bursting into tears. She struggled to compose herself, desperate to avoid the memories of the last time she'd been in the graveyard when she'd said goodbye to Jeff. She'd kept her gaze straight ahead when the ordeal was finally over, and the priest had left the cemetery after giving her a kindly pat on the shoulder, wishing her well, and telling her how much the elderly people in the parish would miss her father.

What an irony, she'd reflected as she'd walked carefully down the graveyard path, trying not to slip on the ice, that Terence, who had smarmed and charmed half the widows and pensioners in the village in the hopes of being left something in their wills, had died suddenly and it was *they* who had prayed over his coffin.

In the space of a month, Valerie had cleared the house and put it up for sale. Now that she had power of attorney for Carmel she took the decision to sell, figuring that there was no point in letting the house go to rack and ruin; she certainly wouldn't be going back to Rockland's to live. It was just before the property crash hit and she'd made a fine profit on the three-bedroomed cottage, bought as a holiday home by an affluent couple from Dublin. Her mother's pension plus a monthly contribution from Valerie paid for the nursing home, and in the meantime the proceeds of the house sale accrued a yearly interest, though it had fallen dramatically in recent years as interest rates fell. Nevertheless, when her mother eventually died, Valerie would have a nice nest egg indeed. It was this knowledge that had made her take a leap of faith and buy the villa in Spain. Yes, life had at last turned in Valerie's favour until Tessa Egan's letter had surfaced. If she'd despised her father she *loathed* Tessa, she thought irately.

She took a swig of her drink and gazed out across the garden to the shadowy dark sea that was starting to roughen up. The waves had ghostly whitecaps smashing against the rocks and she knew the wind had risen. She took another gulp of spritzer, agitated, restless, unnerved by all these memories that were crowding into her mind, unwelcome and unwanted. Even after all these years Tessa's behaviour still rankled unbearably. Tears gathered behind Valerie's eyelids and rolled down her cheeks.

She would never forget the sight of Jeff, as white as the sheet that covered him, in the hospital mortuary. She would never forget the marble cold of his forehead when she'd bent down to kiss him one last time. Now the past had come back to haunt her. Valerie drained her glass and stood up. She was tired. She might as well have an early night. If Briony hadn't got her key she could ring the bell and Valerie would let her in.

She carried the two lounger cushions inside, put away Katie's toys, washed her glass and locked up, leaving just a lamp on for her daughter's return. She padded silently into Katie's room and smiled to see her grandchild sleeping so soundly. Briony would never stop her from seeing Katie, surely? It was a different set of circumstances that had made Valerie take the path she'd taken. It would be unthinkable for Briony to be so cruel. A feeling of dread enveloped her. *Could* her daughter's anger make her take that vengeful step? Had *she* not let anger and bitterness dictate the actions she'd taken after Jeff had died?

'Don't think about it. It was different then,' Valerie muttered. She went back into the lounge to get her glasses and glanced down at the photo album on the sofa where she'd left it. She picked it up and flicked through the pages. Weariness enveloped her and she took the album with her into her bedroom. She loved her bedroom, with its airy pastel colours of duck-egg blue and lemon, and the white shuttered doors that reminded her of an ad for a holiday in the Caribbean. A small passageway lined with wardrobes led to the cream and lemon tiled ensuite. The wide double bed, with its white Egyptian cotton sheets and duvet, and lemon throw, dominated the room. Rugs on either side of the bed covered the cream and lemon speckled marble floor. It was a most relaxing room, the wide French doors fringed on the outside with sweet scented bougainvillaea and honeysuckle.

Valerie undressed swiftly, folded her clothes neatly and laid them on the white cane chair by the French doors. She hated clutter; she couldn't sleep if anything was out of place. She slipped in between the cool sheets and felt some of the tension that was causing her head to throb begin to ease.

She reached for the album and opened it. A photo fell out of a torn plastic covering sheet and she picked it up and her heart gave a painful twist as she saw the image of herself and Lizzie with Jeff in the middle, his arms around them, laughing into the camera. She'd never been so happy in her entire life as she was then.

It had truly been the best time of her life, Valerie remembered, as the years disappeared and her thoughts drifted back to that glorious summer when everything had been absolutely perfect.

CHAPTER SEVEN

'I've something to ask you.' Lizzie Anderson, Valerie's best friend, tucked her arm into Valerie's as they crossed the main street that ran ruler-straight through Rockland's towards the small green, fringed by trees known as The Triangle, which sat in the centre of the village. A block of shops that included a supermarket, a newsagent's, a butcher's, a pharmacy, a café and chipper constituted the heart of the village. In summer flamboyant hanging baskets and window boxes of busy Lizzies, geraniums and petunias lent an air of Mediterranean gaiety and glamour for the tourists who came to buy ice creams, chilled drinks, cold meats and bread rolls for their picnics on the beach, or to have coffee or lunch in the small café. Tonight there was nothing of that Mediterranean buzz as the rain threatened and a howling south-easterly blew in from the sea.

The little whitewashed church with the narrow stained-glass windows on either side of the big wooden doors lay adjacent to the village primary school. On the other side of the church the large Victorian parochial house marked the intangible separation between the posh end of the village where the doctor, bank manager and 'The Elite', as Valerie's mother called them, lived in big detached houses with sea views, and walled gardens whose mostly high, neatly trimmed hedges obstructed the view of the *hoi polloi*. At the end of the posh houses, a cobbled street that bisected the main road led to the railway station on one side and to a curved sandy beach on the seaside. It was a pretty village in summer but once the tourists were gone and the nights grew long, Rockland's was dead boring, Valerie reflected as she and Lizzie skirted a large puddle beside the Ball Alley, where tonight, a hard-fought game of handball was in progress with some of the local lads.

'What do you want to ask me? Something I'm not going to like, I just know by the way you're saying it,' Valerie said warily.

'Please, please. *Pleeeeease* come to the match with me. I don't want to go and stand on the sidelines on my own,' her best friend pleaded. 'I'll do your maths homework for a week.'

'Aw, Lizzie, I hate football.' Valerie made a face.

'You're my best friend. It's your *duty* to stand by me. I really fancy Phil, and he *asked* me to come to the match. Val, please.'

'Oh, all right,' grumbled Valerie, with bad grace. She didn't particularly like Phil Casey, although she wouldn't let on to Lizzie, who was totally infatuated. He thought he was ultra cool, strutting around, showing off with his new Walkman and his punk earring. If a real punk came near him he'd run a mile, Valerie thought scornfully. She couldn't think of anything more boring than watching fellas kicking a ball around, with people screaming in her ear. What a waste of a Sunday afternoon, especially when she had a free house, a very rare occurrence. Her parents were going up to Dublin to visit an uncle in hospital and then they were going to visit Terence's elderly mother. Terence had wanted her to come but she'd lied and said she had a maths exam the next day and she needed to revise. Terence put a lot of store on her studies. When she had got six honours in her Inter Cert he'd boasted about it for weeks afterwards, mortifying her everywhere they went. If she didn't do well in her Leaving Cert he'd be devastated. He wanted her to go to college – preferably to study medicine, but law or accountancy would suffice. Valerie knew Terence well enough to realize that going to college wasn't all about her. He wanted to be able to boast about his daughter 'the doctor' or 'the lawyer' or 'the accountant'. Terence was a social climber and she was his ladder. He wanted to be as good as 'The Elite' at the grand end of the village, and Valerie was his stepping stone, his last chance to improve the family's social standing, unless he won a fortune on the Sweepstakes.

Valerie had given him the one excuse she knew he would accept without question. She'd been looking forward to her few hours of freedom immensely. She had the new Hot Chocolate cassette and she was going to play it as loud as she wished and lounge on the sofa with Lizzie eating crisps and Trigger Bars – their last occasion of sin before going on a diet – and gossiping. Now Lizzie was changing their plans and wanted her to spend an afternoon shivering in a mucky field. But Lizzie was her dearest friend; what else could she do?

Lizzie was mad into boys. Valerie wasn't any more, not since Gary Higgins, she thought glumly, frowning as she remembered that horrible night the previous year when he'd started snogging her under the cordyline trees in the middle of The Triangle.

It was the first time she'd been properly kissed, a French kiss, like the ones she'd read about in the romances she liked to devour. She had found it revolting. Gary Higgins, the village hunk, had walked her home from the hotel one night and told her he'd make a 'real woman' of her. She'd been scared but curious. He was a couple of years older than she. Until then she'd only been tentatively kissed by pimply, gangly youths with moon craters of acne on their faces, and damp, sweaty octopus hands that roamed all over her until she called a halt. She'd begun to think there was something wrong with her. All the Mills & Boons she'd devoured, all the *Cosmo* articles she'd read when she'd worked weekends in the local hairdresser's, had led her to believe that she would feel hot and quivery and have mind-blowing orgasms, but all she felt as those boys slobbered over her and pressed their crotches against her, was dismay and disgust. Fortunately, she wasn't alone. Lizzie confided that she felt the same. They couldn't understand how Frances O'Connor and Anna McKenna and their gang were always boasting about shifting guys and having passionate sessions down on the boat strand behind the sheds.

'I think they're spoofing or else we're frigid,' Lizzie had fretted and Valerie had felt apprehension grip her as her best friend articulated a fear that caused her much anxiety. She wondered if frigidity could be inherited because she felt sure her mother suffered from the condition. Carmel had told her that men only wanted women for one thing and that she would be better off never getting married. 'Be independent, Valerie. Never let a man have power over you. It's different for you – you can have a career, you can earn your own money. Don't give all that up to be some man's skivvy.'

At night sometimes, when she was younger, she would hear the bed creaking in the room next door, Carmel's murmured protests and her father's hoarse guttural grunts. Valerie would jam her fingers into her ears and the growing revulsion she felt for her father deepened into an antipathy that would last until his death. Carmel had collapsed haemorrhaging one day, hanging out clothes in the back garden, and had to have a hysterectomy. She had moved into the small boxroom while she was recovering and had never returned to the marital bedroom.

When Gary Higgins had chatted Valerie up one Saturday night when she had sneaked out of the house to go to a disco at the hotel, she had decided once and for all to prove to herself that she wasn't frigid. Gary was experienced; he'd know how to treat her; he'd know what he was doing, she reasoned. And so when he'd walked her through The Triangle and sat her down on a bench, her heart had thumped with excitement. It was finally going to happen. He would cup her breasts in his hands, just like in a Mills & Boon romance. He'd gently caress her nipples until they were hard peaks of desire and his kisses would be deep and tender at first, but then probing and insistent as she inflamed him with passionate desire. And then she would feel the quivery, aching need herself and *know* that she was normal, just like Frances and Anna, and those women she read about.

When he had stuck his beer-soaked tongue so far down her throat that she almost gagged, and twisted her nipples until she had gasped with pain and dismay, he had mistaken it for a gasp of pleasure. Before she realized what he was doing, Gary had thrust his hand inside the waistbands of her maxi skirt and knickers and roughly jammed two fingers into her, making her cry out in shock and pain.

'Good, isn't it?' he muttered drunkenly, jabbing his fingers in and out. 'Now you touch me.' He was unzipping his jeans as he spoke.

Stunned, she'd managed to pull away from him after a struggle and had jumped to her feet. 'Hey, don't be a prick teaser,' he protested, lurching towards her, but she had raced out of The Triangle as fast as she could, disappearing down the narrow lane that led to the back of the cottages and climbed in through her bedroom window, her heart pounding so hard she was sure the whole street could hear it.

She lay on her bed, sore and violated, trying hard not to cry and had decided if being frigid meant you didn't have to endure men doing horrible things to you, she could live with it. Her mother was right.

'What was it like? Did you come?' Lizzie asked excitedly the next morning as they walked through the village to Mass.

'No, I went,' Valerie giggled. Now that it was daylight and she had accepted her frigidity and resolved never to let a man 'maul' – another of her mother's contemptuous metaphors – her, she felt a huge sense of relief. She related the events of the previous night as they headed to St Anthony's.

'Eewww!' Lizzie uttered, horrified.

'It bloody hurt,' Valerie added indignantly as Mrs O'Connell, the principal of the primary school, click-clacked past them in her shiny patent high heels and green velvet hat, a jaunty white feather curling over the brim. 'Morning, girls,' she saluted brightly.

'Morning, Mrs O'Connell,' they chorused politely.

'Don't be late now and don't hang around the end of the church. Make sure you go up the front,' their former teacher instructed bossily as she overtook them and increased her speed. She was the organist and choir mistress, and she was running late.

'Who does she think she is? Bossy boots! We're in Secondary now; she's not in charge of us any more,' Valerie muttered.

'Could you imagine *her* doing it? She has four kids. Maybe she's a nympho,' Lizzie tittered, and Valerie giggled. As they neared the church gates the air filled with greeting from various classmates who were already congregated inside the church grounds, waiting for them.

'Good night, Valerie?' Frances O'Connor asked slyly. She too had previous experience of Romeo Higgins and his roaming fingers.

'Fab,' Valerie said airily, and marched in through the gloomy porch of St Anthony's with Lizzie right behind her. 'What a bitch,' she muttered. 'She thinks she's the bee's knees with her pink leg warmers!'

'Knobbly knees, more like,' Lizzie retorted smartly as they genuflected and edged into a rapidly filling pew. 'And she's a bandy little cow!'

Valerie smiled at the memory of that Sunday morning last summer. Lizzie was always quick with a riposte. She was a brilliant friend and now she needed support in her new romance. Lizzie was convinced Phil Casey was finally 'The One'.

'He's a great kisser, the best, actually,' she'd admitted, deliriously happy after their first kiss, and Valerie had tried not to feel jealous. It was hard, though. Now it was all 'we' are going here, 'we' are going there, 'we' are doing this and that. Where once it was she and Lizzie who were the 'we', now an interloper had taken possession of her friend, her and Lizzie's friendship was on the back burner and Valerie was lonely. She was going to feel like a real gooseberry when they went back to the pub for a drink after the match. But she hid her dismay with, to her mind, an Oscar-winning performance for fake enthusiasm.

'OK, I'll come. I'll cheer Phil on for you.' She smiled at her friend. Lizzie squealed excitedly. 'You're the best, Val, you'll really enjoy it, and there are some fine things in the team. You might get off with someone.'

'Nope, not interested. Besides, Da would have a fit if I started going with someone. You know that. There's no point in me even thinking about dating until the Leaving is over,' Valerie said as they reached the welcome shelter of Lizzie's house, where her mother had kept them two luscious slices of home-made strawberry meringue. Valerie loved being at her friend's house where she was treated like one of the family. It was a real home, unlike her own, which was fraught with arguments and tension.

She had a precious hour of peace the following Sunday when her parents left for Dublin, but it sped by and then reluctantly she pulled on her coat and a purple knitted hat to keep the cold out, and made her way to Lizzie's house. Lizzie was dressed to impress in new Levi's and a cream polo-necked skinny rib jumper under a cropped denim jacket, and wedge boots. 'You better bring a coat, it's cold out,' Valerie warned, as her friend finished putting on her eye shadow.

'Do I look OK?' Lizzie fretted. 'Should I put on some more blusher?'

'Not unless you want to look like Bobo the Clown. You're fine,' Valerie assured her, whooshing her out the door, wishing the ordeal was over.

To add insult to injury it started raining about ten minutes after the match started; a fine grey mist, which clung wraith-like to her, seeping through her coat and hat, which she had pulled down over her ears. The heels of her boots sank into the soft ground and the bottoms of her jeans were caked with muck. Beside her, Lizzie jumped up and down like a crazy marionette yelling, 'Come on, Rovers! COMMME OOOOOONNNNNNN!!!!! Put it in the net, lads. Put it in the NEEEET. Ref, Ref, are you BLIND? Offside, OffSIIIIDE!'

When, Valerie wondered, had her best friend turned into a football fanatic? Until a month ago, when Phil Casey had first asked her out, she had never shown a scintilla of interest in anything related to football. Now she was even watching *Match of the Day* with Phil, leaving Valerie to her own devices on Saturday nights. Valerie couldn't help the by now familiar feeling of being hard done by. Lizzie had dropped her on Saturday nights and yet she expected her to be by her side at a boring football match. She expected a lot, Valerie thought with renewed resentment, praying Lizzie would shut up screeching.

Valerie was yawning, wishing she had worn a scarf to stop the rain dribbling down her collar, when a violent thump made her jump. The hard leather ball bounced again, spattering her with muck.

'Bloody hell! Look at the state of me.' She glared at Lizzie.

'Kick it back in,' Lizzie instructed.

Valerie was so mad she drew her foot back and let fly just as one of the players was heading in her direction to retrieve the ball.

'Yikes, you nearly got Jeff Egan in the goolies!' Lizzie snorted.

'Pity I didn't. Is this thing nearly over?'

'Stop making me feel bad,' Lizzie snapped. 'Standing there with a face like a slapped ass. I won't ask you to come again.'

'Great, Lizzie, great that's good to hear.' She couldn't hide her irritation.

'Oh my God! Oh my God! Phil's got the ball. Go, Phil! Go, Phil! Go, Phil! *GOOOOOO!!*' Lizzie was dancing with excitement as her new boyfriend scored the winning goal. The hundred or so supporters erupted, yelling and roaring, and then, music to Valerie's ears, the final whistle blew, a long sharp piercing note that led to more yelling and joyous cheering.

Later, while she was sipping a Bacardi and Coke in the Oyster Bar, a local pub near the football grounds, a hand tapped Valerie on the shoulder. 'The least you could do is buy me a drink since you nearly ruined my marriage prospects. Just as well I've got good reflexes.' A pair of smiling brown eyes looked down at her and she grinned when she saw Jeff Egan standing beside her. He had been a year ahead of her at school and they knew each other casually.

'Sorry about that. But you ruined my trousers, buster.'

'Ah, stick them in the washing machine, they'll be fine,' he laughed. 'So what about that drink, then?'

'They won't serve me, I'm under age. I'll give you the money for it but you'll have to get it. Phil got our drinks for us.' She went to open her bag.

'I'm just teasing,' Jeff assured her. 'Did you enjoy the match? I didn't know you were a Rockland's Rovers supporter.'

'I'm not, and no!' she said bluntly. 'I just came because Lizzie asked me so she wouldn't be on her own.'

'Ah, yeah, she's started going out with Phil. So it's kind of mandatory to go to the matches, for the first few months, anyway.'

'Well, I wouldn't be going if I was dating anyone in the team.' She was almost shouting, it was so noisy in the bar.

'And are you dating anyone?'

'Nope. My da would have a fit. I'm doing the Leaving. I'd better be heading off home. The reason I got out of going to Dublin with my folks was I said I'd be studying.' She drained her Bacardi and Coke and turned to find Lizzie, who was submerged in a gang of Phil's mates.

'I'll give you a lift home. I have my da's car,' Jeff offered.

'You're going to miss all the celebrations.'

'I'm getting the bus up to Dublin tonight. I need to put in a few hours at the books: I've got a thermodynamics exam tomorrow.'

'Oh . . . OK, I'll just grab my coat and let Lizzie know that I'm heading off.' Valerie was taken aback. It was the last thing she had expected. And a guy as nice as Jeff Egan offering her a lift, at that. She didn't know if he was dating anyone; now that he was studying in Dublin she didn't see him around much.

'Hey, Lizzie, I'm gonna head home, see you at school tomorrow,' she shouted to her friend.

Lizzie battled her way through the throng. 'Are you sure you have to go? A gang of us are going to the disco in Hanlon's.'

'You know I can't, Lizzie. Da would go ballistic; I just have to accept that until I've done my Leaving I might as well be a prisoner. I don't have easy-going parents like you do.'

'Ah it's just I'm the youngest and I get away with murder,' her friend grinned. 'Thanks a mill for coming today. I owe you one.'

'Forget it, see ya.' She didn't want to tell her friend that Jeff was giving her a lift home. She didn't want to be roaring her business out over the din in the busy bar. She could see Jeff was chatting to one of his teammates near the door, waiting for her.

'Will I be safe? Do I need to protect any delicate parts?' he teased, holding the heavy swing door open for her.

Valerie laughed. 'So how do you like college?' she asked as they hurried through the rain to a blue station wagon.

'It's cool. Very different from St Mel's. It's up to yourself whether you study or not.' He opened the passenger door for her and she was impressed with his good manners. No one had ever held a car door open for her before. 'So what are your plans when you leave school next June?' He started the engine and reversed out of the car park.

'I might do a secretarial course. And of course I'll be applying for the banks, county councils, Dublin Corporation, the usual.' She shrugged.

'Wouldn't you think of going to go to college?'

'Nah, I couldn't bear to be under my father's thumb for three more years. The sooner I start earning my own money the better. I want to be as free as a bird. He thinks I'm going to college. I have all the application forms just to keep him quiet. He wants me to be a doctor or a lawyer or an accountant, so I'm saying nothing, just keeping my head down.'

'They're good aspirations to have. Do you not get on well with your da? He seems like a nice guy, from what I've seen of him. Helping out with the Meals on Wheels and bingo and stuff like that?'

'He's a bit . . . um . . . a bit . . . strict because it's my exam year.'

'Oh . . . right.'

She changed the subject. 'So are you living in a flat?'

'No, I wish I was. I'm in digs. Maybe next year, if I make enough money on the boats. We'll see how it goes.'

'What's your landlady like?'

'A bulldog,' he grinned, a boyish lopsided grin that showed off his white teeth and made his brown eyes glint. 'She caught me trying to sneak my girlfriend in one night and, boy, did I get a tongue-lashing!' He laughed at the memory, a deep hearty chuckle.

'That was the pits for sure,' she said brightly, surprised at how disappointed she felt at hearing he had a girlfriend.

'Well, here you are, home safe and sound.' He drew up outside her house. 'Sorry about mucking up your jeans.'

'No bother, Jeff. Thanks for the lift, and good luck with your exams,' she said briskly, letting herself out of the car.

'Same to you, Valerie, see you around.' He gave a toot of the horn and she waved after him as the car drove down the road. Why wouldn't he have a girlfriend? she thought grouchily. There were loads of girls in Dublin and he was a dishy kind of guy. College had matured him. He wore his brown hair longer, and the black leather jacket was very sexy on him. She might even overcome her aversion to men if she went on a date with him.

She sighed as she let herself into the house. He was out of her league now, for sure, and anyway, she had no time for thinking about boys. She needed to make sure she got enough honours in her Leaving Certificate to get a decent job and take the first steps towards independence.

CHAPTER EIGHT

The next time Valerie saw Jeff Egan she was coming home from evening study, looking a sight in her green uniform and navy gabardine coat. She was standing in the queue in the chipper when he pushed open the door and came to stand behind her. He was scowling, his hands thrust into his duffel coat pockets and she wasn't sure if he recognized her. He seemed rather preoccupied.

'Hi, Jeff,' she said casually, as her heart did a little flip-flop. What bad luck to be caught looking like a school kid. And she had a zit the size of an acorn on the side of her nose.

'Oh . . . oh . . . hi, Valerie, how's it going?' he asked politely.

'Fine.' She was suddenly speechless. 'Er, and how are you? How did your exam go?'

'My exam?'

'The term . . . termo . . . ?' She couldn't remember how to pronounce it.

'The thermodynamics, yeah, it went grand. Got a B. Can I have a snack box and a Coke, please?' He placed his order.

'That was a good result,' she persevered.

'Um.'

'Are you playing a match this weekend?'

'Yep, are you going?'

'Noooo!' She smiled. 'Your marriage prospects will be safe.'

He laughed that deep, hearty chuckle, and she felt ridiculously happy and wished her order hadn't been processed so quickly.

'Well, see you,' she said, with pretend jauntiness as she took her change and her brown bag of battered sausage and chips.

'Hey, listen, walk up the road with me, or are you in a hurry? They're wrapping up my snack box now,' he said easily.

'I'm not in a hurry.' She tried to keep her voice neutral.

'So how's the bulldog?' she asked as they walked past the supermarket, devouring their steaming hot chips, the vinegary aroma scenting the night air.

'Barking mad!' he grimaced. 'I swear to God, her cat gets better fed than us students. Just as well my ma packs me a box of goodies when I'm going back after the weekends.'

'Have you succeeded in getting your girlfriend in yet?' She pretended to be ever so casual when she asked the question.

'Oh, we're not dating any more. We were at a party last weekend and she got off with a guy who I thought was a mate.' His face darkened in a scowl and she understood why he had looked so preoccupied and annoyed when she'd seen him earlier.

'That's awful!' She was genuinely shocked that a dish like Jeff could get dumped.

'She said she was pissed and she didn't mean it and she wants us to get back together, but that's just because

I've got tickets for Queen. She can get lost,' he growled, biting into a chicken leg.

'You've got tickets for Queen! For the Crazy Tour? Wow!' She couldn't hide her envy.

'Yep! Simmonscourt Pavilion. Eat your heart out, Ursula Byrne, 'cos you won't be going.' He took a swig of his Coke. 'So how's the swotting coming along?' he asked, changing the subject.

'I just keep telling myself that this time next year it will be all over, and at least Christmas is coming so I can take a couple of days off.' She tried to take a ladylike bite of her battered sausage instead of chomping half at once, as she usually did, but the grease ran down her chin and she had to wipe it away.

'Once Christmas is over it will fly. The trick is to keep revising and not leave it to the last minute.'

'Yeah, well, that's what I'm doing. I swear to God I'll never pick up another book once my exams are over. Lizzie and I are going to light a bonfire down on the beach and burn them.'

'My ma made me sell mine back to the school to their second-hand shop. Got a few quid for them,' he pointed out as they came to a halt opposite the Ball Alley.

'I guess this is where we go our separate ways. Have a good weekend, Jeff. Hope you win your match on Sunday. And enjoy Queen. It will be amazing.' She was sorry their short stroll together was at an end.

'Do you fancy coming? I have a spare ticket now?' He gave his lopsided grin.

'Are you *serious*?' She couldn't believe her ears.

'Yeah, why not? That's if you want to,' he added, scrunching his chip paper into a ball. 'Maybe you don't like them.'

'I *love* Queen,' she said fervently. 'And I've never been to a pop concert.'

'Me neither. We'll be pop concert virgins. Will your da be OK with you going?'

'I don't see why not,' she replied breezily, but her heart sank. Terence would refuse point-blank to let her go to a rock concert. There was no point in even asking him. She'd have to come up with some plausible fib.

'Great, give me your phone number and I'll give you mine and we'll sort out arrangements. Do you have a pen?' Jeff asked.

'Sure.' She scrabbled in her bag until she found one, wrote his number on the cover of her homework note-book, tore a page out and wrote hers on it. 'The best time to get me is around five,' she said, handing it to him. Her dad wouldn't be home from work until six.

'Right, I'll keep that in mind. Roll on the twenty-second of November. I'll have a Killer Queen on my arm and Ursula Byrne can go stuff herself.' He smiled at her and she smiled back, wondering if she would wake up and find out it was all a dream.

'You're going to Queen with Jeff *Egan*?' Lizzie's voice rose an octave and her eyes were like saucers when Valerie imparted her news that night while they babysat for Lizzie's older sister.

'Yeah. Bad move, Ursula Byrne, whoever you are, dumping your boyfriend who has tickets for the concert of the decade.' Valerie giggled. 'Bet she's kicking herself now.'

'Deadly,' Lizzie declared, pouring them two small vodkas and adding tonic, before replacing the bottles in her sister's drinks cabinet. 'I brought crisps too. And Martina left some sandwiches and cream sponge for us.'

'And I've got chocolate.' Valerie patted her bag.

They settled companionably on the sofa in front of a roaring fire with Sister Sledge singing 'He's the Greatest Dancer' on the tape deck. Valerie hummed along happily, taking a packet of Tayto from her friend.

'Now tell me everything again from the beginning.' Lizzie took a slug of her drink.

Valerie relayed the events of a few hours earlier, with Lizzie interjecting a comment here or there. 'The only thing is that he's just bringing me to spite that Ursula one – it's not as if he actually *fancies* me or anything – so it's not a real date, but at least I get to see Queen,' she said a little regretfully.

'And do you fancy him?' Lizzie eyed her sharply.

'I think I do a bit. He's gorgeous-looking and dead sexy in that black leather jacket, and he's good fun too,' Valerie admitted. 'And it's only a few months to my Leaving so once that's over I could start dating him properly.'

'Eight months, dear, not a few,' Lizzie said drily. 'A college boy is not going to wait eight months. I'm just saying that as your best friend who's always honest with you.'

'We can all have our fantasies,' Valerie sighed.

'Have you said anything to your folks?' Lizzie broke off a square of chocolate.

'What do you think?' Valerie said gloomily. 'I won't be allowed to go and that's it! I'll just have to come up with something.'

'Right . . . I figured that.' Lizzie thought for a moment. 'Here's what we're going to do. Tell them you're going on a field trip . . . geography. Remember the one we went on for the Inter?'

'Yeah, but that's not going to go on all night. The concert doesn't start until eight.'

'I know, you can say you're babysitting with me, and we're revising for the Christmas exams. We won't be home until after midnight tonight so that's nothing unusual.'

'It's on a Thursday night, though, which is a bit of a pain in the ass. If it was on a Friday it would be much easier to spoof!'

'Well, just say Martina's going to a wedding and it's a great opportunity to get some serious revision done,' Lizzie improvised rapidly.

'Do you think?' Valerie asked doubtfully.

'Yeah, go for it.' Lizzie sounded confident. She jumped up and held a pretend mic, belting out 'Crazy Little Thing Called Love'. 'Do you know how lucky you are? I'm pea green with envy. Just as well you're my best friend.'

'I'm glad you are. I wish you were coming. It would be a blast.' Valerie hugged her.

'Bet there's no tickets left. I'll ask Phil if he could get any but I won't hold my breath. Now start rehearsing what you're going to say to your da.'

'It's a comparative study to the one we did for the Inter.' Valerie tried to sound nonchalant the following Saturday as she broached the subject before her father began to look at the afternoon sport. She thought 'comparative study' sounded serious and intellectual.

'Would you not be better off sitting at your desks studying like we had to?' Terence grumbled.

'Well, social geography is different,' she explained. 'We're studying dormitory towns outside of Dublin.'

'And how many of you are going? Is it just an excuse for a doss?' He settled himself in his armchair ready to study the RTE guide to see what was on TV.

'No, no,' she assured him hastily, banishing an image of a bottle of vodka being passed surreptitiously around the back of a tour bus, on a previous field trip, and Ashlynn Callaghan puking her guts up out the window on the way home after drinking half a bottle of Malibu, while her friend told the geography teacher earnestly that she was a very poor traveller.

'Only the honours students,' Valerie lied.

'And how much is this going to cost me?' Her father arched a bushy eyebrow at her.

'Um ... one pound fifty,' she ventured, unable to believe her luck.

'Daylight robbery,' he groused, extracting two silver pound coins from his wallet. Valerie took the money calmly. Now she wouldn't have to fund her trip out of her own money either. This was a real bonus.

'Thanks, Dad.' There was a hint of warmth in her tone. This was an uncharacteristically kind gesture from her father.

'Give me back the change and you can pay me back when you start working again,' he growled, returning to form. He had made her give up her Saturday job at the local hairdresser's until her exams were over and she really missed the money.

'Oh, and I'll be going straight to Lizzie's after we get home. She's babysitting and we're going to do maths revision. We've a big test the next day,' she said flatly.

'I thought you babysat on Fridays.' He eyed her suspiciously.

'Her sister's going to a wedding.'

'Go on,' he grunted, turning his attention back to his magazine.

Valerie walked out into the kitchen, feeling strangely dejected. She should have been on a high; it had all gone so smoothly. But for one brief moment she'd felt her da was like every other dad she knew when he'd handed her the coins. Her heart had actually lifted. There'd been a rare, fleeting moment of happiness and then he'd ruined it all and she felt a fool for thinking anything had changed.

'Oh Danny boy, the pipes, the pipes are calling,' the crowd sang lustily with Freddie Mercury urging them on and Brian May giving it wellie on the guitar. Jeff and Valerie grinned at each other as they bopped exuberantly and sang their hearts out. From the moment the lights had dimmed and the roar of welcome from the crowd had nearly lifted the roof off the pavilion as the Pizza Oven stage rig exploded into light, Valerie had been in heaven. Freddie Mercury was almost within touching distance as he started the show with 'Let Me Entertain You' and then belted out 'We Will Rock You'.

At first she'd been shy about joining in the singing but as the band played all those songs that she sang and danced to at the disco in Hanlon's, she gave herself up to the music, and forgot her inhibitions. She was glad she'd worn her good jeans and a glittery boob tube. It was a perfect look for the concert, she and Lizzie had decided, after much trying on and discarding of outfits. Lizzie had done her make-up for her, in the school loo, and packed her school uniform neatly in a plastic bag before transforming her into a disco diva. Jeff had told her that a private bus was going from Wicklow. It would be leaving after the concert and would stop at Rockland's on the journey back so she'd booked a ticket, delighted that there would be no hassle in getting to and from the venue.

Jeff had met her off the bus and they had gobbled down a pizza, which she had insisted on paying for, before joining the queue. The doors opened at seven and they surged through. Jeff had his arm around her as they made their way to their assigned area and when they got there, he bent down and gave her a kiss on the cheek and pulled her closer, and she was secretly thrilled until she realized he was putting on a show for his mates from college, who also had tickets for the same section, and whom Ursula would have known. They had all been coming to the concert as a group.

It dawned on Valerie that Jeff was pretending she was his new girlfriend, and to good effect. One scrawny blonde with purple eye shadow, tight black jeans that hugged her pipe-cleaner legs, and a bright green halterneck top that showed off her bony shoulders, was giving her daggers looks. A friend of Ursula's, Valerie instantly deduced. Jeff clearly had an agenda and she was his pawn, she thought in dismay. Even though it was the kind of thing girls did all the time, she'd never thought that boys would be hurt enough to try and make a girl jealous.

'So I guess word will get back to Ursula that you were seen at Queen with a new girl,' she shouted into his ear amid the din, determined to let him know that she had him sussed.

'What?' He looked down at her, startled.

'That blonde girl just over there that keeps giving me dirty looks – is she one of Ursula's friends? That's why you brought me, wasn't it, to make Ursula jealous?'

A dull red foamed up over his shirt collar, rising to his hairline, and she knew she had mortified him. Good, she thought viciously. He had just proved her point. All men were bastards.

'Look . . . er . . . yeah. I did ask you to make her jealous, but I don't care now. I'm having fun and I'm glad you're with me. I could have sold the ticket but when I saw you in the chipper that day I thought I'd ask you. It was a spur-of-the-moment thing, honest. And then I thought I could make Ursula jealous as well because I wanted to get back at her . . .' His voice trailed away and he couldn't look at her.

'I don't like being used.'

'Don't be mad,' he pleaded, and his eyes were big pools of dismay. 'I like you a lot, Valerie. Honest!'

She couldn't stay angry with him. If he had denied it she would have despised him, but he'd been straight and she could understand his motives. And she liked that he was embarrassed. It showed he wasn't a bastard after all, just a boy with mixed-up feelings who was capable of being hurt. Someone just like her. She was glad she'd had the courage to bring it up. It had cleared the air between them. They were on a new footing now. It felt right.

'Let's give Miss Ursula something to be properly jealous about then,' she said wickedly, a madness coming over.

Jeff looked at her, stunned. 'Are you not mad at me?'

'I'm at Queen's concert, aren't I?' She laughed. 'It's not as if I *fancy* you or anything.'

His eyes widened. 'Oh!' he said, a touch deflated.

Got you, she thought triumphantly. Now *I'm* in charge.

It was a heady moment, a life-changing moment. One that she would never forget. She had taken back her power. Was this what women's liberation was all about? Turning things around so that you were in control of what was happening to you? Not being passive and just accepting whatever men dished out? Valerie wondered briefly, remembering all those *Cosmo* articles she had read on the subject. Whatever it was, she felt elated.

Before he knew what was happening, she drew Jeff's head down to hers and kissed him full on the mouth. His lips were so firm and dry, not like those wet, slobbery lips of that Higgins toad.

'Bet she'll be good and jealous now,' she laughed, drawing away and slanting a glance over at the scrawny blonde, who was slit-eyed with fury.

Jeff laughed. 'You're *bad*!' he said admiringly. 'And you're a sport. Thanks.'

'Let's just enjoy the concert, it's gonna be fab,' she shouted up at him, and her heart lightened as he hugged her tightly, and this time it wasn't to make anyone jealous, it was just for her.

By the time 'Killer Queen' started to thunderous acclaim from the crowd she didn't care who was looking or what anyone else was thinking, and she sang and danced uninhibitedly, lost in the magic of the best night of her life.

'That's you,' Jeff shouted at her. 'My Killer Queen!' And she wiggled her ass, laughing. She was dancing, waving her arms in the air to 'Crazy Little Thing Called

Love' when her eyes met Jeff's and for an infinitesimal moment it seemed as though the music faded and it was just the two of them looking at each other as if really seeing each other for the first time, and as though no one else existed, and then they were back in real time, dancing and singing. Forever after, Valerie would say that was the moment she fell in love with Jeff.

'It was brilliant, wasn't it?' Valerie turned shining eyes on him when the concert was over. She was fizzing with adrenalin as the freezing night air hit them when they emerged out of the Pavilion in a wave of ecstatically happy fans.

'It's a pity you can't stay later.' Jeff linked her arm. 'We could go for something else to eat. I'm starving again. We could have a last drink in Toner's and then have one of Ishmael's kebabs. They *really* hit the spot. That's the plan, anyway, with the rest of them,' he explained as he walked her to where all the coaches were parked. There were crowds milling around like a swarm of highly excited bees, and she wished she could have had a few minutes alone with him.

'I'd love to stay,' she said wistfully, 'but I've got to get back. My dad would go spare if I'm out too late. He thinks I'm revising for an exam, don't forget.' She'd told him the story she'd concocted with Lizzie's help.

'It was a great night anyway. I had a lot of fun, Valerie.' He dropped an arm around her shoulder. 'And . . . er . . . thanks for being . . . for being so understanding. I didn't mean to hurt your feelings or anything,' he added hastily.

'Ah, forget it. Do you think it will work? Do you think she'll come back to you?' She couldn't hide her curiosity.

'I don't want her back. Doing the dirty on someone, especially with a mate is just not on.' He looked at her and grinned. 'Forget her, I'd a great night with my Killer Queen,' he teased affectionately, giving her a squeeze.

'Me too, Jeff. It was the best night of my life. I can't believe I saw Queen live. They were fantastic. I'll never settle down to studying after this,' she declared happily, loving the feeling of his arm around her shoulder. It would have been nice if he'd said, 'Now that I've been on a date with you I wouldn't want to go back to her,' but it might take time for Jeff to forget his ex. She'd be waiting, Valerie decided, because she felt they were *meant* to be together. There was just *something* about that moment.

'The two of us had better get our heads down, I suppose. Christmas exams are coming up, but I'll see you around over the holidays next month, won't I?' He looked down at her.

'Sure. I owe you a drink at least, for tonight.' She wondered if he would kiss her. A car park thronged with thousands of people wasn't the most romantic place for a goodbye kiss but it would be better than not being kissed, she decided. Much to her disappointment he just gave her another hug as they stood at the steps of the bus.

'You're a real sport, Val. I had a great time. Safe journey home. I won't be down for the next couple of weekends but I'll see you over Christmas,' he said as she hugged him back. 'Good luck with the swotting and the exams.'

'You too, and thanks for tonight. I had a ball,' she assured him, conscious that other people were waiting to get on the bus behind her.

If he had kissed her it would have been an almost perfect night, she decided as she sat on the shabby threadbare seat in the warmth of the coach as it sped along the Stillorgan dual carriageway towards Wicklow. The buzz of animated chatter from her fellow concert-goers hummed all around her, but all she could think of was Jeff. He was so easy to talk to, good-humoured and good-natured, and very handsome. Was he interested in her at all or was he still consumed by the cheating Ursula? And had she scuppered her chances by saying she didn't fancy him? It was hard to know. Saying he'd see her over Christmas was not a commitment to meet up or anything. But then there was that magic moment between them when 'Crazy Little Thing' was being belted out. She hadn't imagined it. She *knew* she hadn't. It was all a bit nerve-racking, Valerie thought sleepily as adrenalin gave way to tiredness, and the heat and drone of the engine made her drowsy so that she fell into a doze as the miles sped by.

Jeff made his way back into town. He was too late for last orders, he reckoned, but he'd meet up with his mates at Ishmael's. He was ravenous, and on a high. It had been a cracker of a night, far better than he had anticipated, and that was all thanks to Valerie. She really was a great girl. He had been beyond embarrassed when she'd asked him straight out if he'd brought her to the concert to make Ursula jealous. Because that had been his intention.

When he had caught Ursula and George Owens snogging in George's parents' bedroom he had been gutted. George was supposed to be a mate. He'd thrown a party when his parents were at a medical conference in Barcelona. The house, a detached red-brick Victorian in Drumcondra, was perfect for an all-nighter. It had been one of the best parties he'd been to since he'd started college, with lots of drink, hash and loud disco music. He and Ursula had been hitting the dance floor, boogying to beat the band, and then she'd said she was going to the loo. He'd gone into the kitchen and cracked open another can of beer and chatted to a few girls who were sitting at the breakfast counter. He'd shared a spliff and felt a bit woozy and had dozed off for a while on a sofa in the conservatory. The music was still throbbing when he'd woken up and gone in search of Ursula.

'I saw her talking to George upstairs, a while ago,' Andy, one of his mates, said when he asked around if anyone had seen her.

They weren't talking when he found them. George had her pressed against a wall with his hands up under her top and she was kissing him, her hands running through his lank black hair.

'You dirty slapper,' he exploded, and both of them looked at him in dismay.

'Hey, mate, it was just a drunken snog,' George mumbled. 'She's a tasty bird and I got carried away.'

'Yeah, well, you can have her, ya big fat dopey bastard,' Jeff had sworn, then barrelled down the stairs and out the door, Ursula calling his name as he went. 'Bitch!' he'd muttered as he walked towards Drumcondra road. 'You and I are finished.'

He'd hailed a taxi near Fagan's, gave the address of his digs in Phibsboro, and leaned back against the smoke-riddled seat patterned with black cigarette burns.

Ursula was studying to be a primary teacher in St Pat's and he'd really fancied her the first time he'd met her at a party in the college. They'd been going together for the past three months and had started sleeping together. He'd thought he was in love and had considered bringing her home to meet his parents. That would not be happening now, he assured himself drunkenly. Ursula was history. That lecher Owens could have her. They deserved each other, although what Ursula could see in George was beyond him. His classmate looked like a lugubrious bloodhound, with bulging round eyes, a lardy physique and a tendency to spit when he got excited in conversation. Ursula must have been well drunk when she snogged him, because that was the only way *any* woman would go near him, Jeff thought bitterly as his heart twisted in pain to think that the girl he loved could betray him so easily.

'Look, I was pissed out of my skull. I can't *believe* I snogged that bullfrog,' Ursula pleaded the following day on the phone. 'Jeff, I'm sorry, *really* sorry. Please don't end it like this. Let's meet up and talk about it.'

'Nothing to talk about. I was pretty hammered too but I didn't go around letting girls maul me and sticking my tongue down your so-called friends' throats. How would you feel if I snogged Barbara?' he retorted, still furious and with an almighty hangover to boot.

'Aw Jeff, grow up and don't be so childish,' she snapped defensively. 'You're not living in the sticks now. Get over yourself. That's what happens at parties in the big city.'

'Ursula, George is welcome to you and you're welcome to him. He's an asshole and you're well suited.' With that stinging put-down he'd hung up and felt quite proud of himself. It was the first time a girl had done the dirty on him. He had always felt quite the ladies' man in Rockland's and his ego was more than bruised. Ursula's derisive implication that he was an unsophisticated hick rankled.

He had made the transition from a small fishing village to the big city pretty damn well, he thought angrily. And he'd been enjoying his life in Dublin until she'd mucked it up. He'd felt extremely sorry for himself as he shoved his sports gear into his bag and set off to the Phoenix Park for a few hours' football training.

Three times that week, Ursula rang him in his digs begging him to meet her. On the last call she said furiously, 'You're *so* childish, Jeff. What about my Queen ticket? We'd better meet so I can get it from you. I'll pay you for it.'

'Oh, I'm not bringing *you* to Queen. You can forget that. And I'm not selling it. See if George can get you a ticket, Ursula, and don't ring me again because I'm studying and I'm telling the landlady I'm not taking your calls,' he said calmly, and wished he could have seen her face as she let out an outraged squawk before he hung up.

He hoped that Barbara Nugent, the skinny blonde Valerie had copped watching them, would relay all the night's events to his ex. But surprisingly he wasn't that pushed about whether he saw Ursula again. After tonight he had a new girl on his mind. Valerie had surprised him . . . a lot. When she'd told him she didn't fancy him he'd been miffed, to say the least, and when she had kissed him so Barbara could tell Ursula all about it, he'd very much liked her spark, and the taste of her soft lips against his. *And* she was good fun, and much less serious than Ursula, who fancied herself as a serious intellectual and liked to appear superior and sophisticated. She wouldn't have let herself go dancing uninhibitedly like Valerie had at the concert. Well, he was going to stick with unsophisticated women and he was going to make

Valerie fancy him for sure. Something had happened between them tonight, something very nice. Nice was better than what Ursula Byrne offered him. Nice would do fine, Jeff decided as he emerged onto Baggot Street, whistling.

A biting sea breeze whistled around Valerie as she stepped off the bus at Rockland's, making her shiver, and she wished she had something warmer on under her coat than the flimsy boob tube. She raced across The Triangle over to Lizzie's house, where she retrieved her school bag from behind the garden wall, where Lizzie had hidden it beneath a shrub for her, and then hurried down the back lane and let herself into the yard. She pulled the bolt back gently on the shed door and rooted for the torch on top of the shelf. She pointed the beam of light to her school bag and took out make-up remover and cotton wool pads. Swiftly removing her make-up, she pulled on her school sweater over her boob tube, and hoisted up her uniform skirt before pulling off her high heels and jeans and slipping into her shoes. She folded up her concert clothes and hid them and her cigarettes in her school bag: necessary precautions just in case her father was still up, although it was unlikely. It was after twelve thirty; he was usually in bed before midnight.

Her mother was reading the paper in front of the fire, the dying orange embers in the grate cosy-looking in the lamplight. There was always a fire burning in the grate. Terence had access to the free fuel vouchers for the elderly at work and he helped himself, much to Carmel's disgust. 'That's stealing,' she'd told him angrily, more than once. 'You're ripping off tax payers, the ordinary people,

Terence. Ordinary people like us have to pay for those fuel vouchers and all that other stuff you pilfer.'

'Yeah, well, I'm a tax payer too. For the pittance I'm paid I deserve it, so zip it,' he'd retorted. He had a shed full of cleaning solutions, paint, paint brushes, ladders and the like, all acquired through nefarious ways, and Carmel was petrified that he would be caught nicking stuff and get the sack and make a holy show of them. It was a source of constant argument between them.

Her mother looked careworn and tired, Valerie thought with a pang. Her once nut-brown hair was liberally sprinkled with grey strands, and the glasses she had to wear for reading prematurely aged her. Her mother lived a drab life, Valerie acknowledged with a flash of pity. Had she ever felt anything like the exhilaration Valerie had felt a few hours earlier? Had she ever felt utterly alive and happy? Looking at Carmel, she was so glad she'd grasped the opportunity that had come her way. The Queen concert would be something to look back on with pleasure, if her life turned out to be as dreary as her mother's, although she had every intention of making sure that it didn't.

'Hi, Mam, just heading to bed. 'Night,' she said, stifling a yawn.

'You're very late.' Carmel raised her head from the paper and lowered her glasses.

'I didn't like to leave Lizzie on her own,' she said quickly. ''Night.' She hated lying to her mother. It was bad enough that Terence treated Carmel so disrespectfully, without Valerie telling her lies.

'Sleep well,' Carmel said tiredly, folding up the paper and putting the guard in front of the fire.

'I will,' Valerie said, removing her shoes to walk silently down the hall to her own room. She could hear her father's snores and felt a wave of relief he was none the wiser about her great adventure. Lying snug under her patchwork quilt in her lilac and white painted room, with the wind whistling down the chimney of the small fireplace, she re-examined every moment of the night's events. Like the miser Silas Marner, counting his gold, she polished those precious memories and stored them deep in the vault of her brain where they would be taken out and mulled over for many nights to come.

Life, she decided happily, had never been this good.

'I want a word with you, madam!' Valerie felt a sudden apprehension as she looked up from her French verbs and saw her father standing at her bedroom door. She had been so immersed in her revision she hadn't heard him come in from the bingo where he called out the numbers every week.

She knew the minute she saw the aggressive jut of his jaw and the thinning of his lips that she was in big trouble. She said nothing, keeping her expression neutral, and just hoped he couldn't hear the telltale thumping of her heart.

'You told me lies, you sly little liar!' He closed the door behind him and she felt a deep fear. 'You weren't babysitting! You were at a concert in Dublin, weren't you? And don't try to lie to me. A lad I know from work was at it and he saw you hanging out of some fella in the queue.' He stuck his face into hers, and she could see the broken veins in his nose and the glitter of hard anger in his watery grey eyes. 'Did you enjoy it, Valerie?' he said viciously.

'Yeah,' she muttered, knowing there was no point in trying to get out of it. She wouldn't put it past him to march her up to Lizzie's sister to see if she'd been babysitting, if she insisted she had been.

'Well, now you're going to pay for your enjoyment. You don't tell me a host of lies and get away with it, you lying little tramp.' He stood up and unbuckled his belt.

'Don't you hit me with that!' she exclaimed, startled, jumping to her feet. He'd never hit her before and certainly not with his belt. She couldn't believe it was happening. She couldn't believe that Terence had such dominion over her that he felt it was perfectly acceptable to inflict physical pain on her. She had never felt so powerless or so vulnerable as he blocked her way to the door. Fury suffused his face as he shoved her back against the bed.

'I'll hit you with whatever I like, miss. You won't make a fool of me again,' he shouted, raising his hand high and bringing the belt down with all the strength he could muster.

As the lashes rained down she clenched her teeth to stop herself from groaning. He would not know how much pain he was inflicting. He would not know how humiliated and helpless she felt. But he would know how much she despised and loathed him, she vowed. And she would never, *ever* forgive him.

CHAPTER NINE

'Hey, stranger, I haven't seen you out much. Where have you been hiding? Happy Christmas.' Jeff's voice made Valerie's heart lurch and she turned to find him looking at her, a broad smile creasing his face. She was in the supermarket getting some shopping for her mother. It was the day before New Year's Eve.

'Hi yourself,' she said flatly. He hadn't been in touch since the concert. For all she knew he was back with Ursula. She wasn't going to pretend to be thrilled to see him. He was a man, they were all the same, and she hated the species.

'So where have you been? I thought I'd see you in the hotel on Christmas Eve or Stephen's Night.' He looked taken aback at her coolness.

'Um, had family stuff, couldn't make it this year,' she said offhandedly, dropping a pint of milk into her basket.

'Are you going to be there tomorrow night? Will we see in the new decade together?'

'Er . . .' she dithered, '. . . Probably.'

'Great, we can catch up. It's good to see you, Valerie.' He was smiling down at her so warmly, his brown eyes staring into hers. She felt confused. Was he really glad to see her or was he putting it on?

'So what's the news? How did your exams go?' he asked as she moved towards the cashier.

'I think I did OK.' She shifted the basket to her other arm. 'How did you do?'

'Here, let me carry that,' he said, taking it from her.

'Thanks, Jeff,' she murmured, wishing she could even pretend to be bright and perky. She just felt completely flat and miserable, and wished that the Christmas festivities would be over so she could be unhappy in peace without having to feign festive cheer. There was no way she would be allowed to go to the hotel to celebrate New Year's Eve. Terence wouldn't even allow her out on Friday nights to go babysitting with Lizzie any more.

'You'll be going nowhere until you have your exams done. I won't be giving you the chance to make a fool of me again, you little liar,' he'd told her the morning after he'd beaten her, as she stood at the kitchen sink, drinking a cup of tea and trying to ignore the scalding pain in the backs of her legs and buttocks.

'At least I'm not a thief,' she said spiritedly.

He would have hit her again only her mother stepped between them and said in the sternest voice Valerie had ever heard her use, 'Don't you ever lay another finger on her, Terence, or I'll phone the guards. You've gone too far this time.'

'If she pulls a stunt like that again she'll get worse,' her father had growled. 'And you won't be out any later than eight o'clock until your exams are over.' He'd pointed a finger in her face before grabbing his jacket and brushing past them to go to work.

'Do you want to stay at home today?' Carmel had asked her dispiritedly. 'Go on back to bed and I'll bring you some toast. I'll write a note for your teacher, and for God's sake don't ever give him an opportunity like that again. Do your exams and get the best marks you can, so you can get out of here.'

'I hate him. How can you stay with him, Mam? He thinks he *owns* us!' Valerie had burst into tears. She was angry with her mother for being so submissive. And deep down, she was also angry with her for not stepping in and protecting her.

'Go back to bed,' her mother had repeated wearily, and Valerie saw that Carmel's eyes were bright with tears. They never spoke of the incident again and a shroud of depression settled around the house that not even Christmas could lift. If anything, it added to the gloom, and Carmel had cooked a chicken instead of a turkey, much to Terence's disgust.

'If you want a turkey cook it yourself. I couldn't be bothered going through all the charade and Valerie's not pushed because I asked her,' Carmel said dully, and turned her back on him when he asked her if she had ordered the bird.

'And what about me? The wage earner in the house who works from dawn till dusk to provide for you pair of ungrateful cows?' he'd demanded, furious. But for once, Carmel had let him rant and she went to her room where he knew never to enter.

Usually Valerie put up the tree and the decorations but this year she stayed mostly in her room and he had to decorate the house himself, desperate that the neighbours would think nothing untoward was going on.

When the memories of the beating invaded Valerie's mind at night, she banished them with thoughts of her much-longed-for reunion with Jeff, but as the days passed and there was no contact from him she'd found no respite there and felt an irrational resentment towards him for letting her down. Now, looking at him as he helped unload her shopping at the cash desk, she felt herself softening. One thing about him, he had great manners, she thought approvingly. It was one of the things she most liked about him.

She paid for her purchases, bagged them, and waited for him to put his few items through. The supermarket was busy with people replenishing their stores for the New Year celebrations and several people greeted them and wished them 'Happy New Year' as they made their way out the door.

'I have Ma's car; I'll give you a lift.'

'No, it's fine, it's only across the way,' Valerie shrugged.

'It's starting to sleet, come on. Look, I got a real handy spot right opposite the door.' He pointed to the car, which was parked practically in front of them. Part of her wanted to tell him to get lost – why hadn't he been around when she'd needed him most? But she could tell that he had no idea that she was pissed off with him. And, she reminded herself, she had told him at the concert that she didn't fancy him so why would he even think she was annoyed?

'OK,' she agreed, and he took her shopping bag and shoved it on the back seat before holding open the passenger door for her.

'You're a bit quiet,' he remarked as he reversed out of the parking space and drove towards The Triangle.

'I won't be at the hotel tomorrow night. I'm not allowed out. My dad found out I'd been to the concert and beat the living daylights out of me with his belt.' It all came tumbling out and her lower lip wobbled as she tried hard not to cry.

'Are you *serious*?' He glanced over at her, looking shocked. 'God, that's the pits. I'm really sorry.' She struggled to compose herself but it was no use, her face crumpled under his concerned gaze and she burst into tears. 'Let's get out of here and go somewhere private,' he said awkwardly. He accelerated up the road and took a left towards the hotel and the sea as she sniffled into her tissue, mortified at her meltdown. He followed the curve of the coast for a half-mile or so and pulled into an empty layby and picnic area.

'Are you OK? Valerie?' He stared at her helplessly. 'Would you like me to speak to your dad and say it was my fault?' That made her cry even harder as he took one of her hands in his.

'No . . . thanks,' she managed before breaking into fresh sobs.

'Is there anything I can do?' he asked tentatively.

'No, it's . . . it's OK,' she hiccuped. 'I just feel what right had he to do that to me? I'm seventeen. I'm not a kid. To take his belt off and wallop me with it and not feel anything about how much it was hurting me. I'm his daughter. His only child. How could he do it, Jeff? How?' Her pain was so raw she felt she was having a heart attack. 'You wouldn't do that to a dog, and it just kills me that everyone thinks he's Mr Nice Guy. I hate him, Jeff. Imagine hating your own father?' The words were tumbling out now in a torrent.

'I couldn't imagine that, Valerie; I get on well with my da. I'm really sorry to hear what you've just told me. I didn't realize how tough things were for you at home.' He stroked her hand gently.

'Sorry for bawling,' she apologized, looking at him through puffy eyes blurred from tears. 'I'm so embarrassed.'

'Don't be embarrassed. Why should you be?' he said gruffly. 'I wouldn't have asked you to come to the concert if I had known it would cause you such problems.'

'I'm glad you did,' she said fiercely. 'I had so much fun, more than I've ever had.'

'I had fun too.' He looked so upset and serious she impulsively reached over and stroked his cheek and then, realizing what she was doing, stopped, her hand dropping to her lap. 'Sorry. I don't know why I . . . oh God, now I'm even more embarrassed,' she groaned.

'I was really looking forward to seeing you again, Valerie. I've thought about you a lot,' Jeff said quietly.

'I've thought about you too,' she admitted.

'Would you be able to come for a drink tomorrow afternoon? We could celebrate New Year's Eve early?'

'I'd like that.' She wiped her eyes. 'Is Ursula back on the scene?' She had to ask.

'God, no!' he exclaimed. 'That's really over. Like I said, I've thought about you a lot and I'd like to take you on a date tomorrow even if it is the middle of the afternoon. That's if you want to. You did say you didn't fancy me.' He gave her a teasing grin.

'An afternoon drink date might change that,' she agreed, giving a wobbly smile.

Their eyes met and he cupped her face in his hands and kissed her so tenderly that she was afraid she might start to cry again.

Lying in bed that night, unwilling to sit watching TV in the same room as Terence, she took comfort from the memory of Jeff and his tenderness towards her. She knew without the shadow of a doubt that he would never do anything to hurt or harm her. He was as far removed from the type of man her father was as could be. Maybe the new decade was going to be the best time ever in her life. She knew for certain that the eighties would see her leave her family home to stand on her own two feet, and even though the thought scared her, it invigorated her as well. She would get good marks in her Leaving Cert because she was working like a Trojan and it would pay off. This time next year, if she was lucky, she would have a job, she comforted herself. She would be earning her own money and Terence would have no power over her ever again. And tomorrow she was going on a date, and her father wouldn't even know about it. Jeff was a *real* man, a gentle man and he wanted to date her. Maybe good things were going to happen at last. Her spirits began to lift and the awful cloud of darkness that had being smothering her for the past few weeks began to dissipate.

Valerie smiled at the memory of Jeff's kindness and tenderness towards her. Even all these years later she could remember that moment as though it had happened yesterday. For the first time in her life she had realized that men could be kind and loving. It had been a revelation. She had never seen her father act tenderly towards her mother. Terence had never been affectionate with her, but as Lizzie had pointed out to her not so long ago when they had been discussing her relationship with her father,

Terence had never received love and, consequently, didn't know how to give it.

Valerie sighed, fingering the gold cross that hung around her neck and which had been one of Jeff's first gifts to her. He knew what it was to be kind and loving because he had experienced it. She was lucky, she supposed, that Carmel had made up for Terence's failures as a parent, in her own quiet way. It was thanks to her mother that Valerie had enjoyed one of the most momentous occasions of her life when she had crossed the threshold of adulthood and never looked back.

CHAPTER TEN

'I'm a free woman!' Valerie danced around Lizzie's bedroom as she ripped off her school blouse and stepped out of her uniform skirt.

'Me too. Yippeeeeeeee!' Lizzie hollered, flinging her tie out the window. They had finished their last exam, and they were elated. School days were finally behind them and the future beckoned. And the beginning of that future was the End of Exam Barbecue, which was taking place down on the beach in a few hours' time.

Valerie had told her mother about the planned celebrations the previous week. 'And I don't care what Dad says, I'm going, Mam, and if he takes the belt to me again I'm going to have him charged with assault,' she'd said heatedly.

'Go to your barbecue, I'll deal with him,' Carmel had responded with uncharacteristic decisiveness. 'It might be a good idea to stay with Lizzie for the night. Then you won't have to be worried about what time you get in and he won't be getting himself worked up.'

'Thanks, Mam.' Valerie flung her arms around her mother and hugged her. Carmel's arms tightened around her. They didn't usually show much affection and because it was so rare, it was a precious moment.

'You're a good girl, and a good daughter. I want you to have fun and be carefree when your exams are over. You've worked so hard you deserve it, and I'm very proud of you. I'm sorry I didn't do more to stop your father beating you. I didn't realize that was his intention.' Carmel's cheeks were pink as she made her speech, and her eyes were dark with a sad weariness that caught at Valerie's heart.

'It wasn't your fault, Mam. Don't think it was. I certainly don't blame you,' she'd said earnestly. 'I just don't think Dad likes me very much. I know he always wanted a boy.'

'Well, I'm glad I had you,' Carmel had replied fiercely. 'And now you can live your own life and be independent. Always stand on your own two feet, Valerie. Don't end up like me, dependent on a man like your father, with no life of my own.'

'But why don't you get a job, Mam? Earn your own money?' Valerie had asked, surprised to be having such an unexpectedly intimate conversation with her mother. Carmel rarely spoke of her feelings.

'I suppose I could. I could try to get work in the hotel, or in some of the B & Bs now that the summer season's upon us. Your father would probably be all for it. You know what he's like about money – the more there is the better.' She gave a wry smile.

'I think that's a great idea, Mam. It feels so good having your own money. Lizzie and I and all the girls in our class have applied for jobs all over the place. We've done the Civil Service, Corporations, and County Council exams, and the banks, and hopefully we'll get high up on the selection panels,' Valerie said cheerfully.

'Aahh, don't worry, you'll get a job with no bother, a bright girl like you. And I should stop being such a stick-in-the-mud, shouldn't I?' Carmel had said, displaying a bit of spark.

'Yes, Mam. Get out there and be independent the way you're always telling me to be. And when I get a car, we can learn to drive together. We don't have to depend on him. He won't let you drive his car and he's told me I won't be getting behind the wheel either, so stuff him. We'll learn to drive ourselves,' Valerie had said excitedly, relishing the thought of the look on her father's face when she and her mother would no longer be obliged to him to be taken anywhere.

'I don't think I'd have the nerve to drive,' Carmel said doubtfully.

'You will, I'll help you,' Valerie had urged. 'We won't tell him and then when you're confident enough you'll just drive off one day in my car and leave him gobsmacked.'

'We'll see.' Carmel had laughed, and Valerie had never felt so close to her.

Life was certainly improving, she thought now, as she stood under the shower in Lizzie's untidy bathroom, lathering sweet-scented peach shower cream all over. Jeff would be at the barbecue tonight. His exams had finished a few days ago, so tonight would be a double celebration. She couldn't wait.

Since that first afternoon date at New Year they had met most Sunday afternoons when his football match was over, going for a walk on the beach and a drink in the hotel afterwards. Jeff was great fun to be with, but he had a sensitive side that helped her through the lonely months of her curfew. Looking forward to their Sundays together kept her going.

They would walk along the beach holding hands and catch up on the events of their respective week, before going back to the car, if he was able to borrow either of his parents'. They would drive to a secluded spot, and kiss and cuddle, and Valerie was never happier than when she and Jeff were in that special little bubble of time that was theirs alone. All the worries of exams and her unhappy home life would evaporate for a while. As dusk began to fall they would drive back to the hotel for a drink before he would take her home around six. Then she would feel sad, knowing that he was heading up to Dublin and she had a long week of study ahead of her.

'We're soulmates, Lizzie,' she would tell her best friend, who, tragically, had become manless at Easter. Phil Casey had turned out to be two-timing Lizzie with a Goth from Bray, and she was devastated and furious while trying not to be envious of Valerie's blossoming romance.

Lizzie was hoping that tonight her dry spell would be over and she would meet 'The One' at the barbecue. Valerie hoped she would too, so that she and Jeff could double date with her friend. She hated seeing Lizzie lonely and distressed after her break-up with Phil. She wanted them both to have fun. Now that the exams were over Terence could stick his curfew, blunt end first, up his skinny ass, she'd told her best friend. She was going to make up for all those months of isolation. She was going to party and she wanted Lizzie to be as happy as she was.

In high spirits they pulled on bikinis and denim shorts. Lizzie selected a white V-necked T-shirt from her wardrobe, which emphasized her pert boobs and her golden tan. Valerie put on a pink and blue stripy cheesecloth shirt and tied it in a knot at her breastbone and slipped into a pair of white espadrilles. They looked great, they assured themselves as they studied their reflection in the chipped bevelled mirror in the corner of Lizzie's bedroom.

Lizzie was tall, and with her jet-black hair that fell in a silky curtain around her face, she reminded Valerie of Ali MacGraw. She studied herself critically. At five foot two she wished that she were a couple of inches taller, but at least she was slim enough, with curves in the right places. Her blond hair, worn in a shaggy cut, gave her an air of sophistication *à la* Jane Fonda in *Klute*, she decided, as she fiddled with the knot of her blouse to get it dead centre. At least they didn't look like schoolgirls any more, she thought, as she applied another coat of mascara to her eyelashes. They had their beach bags packed and a bottle of vodka wrapped in a towel. It was time to go party.

'You pair better have something to eat to line your stomachs,' Ciara Anderson called up the stairs, and Valerie marvelled at how free and easy Lizzie's mother was. She had cooked lasagne for dinner and they tucked into it with enthusiasm before setting out across The Triangle on their way to the hotel.

> *'All in together, girls*
> *This fine weather, girls.*
> *He saw. I saw. Sitting on a see saw.'*

The chants of a group of little girls skipping filled the air. The thwack of a ball against the wall of the Ball Alley, as a trio of boys played handball, and the singsong rhythm, 'Plainy a packet of Rinso, Uppy a packet of Rinso', as two friends played a game of Two Balls, made them smile. The Triangle was a favourite spot for children to play, as it had been for Valerie and Lizzie, and their parents' generation too.

'Remember when we used to play Two Balls? We just play it a bit different now,' Lizzie giggled, and Valerie snorted with laughter. Lizzie was irrepressible and Valerie loved that wicked streak. She hoped her friend would never change.

The village was buzzing in the early evening sun. Day-trippers coming up from the beach thronged the shops and café. The flowers were blooming voluptuously, vivid splashes of colour against the freshly painted buildings. Even the cordylines in The Triangle waved languidly in the balmy breeze. Rockland's was glorious on a summer's day and the Tidy Town committee had worked hard to get the village looking its best. The contrasts between the deserted, drab, gloomy grey of winter and the manic, bright, exuberant energy of summer was hard to believe. Some of the inhabitants hated summer, with the daily invasion of noisy tourists, and loved the peace of winter when the villagers reclaimed Rockland's for their own. Others thrived on the summer energy when the village was alive, and dreaded the long dark nights of winter when the village went into hibernation, and was forgotten about by the rest of the world. Now, though, the buzz and high spirits that permeated Main Street and The Triangle matched Valerie's mood, and she and Lizzie called out greetings to people they knew as they made their way down to the seafront to where Jeff and the others were waiting.

CHAPTER ELEVEN

Jeff was waiting for them in the hotel's beer garden, and he and Valerie hugged tightly.

'How did it go?' he asked. He was drinking beer and she took a sip of the cool golden liquid.

'I think I did OK. The only one I'm a bit worried about was maths. The trigonometry question was really hard, but there's nothing I can do about it now,' she sighed.

'You'll be fine,' he said reassuringly. 'Right, women, what are you drinking?' He raised a dark eyebrow and she thought how handsome he was with his thick hair that curled down over his collar and wide brown eyes that looked like smooth velvet.

'Dubonnet and white, and vodka and orange,' they chorused, settling themselves on the white plastic chairs that Jeff had kept for them. A big green and orange parasol flapped in the breeze, overhead, shading them from the glare of the sun, and behind them exotic-coloured butterflies feasted on an enormous buddleia whose purple branches drooped with pollen-filled blooms. The garden was thronged with school leavers, the young waitresses kept busy as rounds of drinks were bought and consumed with zest. Knowing that they were finally finished with school, and on the threshold of adulthood

and freedom lent an air of manic excitement to their
drinking. Several of Valerie's classmates were already the
worst for wear. It was a scorcher, the temperature still in
the high seventies, although the sun was throwing long
shadows, and Jeff and Lizzie and Valerie were eager to
get to the beach and go for a swim before the barbecue.
They finished their drinks and made their way down to
the sea, crossing the hot steel railway tracks onto the
sand. They could see the flames of the bonfire in the
distance, and the smell of charcoal mixed with the aroma
of charred pork ribs wafted across the strand. Shouts of
welcome and the waving of beer bottles greeted them.
Valerie knew that when she looked back on her life this
would be one of the highlights. She had never felt as carefree, happy and optimistic as she was right now. Jeff
squeezed her hand and held her steady as she skirted
some seaweed-covered rocks, and she relished the way
he always took care of her, treating her as though she was
something precious and fragile.

The sea was lukewarm after the heat of the sun, and
she raced out into the surf, followed by Jeff and a squeal-
ing Lizzie, who would never get straight down but stood,
arms wrapped around her, yelling as the waves whacked
her. After paralleling Jeff for a while as he sliced through
the water with a powerful breaststroke Valerie fell behind,
turned on her back and floated, staring at the feathery
wisps of clouds that were turning pink in the setting sun,
and feeling utterly relaxed. The sound of 'Yes Sir, I Can
Boogie' drifted down from the beach. She could see
people dancing and smooching, while others sat with
plates of food on their knees, laughing and chatting. Jeff
swam up to her and they lay side by side with the water

lapping between them, a dazzling silky sheet of molten orange and gold, and watched the sun sink below the horizon. This is bliss, she thought as the water rippled over her tummy and caressed the tips of her toes. The first night of my new life and it's only just starting.

'I'm going down to that beach and I'm bringing that one home. It's no place for her. If you'd see all them young ones wearing next to nothing around the place, locked out of their minds, some of them . . . I'm telling you, Carmel, she had no business going without asking my permission. She's getting notions about herself and I'm going to put a stop to any wild behaviour before it starts. She needn't think she's going to be doing what she likes in this house. I'm the boss and she'd better realize it. While she's living under *my* roof, she'll obey *my* rules.' Terence took a slug of tea and ate a slice of fruitcake, his face puce as he fumed over his daughter's lack of parental respect.

'She asked my permission and I gave it,' Carmel said tightly, drying the bread knife and wishing she could stick it between her husband's shoulder blades.

'What do you mean, *you* gave permission?' he blustered, staring at her.

'I gave her permission to go to the barbecue and to stay the night in Lizzie's,' Carmel repeated dully.

'Without asking *me*?' Terence couldn't hide his incredulity, his hand with its slice of cake suspended in mid-air.

'I'm Valerie's parent too. I'm her mother. I gave birth to her and I've as much right, if not more, to give her permission to do something. She's worked very hard this year,

she deserves her night out. And I'm telling you one thing,
Terence Harris, if you do anything to spoil this night for
her, if you say one word to her, I'm writing to the council
and I'm going to tell them about all the stuff you've been
thieving from them over the years—'

'Have you gone *mad*? Who do you think you are, talking to me like that?' He jumped up and slammed the
table with his fist so that his cup shook.

Carmel stood her ground although she was quaking
inside. 'I should have put my foot down with you long
ago, you big bully. If I had known you were going to beat
Valerie with your belt you would have had to get past me
first. Did it make you feel good? How brave you are,
hitting a young girl half your size with your belt. You
sicken me. It was the sorry day I agreed to marry you,
Terence Harris. I only did it to get away from home
because I had a father like you, a father who was fond of
using his fists. You're not men at all, you're sad, pathetic
excuses for men – cowards, bullyboys and uncouth igno-
ramuses with no breeding – and if you ever touch Valerie
again you'll be sorry. And if you get the sack it will be
good enough for you, going around the village pretending butter wouldn't melt in your mouth.' The anger, rage
and bitterness she'd been swallowing down all her life
erupted like lava from a volcano, unstoppable.

Terence stared at her, his mouth open. If Carmel hadn't
been so angry she would have laughed at the perplexity
in his eyes. Why had it taken her so long, she wondered
as she glowered at him. Why had she let him walk over
her, repeating the pattern she had endured with her
father and her brothers? They had treated her like dirt,
like an unpaid skivvy, and when she had married she'd

endured more of the same. Well, now it was finished. The pattern was finally broken. With elated satisfaction she turned her back on her baffled husband and walked from the kitchen. The worm had turned and Terence Harris had lost his power over her. She would never give it back to him, Carmel vowed, walking into her small cell of a room with its narrow single bed and lilac nylon bedspread.

Valerie was right, she should get a job and learn to drive, not surrender to a life of tyranny. She was only fifty, not an old crone. Valerie would fly the nest eventually and then she was responsible for no one but herself, she thought with a little jolt. Her mother was dead. Cancer had claimed her after a short vicious onslaught. Once the funeral was over she had left her father and her brothers boozing in the parlour, taken a few keepsakes from her mother's dressing table, walked out of the house and never gone back. She hadn't seen any of them in three years and she had no desire ever to see them again. She was free compared to many women who were tied with family responsibilities. She should make the most of it. It was a new decade, and women were becoming vastly empowered; she too would be an empowered woman of the eighties, Carmel thought with a little smile, wondering if she would have the courage to see it through.

Terence poured himself another cup of tea and noticed that his hand was shaking. What had come over Carmel? What a mouthful of impudence she had given him. The anger she had lashed him with, the look of derision in her hazel eyes, which sparkled with hostility. She'd never raised her voice to him before. And she'd certainly never threatened him. It must be the change of life business that women of a certain age went through. Didn't their hormones go rampant and they behaved like termagants? He frowned. She'd gone through that when she'd had the hysterectomy, he thought, perplexed. Was this something new?

Maybe she was starting to go doolally! Whatever it was, something had changed. He wasn't the boss of his own house any more. That Valerie one was too smart for her boots and needed discipline, but now that she had finished her exams she felt she could do as she pleased. Well, let her have her illusion for the rest of the summer, if that would shut Carmel up and bring her back to her senses. He couldn't risk her shopping him at work, and the way she was carrying on he wouldn't trust her not to. The woman was downright irrational! But come the autumn, when he was paying college fees, his daughter would be rightly under his control and *then* she'd find out who was boss. He'd lay down the law in no uncertain terms, and she'd know her place, by God she would, Terence vowed, his lips a thin mean line in his mottled red face.

'Let's go over to the dunes,' Valerie murmured, drawing away from a long lingering kiss with Jeff. The moon was throwing silver streamers on the sea and the flames of the big bonfire crackled and sparked in the dark. Disco music blared from a boom box and people bopped exuberantly under the stars. Others were skinny-dipping, splashing and yelling in drunken merriment. Lizzie was snogging a bearded six-footer whom Valerie recognized as a chef from the hotel.

Valerie didn't want to be kissing her boyfriend with a load of her classmates looking on; she wanted to be on her own with Jeff. She wanted to touch him everywhere and feel his skin on hers, and feel his hands doing the things that had, at long last, made her feel deliciously hot and quivery. She slipped her hand into her beach bag and took out her crumpled towel. Hand in hand, they stole quietly away to the inky darkness of the high dunes that ran like a mountain range along the beach. They found a ferny hollow and spread out the towel and then they were in each other's arms, kissing, touching, hungry for each other. Jeff unhooked the top of her bikini and gently cupped her breasts, his thumbs giving her unimaginable pleasure as they caressed her nipples.

'Let's go the whole way,' she murmured against his mouth as her hands slid beneath the waistband of his shorts.

'No, you've had too much to drink. I don't want to take advantage. It should be something special the first time we do it,' he muttered hoarsely.

'You wouldn't be taking advantage – I *want* to. I want you to be the first, Jeff. I never thought I'd even *like* doing it after one experience I had, and you changed all that,' she said earnestly. 'I'm not drunk, just lovely and floaty. Even if I hadn't drunk anything I'd still want to,' she assured him. 'It's such a beautiful night, and I'm having such a wonderful time, it would be really special for me and I hope it would be special for you.'

He took her face in his hands. 'It will be, Val. You're beautiful and amazing, and being with you these past few months has been a great time in my life.'

'Better than with Ursula?' She just *had* to know.

'Much!' he said emphatically.

'Jeff, I'm really happy when I'm with you, happier than I've ever been. I love being with you.' Her eyes were shining. She loved that he didn't want to take advantage of her because he thought she'd drunk too much. It showed he *really* cared.

'We have to use a condom. I don't want to get you pregnant.'

'Have you got one?'

'I can get one,' he grinned. 'And I'll bring another towel.'

He jumped up, adjusted his clothes and disappeared over the top of the dunes and she sat in the moonlight watching the Plough and Venus and Orion's belt twinkling in the black velvet sky. The waves lapped against the shore in a soothing lullaby that not even the sound of the Rolling Stones in the distance could dissipate. She was nervous and excited. She trusted Jeff implicitly. He had proved himself to her these last six months. They had something really special going on between them and he had been like a balm to her wounded spirit, bringing her back to herself when she had been drowning in hate, bitterness and helplessness. Jeff's love had been her salvation, Valerie knew. Now she wanted to take things a step further and it seemed he did too. Some of the girls in her class had done it with blokes they didn't have real feelings for. She was lucky. Her first time was going to be with a boy she loved. At this very moment, Valerie knew she would never be as happy as she was right now. She was on the threshold of a whole new life in every way and she was ready for it.

Jeff was breathless when he returned, and she threw her arms around him and kissed him. He kissed her back ardently and she was secretly delighted that she could arouse him so much and so utterly relieved that her fears of being frigid had long since been put to rest.

'Are you sure?' he asked once more when he lifted his head a little while later.

Her heart was beating madly with nervous anticipation. She wondered would it hurt, and then she couldn't help remembering a conversation at school about girls getting so tense, the boys couldn't get out of them. Vagi something it was called. How scary would that be?

'We don't have to if you don't want to,' he said reassuringly when she hesitated.

'I am sure,' she whispered. 'Just be real gentle, won't you?'

'I will, Valerie. I swear I won't hurt you . . . ever,' Jeff murmured, and she drew him close to her and wrapped herself around him, sure that he never would.

CHAPTER TWELVE

'Don't you stay out all night, miss. And don't forget, don't come back to this house with any news that we don't want to hear. Keep your legs closed when you're out with that Egan fella,' Terence warned, as he lay sprawled on the sofa watching *The Dukes of Hazzard*.

'*Terence!* Don't be so crude. There's no need for that kind of vulgarity.' Carmel flushed a dull red.

'You are pig ignorant,' Valerie said contemptuously, grabbing her cigarettes from the coffee table and stuffing them into her bag.

'And you look like a little tart with all that muck on your face. Those jeans are too small for you, too. I don't want the people of Rockland's thinking I've reared a tramp, and well they might think it the hour of the night you come home at and the state you come home in, so don't give me any more of your lip.'

Valerie's fingers curled into her palms so hard she left nail marks. She would love to rake her fingers down her father's face and draw blood. He had become more obnoxious, more intent on demeaning her since she'd started working at in the County Council that September, and his parental authority over her had diminished.

'For God's sake!' Carmel exclaimed, disgusted. 'You

should be ashamed of yourself, Terence Harris, saying things like that to your own daughter.'

'Ah, shut up, you, and don't be annoying me.' Terence dismissed her with an imperious wave and turned up the sound on the TV.

''Night, Mam,' Valerie muttered, brushing past her mother to get out of the house as quickly as she could. She *hated* that her father belittled her mother, telling her to shut up, but she hated it even more that Carmel took it from him. Despite having put her foot down a few times over his behaviour, Carmel still let him get away with far too much, Valerie felt.

She hurried down the garden path, fuming. She'd had enough. She was getting the hell out of Rockland's as soon as she could. Lizzie had moved to Dublin a few weeks ago and was living in a poky bedsit. She was always begging Valerie to move to the capital and share a flat with her, but Valerie had a car loan to pay off in the Credit Union and she felt she couldn't afford to pay rent as well.

'But you're paying for your keep at home,' Lizzie pointed out. 'There won't be that much in the difference, and you'd be able to see Jeff a lot more during the week. You've got a good salary, you can well afford it. I think you're just making excuses,' her friend said perceptively.

'Maybe you're right,' Valerie conceded, 'but it's different for you, Lizzie. You know you can always come back home if anything goes wrong and you can't afford the rent. Once I leave I'm gone for good. Da won't ever let me come back unless I crawl, and I won't be doin' that! So I'll be on my own.'

'Sell the friggin' car, pay off the loan and start saving again,' Lizzie had urged.

'No. It took me ages to save enough to secure a loan. I don't want to go back to square one. And anyway, I'm letting Mam practise in it. We're taking lessons. It gives me freedom. I couldn't give it up. As soon as I pay off the loan I'll apply for a transfer to Dublin or the County Councils, and come and live with you,' she'd promised, wishing she had the nerve to up sticks like Lizzie had. She wanted to move to Dublin but she also wanted to have a little nest egg for emergencies. Life had taught Valerie to be as well prepared as she possibly could for any eventuality.

But this time Terence had gone too far and given her the kick in the ass she needed. Lizzie was right: what she paid her parents for her keep would be almost enough to pay rent. It was time to leave home and get out from under Terence's thumb. She was only being a coward, she admonished herself angrily. But never the less, as much as a part of her longed to leave home, a small part of her felt daunted. Making the transition from schoolgirl to career girl was more overwhelming than she'd anticipated.

Those first weeks in her new job when she had felt like such a 'new girl' and everything had been so unfamiliar had been nerve-racking. People had been kind but everyone had their own little clique and she felt like an outsider going into the staff canteen, wondering where to sit. She had been working in the car tax department and the work was so mind-numbingly boring she had even longed to go on the public counter, despite the tales she heard about people losing their rag and hurling abuse at the counter staff.

As the first few weeks went by she had filed what seemed like a million green documents in their beige folders, and the hours had dragged on interminably. She had wondered despairingly if this was what her life was to be like. Should she have gone to college? One morning she had woken up feeling sick and shivery and had lain in bed wondering if it was too soon in her career to call in sick. When she was at school it wouldn't have been an issue: she would have just turned over and gone back asleep, and her mother would have given her a note for her teachers the next day. But she wasn't at school, she was at work – 'real' work – where notes from your parent didn't count. The probationary period could be extended. She could lose an increment for taking too much sick leave or having too many lates. At the very least a higher-ranking officer in the Personnel Department would interview her. Sometimes being 'grown up' wasn't as liberating as she'd imagined, Valerie thought miserably as she'd made her way into work on the bus, hoping she wouldn't puke.

When she'd heard that she was only entitled to twenty-one days' annual leave she'd been shocked. Memories of all those long lazy school holidays every summer came racing back. How she had taken for granted carefree days on the beach with Lizzie, reading and listening to their favourite pop programme, *Solid Gold McNamara*, playing brilliant music on her trusty little tranny. Then they would maybe knock a few balls around with tennis rackets on the hard sand near the sea's edge, before going for a swim. Afterwards, there'd be a snack of crisps and a juicy Granny Smith washed down with Coke, before a delightful snooze in the dunes, the sun warming sea-cooled limbs. Or, on wet days, lazing in bed reading Mills & Boons, or her absolute favourite, Georgette Heyer, borrowed from the library, which she passed on to her mother when she was finished with them. If her period knocked her for six she could curl up on the sofa with a hot-water bottle on her tummy and watch afternoon TV while Carmel made a fuss of her and brought her hot chocolate and paracetamol. Only now did she appreciate all those things that she had taken so much for granted. From now on such luxuries would be hard-earned, she realized with a jolt one hot afternoon when the sun shone unrelentingly down on her head through the office window as she filed those detested forms and her stomach ached with cramps.

But then came the joy of her first pay cheque. Her own money at last! Much more than her meagre wages for working on Saturdays in the village hair salon. She had taken the bus up to Dublin the following weekend and met Lizzie outside Roches Stores. They'd gone on a mini clothes-shopping spree, as well as treating themselves to lunch in Arnotts' restaurant. They had taken the five o'clock bus home and that night they had dolled themselves up in all their new finery and make-up, and headed off to the hotel.

Being able to stand at the bar and be served drink made them feel so hip. They saw some of the sixth-years from their old school giggling in one of the booths and felt utterly sophisticated in comparison. They were career women now, on the ladder to success, grown up at last. And Valerie had a boyfriend she was sleeping with, how cool was that? She had it all.

Parts of growing up were wonderfully emancipating, Valerie reflected, but sometimes she felt out of her depth and unsure. Once she moved to Dublin she would really be standing on her own two feet without the safety net of home and familiarity to cushion her. The prospect gave her flutters of apprehension as well as anticipation.

Terence tried to concentrate on Daisy Duke's never-ending legs, as she sat atop a fence hollering at Bo and Luke as they tore around a muddy field in The General Lee. *The Dukes of Hazzard* was one of his favourite programmes and all he wanted was a bit of peace to look at it. But there was no peace to be had in this damn household with that crabby pair it was his misfortune to live with. Since Valerie had left school and started working she was growing increasingly defiant and disrespectful. And she was staying out until all hours at the weekends with that Egan fella. He didn't like the Egans. You'd think by the way Tessa behaved they owned the *Christina O*, instead of a clunky, rusty little trawler. Tessa Egan had snubbed him once and he'd never forgotten it. He'd offered her a bag of coal at half price. Coal got with the fuel vouchers he helped himself to, and she'd looked at him as if he'd crawled out from under a stone and said snootily, she had a coalman who supplied her with coal, thank you. But other people in the village were eager to get the cheap coal and he was delighted with his profit. He hated these goody-goodies like Tessa, who thought they were superior to him.

Terence sighed deeply. People had looked at him as though he'd crawled out from under a stone all his life. His eyes darkened as the memory he could never erase danced around his brain. Brenda Ryan yelling, 'Get away from me, get away from me, you horrible stinky boy. How *dare* you try and kiss me? I don't kiss the hired *help*!' And then her father, hearing her screeching, coming thundering around the side of the barn and nearly knocking him into kingdom come, roaring, 'Get out of here, ye little cur, and get back to that slum ye crawled out of. You're sacked. Don't step foot on this farm again, and if I catch ye sniffing around my daughter again, I'll break yer bloody neck!'

But it was Brenda's sneer that stayed with him. Her blue eyes flashing with derision, her nostrils flared as though she were smelling something nasty, and the way she'd called him the 'hired help'. He was fourteen, a farm boy on her father's dairy farm. Brenda, six months younger, had spent the summer flirting with him, tossing her golden curls and fluttering her eyelashes as she sought him out every day to bum a smoke off him.

'You're very strong. I like strong boys,' she'd told him with a smouldering sideways glance that particular day, as she'd held his hand steady while he lit a match for her. When he'd grabbed her and tried to kiss her, she'd started yelling blue murder.

His father had beaten him black and blue for losing his summer job, and Brenda had put out the rumour that he'd nearly raped her. A severe beating from three youths one night soon afterwards had convinced his mother to send him to live with her brother and his wife on the other side of the country, where he'd been treated like an unpaid slave for the rest of his school days.

Carmel and Valerie knew nothing of these dark days, and he'd never tell them. He wouldn't shame himself, but it grieved him that Valerie wouldn't go to university and study, to make something of herself. The professions were *respected*, and if he couldn't engender respect for himself, he could make sure that Valerie's position in society would be far higher than his ever was. It was so frustrating that she was being given the chance and was turning it down with a sneer that reminded him of the way Brenda Ryan had looked at him all those years ago. It was that sneer that had made him lose control and roar at her, 'You got five As in your Leaving Cert. I've told you I'll pay for you to go to college. You can study any subject you want – medicine, law, accountancy – and you're telling me you're going to take a job in the County *Council*! How stupid are you?'

'I got a very high place on the panel. I can start immediately. I want to earn my own money. I can always go to college at night and pay for it myself,' she'd said coldly.

'But I've just told you *I'll* pay for you to go to college. You've a chance to become a professional, a chance to make something of your life. Are you *mad* to turn down an offer like that? There are young people in Rockland's who would give their eyeteeth for the opportunity I'm giving you.' He had never envisaged that she wouldn't go on to do her degree. She was a very bright girl. He had high hopes of her. But she wasn't having any of it.

'Thanks, but I don't want anything from you,' she'd replied scathingly. 'I'm being offered a good job as a clerical officer with excellent prospects of promotion, and I can pay for my university education if I want to.' She'd turned and walked away from him, and he knew she was exultant that she could throw his offer back in his face.

'You talk to her,' he'd ordered his wife. 'Get her to see sense.'

'Terence, Valerie can make her own decisions regarding her future, and whatever she decides is good enough for me,' Carmel retorted.

Fury engulfed him. 'You're a pair of ungrateful bitches,

that's what you are. I'm sick of you,' he'd raged, slamming the door behind him. He'd sprayed gravel as he'd gunned the car engine and driven off in high dudgeon. That daughter of his was an ungrateful biddy, he'd fumed, driving like a madman out of the village to get well away from them. He hadn't spoken to Valerie for weeks.

Terence sighed, remembering how hurt he'd been that his magnanimous offer had been so ungraciously rejected.

Valerie had never forgiven him for taking the belt to her, he reflected. Maybe he *had* overreacted at the time, but catching her out in those blatant lies had maddened him and brought back one of his greatest fears. A fear that he hardly dared admit to himself and only did in his darkest moments. A fear that she would end up a lying thief. A person of no value. Someone just like him. Valerie was a disappointment to him and always had been, just as he'd been a disappointment to his father. He had hoped for a son, a son who would make him proud, and instead he had a wilful, defiant daughter who cared nothing for him, and a wife who had ceased to care for him many years ago, and who, by her own admission, had only married him to get away from being a skivvy at home.

The old dears he brought Meals on Wheels to and called out the bingo numbers to had more feeling for him than his own kith and kin, he thought sorrowfully as a strange mixture of sadness, loneliness and bitterness soured his stomach and made his ulcer ache. Not even Daisy Duke's curves could comfort him. He closed his eyes, lay back in his chair and hoped he could regain his composure enough to wear his hail-fellow-well-met mask when he was calling out the bingo numbers later that evening.

CHAPTER THIRTEEN

Valerie lit a Dunhill and drew it deep into her lungs, exhaling a long thin stream of smoke as she sat in her little red Mini and put the key in the ignition. Normally she would have left the car at home and walked to the hotel but it was pissing rain and she didn't want to meet Jeff looking like a drowned rat. She could leave it in the hotel car park and collect it in the morning. She glanced at herself in the rear-view mirror. How *dare* her father tell her she looked like a tart? She scowled as a pair of mutinous blue eyes outlined in blue eyeliner and shades of smoky grey eye shadow reflected back at her. She took her long-pronged Afro comb out of her bag and stabbed it angrily into her blond, recently permed curls, before spraying herself with *Charlie*.

Revving the engine, she pulled out from behind Terence's Cortina and drove down the narrow street of railway cottages. She was *so* looking forward to seeing Jeff. He hadn't been down the previous weekend. His team had been playing an away match in the midlands and he'd travelled there from Dublin. She wished he didn't have to spend so much time training and playing football. It took him away from her and that she found hard to deal with. If he loved her as much as she loved him surely he'd *want* to spend more time with her, she reasoned.

She glanced onto the floor of the passenger seat and saw an empty crisp packet and Lion Bar wrapper, and made a mental note to shove them under the seat so Jeff wouldn't think she was a slob. She reached the main street, the rain sluicing down, dancing into puddles that formed around the cobbles at the church gates. A couple of teenagers hurried into the warmth of the chipper, and then the street was deserted again. Rockland's reminded her of a ghost town or film set. She waited for a black cat to dawdle its way in front of the car before she could move from the side road.

She was proud of herself, Valerie decided, still angry at her father's words. She was eighteen, six months out of school, and she had been working full time since the end of September. Some of her classmates were dossing their way through commercial college but she had got a job as soon as she could. When Terence had heard that she wasn't going to university he had gone ballistic. She'd taken immense pleasure at the sight of him, his Adam's apple bobbing up and down, his eyes bulging in disbelief, when she'd told him she was turning down his offer and starting work at the County Council.

'Are you sure you don't want to go to college? Might it not be a good opportunity to grasp, even if you are stuck with him financially for another few years? You could live in Dublin and be far enough away from him. I'm asking you just to make sure you at least think about your future and what your father wants to do for you.' Carmel had followed Valerie into the kitchen when Terence had stormed out the door.

'Mam, I couldn't bear to be beholden to him. I'd never hear the end of it. I just don't want anything from him,' Valerie reiterated.

'Use him,' Carmel said bluntly. 'He's your father, it's his duty to provide for you.'

Valerie laughed. 'I wish he could hear you saying that. No, Mam, my mind's made up. I'm going to take the job and save for a car, and then I'm going to live in Dublin with Lizzie.'

'Well, for what it's worth, I think you're right. But I just had to make sure you weren't cutting off your nose to spite your face. I wouldn't like you coming back in a few years' time telling me I should have made you go to university.'

'Don't worry, Mam, that's the last thing I'd do. I can always go to university at night. You've nothing to feel bad about.' She had given her mother a reassuring hug.

She had been half expecting Terence to kick her out of the house but he had never spoken of her going to college again. When she got paid her first month's salary and handed over the amount he decided she should pay for her keep, it dawned on her that the extra money she was bringing in was the reason he'd zipped his lips. Money was his god and always had been. He'd milk her for sure.

She saved hard, also working Saturdays in the hair salon, and got the loan for her car. She'd planned to pay it off in the next couple of months and then move to Dublin but tonight's spat was the last straw. Enough was enough. She had her pride and her father would never get the chance to speak to her like that again, she vowed. She wanted to ring Lizzie from the hotel to tell her that she was coming up to live in Dublin as soon as she could get a transfer. Her best friend would squeal with delight. Lizzie hadn't come down for the weekend; there had been some overtime going and she'd taken it.

Pools of light from the orange sodium streetlamps cast eerie shadows through the slanting rain. Suddenly Valerie wanted to be in one of the warm snugs in the hotel, sipping a Guinness and blackcurrant, with Jeff's arm around her. When the black cat was safely on The Triangle, she made a right turn and drove past the public tennis court, a regimented row of red-brick two-storey houses, and a couple of fishermen's cottages, until she came to the road that sloped down to the harbour. She indicated left but didn't turn, gazing through the blurry windscreen stroked by the swishing wipers, towards the cluster of houses up on The Headland where Jeff lived, wondering if he had left for the hotel yet.

She supposed she could drive up and check but she didn't particularly want to see Tessa. Valerie couldn't quite put her finger on it, but she had the feeling that Jeff's mother didn't like her that much. Even though she had been dating Jeff since January, almost a year now, she had never warmed to her boyfriend's mother either.

'Don't distract Jeff from his studies, now,' Tessa would say, pretending it was a joke, with a smile that never quite reached her eyes. Or her last little snide remark: 'You remind me of someone out of *Dallas*. You're too sophisticated for the likes of us country folk now, isn't she, Jeff?' This when she'd worn a royal-blue double-breasted jacket with padded shoulders and nipped-in waist, over a pair of white trousers. She'd bought the outfit in A I Wear on Henry Street when her probationary period had ended and she'd been made permanent. She'd felt as stylish and sophisticated as Sue Ellen or Pamela Ewing as she'd left the boutique, jauntily swinging her carrier bags, although she couldn't imagine either of those glamorous ladies tucking into chips and big fat sausages in Woolworths' cafeteria after a shopping spree, the way she had. It was the second time she had driven to the capital in her new Mini. She'd felt as if she had the world at her feet as she'd parked behind Penny's and walked up to Henry Street, the bustling thoroughfare full of Saturday shoppers like herself.

No, Tessa didn't like her for some reason. That was a big problem because Jeff was her youngest child and, as far as Valerie could see, Tessa's favourite. Maybe she wouldn't like *any* girl who was dating Jeff. Maybe she was one of those possessive mothers Valerie often read about in the agony aunts' columns. Jeff had a very good relationship with his mother – they were always teasing each other – and he didn't like it if Valerie criticized her. She had learned very quickly to keep her criticisms to herself and put on a mask of polite amiability when she was around the other woman, who did likewise. But there was no love lost between them.

Tessa would not be best pleased to see her, but tough, Valerie thought defiantly, putting her foot on the accelerator and driving towards The Headland. She didn't want her boyfriend getting soaked to the skin. Tessa would have to put up with her coming to the door. Jeff drove a motorbike now and he wouldn't drink when he was driving it, having once come off it in a skid when he'd ridden it home the worse for wear after a party. Tessa and his dad, Lorcan, had warned him if he ever pulled a stunt like that again, he could pay his own college fees and get out of the house.

Valerie left the main street and took the curving ribbon
of road that led gently up to The Headland. To her right,
further down the coast, she could see the lights of
Wicklow town, an orange splash in the gloom of the
night.

The Egans' house was right at the point, affording them
panoramic sea views as well as over the harbour and the
village. It was a beautiful setting, Valerie conceded, even
if they were open to the elements. Tessa's green Toyota
was parked outside the blue and white house. And
Lorcan's battered old Peugeot station wagon was beside
it. She liked Lorcan. Jeff's dad was a quiet, good-
humoured man who was content to let his wife do most
of the talking while chipping in the odd pithy comment
here and there, his blue eyes twinkling when he took the
wind out of Tessa's sails.

Valerie took a deep breath. Would it always be like
this? If the relationship between her and Jeff developed
into something more – and she fervently hoped that it
would – she could be stuck with Tessa for a mother-in-
law. Now there was a thought to put her off marriage,
she reflected drily as she ran for the front door. She didn't
like to take a liberty and walk around the back and let
herself in like most people did. She felt Tessa would think
it too presumptuous if Jeff wasn't there. She took a deep
breath and pressed the doorbell, hoping that Tessa
wouldn't be the one to answer it.

CHAPTER FOURTEEN

'Valerie!' Lorcan opened the door, his rugged face creasing into a smile when he saw her. She blinked in the light that spilled out into the darkness and stepped inside as he held the door open for her.

'I was just wondering, has Jeff left? It's such a bad night I thought I'd give him a lift—'

'Who is it?' Tessa's voice rang out and then she was emerging from the kitchen wiping her hands on a tea towel.

'Oh it's yourself,' she said unenthusiastically. 'You should have come around the back, and not be knocking on the front door like a visitor.' Valerie wasn't sure if Tessa was issuing a subtle rebuke, implying that she thought herself too grand to come in through the back door like everyone else. You just couldn't win, she thought irritably.

'I didn't want Jeff to get wet – it's an awful night – so I thought I'd call and see if he'd left yet.' She knew she was babbling and she just wished Jeff would come and put her out of her misery so they could leave immediately.

'Come in, come, in,' Lorcan urged, shutting the front door behind her.

'Ah, if Jeff's gone I'll get going myself,' she said hastily.

'I gave him a lift down about ten minutes ago,' Tessa said smoothly. 'You should have phoned and saved yourself a journey.'

'Oh!' Valerie was thrown. It hadn't dawned on her to ring, she'd been in such a rush to get out of her own house. Besides, Terence was always giving out about the phone bill, even though she contributed to it every pay day.

'I won't come in then. I'll . . . I'll get going.'

'Enjoy your night.' Lorcan smiled kindly at her. 'See you, Valerie.'

'See you, Mr Egan.' She smiled back at him.

'Lorcan, call me Lorcan. "Mr Egan" make me feel like an ancient,' Jeff's father chided good-naturedly as he went into the big kitchen where she could see a fire roaring up the chimney. She thought how snug it was compared to their small functional kitchen at home.

'Good night,' she said to Tessa, who was tucking a stray strand of hair behind her ear. Even in her late forties, Tessa Egan was still an attractive woman, Valerie admitted. Dressed in jeans and a bottle-green polo jumper, Tessa had a curvy figure and long, slim legs giving her a good three inches over Valerie. She wore little make-up, just a hint of lipstick, and her tanned face, framed by a curtain of thick chestnut hair, exuded a healthy, vibrant glow. Only the faint spider's web of fine lines around her dark eyes, and the odd glint of grey in her hair betrayed her age. It was from Tessa that Jeff got his melting brown eyes.

She and Lorcan were a handsome couple, and they were still mad about each other. Valerie could see it in the way Tessa would lay a hand on her husband's shoulder when she was giving him a cup of tea, or how he would meet her gaze when he said something to make her laugh, his own blue eyes glinting with enjoyment. They were so different from her own parents. Terence and Carmel's coldness towards each other permeated every nook and cranny of their house, such a contrast to the warmth and conviviality that radiated from Jeff's home.

'Good night, Valerie,' the older woman said levelly. 'Enjoy your evening and make the most of it. Jeff's going to need to knuckle down and study for his exams; he won't have time to be gadding around. He needs to get good results because we can't afford to be paying for him to be repeating. You're lucky you don't have that kind of pressure on you with your *permanent* and *pensionable* job.' Tessa added extra emphasis to the last bit of her sentence, as though trying to induce some form of guilt in Valerie.

'Yes, I've told him he needs to get his head stuck into Rogers and Mayhew,' Valerie responded coolly, letting Tessa know she knew all about Jeff's need to study and dropping in a reference to a well-known engineering textbook for good measure.

'Excellent, we both know then what Jeff needs right now.' Tessa's eyes were cold, belying her smile as she opened the door to let her out.

'If Jeff doesn't pass his exams it won't be because of me.'

'Good. Oh, and by the way, he's playing a match tomorrow so don't keep him out *too* late. He knows not to be drinking either. Good night, Valerie.'

'Good night, Mrs Egan,' Valerie said politely, pulling her collar up over her ears and hurrying to the car without a backward glance. 'Snooty bitch,' she muttered, revving the engine and doing a U-turn to head down to the hotel and her boyfriend's welcoming arms.

'I can't take to that young one at all. Jeff could do much better for himself,' Tessa grumbled as she plonked down beside her husband on the shabby fat-cushioned sofa in front of the kitchen fire.

'Aah, don't be giving out, she's grand.' Lorcan lowered his paper and reached out to draw her into the crook of his shoulder.

'It's the airs and graces she gives herself with her fancy clothes and her car. You could scrape the make-up off with a trowel!' Tessa nestled in against him, loving the comfort of his hard muscled torso.

'Sure, that's the fashion now. Look at Lisa, she always has her eyes done up and her lipstick on,' Lorcan pointed out, referring to their daughter, who had recently got married to the son of a neighbouring fisherman. Valerie had been Jeff's guest at the wedding, much to Tessa's chagrin.

'Lisa's twenty-eight, she's a grown woman, not a flighty little article just out of school, with an attitude problem.' Tessa kicked off her shoes and wriggled her toes, allowing the heat of the fire to warm them. 'I know she and Jeff are having nookie; they sneaked off to a room at the wedding. I've warned him about not getting a girl pregnant, for all the good it's doing.'

Lorcan yawned. 'All we can do is advise him, Tessa, you know that.'

'His life will be ruined if she gets pregnant—'

'Stop worrying, it will get you nowhere,' he said gently.

'I can't help it, Lorcan. I know—'

'Shush, Tessa, we have the house to ourselves and what's rare is wonderful. I bet we could show those youngsters a trick or two.' He silenced her with a kiss and slid his hand up under her jumper and cupped her breast. Tessa's mouth curved into a smile beneath his and she traced a finger along his blue-jeaned leg. She slid her hand along his crotch and felt his answering response.

'Mr Ever Ready,' she murmured against his lips as he pressed her back against the sofa, his leg parting her own. 'Here or up in bed?' she said, unbuckling his belt.

'Here first and *then* upstairs,' Lorcan said, laughing, undoing the top of her jeans and sliding them down over her hips while she did the same to him.

Later, as she lay in their bed, spooned beside her husband in the dark, his arm around her midriff, Tessa's thoughts returned to Jeff and Valerie. Were they lying somewhere – the back of her little Mini, perhaps – similarly sated after lovemaking? It was a bitterly cold night; there wouldn't be much comfort in it for them.

It was so hard to think of her younger son as a man, in a relationship of his own. She didn't want him to be all grown up, ready to fly the nest, her lovely light-hearted boy. He should be having fun with his friends, playing football, enjoying his college days, and not getting tied down in a serious relationship. And if Valerie Harris had her way, it *would* be serious, Tessa thought grimly. She'd seen the way the young woman hung out of him possessively, as though she *owned* him, the day of the wedding. The possessive ones were the worst. Her elder son, Steven, had dated a girl once who stuck to him like a limpet and threw a tantrum every time he so much as glanced at another girl. And she had hated when he spent time with his family, kicking up a rumpus when he had spent a couple of hours doing the garden for Lorcan instead of being at her beck and call.

That relationship hadn't lasted, luckily, and Steven was now dating a lovely girl from Galway. Perhaps once Jeff got tired of Miss Clinging Vine he'd end it and go and enjoy his life. She certainly hoped so, Tessa thought as her eyes grew heavy and she drifted off to sleep.

CHAPTER FIFTEEN

The smell of engine oil and wet sand mingled with the scent of Jeff's aftershave, and his mouth tasted of mints as they leaned against the old wooden walls of the boat shed, his breath coming in raspy gasps as he held onto the last shuddering moments of orgasm.

'Was it good for you?' he breathed into her hair.

'Yeah,' she whispered back. 'It was great.'

'I wish we had a place of our own to go to. I feel like going to sleep now.' He smiled down at her and she could see the gleam of his teeth and just make out his eyes in the dark. It was freezing cold and her bum was numb. She shivered and pushed him away, bending down to pull on her jeans. She straightened her clothes and pulled her coat close around her.

'We might have one soon.' She nuzzled in against his neck again. 'I'm going to try for a transfer to Dublin, the Corporation or the Council – I don't care as long as I get one of them – and then I'm moving into a flat with Lizzie. I've had enough here. I can't stand living with Da any more. He's being even more obnoxious than normal and I hate having to make love here or in the back of the car. It was OK when the weather was good but it's winter now and it's the pits. And I'll be able to cook for you when you're studying. You won't be at the mercy of that ould landlady of yours.'

'Sounds good to me.' Jeff tucked his shirt into his waistband. 'But what will we do when I'm working on the trawler in the summer and you're up in Dublin?'

'Why do you have to work on the trawler? Get a job up in Dublin,' Valerie replied tartly. Now that the high of their lovemaking was over she felt flat and dispirited. There was no place to have a comforting cuddle. They were going to get drenched walking back over to the pier and up to the village because the car was in the hotel car park. She hadn't driven to the boat shed. She didn't dare risk it. She had drunk Guinness and then a couple of Bacardis and she knew she was on the far side of sober.

'I can't let Dad and the lads down. I need the money for my fees,' Jeff said cheerfully. 'C'mon, Val, don't let's argue and ruin our lovely night.'

'What about letting *me* down? It would be nice to know I was somewhere near the top of your ladder rather than hovering on the bottom rung to get kicked off when your dad and "the lads" need you, or you have to go training,' she grumbled petulantly.

'Look, I shouldn't have been drinking tonight, because I've a match tomorrow but I *did* drink to keep you company. So don't be giving out to me. You always get like this after we make love.'

'I just want to be able to cuddle in a bed like normal people and not have to do it in a smelly old boat shed in the middle of winter.' She wrapped her scarf around her neck.

'I don't like it very much either,' he retorted. 'Do you want to stop having sex?' He dropped the used condom into a bag of rubbish and turned to look at her, holding the torch at a low angle.

'Do you?' she asked, startled. Maybe he was going off her, she thought fearfully. Maybe Ursula was back on the scene.

'I asked you first?'

'Well, if you don't want to, that's fine with me,' she said huffily. 'Let's go home.'

'Don't be cranky. I just want to do what you want to do,' Jeff growled as he held the door open for her. They walked across the sand, trying to avoid the slippery seaweed thrown up by the stormy inky sea, and climbed the ramp to the pier in silence. It had stopped raining and the moonlight, when it fleetingly appeared from behind sullen banks of bad weather, was reflected in the puddles along the uneven paving slabs. The fluorescent glow of the village streetlamps glimmered up the hill ahead of them and the pools of light spilling from curtained windows in the houses dotted around The Headland conjured up visions of welcoming homes and hearths for weary travellers and sailors.

How she would love to live in a cosy cottage with a big blazing fire, and a huge double bed, somewhere up on The Headland, with beautiful views and a garden filled with roses and flowering shrubs. They would be deliriously happy, she daydreamed as she trudged by his side over the railway line towards the hotel.

'You don't have to walk me home,' she said curtly, determined not to be the one to make up first, when they reached the main street.

'Fine,' he said coldly. 'See you.'

Bastard. Valerie swore silently, racing across The Triangle without looking back. Her mother was right:

men were only after one thing. She slowed just in case he followed her to apologize for his churlish behaviour. It was a forlorn hope – Jeff was nowhere to be seen – and she let herself into the house and bypassed the sitting room where her father was watching a cowboy film. She hurried in to the succour of her bedroom where she flung herself down on the bed and cried silent bitter tears. Their first row might well be their last. Perhaps he wanted out of their relationship, but Jeff was so much a part of her life now she just couldn't imagine it without him.

Women were the oddest creatures, Jeff thought. They got into huffs over the least thing. One minute they were bright and bubbly and full of fun, the next they were glowering and spitting like cats, full of fury and indignation.

It wasn't as if he *wanted* to be making out in the boat shed. They couldn't really do it in the back of the car in the hotel car park. There were too many people toing and froing. Neither of them had a free house. They had no money to go to a hotel. At least he had the key to the shed and it afforded them some shelter. Some of his mates had to do it up against the wall at the back of the Ball Alley. Valerie had been all eager at first, but it was always afterwards, when the thrill of their lovemaking was over, that she got cross and grumpy. Their row had spared him the ear-bashing about his football match tomorrow and how much time he'd be able to spend with her afterwards before heading up to Dublin.

At least she hadn't burst into tears before storming off. He hated when girls cried. Ursula had been a great crier, far moodier than Valerie, and he was absolutely certain she would never have done it standing up against the walls of a cold, smelly boat shed. She had been a bit prissy sometimes, and she had expected him to spend a lot more time with her than Valerie did, in fairness. But sometimes, like now, he wondered if he would be better off single, just having fun and concentrating on his studies and his football. Of course, that's what his mam would say, he thought wryly, letting himself into the back porch. He could hear her moving about in the kitchen. He had expected her to be in bed.

'Nice night?' Tessa asked as he took off his duffel coat and scarf. She was in her dressing gown, making hot chocolate.

'It was OK.' He shrugged.

'Only OK?' Her eyebrow rose at his grouchy tone. 'Did you have a row?' she asked perceptively. She knew his moods, knew him inside out.

'A bit of a one,' he admitted, coming into the kitchen where the fire still glowed brightly.

'Do you want a mug of hot chocolate and a slice of tea brack?' Tessa asked kindly.

'Sounds good.' He stood in front of the fire and warmed his hands. A low faint rumble overhead told him that his dad was sound asleep. Tessa bustled around the kitchen, stirring powdered chocolate into hot milk and buttering a doorstep-sized slice of brack for him. Jeff felt some of his irritation ease away in the familiar comfort of the kitchen.

'There you go, son, that will warm you up.'

'Thanks, Ma, you're the greatest,' he grinned, sitting down on the sofa.

'Where did you go? It's a horrible night.'

'Just to the hotel.'

'Valerie called earlier but I told her I'd given you a lift down. She's gone all glam and sophisticated since she started working.'

'She's a good dresser all right.' He took a slug of the hot chocolate.

'Just let me give you a word of advice, Jeff. You need to focus on your exams now. Valerie hasn't the burden of studying like you have. She's a free agent so make sure you keep sight of your goals and don't be distracted. There'll be plenty of time for you to have fun and go places and enjoy yourself when you have your qualifications. You only have another year and it will be worth it in the end. Maybe tell Valerie you need to concentrate on your studies for now and not let things get too serious.'

'Yeah,' he sighed. He'd had this lecture before. He knew Tessa was right, he needed to focus on his engineering studies if he wanted to graduate and get any sort of a decent job, but a guy had to have some diversions. And besides, he really liked being with Valerie – well, most of the time, when she wasn't in a snit.

'Leave that, I'll wash it up for you when I'm doing mine,' Tessa said, curling back up on the sofa with her book.

'Thanks. 'Night, Ma.' He leaned over and kissed her and put his mug in the sink before taking the stairs two at a time. He was looking forward to his bed as the wind got up again and sheets of rain pelted the windows. Tessa had already turned his electric blanket on. She was a sound mother, he thought gratefully as the heat infused his cold body. He wished Valerie was in his arms. Body heat was the best for warming you up, he thought tiredly, yawning so widely he nearly dislocated his jaw. Moments later he was asleep.

Tessa opened her candlewick dressing gown and flapped her hands up and down over her face as the rising tide of heat flashed yet again through her body. The top of her scalp was so hot she could fry an egg on it, she thought glumly, hating this now frequent occurrence over which she had no control. She'd had to leave the comfort of her bed to cool down. Her post-coital lethargy had evaporated and she felt wide awake. Nothing in life had prepared her for this sudden hard slap of middle age: the aches in her feet and hands, the memory loss, having to wear glasses now at nighttime to read. How had this happened? It wasn't as if it had crept up on her as such. It had seemed that one day she was youthful and fit, and then overnight, after that horrible first hot flush, when she wasn't sure, couldn't believe it was happening, the realization that her youth was gone and there was nothing that she could do about it. It grieved her, truly grieved her.

She felt that she had achieved so little with her life. She had been a wife and mother, reared her children, and now had a part-time job in the local pharmacy, which paid for luxuries like her own car and the odd holiday. But her life had been predictable; happy enough for the most part, she supposed, but looking back, things could have been so different. When she saw Valerie Harris and Lizzie Anderson, parading around in their up-to-the-minute fashions, and Valerie whizzing around in her little red Mini, an ache of loss would surprise her every so often and she'd have one of her 'what if' moments.

Those girls had it all. Not for them the grinding monotony of the kind of life she'd led, especially in the early
days of childrearing. Did they know how lucky they
were to have choices? Or did they take it all for granted?
she thought crossly as another flush enveloped her. It
had been a mistake to drink hot chocolate. But a glass of
wine would have set her off as well. She heard Lorcan's
rumbling snores upstairs. Did men know how lucky they
were? Jeff was probably snoring his head off too, but she
was damn sure Valerie would be awake fretting after
their row, because that was what women did.

Well, a bit of fretting wouldn't do her any harm. Jeff
had his exams to pass and his life to live, and Tessa wasn't
one bit sorry to hear that all was not rosy. Let Valerie
Harris go and hook her claws into someone else. She was
just a bit *too* smart for her boots, a bit *too* sophisticated
and a bit *too* smug.

And you're jealous of her! The realization made Tessa's
jaw drop as she sat staring into the dying embers, feeling
thoroughly disgruntled, wondering where all this had
come from. She remembered how a friend of hers had
once told her that issues that hadn't been dealt with
always seemed to surface with the menopause. Well, she
just wasn't having any of it. She'd dealt with her issues
and that was that. There was no point in looking back.
No point at all!

'Do you think I should go to his match?' Valerie curled
her hair around her finger and dropped the last of her
coins into the call box outside the supermarket. She had
phoned Lizzie from the call box to have some privacy
and tell her of the events of the night before.

'Why don't you go about ten minutes before the end so you don't have to stand shivering for the whole of it?' Lizzie, ever the pragmatist, suggested.

'Oh, that's a good idea.' Valerie brightened. 'What will I do if he ignores me?'

'He won't ignore you, he's mad about you,' Lizzie snorted.

'I'll ring you tonight to tell you how it goes,' Valerie said hastily as the phone started beeping.

'It will be fine,' Lizzie assured her comfortingly before the line went dead.

Valerie took extra care with her appearance and added another layer of foundation and blusher. She had been so tense she had barely touched her roast beef dinner, telling her mother she'd have it later.

At least the sun was shining and the rain of the night before had moved out over the Irish Sea. It was difficult driving with the sun so low in the sky. The glare bounced up off the road and dazzled through the bare-branched trees, almost blinding her in spots as she drove to the football pitches where the Rovers were playing a home game. She could hear the roars as she drove along the narrow road that led to the playing field. The cars were parked up by the ditch on either side of the road and she spent five minutes or more trying to squeeze in between a rusty Toyota and a Renault, breaking out in a cold sweat when she misjudged and thought she was going to grind up against the side of the Toyota. She was a nervous wreck by the time she got out of the car and she had to take a couple of deep breaths as she made her way to the sidelines. She asked a middle-aged woman who was minding a child in a buggy what the score was and was told, 'It's a draw and we're into injury time.'

Just about made it, Valerie thought with relief, scanning the swarm of players as they raced down to the far goal-mouth. And then she saw Jeff, elbowing a player out of the way and kicking the ball to a teammate as the crowd roared their approval. Her heart lifted at the sight of him.

The player raced towards the opposite goalmouth as the opposing team defenders surged around him and then the final whistle blew and the Rovers supporters groaned, and consoled each other. The players back-slapped each other, shook hands with the opposition and began strolling over to the sidelines to greet supporters before heading back to the clubhouse.

'Jeff, Jeff,' Valerie called his name, waving her green Rovers scarf to catch his attention. She saw him glance over his shoulder and then he saw her and his face split in a broad grin as he made his way over to her.

'I'm sorry for being a cranky cow,' she blurted as she threw herself into his arms, not caring that he was manky dirty and hot and sweaty.

'I'm sorry too.' His hug was tight.

'I love you, Jeff.' It was out before she knew it. The first time she'd said it.

'I love you too, Val,' he said easily, and they gazed at each other, oblivious to the crowd around them.

Further up the pitch, Tessa stood, her hands shading her eyes as she watched them.

Row over, she thought as she watched her son lean down and kiss his girl. It looked like Valerie was here to stay for the foreseeable future.

CHAPTER SIXTEEN

Tears slid down Valerie's cheeks onto the photo album as memories she had long suppressed overwhelmed her. Lying against her pillows, thousands of miles from Rockland's, in the balmy heat of a Spanish night, she felt as if she had never left home. The years had reeled back and it was almost like watching a film of her life. The intensity of the emotions and feelings that churned within shocked her. She'd thought she'd got over all those years of hurt and grief. She thought she had buried deep the feelings of antipathy and rancour, and got on with her life.

And now this fresh horror. Briony's discovery of Tessa's letter had brought that woman back into her life again. Hadn't she caused enough damage? Was Valerie to be eternally punished? How could life be so unfair? Hadn't she suffered enough? Jeff had been taken from her. Her own father had practically disowned her once she'd got pregnant. Carmel had Alzheimer's and didn't even recognize her any more, and now Briony hated her and was threatening never to let her see her beloved Katie again. Just when she'd finally got her life on an even keel, she was back in upheaval. A place she'd been many times in her life.

She heard Katie give a little whimper and jumped out of bed, hastily wiping the tears from her cheeks as she hurried into her grandchild's bedroom.

'What is it, chicken? I'm here, Valerie's here.' She leaned down and kissed the little girl.

'I's having a bad dream. Can I come into your bed?' came the plaintive plea.

'Of course you can, darling.' She leaned down and lifted her up. She loved the way Katie snuggled into her neck, with one small thumb tucked into her mouth.

'Can I have a biscuit, Valwee?' she asked sleepily.

'Does Mammy give you biscuits at night?' Valerie smiled as she carried her into her bedroom.

'Sometimes,' Katie yawned.

'Just this once then.' Valerie laid her gently on the bed and pulled the sheet up over her. She loved the way Katie called her Valwee. She had never wanted to be called 'Gran' or 'Nan' or the like. She was too young, she'd told Briony firmly.

She went out to the kitchen, shook a few biscuits onto a plate and poured a small amount of milk into two tumblers. Her hand hovered over some cupcakes but she decided against them. It was late; she didn't want her granddaughter to get a tummy ache.

'Are we having a midnight feast, Valwee?' Katie's eyes widened with pleasure and she sat up when she saw her grandmother bringing the goodies in on a small tray. She adored midnight feasts.

'We are, love, but then you've got to lie down before Mammy comes home because we don't want her to be cross,' Valerie warned.

'OK,' her granddaughter agreed, and reached for her milk and biscuits.

Valerie watched her enjoy her snack and felt an ache of sadness as she took a drink of her own milk. It was inconceivable that Briony would prevent her from seeing Katie again. It just *couldn't* happen.

But it could, a little voice in her head said. *You stopped Tessa from seeing Briony. You got your own back there. Now it's your turn to suffer.*

Valerie stared at Katie as she licked her fingers, drained her tumbler of milk and handed it to her before settling down against the pillows, a smile curving her rosebud mouth. 'That was brill, Valwee, thank you. Will you sing me a song? Mommy always sings me Sugar an' Spice an' all things nice.'

A flashback of Tessa singing that little song to Briony made Valerie catch her breath. Imagine that her daughter had remembered it and now sang it to her own daughter. Valerie wondered whether Briony could possibly remember Tessa singing it to her. She fervently hoped not.

'I don't really know that one,' Valerie said faintly. 'I'll sing you "Christopher Robin".'

'Oh, yes, please. I *love* that one!' Katie stuck her thumb in her mouth and her eyelashes fluttered down onto her cheeks. She was practically asleep.

Valerie sang, trying to keep the quiver out of her voice as the impact of what she had done all those years ago shook her to her core. Don't think about it, sing the lullaby, she told herself fiercely as the evocative words floated over Katie's drowsy head. She trailed off, aware that her grandchild was now fast asleep.

Tessa Egan had once sung lullabies to a much-loved grandchild. Had once comforted a distressed little girl and brought her to her bed. Had once had midnight feasts, and played in playgrounds, and painted and told stories, and sang songs. Tessa had done all those things with Briony, and Briony had loved her with all her little heart. Sometimes Valerie had felt that Briony had loved Tessa more than she had loved her.

And she had put an end to it. Had separated grandmother from grandchild. Only now when she was facing the same prospect did Valerie begin to realize the enormity and consequence of her act. If she felt Tessa had been spiteful, Jeff's mother could say the same about her, she thought dully. She felt sick. People who believed in karma would say she was getting what she deserved. Something Lizzie was fond of quoting came to mind.

> *There is a destiny that makes us brothers;*
> *None goes his way alone;*
> *All that we send into the lives of others*
> *Comes back into our own.*

She had caused Tessa unimaginable grief. Only now was she beginning to understand just how much. Because she had caused such grief to Tessa, was she now going to be the grieved one? The one to suffer even more heartache?

But Tessa had *ruined* her life, Valerie thought angrily. She *deserved* what she got.

But *Briony didn't deserve what had been done to her*, that voice that would give her no peace whispered. Was this what was meant in the Bible when it said, 'As ye sow, so shall ye reap'?

Oh my God! Please, please, don't let me lose Briony and Katie, please, God. Don't do this to me, Valerie begged silently, distraught as she went back to her bedroom.

Her gaze rested on another faded photo, one of her and Jeff, and she picked it up and studied it, then felt a savage dart of anguish.

'Jeff, please, if you're watching over us, help us,' she whispered.

His eyes, so happy and relaxed, stared back at her from the photo. He had his arms around her and she was looking up at him adoringly as he gazed towards the camera. The picture was taken the day of the Royal Wedding. The day Lady Diana Spencer and Prince Charles had married. The day Briony was conceived. It had been one of the happiest days of her life, and a day when it seemed all her dreams had come true.

It was Tessa who had shattered her dreams. Tessa and her interfering ways. She gazed at the photo with bleak sadness, remembering the pure optimism and joy she felt when life had been the best it had ever been for her and no dark clouds loomed on her horizon.

It was the last time in her life when she was truly carefree, and her thoughts drifted back to that sunny July day in 1981, when millions of people around the world watched a magical wedding and every young girl, including herself, dreamed of being a fairytale bride.

CHAPTER SEVENTEEN

'Right, we have the goodies, bacon and sausages for butties, vino for later, and plenty of chocolate and crisps,'
Lizzie declared, surveying their stash on the coffee table
in their small shabby sitting room. A chintz sofa that had
seen better days and a matching armchair took up most
of the space. A standard lamp with a pink bockety shade
that matched the pink roses in the wallpaper stood in the
corner beside it. Opposite them, a narrow fireplace with
chipped green tiles. A wooden china cabinet with a
cracked pane of glass sat in one chimney alcove, another
coffee table holding their stereo unit and TV sat in the
other. A wooden sash window with white lace nets
looked out over an overgrown back garden. The elderly
lady who owned the house and lived downstairs allowed
them to use it. It was south-facing and perfect for
sunbathing.

They had the upstairs flat in a large red-brick bay-
windowed semi in Daneswell Road, close to Glasnevin
Village. Shabby and old-fashioned as the flat was, they
loved it. The rooms were big and airy and they had plenty
of space compared to some of the matchboxes a couple of
their friends lived in. They were having the time of their
lives, free from parental restraint, with Valerie's car,

money in their pockets, new people to meet and places to see. They were in their element. The icing on the cake for Valerie was that she could now see Jeff in the evenings whenever she wanted, and occasionally spend blissfully happy intimate moments cocooned in a bubble of love. In the space of a couple of months her life had changed radically in a way that she had only dared to dream about.

Valerie had got her transfer to Dublin Corporation, and Lizzie was working in the P&T. When the letter of confirmation came from the Corporation telling her that her transfer had been accepted, and to present herself at their personnel department in Aungier Street, she had been dizzy with excitement.

Telling her mother that she was moving up to Dublin had been difficult. Valerie felt as though she was abandoning Carmel. 'You'll be able to come and stay with me and we can go shopping in Grafton Street, and have our lunch in fancy restaurants and go to the pictures and the theatre,' Valerie had said comfortingly when she'd seen the stricken expression on Carmel's face.

'You don't want your mother hanging out of you up in Dublin. Go on and live your life and have fun up there, Valerie,' Carmel had said firmly.

'No, Mam, I'd really like to do things with you. You could come up once a month, couldn't you? You could take the bus up and I'll meet you at Bus Aras, and we could have dinner and go to a show or to the pictures and you could stay the night.'

'You haven't even got a place to live yet.' Carmel had laughed at her daughter's enthusiasm, secretly delighted that she was so insistent about spending time with her.

'We're going flat-hunting at the weekend. Lizzie can't wait because she's living in a bedsit. You should see it, Mam, it's tiny and she just has a little two-ring cooker and a fridge right beside her bed! And all her clothes are in black bags because the wardrobe is just a cupboard, and she has to share a bathroom. She can't wait to move.'

'I'm going to buy you some nice sheets and pillow-cases, and some towels, and you can take some of those mugs and that matching jug and sugar bowl set that your aunt Alice gave me last Christmas,' Carmel had offered.

'Thanks, Mam, you're the best.' Valerie had hugged her, before getting a map of the city and putting it on the kitchen table, where they pored over it, looking for Aungier Street.

'What are you two looking for? Where's my dinner?' Terence came in from work and stood staring at them, disgruntled that the table wasn't set and his dinner wasn't ready for him.

'It's a casserole. I'll dish it out now,' Carmel retorted.

Valerie started folding the map.

'What are you looking for that's so important?' He'd slumped down on a chair.

Valerie had glanced at her mother and taken a deep breath. She had imagined this moment many times, and now that it was finally here all the eloquent speeches she'd composed about gaining her freedom and no longer being under his dominion, and particularly about her lack of respect for him because of his absolute lack of respect for her, and his total failure as a parent, evaporated. 'I'm moving up to Dublin. I transferred to the Corporation,' she said coldly.

'You could have moved up to Dublin and gone to college and made something of your life.' He scowled at her.

'Oh, I will make something of my life, don't you worry.' She recovered some of her brio. 'Lizzie and I are going to study for an Arts degree at UCD at night, when we have the money saved for it.'

'Another hot thing, that Lizzie one. I'll believe it when I see it,' he'd said derisively and stuck his head in the newspaper he'd pulled out of his jacket pocket. That was the last time he referred to her moving away from home. When she actually moved to Dublin two weeks later, having found a flat that suited her and Lizzie perfectly the previous weekend, Terence had gone to do his Meals on Wheels stint long before she finally climbed into the Mini, the little car bursting at the seams with bulging black bags of clothes and boxes of books, tapes and personal belongings, which Jeff had helped her to pack. He was travelling back to Dublin with her to help her move in. But the fizz of excitement went flat when she saw Carmel standing in the doorway waving at her as she started the engine. She'd waved back but the lump in her throat nearly choked her, and her eyes were blurry with tears as she drove out of Rockland's. What had Carmel to look forward to? A tedious existence living with a husband she didn't want to be with. At least Valerie had her life ahead of her.

'You'll be able to come back to visit; it's only an hour away,' Jeff had said comfortingly, remembering his own mixed emotions when he had left home to go to college.

'I know, I just hate leaving Mam. I won't ever be going back to live there and she knows it,' Valerie sniffed.

'Um,' he murmured, and she figured he didn't know what else to say and that her tears were making him feel uncomfortable.

'Sorry.' She swallowed.

'It could be worse, you could be emigrating or something,' he had said awkwardly.

'Yeah,' she'd agreed. It was true she was only an hour away. As they drove along the N11, playing Queen on her tape deck, her anticipation kicked back in. When she pulled up outside their new flat and saw Lizzie waving excitedly out of the top window, she waved back, grinning broadly. This was going to be fun, she knew it was. She had left childhood back in Rockland's, now she was going to spread her wings and fly high.

She had taken like a duck to water to living in the city and had settled into her new job relatively quickly, much more confident in her abilities than when she had first started working. She and Lizzie had decided to make a day of it when the date of the Royal Wedding had been announced and had taken leave. They were bunkering in with plenty of supplies to enjoy the royal pageant, and the smell of sizzling rashers and sausages was making her mouth water.

Valerie sighed happily as she turned on the TV and saw the crowds of well-wishers outside Buckingham Palace waiting for Lady Diana to emerge from her state carriage.

'I'm dying to see the dress.' Lizzie arrived in from the small kitchen with a mug of tea and a plate of crispy fried white pudding. 'Starters,' she grinned before hurrying back to the pan.

Valerie munched on the tasty fare. She and Lizzie had been out drinking with Jeff and some of his classmates in the Bolton Horse the night before, and she was feeling a bit under the weather. A fry-up was just the antidote she needed.

'Hurry,' she called. 'The guests are arriving at St Paul's.'

'Coming,' yelled Lizzie, hurrying in a minute later with a plate piled high with bacon and sausage butties slathered with tomato ketchup.

'Imagine wearing white to a wedding! Is that not considered a fashion *fax pas*?' Valerie commented noticing how many of the guests were wearing white. 'Oh look there's the First Lady,' she added as a reed-thin Nancy Reagan made a gracious entrance.

'It's a long time since she was a virgin bride! Look, she can hardly smile her face has been lifted so much; she's like a waxworks model.' Lizzie curled up on the sofa and bit into a sandwich.

'Princess Grace's hat is going to block the view of half the congregation. I'd hate to be stuck behind her.'

'Good God, look at that one in the green, it's hideous!'

'Oh! Here come the real Royals! Oh, wow, Anne's a bit floral.'

'Oh, the Queen's lovely! Isn't this the life, Valerie?' Lizzie grinned over at her and Valerie thought how lucky she was to have such a great friend. They sat companionably enjoying the spectacle, interjecting comments and both exclaimed in dismay when Diana emerged from her coach.

'Oh, no, it's all creased!'

The Emanuels fussed about the bride, and the creation there had been so much speculation about.

'Don't like those mutton sleeves. I hope her dad makes it up the aisle OK. It's an awful long walk,' Lizzie observed as Earl Spencer, resplendent in tails, took his daughter's arm to begin the walk along the nave, and Valerie went to the kitchen to refill their mugs.

A thought struck her: if she were getting married to Jeff, her father would have to walk her up the aisle! That would ruin her wedding day, she thought, horrified. Imagine having to paste a smile on her face and pretend to be enjoying the farce of having Terence give her away. And that was another thing that irritated her – the 'giving away', as though the bride were a chattel. Until she had left home her father had always thought he had complete authority over her, but not any more. She was her own woman now, and if she didn't want to be 'given away' by her father she didn't have to be. Valerie banished the thought and hurried back with their steaming mugs to drink in the joyful pageant that was the Royal Wedding.

Several thoroughly enjoyable hours later, showered and dolled up, they made their way into town. Valerie was going to meet Jeff for a drink in the Parnell Mooney. He was working on his dad's fishing boat for the summer and was coming up to spend the night.

The only fly in the ointment was that Jeff was back in Rockland's, working all hours to help pay for his college fees and digs. Valerie couldn't wait to see him. Lizzie, being the understanding friend that she was, had arranged to meet her cousin to go to the pictures and she was going to stay the night at her house. Her cousin was sharing a house with a few friends, one of whom, Dara, Lizzie was dead keen on. Valerie hoped that he fancied her back. She'd love to see Lizzie with someone nice. Her friend's choice in men had been rather disastrous since Phil Casey had done the dirty on her, and she seemed to lurch from one totally unsuitable man to another. The last one, a chap from work, had kept her dangling and waiting by the phone, and allowed her to spend a fortune wining and dining him, rarely putting his hand in his pocket until Valerie had bluntly told her that she was being a doormat and she had reluctantly agreed and given him the boot.

'Tonight's the night; I think something's going to happen. My horoscope in *Company* was great. "A life-changing event," it said.' Lizzie oozed optimism as she got into the car beside Valerie and waved at Mrs Maguire, their landlady, who was deadheading her roses. Mrs M waved grandly back in a rather regal manner and the girls smiled at each other. The sherry fumes had been rather overpowering when they had stopped to say hello to her on their way out.

'You gels look delightful,' she declared. 'Did you enjoy the wedding? I rather fancy Philip myself. Looks marvellous in uniform, deah. So straight and erect,' she said to Valerie, while Lizzie tried to keep from laughing.

'Indeed, very handsome,' Valerie agreed as they edged forward along the path. The trick was not to stop when you got the whiff of alcohol from her. Once you stopped it was impossible to get away. 'Enjoy your evening, Mrs Maguire,' she said, putting on a spurt, Lizzie close behind her.

'Straight and erect, hmm! I could do with a bit of that.' Lizzie pulled down the visor and studied her reflection critically as Valerie snorted with laughter and put the key in the ignition. 'Drive on, Macduff,' her best friend ordered. 'Let's hit the town.'

The traffic was light and Valerie parked just down from

Findlater's Church. As they strolled past the Gate, towards O'Connell Street, she sighed with happiness. By now the centre of town was busy. She could see the queues forming for the Savoy, the Adelphi and the Ambassador Cinemas, and a busker played a lively version of 'Dirty Old Town' on the corner of Parnell Street. Couples strolled along in the evening sunshine and a group of giggling teenagers yelled flirty comments at a couple of Russian sailors who were out for a night on the town. It was all so different from Rockland's. So cosmopolitan, Valerie thought, as a gaggle of Spanish students overtook them, chattering away in their native tongue, and a coachload of American tourists poured off their bus to see a play at the Gate Theatre.

'Have a great night. Tell Jeff I was asking for him,' Lizzie said as they stopped to go their respective ways. Valerie was turning right to head past the Rotunda Hospital and Lizzie was meeting her cousin at the Savoy.

'I hope you shift Dara. Give me a buzz at work tomorrow to let me know.'

'Sure I will. Have a great night with lover boy!' Lizzie smirked. She burst into the Pointer Sisters' new smash hit, 'Slow Hand'.

'Stop it, you,' Valerie giggled, digging her in the ribs, pink with embarrassment at the sexy words.

'At least you won't have to worry about Mrs M hearing. She was tipsy when we were leaving so she'll be out for the count later,' Lizzie remarked as the leaves on the trees under which they stood caught the evening sun.

'You're a pal,' Valerie said, and they waved at each other before going their separate ways. The Parnell Mooney was humming, busy with tired workers having a drink before going home, and revellers out for drinks before going to the cinema or the theatre. A young man, flushed and excited, was toasting the birth of his first son in the Rotunda Hospital across the street. Valerie peered around the dim, dusky bar. Particles of dust suspended on sunbeams seemed to dance over the drinkers' heads, and the smog of smoke, and the smell of Guinness and beer and furniture polish was a heady mix as she made her way through the throngs, wondering if Jeff had arrived yet. She hated waiting in a pub on her own, and hoped he wouldn't be long.

He was over an hour late when she saw him make his way towards her, looking faintly apologetic when he saw her scowling.

'Sorry,' he said, bending down and kissing her on the cheek. 'The bass were biting and we just had to fish them, and then the last line of lobster pots we threw out got tangled. It was just one of those days,' he said tiredly. His face was tanned and weather-beaten, giving him a faintly swarthy air. She melted a little.

'I just hate waiting in pubs on my own,' she said, scooting along the banquette to make room for him. She'd managed to get a seat at a table and had sat sipping a spritzer and reading the latest Jackie Collins novel while she waited for him.

'Do you want another drink?' he asked.

'Just another spritzer,' she said, putting her book into her bag.

'So what do you want to do? Did you come up in your mam's car or on the bike?' she asked when he came back from the bar.

'Ma gave me the car. I've to be back to catch the tide in

the morning so it will be an early start. What do you want to do?' He leaned over and kissed her again, and she threw her arms around him and hugged him.

'You decide,' she said happily, snuggling in against him. She didn't care what they did so long as they were together.

'Would you fancy going to *see Raiders of the Lost Ark*? Everyone's saying it's a brilliant film,' he suggested hopefully. Jeff loved going to the cinema, but sometimes the action films he chose were not to her taste.

'Oh, that's the one Lizzie's going to. OK,' Valerie agreed. 'Do you want to go for something to eat and we can go to a later showing? Lizzie's staying over with her cousin so we have the room to ourselves. She's a great friend.'

'Deadly.' Jeff's eyes lit up. 'We'll make the most of that.'

'You bet.' Valerie squeezed his hand tightly. She couldn't wait to make love to him. If it were up to her she would have gone straight home to bed. They strolled along O'Connell Street, chatting away, when Jeff heard his name being called just as they reached North Earl Street.

'Ah, Eddie, how are you?' he said, smiling. 'Valerie, this is one of my classmates in college; he was at Queen the night we were there. You remember Valerie?' he asked his friend.

'I do. Hi, Valerie. This is Lindsey.' He introduced the girl he was with. They chatted for a while and then Lindsey rooted in her bag and pulled out a camera. 'Would you take a photo of us under Clerys Clock?'

'Lindsey!' Eddie exclaimed. 'She has *hundreds* of photos. She's a photo fanatic,' he groaned, throwing his eyes up to heaven.

'Sure,' agreed Jeff. 'I'll do my Lord Snowdon impression.'

'And I'll take one of you and Valerie,' Lindsey said, posing under the clock, a famous landmark for meeting on a first date.

There was much laughter as they took the photos and said their goodbyes.

'I hope she gives you the ones she took of us,' Valerie said as they retraced their steps back towards North Earl Street to eat in one of the small bistros.

Raiders of the Lost Ark was one of the best movies they had ever seen, they both agreed several hours later as the crowds spilled out onto O'Connell Street. In spite of herself, Valerie had really enjoyed it, hiding her face in Jeff's shoulder when she thought it was going to be scary, and cheering Indiana with the rest of the audience when he got out of a tight spot.

'Harrison Ford is almost as sexy as you,' Valerie teased as they walked hand in hand up towards North Frederick Street where her car was parked. Jeff had parked close by in Parnell Square so he walked her to the Mini, and she waited until he drove past in his mother's car before moving out into the traffic to follow him. Driving past the Black Church she caught up with him and flashed him and saw him wave back. Her heart was singing. Soon she would be in his arms. She sang along to 'The Tide is High', at the top of her voice. In her wildest imagination she had never dreamed she could be so happy. She was almost afraid it was too good to be true, she thought a little fearfully as they sped home.

'Don't say anything, don't make any noise,' Valerie warned Jeff, as usual, when they walked hand in hand up the small garden path to the front door. Although Jeff had stayed over regularly ever since she'd moved in, she didn't want to take any chances of Mrs Maguire hearing him coming in, just in case the landlady got stroppy. Mrs Maguire generally left the girls to their own devices, far more interested in sipping Buckfast Tonic Wine, or Harvey's Bristol Cream while watching soaps and playing Patience with a tatty pack of dog-eared cards, than worrying about her 'gels' upstairs.

Valerie had put fresh sheets on the bed and bought herself a sexy spaghetti-strap nightdress in Roches Stores, and now she busied herself lighting candles and putting some mood music on her cassette recorder. Jeff was in the kitchen opening a bottle of Blue Nun, and preparing a treat for their supper. She rubbed some body lotion into her arms and legs, sprayed some Charlie onto her wrists and slipped into the pale aquamarine nightie, which slithered down over her hips and made her feel deliciously sophisticated and sexy, just like her heroines in *Dallas* and *Dynasty*.

'Hey, that's gorgeous on you!' her boyfriend exclaimed when he came into the bedroom, carrying a tray with two glasses of wine, and two full dishes of prawn cocktail.

'Oh yummy!' Valerie licked her lips, forgetting her sophistication when she spied the treat he'd made.

'Fresh off the boat. Ma cooked them when I was having my shower, and made the Marie Rose sauce. I really only had to wash the lettuce and arrange them in the dish and sprinkle the paprika on them,' he admitted, laying the tray on the bed and handing her a dish and a serviette.

'You have the room nice,' he said as they sipped their wine and ate the plump luscious prawns. 'The candles are sexy.'

'Thanks.' Valerie didn't let on that a lot of her clutter had been kicked under the bed. In the candlelight the faded cream wallpaper didn't look quite so old and marked, and the pink floral curtains weren't as garish as in daylight. She and Lizzie had bought two pale pink nylon bedspreads and pillow shams to dress their divan beds and two pink lamps for their bedside lockers, and in the candlelight the room looked inviting and romantic.

'Better than the boat shed, isn't it?' Jeff grinned as he scraped his dish and took a slug of wine.

'Much,' Valerie said fervently, taking the dishes and tray and laying them on the floor. 'Now ravish *me*.' She couldn't stop smiling at him. Their relationship was getting better and better. They could talk about anything. It was the most sustaining relationship of her life. She had never thought such joy was possible between a man and a woman, but then all she'd known was the toxic relationship between her mother and father.

'Come on, my little sex kitten.' Jeff reached for her. 'Let's make this a night to remember.'

CHAPTER EIGHTEEN

'Oh, Lizzie, it's a disaster. I've made such a mess of things.' Valerie cradled the phone under her ear, wishing that she could be with her best friend. They had been through so much together over the years – shared the good times and the bad – and it was to Lizzie Valerie still always went for sound advice.

'Calm down, Valerie,' Lizzie soothed. 'Everything will be OK.'

'It won't, Lizzie! Briony's so mad at me she says she's booking a flight home. She never wants to see me again and she's going to stop me from seeing Katie,' Valerie explained agitatedly.

'She won't do that, Val. I *know* she won't,' Lizzie replied sombrely. 'Where is she now?'

'I don't know. She stormed out of here about an hour ago and she's not back yet. Will you talk to her, Lizzie? Will you tell her I had good reasons for what I did? She'll listen to you. She's always listened to you.'

'That's what godmothers are for,' Lizzie said wryly. 'How did she find out that things weren't what they seemed?'

'She found a letter from Tessa,' Valerie sighed. 'I should have told Mam to burn the bloody thing years ago.'

'What a strange day for it to happen,' Lizzie remarked.

'I know. It's hard to believe that she'd find a letter from Jeff's mother after all these years, on his anniversary.'

'Maybe he planned it to happen. There's no such thing as coincidence. Everything happens for a reason. You know I believe that, Valerie,' Lizzie said gently.

'Ah, Lizzie, don't give me any of your spiritual mumbo jumbo stuff, not now, I'm too upset,' Valerie said irritably. Much as she loved her friend, she did not want to hear that 'perhaps we choose our life events to help us grow spiritually' sort of rubbish. When, years ago, Lizzie had had two miscarriages in a row, soon after she and Dara had first married, she had been distraught and had gone to see a spiritual healer. It had set her on a whole new path and she thought about things very differently now, believing that there was always a reason for everything. It was very interesting to listen to her talking about it sometimes, but not now, not today of all days.

'Sometimes when you think that what's happening is the worst thing that can possibly happen, you look back and see that actually it was one of the best,' Lizzie was saying. 'If I hadn't had my miscarriages I would never have opened up my mind to all that I know today. That was my babies' gift to me. This could be Jeff's gift to you and Briony.'

'How can you possibly think that Briony finding out that I'd lied about her grandmother rejecting her is a *good* thing? You're for the birds, Lizzie?' Valerie said crossly. 'And if that's the best you can do I've wasted my time ringing you.'

'It might lead to a reconciliation,' Lizzie said, unperturbed.

'That is never going to happen. *Never!*' Valerie added emphatically. 'You should know that better than anybody.'

'Well, whatever you think, everything does happen for a reason, Valerie,' Lizzie said calmly. 'Now I'd better go upstairs and see what's happening and why in my back bedroom. Michelangelo is painting the ceiling and I swear the Sistine Chapel has nothing on it. I hear a litany of curses which leads me to think something's gone awry.'

'Give my love to Dara,' Valerie grinned. 'When are the two of you going to come out?'

'We're saving our coppers,' Lizzie said drily. 'There's a recession on and our children are bleeding us dry!'

'Just book a flight, that's all you need. We can live very cheaply out here.'

'Um, leaving a fourteen-year-old with an attitude problem in the house on her own, currently thinking we are the meanest parents because we won't allow her go to a mixed sleepover? I don't think so,' Lizzie replied.

'And how is my godchild?' Valerie smiled.

'Lucky to be alive, I'd say. Yesterday she was asking me something and she actually said, "in your day". God, I felt like an ancient. I'm still young, hip and cool, aren't I, Valerie?'

'No one hipper or cooler on the planet,' Valerie grinned, glad she'd rung her friend just to hear her voice.

'I better go, Val. I don't know what Dara's done but he's roaring at me. It could possibly be more of a Jackson Pollock episode than a Michelangelo moment,' Lizzie groaned. 'Don't worry, I'll have a chat with Briony.'

'Thanks, Lizzie, you're a pal.' Valerie felt somewhat calmer as she hung up. Briony was very close to her 'Auntie Lizzie' and had always listened to her in the past.

She might look at things differently when she'd had a word with her.

She wandered out to the terrace. The breeze had changed direction and she could hear the sea breaking against the shore. It was a sound that evoked a memory of sitting with Jeff in the moonlight on top of the bank at the end of his garden when she was pregnant with Briony. He had his arm around her shoulders and she was leaning in against him and he was telling her not to worry, that everything would be fine.

'Ahh, Jeff, why? Why did you leave me? And why is all this happening now?' she asked angrily. 'You better do something to sort out this mess, mister. You were as much a part of it as I was.'

She stared up at the sky. Could he hear her? Was his spirit up there somewhere or was it all a fairy tale, this eternal life stuff? And yet there were times, she couldn't deny it, when she'd felt his presence around her strongly, especially when Briony was young and very sick with chickenpox and running a dangerously high temperature, and she had felt isolated, alone, scared and helpless. Was Lizzie right? Could it possibly be true, that this was a good thing to be happening and that Jeff was very close to them? Valerie pondered. Lizzie had such belief that her grandmother and Jeff and all who had 'passed', as she called it, were around them. Even her babies were very close to her, she told Valerie.

Lizzie had gone through such dreadful torment when she'd lost the two babies, each late in pregnancy. She'd been so devastated she'd started drinking heavily and Dara had been at his wits' end. After losing the second baby she'd come to stay with Valerie. Watching her best friend distraught and drunk every night had been scary. Valerie knew Lizzie was on a slippery slope.

One night, when Briony was in bed and Lizzie was preparing to open a bottle of red, Valerie had taken it from her. 'We're not doing that tonight.'

'What?' Her friend looked at her, astonished.

'We're not drinking tonight, or tomorrow night or any other night you're here with me. I'm not going to stand by and watch you turn into a lush, Lizzie.'

'I'm not turning into a lush! I just need something to take away the pain for a while. You don't understand what it's like. It's unspeakable, unbearable. You've never lost a child. You have Briony,' Lizzie said furiously.

'I lost Jeff. I do understand pain,' Valerie retorted. 'How mean are you, Lizzie, acting like this and having Dara up the walls with worry? He's grieving too, you know. He's lost his children too, and have you ever considered him in all of this when you run to the bottle and drink yourself into a stupor? You have a wonderful husband and you're treating him like dirt. I never thought you'd be so selfish.'

'You're a *bitch*, Valerie! How dare you say things like that to me? I might run to the bottle but I would never take my child away from its grandparents – if I ever had a child that lived, that is.' She burst into tears, grabbed her bag and left the house, incandescent. It was their worst row ever. She'd booked into a hotel, although Valerie hadn't known that, and Valerie was sick with anxiety, imagining all sorts of terrible scenarios involving a drunken Lizzie.

Lizzie had phoned the following day and asked if she could come back. They'd fallen into each other's arms crying and had stayed up talking until the early hours, drinking only tea. But it had been a turning-point for Lizzie, and when she had gone back to London she had set about seeking help. Having been brought to her knees she'd found solace in spiritual knowledge, which had sustained her ever since. She'd eventually had two more children, a boy and a girl, and had gone on to study and specialize in counselling for women who had lost children through miscarriage and childbirth. If she hadn't lost her precious babies she'd never have gone down that road.

Valerie admitted that when Lizzie gave her advice it came from hard-won knowledge and experience. Her best friend really wasn't an airy-fairy sort of person at all. Lizzie was one of the most practical and down-to-earth people that she knew, not one to suffer fools gladly and never had been. And if her friend had something to say she came straight out with it. But yet there was a side to her that coloured every aspect of her life and that was as natural to her now as breathing. She truly believed that death was just another path, and it most certainly wasn't the end of existence.

Valerie made a mug of tea, then went back out to the terrace and sat gazing out to sea. Sometimes, she *had* felt that Jeff was around her, especially that first year in Dublin when she had struggled with her grief. She wished she could believe like Lizzie did. Lizzie's beliefs took the sting out of death.

What would Jeff think of the mess she was in now? A mess of her own making. That was the hardest thing to accept, Valerie thought gloomily. What a change a few minutes could make in a person's life. It had taken Briony only a few moments to read that letter and now all was changed utterly. This morning she'd been so happy at the prospect of spending the day with Katie and Briony and now her daughter was furious with her. Why *had* she kept that damn letter? she berated herself again. Why hadn't she severed the link completely? Now it was too late. Whether she liked it or not, Tessa Egan was back in her life, and causing havoc as usual, and there was nothing she could do about it.

CHAPTER NINETEEN

'Why are you on such bad form, Jeff? Is anything wrong? Forget about the exam results. If you've done badly you can repeat.' Tessa studied her son critically as he pushed a half-eaten chop around his plate.

'I'm not on bad form,' he growled. 'I'm just tired. It was a long day.'

'Are you going up to Dublin? You can have a lend of the car if you want it,' she offered brightly.

'Nah, I'm not going up tonight. I think I'll just go for a run and hit the sack.' He sighed, a sigh that came from his toes, only reinforcing her gut instinct that something was bothering her youngest child.

He pushed away his plate and stood up. 'Thanks for dinner.'

'Leave it, I'll wash it up,' Tessa said irritably. It annoyed her when Jeff was uncommunicative and surly. He was normally such a cheerful, chatty lad. Even puberty hadn't dented his sunny nature like it had some of her friends' sons, turning them into sullen little grumps. It annoyed her even more that something was going on in his life that was upsetting him and he wasn't telling her about it. Tessa liked to know what was going on with her children. Lisa and Steven, her two eldest, had recently flown the nest, but she still had Jeff and she wanted to keep him for as long as she could.

Why wasn't he going up to Dublin to see Valerie? Had they had a fight? Was she being demanding? Putting pressure on him for spending too much time training? Maybe that was it, Tessa decided as she cleared away the detritus of the meal. She stood at the sink, her hands in hot soapy water, staring out at the panorama that unfolded outside her big kitchen window. The big sweep of blue speckled sky. Drifts of feathery clouds scudding gaily overhead. The sea a shimmering palette of blues, greens and navys, depending on where the sun was shining through. Golden wheat fields on The Headland ripe for cutting, the non-stop droning of tractors and farm machinery as they gathered up the harvest, working until long past midnight to make the most of the fine weather. The trawlers in the bay at rest for a few hours before their next foray to harvest the bounty of the sea. This tapestry of the life of her village, her home, usually brought a sense of comfort and gratitude to Tessa, but today she hardly noticed it. She was too agitated. She just had a *feeling* all was not right.

If Jeff did break up with that young Harris one it wouldn't be a tragedy. He'd get over it and be far better off not being restricted and tied down at his age. He was spending a lot of time in Dublin and had even decided against going on an InterRail holiday with some of his mates, which she knew he'd been looking forward to. When she'd pressed him on it he'd just said he'd prefer to save the money. He'd be back in college in September and he might try and move into a flat rather than stay in his digs, he'd said. 'Everyone needs a holiday and you've worked hard; go off with the lads and enjoy yourself,' she constantly urged but to no avail. If she found out that Valerie had put him off going Tessa would have something to say to the little madam, she thought, clattering saucepans into the press, cursing when they wouldn't fit neatly in because Lorcan or Jeff had put the frying pan in the wrong place despite her telling them on numerous occasions that it went on the *bottom* shelf and not the top. She rearranged them the way they should be arranged and slammed the cupboard door shut.

She was getting into one of her irritable moods when anything and everything annoyed her. She should go for a walk to try and clear her head, but then Lorcan would come home to an empty house and he'd had a very long and tiring day at sea, and she'd feel mean. Once again her life revolved around the men in it. Tessa scowled, feeling quite sorry for herself for no real reason that she could think of except that she had menopausal PMT, which far outweighed ordinary PMT and anything that men would ever suffer from. She'd felt she was getting a period for the past two weeks, even had the headache, spots and dull back and stomach ache to prove it, and so far no sign. This was *not* a good week for Jeff to be having a crisis.

'Cop on to yourself,' she chided aloud, knowing that she was being irrational. In fairness to her family they were pretty stable and sound. *She* was the one who was verging on being unreasonable lately. It wasn't fair to be taking out her moods on her family just because she wasn't happy to be galloping into middle age and all the horrors it entailed. 'Oh stop it,' she groaned. She was fit and healthy. She had a great husband, lovely children and a part-time job, she was bloody lucky, Tessa lectured herself, massaging her temples.

The sun was beginning to set so she walked into their airy west-facing sitting room and put an Acker Bilk cassette into the tape deck, letting the pure, crystal-clear notes of 'Stranger on the Shore' float over her as she stretched out on the sofa and watched the setting sun tint the sky and sea. No matter how many times she watched the sun set Tessa never failed to delight in its beauty. And tonight was no different. Soothed by the music and the spectacular vista unfolding in front of her, her agitation lessened and she was asleep when Lorcan woke her by dropping a blanket over her.

'Sleeping beauty.' He smiled down at her as she woke with a start.

'You're very late,' she remonstrated. It was almost dark outside.

'Denis and I stayed down at the boat shed repairing one of the nets. It got badly holed and it needed to be done.' He yawned.

'Go on,' she teased, getting up from the sofa, 'you have another woman.'

'Indeed I do, how did you guess?' Lorcan's blue eyes crinkled in amusement as his wife kissed him.

'You've been spending a lot of time in that boat shed.' She linked her arm in his as they walked out to the kitchen.

'It's the fishnets. They drive me wild. Very sexy, especially when the seams are straight!' He smiled down at her and she cuddled in against him, loving their easy banter. How lucky was she to look forward still to Lorcan coming in from work, to fancy her husband still after all these years.

'I'll give you fishnets . . . Sit down and I'll heat up your dinner. It's too late at night to be eating,' she scolded. They still had a lot of fun in their marriage, she thought gratefully as she busied herself at the cooker.

'Did Jeff say anything to you about what's bothering him? He's in terrible bad form these last few days,' she asked her husband when they sat together on the small kitchen sofa, drinking tea, after he'd finished his meal.

'He's a bit quiet, all right, not his usual exuberant self, but he didn't say anything to me, Tess.' Lorcan shrugged. 'Everyone's entitled to an off day or two.'

'But it's not like him,' Tessa persisted. 'Not like him at all.'

'He'll tell us soon enough if something's wrong.' Lorcan wolfed down a slice of home-made cherry and walnut cake, his favourite.

'I bet it's that Valerie one,' Tessa grumbled.

'Ah, leave her be, Tessa. You never have a good word to say for the girl,' Lorcan remonstrated.

'Don't say that,' Tessa retorted, stung at his criticism, knowing he had a point.

'Look, he's happy with her and that's all that counts.'

'He's not happy lately,' she snapped.

'Give it a break, Tess. He can't always be on good form, now, can he? You should know that,' he added.

'What are you saying? That *I'm* on bad form?' She sat up ramrod straight and glared at him.

'There you go, flying off the handle for no reason. I rest my case,' he said drily, picking up the paper.

'It's called the menopause and you'd better get used to it,' she retorted.

'No wonder I'd prefer to be in the boat shed,' he remarked from behind the paper.

'Lorcan Egan!' she raged, pulling the paper down to see him grinning at her.

'God, you were always easy to wind up.' He started laughing.

'Bastard!' She was furious with herself for laughing, but she could never fight with Lorcan. He always ended up making her laugh.

'There, there, there, pet, you'll be all right,' Lorcan teased, laying the paper down and putting his arm around her. 'Don't be worrying about Jeff, he's well able to take care of himself. He's not a child, Tessa, you have to remember that.'

'He's my baby, the only one left,' she sighed.

'Well, don't smother him, because men hate to be smothered,' he advised.

'Are you saying I smother *you*?' she demanded.

'What is *wrong* with you? You're like a briar.' He threw his eyes up to heaven.

'Sorry,' she muttered.

'I'd better put the bins out.' Lorcan stood up and walked to the back porch. She could have kicked herself for putting him in a bad humour with her crankiness. He was right, she *was* like a briar. She was even starting to annoy herself with her mood swings.

She heard Lorcan talking to someone and then Jeff came into the kitchen wearing his football kit. His T-shirt was stuck to him in damp patches after his run.

'Just going to wash these, is that OK?' He glanced over to see if the washing machine was empty.

'Sure, go ahead,' she said, glancing at him

surreptitiously to see if he still looked grumpy. 'Would you like a cup of tea?' she offered.

'Nah, thanks, I'm gonna hit the sack.' He gave another of his gale-force sighs.

'Jeff, if there's anything wrong you can tell me, you know that,' she said tentatively, just as Lorcan came back into the kitchen.

'Valerie's pregnant!'

Tessa's heart started to pound. Had she heard him right? 'What!' Her mouth was dry and she had to swallow hard.

'Valerie's pregnant!' he repeated, unable to meet her gaze.

'In the name of God!' she exploded as Lorcan laid a restraining hand on her arm. 'I knew it, I knew something like that was going to happen with that one.'

'Stop it, Tessa,' Lorcan said sternly.

'I won't stop it, Lorcan. In this day and age there's no need for girls to get pregnant. They have access to contraception, not like in our day,' she ranted. 'Were you using contraceptives?' she demanded, her face contorted with anger.

'Yes, condoms,' Jeff muttered miserably. 'One burst on us.'

'Why wasn't she on the pill if you were having sex? Was she afraid she'd put on weight? It's not good enough, Jeff. You've ruined your life. *She's* ruined your life.' Tessa burst into tears.

'When is the baby due?' Lorcan asked quietly.

'April.'

'*April!*' Tessa screeched. 'You have your finals coming up. Have you any idea what it's like having a new baby?

And where are you going to live? And what are you going to live on? Jesus Christ Almighty, Jeff, how *could* you?' She was devastated as she stood looking at her woebegone younger son, his head hanging, his fists clenched tightly.

'I'll look after Valerie, don't worry about that,' he shouted back at her. 'We're going to get married as soon as we can.'

'Oh, by God you are *not*!' Tessa stood with her hands on her hips. 'You're not marrying that one. You're not marrying *anyone* at your age, do you hear me?'

'I have to marry her,' he said desperately. 'I have to do the right thing.'

'The lad is right—'

'No, Lorcan, no!' Tessa turned on her husband, eyes blazing. 'I won't allow it. He's too young to marry anyone. You should never marry because you have to, only because you want to.' She stared at Lorcan, wiping the tears from her eyes and saw the pain in his. She hated Jeff for inflicting this torment on his family.

'We'll talk about it tomorrow,' Lorcan said firmly. 'Have you told Valerie's parents yet?'

'No, we were leaving it for a while until we have our plans made,' he said miserably.

'Oh Jesus,' Tessa moaned. She'd forgotten about Valerie's parents. 'Whatever about Carmel, that other yoke is a piece of work. What did you get involved with the likes of them for?'

'Stop it, Tessa. Go to bed,' Lorcan said grimly. 'And you too, Jeff. We can talk about it tomorrow and see what has to be done. We'll stand by you and Valerie, won't we, Tessa?'

He directed a laser-like stare at his wife and Tessa knew him well enough to realize that she could only push it so far with him. Lorcan was a quiet man and rarely had to assert himself, but when he did he was formidable.

'Tessa?' Lorcan repeated.

'Yes, we'll support you,' Tessa said dully, and turned on her heel and walked out of the kitchen. She picked up her bag from under the hallstand and rooted for her car keys.

'Where are you going?' She hadn't heard Lorcan following her out into the hall.

'I need to be on my own. I'm going to drive over to The Point and sit in the car for a while.'

'You need to be with me, with your family.' He took her hand in his and held it to his heart, his face creased and tired as he looked at her with concern.

'No, Lorcan, I need to be on my own, I'm sorry.' She touched his cheek with her free hand and he let her go.

'Take a jacket, it's chilly out tonight and don't stay out too late,' he said heavily before going back to Jeff.

She took one of his fleeces off the hallstand and walked out into the cool night air. Autumn's chill had come early, even though it was only late August, and once the sun went down they were back to lighting fires in the kitchen. She got into the car and found that her hands were shaking as she went to put the key into the ignition. She felt weighed down with worry. Once you had a child there was always worry. Jeff would find that out soon enough. His relatively carefree existence was gone, never to be regained. All her dreams for him had just evaporated with those two words: 'Valerie's pregnant.'

Valerie. Valerie. Valerie! Now no matter how much Tessa hated the idea, their lives would always be entwined now. Valerie was the mother of their first grandchild whether Tessa liked it or not and, more to the point, whether Tessa liked *her* or not. That was the worst of it. After hearing Jeff's news, Tessa felt even more hostile than ever towards her son's girlfriend. Well, she was not going to become her daughter-in-law if Tessa had anything to do with it. Her precious son was not going to be trapped into a marriage with that girl and have Terence Harris for a father-in-law. She had no time for the way Valerie's father ripped off the welfare system, shamelessly selling fuel to which he was not entitled, and making a fine profit at tax payers' expense. Jeff had told her that he treated Valerie harshly and was very dictatorial. Poor Carmel never looked happy. She didn't want that man in their lives. Over her dead body, Tessa vowed as she started up the engine and drove into the velvet darkness.

Lorcan lay in bed, waiting for the sound of the car driving up to the house. It was nearly midnight. He wished Tessa would come home so that he could put his arms around her and try to offer her some comfort. He knew she was devastated. He knew that as well as worrying about Jeff and his future she would be dreading the whispered talk in the village. The busybodies would have a field day. That aspect of it didn't bother him too much, Lorcan thought sourly. He didn't give two hoots about the village gossips. What he was worried about, apart from Tessa's pain, was his wife's attitude towards Valerie. She was very hard on the girl, for some reason. He found her a nice enough young lady. Jeff seemed happy with her and that was the important thing. And he was proud of his son for wanting to do the right thing by her. That was the mark of a man.

Lorcan studied the golden harvest moon, framed by the big sash windows in their bedroom. It would be lovely to be out fishing under it. Peaceful, calm, serene. The sea was the only place he'd find peace and quiet for the next few months, he thought glumly. The family would be on a rocky road for the foreseeable future, but he'd been on a rocky road before, he and Tessa, and they'd survived and regained their equilibrium. There was no point in crying over spilled milk and pointing the finger of blame. This too would pass.

He heard Tessa's car crunch over the gravel and hoped she'd calmed down. He yawned again. He longed for sleep but his wife needed him tonight of all nights. Lorcan took a deep breath and lay patiently awaiting his poor beleaguered beloved.

Jeff lay wide awake and heard his mother make her way up the stairs. He heard the creak of his parents' bedroom door and the low murmur of voices.

At least they knew. There was some relief in that. He hadn't intended telling them so soon and had just blurted it out when Tessa had pressed to know what was wrong with him. He had expected her response, if he was honest. Tessa never kept her emotions reined in. She was so different from his father. That was why they worked so well as a couple, he supposed, looking at his parents' relationship for the first time with adult eyes. Lorcan and Tessa were like him and Valerie. She was the hot-tempered, shoot-from-the-hip sort, and he was the laid-back, anything-for-an-easy-life type.

Well, life would be anything but laid-back from now on. He was going to have responsibilities. He was going to be a father. It all seems so surreal, he thought tiredly. If he had ever thought anything like this would have happened he'd never have had sex . . . ever.

Valerie was up to ninety, his mother was up to ninety. She was disappointed in him and Valerie was disappointed that he hadn't come up to Dublin tonight. She wanted to get married, he knew that. She'd been so relieved when he'd suggested it, hoping against hope that she'd want to at least wait until he had finished his exams, and maybe by then she might have cooled on the idea. He might very well have to give up college and stay fishing to have a steady income to provide for his child.

His father expected him to get married and do 'the right thing'. He had got a girl into trouble and he couldn't walk away, would be Lorcan's thinking on the matter. In fairness to his mother she understood how trapped he felt. Trapped, cornered, ensnared . . . these words couldn't even *begin* to describe how he felt. He cared an awful lot for Valerie, he really did, but even though he'd told her he loved her, now he wasn't quite so sure. He hadn't planned on getting engaged or married or any serious stuff like that. Let alone having a baby. All he'd wanted was to have fun and plenty of sex, just like all his mates. Why did he have to be the one to get caught? It wasn't bloody fair, he raged. Tonight had been the second worst night of his life. When he'd found out Valerie was pregnant had been the first.

And another dread-inducing ordeal awaited. Valerie's

folks had to be told the shattering news and old man Harris was going to have his guts for garters.

Jeff felt utterly tense as he lay with his hands damp with perspiration and his heart beating a tattoo under the sheet, wishing he could pack up his kitbag, climb out the window and take to his heels, away from Rockland's and all the responsibilities and hassle that now awaited him.

CHAPTER TWENTY

Valerie lay in bed, desperate for sleep. She felt nauseous, stressed and very tired. Lizzie, asleep on the divan beside her, gave a few gentle ladylike snores, oblivious to her best friend's desperation. Valerie tried hard not to be resentful. Lizzie was a true friend. From the moment Valerie had tearfully confided that she feared she was pregnant, Lizzie had proved that she was pure gold. She had got Valerie through those first shattering days when her world had been thrown into upheaval. She had sat beside her on the chipped edge of the old-fashioned cast-iron enamel bath, holding her hand while they waited for the results of the pregnancy test, a result that Valerie had known instinctively would be positive. From that heart-stopping moment when the condom had burst when she and Jeff had made love, after their happy evening at the pictures, Valerie had known that she had fallen pregnant.

'It will be OK,' Jeff assured her, trying to ease her panic. 'It happens lots of times to people and nothing goes wrong.'

'Did it ever happen to you and Ursula?' She was frantic for reassurance as she wriggled out from under him.

'Yeah,' he'd muttered. 'It was fine, though. Have a bath. It will be OK. Stop panicking.' He yawned and seemed unconcerned as he lay back against the pillows.

Easy for you to say, she thought edgily as she got out of bed to run a bath.

'Maybe you should think of going on the pill,' Jeff suggested warily as they sat at the kitchen table a while later, having a cup of hot chocolate to try to ease her agitation and induce sleep. Her fears were beginning to impact on him and he was starting to feel jittery.

'Yeah, I'll go to the Well Woman,' she agreed, knowing in her heart of hearts that it was already too late.

She would never forget the look on his face, a few weeks later, when she told him that the pregnancy test she'd taken was positive. They were sitting on a bench under a massive oak tree in Phoenix Park, the sun-dappled leaves dipping down over their heads in the late evening sun. The park was buzzing with joggers, dog walkers, and families and couples out for a stroll after work. She had met Jeff after a training session and he was tired, thirsty and keen to go for a pint.

'I'm pregnant,' she said hesitantly, and saw the last vestiges of his boyish carefree *joie de vivre* disappear before her eyes as shock, horror and dismay took up residence in his psyche.

'God, Valerie, are you sure?' he demanded, jumping to his feet.

'Positive,' she retorted, her heart sinking as she saw the trapped desperation in his eyes. 'What are we going to do?'

'Well . . . ah . . . could you do something to bring on a miscarriage? Can you have very hot baths or . . . or lift something heavy?' He was pacing up and down in front of her, grey-faced beneath his tan. 'This is a disaster,' he burst out.

'Oh, Jeff,' she murmured in dismay, and burst into tears.

'Sorry, sorry, I didn't mean to upset you,' he said gruffly. 'Come on, let's get out of here.' He took her hand, embarrassed that people were looking at them as Valerie wept uncontrollably. They walked to the car in silence and she struggled to compose herself.

'Where do you want to go?' he asked.

'Home,' she muttered, distraught.

'Will you be OK to drive? I can't leave the bike here. I'll follow you.' He held the car door open for her.

'OK,' she said even though her hand trembled as she put the key in the ignition.

He's going to dump me, she thought fearfully as she drove past the American Ambassador's Residence. The Stars and Stripes fluttered gaily in the breeze, mocking her with its carefree abandon. People were walking along talking, laughing. Anger and resentment ripped through her. Her life was in tatters and no one cared.

She drove towards the North Circular Gate, glancing in the rear-view mirror to see if there was any sign of Jeff following her on the bike. She might never see him again, she thought in sudden terror. She'd seen the horrified look in his eyes when she'd told him that he was going to be a father. He wanted to be a million miles away from her. She was a fool to think otherwise. He was probably blaming her for what happened. If blame was to be apportioned it had to be half and half, she screamed silently. It took two to make a baby. That was always forgotten when a girl got pregnant outside of marriage.

The boys more often than not got away scot-free to continue their lives unhindered and unfettered. It was the girl who paid the price. She was now one of those girls that everyone judged so freely. People would whisper about her behind their hands at work. She would be the talk of the village and her parents would be ashamed.

She had believed the myth of liberation perpetuated in all those glossy magazines she devoured avidly. She had believed that women were free to have it all, including a sex life outside of marriage. How many articles had she read about 'Pleasing Your Man'? She'd bought sexy lingerie and slathered herself in moisturizers and lotions to keep her skin silky soft, and believed she was a 'liberated woman', 'A Woman of the Eighties'. She'd looked at the glitzy soaps, *Dallas*, *Dynasty* and the like, and wanted to be just like those characters. And look at where that had got her. What a fool she'd been to take such a risk. She'd been so shallow and impressionable, thinking that she was cool and sophisticated, especially when she was back in Rockland's socializing with Jeff in the hotel, impressing the hell out of her peers. The girls she'd been so desperate to keep up with. For the first time in her life she'd felt she was as good as they were. How sad was that, she thought, to define herself as being a success because she had a boyfriend and she was sleeping with him, and she was a so-called 'liberated woman'. How sad, and how utterly immature.

She and Jeff had never even discussed what would happen if she got pregnant. She had taken no responsibility for her own state of being. She should have been proactive and used some sort of contraception other than condoms. At least then she would have had a degree of control. She'd been completely irresponsible, sickening though it was to admit. She'd thought she was mature, but *this* was the beginning of maturity, she realized, her first instance of real self-awareness.

She had Lizzie and she had her mother to depend on, otherwise she was on her own. Fear swamped her again as she emerged onto the North Circular and had to brake suddenly when a taxi cut in front of her. 'Bastard!' she swore viciously, pressing hard on the horn. The taxi driver flipped the finger at her and she felt hatred for every man she knew. She hoped her baby would be a girl, she thought bitterly.

Jeff *wanted* her to have a miscarriage. He had been surprisingly direct about it. It would solve everything. She wondered if he would ask her to go to England for an abortion. Rita Gallagher, who worked in the village post office, was supposed to have travelled to a clinic in Liverpool for a termination, or so the rumour went. She was having an affair with the local Garda sergeant, who was married with two grown sons. It had been going on for years. Rita ignored all the gossip that swirled around her and held her head high always; much to the disgust of some of the Altar Crawlers, who held the high moral ground and conveniently forgot the biblical precept of not judging lest you be judged. Valerie sighed, thinking of Rita. She couldn't bear to have a rumour like that following her around. What a difficult and lonely journey that must have been if it was true. Valerie knew that no matter what happened she would not be taking the boat to England, but she would never judge anyone who did. Being unwantedly pregnant was something she wouldn't wish on her worst enemy.

Let Jeff abandon her. That was what men did and she was a mug to expect otherwise, she thought as she drove towards St Peter's Church, with no sign in the mirror that her boyfriend was following her on his motorbike. She swung left at Doyle's Corner, speeding through Phibsboro and Cross Guns Bridge, desperate to get home.

Lizzie was out on a date with Dara Fallon, the guy she'd fancied for ages, and the flat had never felt so quiet, the silence amplifying the thudding of her heart. She felt so utterly alone. 'What am I going do?' she asked aloud as she studied her reflection in the big gilded oval mirror that hung over the mantelpiece and saw how pale she was, how sunken and dark her eyes were. Eyes that were full of fear and apprehension. She was going to be a *mother!* She was going to have a little being depend on her totally. What did she know about babies? Nothing! Carmel had never been pregnant after she'd had her. There had been no babies in their house for her to help rear. She'd never even fed a baby its bottle, she thought in blind panic as her stomach lurched and her thoughts whirled around her brain until she wanted to scream, 'SHUT UP!'

She heard the sound of a motorbike growing louder along the road and hurried to the window. She actually felt weak with relief as she saw Jeff dismount and lock the bike to Mrs Maguire's railings. 'Thank God! Thank God! Thank God!' she breathed. He hadn't abandoned her . . . yet.

She hurried down the stairs to let him in. 'I thought you weren't going to come back,' she blurted. 'I thought you were going to leave me.'

'I won't leave you, Valerie,' he said stoutly, and she felt more love for him at that moment than she'd ever done.

'Come on, let's go upstairs and decide what we're going to do.' He took her hand and started up the stairs ahead of her.

Oh, no, he wants me to have an abortion. Relief was superseded by dismay as they reached the top of the stairs.

'Do you want tea?' she asked hesitantly as he stood back, then followed her into the kitchen.

'No, no, thanks.' He ran his hand over his stubbly jaw. He looked shattered as he leaned against the doorframe. 'We'll have to tell the folks, but before we do we better make our plans. We should try and get married around Christmas when I've finished my term exams. It will give us a few months to try and save. What do you think?'

'That's sounds . . . er . . . fine,' she said weakly, and had to sit down on one of the kitchen stools because her legs had started to shake. Jeff was going to *marry* her. Everything was going to be OK. She felt faint with relief.

It wasn't ideal. She would love to have had a long courtship when they were free to do as they pleased, travel and see the world, save for a house, and celebrate their engagement. She would have liked all those things but they weren't going to happen now. But at least she'd have a wedding ring on her finger and she wouldn't be an 'unmarried mother', as girls in her position were so disparagingly called, she comforted herself. She loved Jeff with all her heart. He was the love of her life, there were no doubts in her mind about that. And he *had* told her before she got pregnant that he loved her. But was *she* the love of his life, she couldn't help wondering. If she wasn't pregnant would they have got engaged eventually or would he have tired of her and feel he didn't want to be tied down? Now she'd never know. And that was something that would always niggle at her, no matter how much she tried to suppress it. *Stop it*, she told herself silently. Circumstances had ensured that they would marry, and far quicker than she had anticipated in those fantasies she'd happily indulged in every so often. This was her reality now and she had to deal with it.

'I'll come with you to tell your parents,' she heard him say.

She jumped up off the high stool and threw her arms around him. 'Oh, Jeff, you're so good to me.' She rested her head on his shoulder and felt a measure of peace descend for the first time since her life had been turned upside down.

He gave her a squeeze. 'We'll be OK,' he said, and because she wanted to believe him she did.

It would be a lovely wedding, Lizzie assured her the following day when Jeff had gone. She, of course, would be the bridesmaid, she grinned. Valerie could wear ivory; it was becoming a popular colour for wedding dresses now. She could have her dress cut in the empire-line style, which would hide a burgeoning bump. Lizzie was enjoying being in charge as she handed the mother-to-be a mug of hot milk and pepper, with dry cream crackers, her own mother's remedy for nausea.

Valerie burst into tears at her friend's kindness. 'I don't want to be looking like a beached whale waddling up the aisle,' she wept. Her hormones were all over the place. One minute everything was fine and she was feeling normal and even a little excited, the next she was in floods and everything loomed like a big dark cloud on her horizon. It was most unsettling.

'You won't be like a beached whale. You'll be gorgeous and voluptuous and sexy,' Lizzie soothed, patting her back.

'Why did the fucking condom burst?' Valerie raged between snotty sobs. 'It's God's punishment for us having premarital sex, that's what it is.'

'Don't be *ridiculous*,' Lizzie scoffed. 'It was bad luck, nothing more, nothing less. A child is a *gift* not a *punishment*, Valerie.' Lizzie looked at her sternly. 'So stop that nonsense.'

'Easy for you to say,' sniffed Valerie. 'I'm just saying what Da will be saying when I tell him.'

'Stop fretting and worrying about things until you have to worry about them,' her friend advised as she settled down on the sofa with a crisp sandwich and a mug of tea, to watch *Star Trek*.

Terence wouldn't pay for a big wedding; of that there was no doubt, Valerie mused as she washed up some dirty dishes. She'd be lucky if he didn't throw her out of the house for good and tell her never to set foot in it again. She felt even more nauseous as she thought of telling Carmel her news. Her mother would be so disappointed for her. She took such pleasure listening to her daughter's tales of life in 'the big smoke', as Carmel called Dublin. They had had a few most enjoyable mother-and-daughter days, including trips to the cinema, theatre and, on Carmel's birthday, lunch in the Royal Dublin Hotel, a special treat that Carmel had thoroughly enjoyed.

There'd be no more luxuries like that, Valerie thought sadly. Every penny counted now. Jeff was still in college and wouldn't have finished his final exams before the baby was born. They would have to find somewhere to live and find someone to look after the baby while she was at work, but at least Jeff would be by her side. They would be a family. It was all she'd ever wanted really, even if it was all happening much sooner than she'd anticipated.

Would it be a boy or a girl, she wondered. She'd like a little girl. Jeff would be a very kind and loving father, very different from Terence. Theirs would be a happy home, she thought with rising optimism as she hummed 'Crazy Little Thing Called Love'.

Now, two weeks later, as she lay awake in the light of the full moon, her mind racing, her heart was sad. Very sad. Jeff hadn't come up from Rockland's. He'd phoned her around six thirty to say he was only getting ashore and he had to be up before the dawn to catch the tide. If it was OK with her he'd give it a miss for tonight and see her at the weekend. What could she say but that it was fine? She could do with an early night, she'd lied.

Valerie felt that by now familiar fear in the pit of her stomach. Jeff was cooling off, she was sure of it. They were supposed to be telling their parents at the weekend and discussing the arrangements for the wedding. It was clear he was having second thoughts and didn't want to go through with it. As she'd always dreaded, she was on her own.

She tossed and turned for hours, frantic for sleep, knowing that she had to go to work in the morning, and almost cried when the moonlight waned and the first faint glimmers of daybreak whispered across the eastern sky, and the birds began their inexorable dawn symphony, celebrating the start of a new day.

Chapter Twenty-One

Something was up, Carmel thought in dismay as she saw her daughter pushing a piece of bacon around her plate. She had cooked Valerie's favourite meal: bacon, cabbage, floury potatoes and parsley sauce. It had been a while since her daughter was home for the weekend and she had been really looking forward to seeing her.

They had grown much closer since Valerie had moved up to Dublin. Carmel was immensely proud of the way she had made a whole new life for herself. She was blossoming into a beautiful, self-assured, happy young woman, living the life she wanted, a far cry from her own dreary existence. Valerie was *living*, she was *existing*, Carmel often thought, wishing she had the get-up-and-go to improve her life. Valerie had bought a car and learned to drive. At least Carmel was taking lessons, which was a big leap for her, if somewhat nerve-racking.

Valerie loved living in the flat with Lizzie and they had made a very good job of decorating it. Carmel, impressed with how they had updated their old-fashioned bedroom, had taken a leaf out of her daughter's book and done a little redecorating of her own. She'd bought some new mint-green and cream floral-patterned material and made curtains, and a matching bedspread with a little frill around the end. It gave her small bedroom a bright fresh new look. Valerie had been very complimentary when she'd seen it and had bought a few scatter cushions to throw on the bed.

Carmel loved spending a Saturday in the city with her daughter. She would travel up on the bus and Valerie would pick her up at Bus Aras. Carmel was amazed at how unfazed she was driving around in the traffic and how well she knew the city after only a few months living there. She brought her to places she'd never been to before. They had spent a lovely day on Carmel's birthday, shopping in the Dandelion Market and Grafton Street before having a posh lunch in the Royal Dublin Hotel. Valerie had ordered smoked salmon for her starter. Carmel had had a little taste but hadn't liked it very much. She'd played it safe and had a prawn cocktail but at Valerie's urging she had tried the chicken supreme with rice and had really enjoyed it. Her daughter had insisted that she have a glass of wine to celebrate and Carmel had felt on a par with 'The Elite' in the fancy houses in the village. They were always lunching in fancy hotels. Afterwards, Valerie had taken her to the National Botanic Gardens just across the road from where she lived. The beauty and scents of the magnificent rose garden had been breathtaking. The weeping willows dipping into the river that curved around the boundary gave off such a tranquil air she could have stayed there for hours.

When she'd heard Valerie was coming home for the weekend, Carmel had made an effort and decorated the table with her good linen tablecloth and silverware, and had bought a bottle of Black Tower as a special treat. In a fortunate turn of events, Terence had had to work over-time and wasn't due home until after ten so they could have a lovely relaxed dinner with no tension. She hadn't anticipated Valerie arriving home looking pale and wan, with dark circles smudging her eyes, and unable to eat her dinner, let alone drink the wine that sparkled in her Waterford crystal glasses, a wedding present from an aunt all those years ago. They'd never been used until now and she had shined them until they sparkled before pouring in the golden liquid.

'Are you not feeling the best? You look a bit pale,' she queried as Valerie ate a small portion of potato that she had mashed into the sauce.

'I'm a bit off,' Valerie admitted.

'That's a pity. I was hoping you'd enjoy the wine. I bought it as a bit of a treat for us.'

'Thanks, Mam.' Valerie smiled at her.

'And how's Jeff?' Carmel asked lightly, hiding her disappointment. 'Will you be seeing him later?'

'He's fine,' Valerie said heavily. 'I'll be seeing him tomorrow. He's at a friend's stag party tonight. Mam, I've something to tell you.'

Carmel felt an icy hand grip her guts as she saw her daughter's expression. The pallor, the lack of appetite, the air of ennui. *Please, not that!* She sent up a silent prayer. 'What's the matter?' she said quietly, folding her hands in her lap.

'I'm pregnant.'

The words hung like giant boulders over Carmel's head, crashing down into her as all the dreams she held for her daughter smashed into smithereens. 'Oh, Valerie!' Carmel whispered, sick to her stomach.

'I'm sorry, Mam,' Valerie said miserably, twisting her serviette in a knot.

'But didn't you protect yourself? Girls can do that now, it's different than in my day.' Carmel tried to keep her voice steady. She wanted to slap Valerie and shout, '*You stupid, silly girl, you had every chance and now you've ruined it. And you've given your father the chance to have a real go at you. He'll never forgive you. You'll be able to go back to Dublin but I'm the one who will have to sit and listen to him. How could you, Valerie, how could you?*' The words shrieked around in her head and for a moment she thought she'd actually uttered them.

'We used condoms,' Valerie muttered.

'You can't depend on them,' Carmel said crossly. 'You know your father is going to go mad. Oh, Valerie, you've given him the opportunity to have such a go at you and there's nothing I'll be able to do about it.'

'Don't worry, Mam, it will be OK. We're getting married at Christmas. Jeff's going to be here when I tell him. I was going to wait to tell you together . . .' She bit her lip.

'*Married!* You don't want to rush into marriage, Valerie,' Carmel said in alarm.

'But then I'd be an unmarried mother!' Valerie exclaimed, astonished at her mother's reaction.

'There are worse things, Valerie. Better to be an unmarried mother than an unhappy wife.'

'We love each other,' Valerie ventured, lowering her eyes, and Carmel felt a fresh rush of worry as she wondered what Jeff's true feelings for her daughter were.

'Why don't you go and lie down for a while?' she said tiredly, standing up from the table. 'I'll clear away here.'

'I'm sorry, Mam.' Valerie was near to tears.

'Go and rest,' she repeated. 'We'll get through it step by step and I know Lizzie will be a big help to you.'

'She is already, Mam, she is,' Valerie said with heartfelt emotion. 'I can always depend on her.'

'Well it's good to have someone in life to depend on. My advice to you is to wait until Sunday to tell your father. Then you can leave for Dublin and it will give him time to cool down,' Carmel said, scraping the uneaten meals into the bin. 'And make life easy on yourself, Valerie. For once in your life, do *not* argue with your father, no matter what he says to you,' she warned.

'OK, thanks, Mam.' Valerie stood up from the table. 'I *am* sorry.'

'Stop apologizing. What's done is done, and we have to get on with it,' Carmel said sharply, flinging the plates into the basin none too gently, before filling it with water and washing-up liquid.

She heard her daughter walk down the hallway and shook her head in despair. Terence would lose the plot completely. The family's name would be shamed. There'd be talk and speculation, the way there always was when something like this happened in Rockland's. It was like every other village in the country: claustrophobic, smothering, a hotbed of gossip and exaggeration, Carmel thought wearily as she immersed her hands in the soapy water.

She kept herself to herself mostly, but Terence was very involved in the parish activities and liked to be seen doing good deeds. His reputation and how their neighbours viewed him had always been important to him. This would be a harsh blow. A very harsh blow indeed. For the first time in a long time, Carmel actually felt sorry for her husband. He tried so hard to be a people pleaser. There was some need in him, some want that made him crave approval and acknowledgement, and from individuals who were only really on the periphery of his life, and all the while the two people who should mean the most to him hardly rated at all. Now a grandchild was coming, and instead of the baby bringing joy there would be more division in the family, more trauma. Would it never end?

But Valerie needed her, and her grandchild would need her, and Carmel would do her best for them. That was all she could do. Terence would have to be responsible for his own feelings and behaviour; she wasn't going to indulge him any more. Those days were gone.

She had meant what she had said to Valerie. Better no marriage than an unhappy marriage. She had learned that the very hard way. She had to take responsibility for her own part in the unhappiness of her own marriage, she thought with a dart of shock. She should never have married Terence. But she had married him to get away from an unhappy home life, afraid to strike out on her own, and had gone from the frying pan into the fire. He wasn't all to blame.

She must speak of this to her daughter soon to try to prevent her from making the same mistake. Although in fairness Jeff Egan seemed like a very nice lad and she had never felt any cause for concern for her daughter's welfare because of him. But even the nicest chap in the world would change in an unhappy marriage, especially if it was a marriage they felt coerced into. No matter what Terence said – and Carmel knew without the shadow of a doubt that he'd want Valerie up that aisle the sooner the better – she was going to do her best to persuade her daughter to give it time before rushing into a marriage that could end in tears. Carmel felt a firm resolve that brought an unexpected calm to her spirit as she stood at the kitchen sink washing the dishes.

'I've told my mother,' Valerie said to Jeff as they walked along the beach under The Headland.

'What did she say?' Jeff kicked a piece of driftwood out of his way. He had his hands in his jacket pockets and she wished he would hold hands with her. The weather had turned and a south-easterly blew up along the beach, swirling the sand around them. She hadn't wanted to sit in the stuffy lounge of the hotel. She wanted fresh air and had asked him to go for a walk on the beach. He was subdued and had given her only a peck on the cheek when they'd met up.

'She was OK after the shock. She thinks we should wait until Sunday to tell my da, so that I can leave for Dublin afterwards because he will go berserk.' She didn't tell him that Carmel had, surprisingly, declared that rushing into marriage was not the course of action to take.

Her mother had broached the subject again when they'd gone for a driving practice earlier in the day before going to Mount Usher Gardens. Carmel had said very frankly that she had married Terence to get away from home and to escape looking after her father and brothers. It was the biggest mistake of her life and if she had her life over again she would not repeat it. An unhappy marriage was a hard cross to bear for both her and Terence, she'd admitted. She didn't want Valerie to end up unhappy by rushing into marriage because she was

pregnant. Valerie was astonished at her mother's direct-
ness. Carmel had always been very private about the
state of her marriage. Valerie had assured her that her
relationship with Jeff was different and had changed the
subject. She did not want to *hear* this type of talk. It was
too unsettling.

Valerie felt that if she gave Jeff any leeway in the
marriage department he'd take it like a drowning man
grasping at a life raft. It was a thought she tried hard to
ignore. She just couldn't face the long lonely road ahead
without him.

'I told my folks,' he sighed.

'What did they say?' she asked warily. She was sure
Tessa Egan was far from impressed with the news.

'Ah . . . not much. They were a bit shocked and disappointed. You know yourself.' He shrugged. 'Dad was
calmer than Mam. She was a bit . . . er . . . put out.'

I bet she was, thought Valerie. 'Well, my da won't be
calm, that's for sure, just to warn you,' she said emphatically. 'Should we talk to the priest about the wedding?'
she ventured.

'I suppose we should,' Jeff said unenthusiastically. 'But
we should wait until we've told your da.'

'He'll want us to get married as soon as possible, I
know that.' Valerie slanted a glance up at him.

'Right,' he said, staring out at the horizon.

'Jeff, please talk to me,' she pleaded. 'You're so cool
and distant. It's scaring me.' Tears brimmed in her eyes.

'Oh, don't cry, Val,' he groaned, putting his arms
around her. 'I just feel a bit overwhelmed by it all. I can't
imagine being a father and having a baby to look after.'

'I can't imagine being a mother,' she said into his neck.

'We have a lot of decisions to make.' He buried his face in her hair.

'I know.' He was struggling just like she was, she reminded herself. It was all new to him too. They held each other tightly as the wind whipped the sand around their ankles and the waves crashed in on the beach, pounding the shore in fury.

'Oh, look.' Valerie pointed out to sea where a rainbow arched across the sky in glorious Technicolor splendour. 'What a gorgeous rainbow.'

'Just for us.' Jeff smiled down at her and put his arm around her shoulder and they stood in silence looking at nature's magnificent spectacle. Valerie snuggled in against him, glad that they had acknowledged their fears, at least, and wishing that the ordeal of telling her father was behind them.

'What's she bringing that fella here for?' Terence grumbled as he saw Valerie and Jeff walking hand in hand towards the house. He was just about to sit down with a cup of tea and the Sunday paper while Carmel prepared the roast dinner.

'Just be polite, Terence. Manners cost nothing,' Carmel said exasperatedly.

Terence looked at her. She was in one of her odd moods again. Edgy, he decided. Best to keep out of her way and let her get on with things. She had been in bed when he'd got home tired and hungry from his extra long day at work on Friday night and he'd had to heat up his own dinner. And then, yesterday she'd gone driving with Valerie and they hadn't come back for ages, and he'd had to have a fish-and-chip dinner, and, to add insult to injury, she'd told him to go and get it himself. Definitely edgy stuff, Terence decided, opening the paper at the sports pages.

'Dad?' Valerie stood in the door with the Egan chap behind her.

'Ah. Hello. Nice day out there; better than yesterday, anyway,' he said, remembering his wife's exhortations.

'We've something to tell you.' Valerie was ashen-faced, he noticed, and the Egan fella didn't look much better.

'What's that, then?' Terence felt a sudden trepidation. This was not good news of any description, he knew by their demeanour.

'We're going to have a baby.' Jeff put his arm protectively around Valerie.

Terence felt the way he'd felt when Brenda Ryan's father had called him a cur and told him never to set foot on his dairy farm again. Worthless. Helpless. Furious. Inadequate. Panic-stricken. Slowly he put his paper down. He wanted to jump to his feet and roar at her. He wanted to call her a slut, a whore, a tramp. A stupid little fool. He'd done his best for her, offered her a university education, and she'd turned her back on him with a sneer on her face and now look at her, up the duff, with no chance of bettering herself. Valerie Harris, Terence Harris's daughter, who couldn't keep her legs together, that's what they'd be saying in the bingo hall. The ould ones would be saying, 'She went before the whistle.' He knew what they were like, gossiping in the bingo hall. It would be the Harrises that would bear the brunt of the gossip. That snooty bitch Tessa Egan wouldn't have her nose rubbed in it like Carmel and himself would. A cold rage enveloped him. He stood up and pointed his finger at Jeff.

'Have you told your parents?' He glowered at him, ignoring his daughter.

'Yes, I have.'

'And what did they have to say?'

'They weren't too pleased,' he muttered.

'Well, we're going to your house now to sort this out. Carmel,' he yelled.

'I'm here,' his wife said from the doorway. 'There's no need to shout, Terence. Shouting won't help the situation.' She was pale but composed.

'Oh, so you know, do you? Well, get your coat. We're going up to this fella's family, and we're going to make sure he does the right thing by her.' He looked at Valerie as if she had crawled out from under a rock.

'I've every intention of marrying Valerie, Mr Harris,' Jeff said quietly.

'Oh, indeed you have, sonny. Make no mistake about it, the pair of you will be up that aisle before you know it.'

'No, Terence—'

'Get your coat, Carmel,' Terence gritted.

'Dad, it's not a good time—'

'I don't want to hear a word out of you, miss. Keep your trap shut the way you didn't keep your legs shut,' Terence snapped at her.

'Terence, do *not* speak to Valerie like that.' Carmel was crimson with annoyance and embarrassment.

'We could meet in the hotel in an hour's time, if that would suit you. My mother will be getting the Sunday lunch now,' Jeff said tightly.

'Sonny, we won't be having any public meeting in any hotel,' Terence said truculently, barging past him. 'Now the pair of ye follow me up to your house and let's have no more discussion.'

'Oh Jesus!' Valerie whispered, afraid she was going to puke.

'We'd better get it over with,' Jeff growled. 'If he calls me "sonny" once more, I'll deck him,' he muttered to Valerie, and didn't care if Terence heard him.

'I'll just go and turn down the oven.' Carmel's lips were a thin line as she walked past her husband.

'Go on, you pair, and tell the Egans that we're on our way.' Terence opened the front door and was tempted to kick the two of them in the ass as they walked out past him.

'Don't you make a disgrace of us with the Egans,' Carmel warned him as she slid into her Sunday coat. 'And don't for God's sake make vulgar remarks about our daughter.'

'I'll say what has to be said,' Terence retorted furiously. 'And you make sure to back me up.'

'I'll have my own say, Terence. Now come on and get this ordeal over with,' his wife said curtly and he followed her out, wondering what she meant by that.

He followed Valerie's Mini through the village, his thoughts racing. If she got married as soon as possible it would take some of the sting out of the sorry mess she, and now they, were in. At least she'd be living up in Dublin so she wouldn't be parading her shame around the village. At least that was some small mercy.

And he wouldn't be taking any nonsense from that Tessa Egan. It was her son who had got his daughter into trouble; he wouldn't be letting her forget it. She needn't look down her snooty nose at him and his family. Terence's hands tightened on the wheel as he prepared himself for the battle to come.

CHAPTER TWENTY-TWO

'Oh Lord, Jeff never told me he was bringing *her* here today,' Tessa groused as she saw Valerie's Mini turning into the drive. The mushy peas had just boiled over in a green foamy spume on top of the cooker and that in itself had put her into a bad mood. Now she was going to have to deal with Jeff's pregnant girlfriend.

'Now, Tessa, be kind,' Lorcan admonished from the table where he was hulling strawberries.

'Jesus, Mary and Joseph, Lorcan. Her parents are with them!' Tessa exclaimed in dismay as she saw the Harrises' car pull up outside their garden.

'The word is out,' Lorcan said wryly.

'The feckin' nerve of them, coming up here without a by-your-leave,' Tessa bristled. 'The lunch will be ruined if I have to go entertaining them. They might have had the manners to phone and arrange to meet, instead of arriving unannounced.'

'The lunch will be grand. Turn off the peas and the spuds, and turn down the oven,' Lorcan said calmly as he shook caster sugar over the strawberries and placed them in the fridge. 'I'll show the Harrises into the sitting room.'

'I hope they don't come in the back, I hope Jeff has that much cop on. I'll kill him,' Tessa fumed. 'And I hope we won't have to listen to any old guff from that Harris fella.' She tucked a strand of hair behind her ear, turned off the cooker, and saw with relief that her son was leading his unwelcome guests to the front door.

'Don't lose the cool, Tessa. Remember, least said soonest mended,' Lorcan threw over his shoulder as he went out to the hall. 'Hello, Valerie, come in,' she heard him say kindly, and she wished she could be as composed as he was. She would not let the Harrises see that she was rattled, she resolved, catching sight of her flushed face in the small mirror over the fireplace.

Tessa took a deep breath and went out to the hall. The first person she saw was Valerie, looking drawn and apprehensive, hardly able to meet her eyes. Not looking so cocky today, are we? she thought nastily as she swept a glance over her. 'Hello, Valerie,' she said coolly. 'Go in and sit down. Jeff, go and put the kettle on.'

'OK,' he muttered. 'Sorry about this. *He*,' Jeff jerked his thumb over his shoulder, 'wouldn't wait. I did try to put him off or say we'd meet in the hotel later but he insisted on coming.'

'Did he now?' Tessa retorted.

'Carmel, Terence, come in,' she heard her husband say in his calm tones, and was so glad he was here to stand by Jeff's side.

She saw Carmel's pinched white face, her eyes dark with trepidation. Despite her anger and indignation she felt sorry for Valerie's mother. It wasn't the poor woman's fault that her daughter had got pregnant and that she had a boor for a husband.

'Come in, Carmel. Let me take your coat and go in and sit down,' she said politely.

'Thank you, Tessa. I'm sorry for springing this visit on you. I hope it's not putting you out. You were probably getting the lunch,' Carmel said, clearly uncomfortable as she divested herself of her coat.

'I was but it will wait.' She glared at Valerie's father. 'Hello, Terence,' she greeted him, her voice a couple of degrees cooler.

'Tessa.' Terence was equally cool.

'Tea or coffee?' Lorcan interjected, following them into the sitting room.

'No, no, nothing like that,' Terence said brusquely. 'This isn't a social visit, as I'm sure you know.'

'There's nothing like a cup of tea to ease the chat,' Lorcan said evenly. 'Carmel, will you have a cuppa? Valerie?' He raised an eyebrow at her.

'Thank you, Lorcan. I'll join you in one,' Carmel said quietly, ignoring the daggers looks her husband was giving her.

'Grand. And Tessa and I will have one too. Valerie, why don't you give Jeff a hand out in the kitchen, and we'll sort things out over the tea?' he suggested. Valerie took up his suggestion with alacrity and hurried out to join her boyfriend.

'You have a lovely view, Tessa,' Carmel observed as she sat on the edge of the sofa and stared out of the French windows.

'We didn't come here to talk about views,' Terence blustered. 'Now your son has got my daughter pregnant and I'm here to see that he's going to do the right thing by her.'

'Jeff has every intention of fulfilling his responsibilities and doing the right thing by Valerie, be assured of that, Terence,' Lorcan said in a voice of quiet authority.

'Right then, well, we better discuss wedding plans.' Terence sat down beside Carmel. 'I'm not going to spend a fortune on it, just so as you know.'

'Perhaps we should wait until Valerie and Jeff are here; after all, it is their future we're discussing,' Lorcan suggested mildly.

'I don't think they should rush into marriage,' Tessa said firmly and saw Carmel look at her in surprise.

'I want her married before she has that baby,' Terence declared trenchantly, sitting up straight, lower lip sticking out like an angry little gnome just as Jeff pushed Tessa's hostess trolley, laden with mugs of tea and a plate of chocolate biscuits, into the room. Valerie followed him, head down, and it was clear she had been crying.

'You should have used the china cups,' Tessa chided testily as she handed her a steaming mug.

'Ah sure, what difference does it make once it's tea, isn't that right, Valerie?' Lorcan tried to lighten the atmosphere when he saw the girl flush at the rebuke as she handed him a mug of tea, and placed one on the coffee table for her mother.

'Right, we're all here now,' Terence began impatiently. 'I was just saying to your father,' he looked up at Jeff, 'I expect you to marry my daughter before this baby is born.'

'Now look, Terence,' Tessa stood up. She had had enough of the little dictator sitting on her sofa. 'Rushing up the aisle is not necessarily the wisest course of action. They're too young – they're not even twenty-one – it would be—'

'I'm telling you now, Tessa, your son is going to walk her up the aisle before that baby's born. I'm having no bastards in my family, thank you,' Terence said furiously.

'There's no need for that sort of language, if you don't mind,' Lorcan reproved sternly.

'I think Tessa's right.' Carmel sat tombstone straight, her handbag on her knees, her hands curled so tight around the handle her knuckles were white. Two bright spots of pink stained her pale cheeks.

Terence's eyes bulged, his Adam's apple bobbed up and down and he looked as if he was about to have apoplexy. 'Are you *mad*?' he demanded, glaring at her in astonishment.

Valerie looked stricken at her mother's startling inter-vention. Jeff shot a surprised glance at his mother.

'No, I'm not mad, Terence. I agree with Tessa. They are far too young. There's plenty of time for them to get married. They have their whole lives ahead of them to do that.' Carmel didn't look at her husband as she made her speech.

'I agree wholeheartedly, Carmel,' Tessa said, delighted to have an unexpected ally. 'Getting married and having a child are major life-changing events. Jeff is doing his finals next year; he's not going to be able to concentrate on his studies if he has all—'

'I'm not interested in your son's *finals*! They're no concern of mine. I'm not having my daughter going around as an unmarried mother,' Terence fumed.

'With respect, Terence, Jeff's exams and his results will have a *most* important bearing on their child, *our* grand-child,' Tessa said sharply. 'The better he does in his exams the easier it will be for him to secure a good job, and provide for Valerie and their child. Surely they can wait for another year or two until they're on a steadier footing? Things have changed, it's not the . . . the stigma it used to be,' she added, glancing over at Valerie, who looked stunned. 'I'm sure you agree with me, Valerie. I'm sure you wouldn't like to see Jeff's last two years of study wasted. I know he's said he'll work on the boat but I can tell you it's hard work and long hours, and we haven't worked all these years to provide Jeff with an education only for it to be thrown away. The best thing Jeff can do for you and the baby is get his qualification, and I know if you love him you won't stand in his way.'

Valerie swallowed hard. Tessa's hard stare was unnerving. Jeff was staying mute. She was disgusted and disappointed with him. She wanted him to jump in and say, 'I'm going to marry her,' but he was keeping out of the conversation and she knew then that his mother and Carmel had thrown him a lifeline and he was going to grab it.

'Now wait here a minute,' Terence exclaimed as he saw what was happening. 'Have the men no say in this at all? You women aren't thinking straight.'

'Tessa, I can understand Terence's concerns, and Jeff *has* expressed his willingness to marry Valerie before the baby is born.' Lorcan eyed his wife keenly.

'It's up to Valerie. Let *her* decide,' Tessa declared. 'I know she loves Jeff, and I know she'll make the right choice for all of them, and of course, Lorcan and I will give every help we can to them.'

Valerie knew she was trapped in a no-win situation. Tessa had skilfully manoeuvred her into a corner. If she said she wanted Jeff to marry her, he could say goodbye to his chosen profession and spend his life on the boats in a tough occupation that would mean they would have to live in Rockland's. Tessa was right in one way. Even she could see that. Getting married now would be a short-term solution and would have a huge impact on their future options. There was nothing she could do about having the baby, but by choosing to wait to marry, she could take the pressure off Jeff and let him continue with his studies and marry him when, as Tessa had put it, they were on a 'steadier footing'.

'What do you think?' Valerie turned to Jeff. She wasn't going to let him off that lightly.

'Well, er . . . um . . . I think your mother and Ma have a point, and it would be good to get the qualification,' he hedged.

'So are you saying you want to wait?' she persisted.

'It's up to you, Valerie. I'll do whatever you want.' Jeff landed it right back at her. Lorcan looked at her with eyes full of sympathy and she felt that he was the only one who understood how she was feeling right at that moment.

'OK, we'll wait,' she said, defeated. She wasn't going to *beg* him to marry her.

'Well, I wash my hands of the whole affair.' Terence's voice shook as he put his mug down and stood up. 'I did my best for you,' he said to Valerie. 'You've made your own bed, now lie in it. I'm finished with you. You can give your mother a lift home.' He marched out the door without a backward glance and they heard the front door slam.

'He'll calm down; he's only trying to do his best for you,' Lorcan said comfortingly.

'We're all trying to do our best for you,' Tessa said more kindly.

'It's been a difficult few days. If you don't mind, I'm going to head back to Dublin. I'll give you a lift home and get my stuff, Mam,' Valerie said with as much dignity as she could muster. She didn't look at Jeff.

'Would you like some lunch? You can't be driving up to Dublin with nothing in your stomach, sure she can't, Tessa?' Lorcan looked at her in concern.

'Stay and have a bite of lunch with us. And what about yourself, Carmel? You're welcome to stay too.' Now that she had got her own way and given her son some time to adjust to his new circumstances, Tessa felt she could be magnanimous.

'No, thanks, Mrs Egan,' Valerie said coldly. 'I'd like to get on the road so I can get to Dublin before the heavy traffic.'

'You need to mind yourself on that road now.' Lorcan patted her on the back, looking over at his son.

'I could drive you up and get the bus back,' Jeff offered, catching his father's gaze on him.

'That's an excellent idea, Jeff,' Lorcan said. 'You need to take good care of Valerie. She's your responsibility now.'

'Well, just let him have a bite of lunch then.' Tessa got to her feet. 'Why don't you go home and get your bits and pieces and Jeff will be ready to go when you come back?' she suggested.

'That's a good idea,' Carmel said, looking at her daughter's mutinous face. She stood up and straightened her clothes. 'We all need to mind Valerie and the baby.' She looked directly at Tessa. 'Especially now that she's made the brave decision to have the baby without the protection of marriage for the time being.'

'It's all for the best, and we won't be found wanting, Carmel,' Tessa assured her as she handed her her coat. 'That baby will be much loved when it arrives, Lorcan and I can promise you that.'

'I'm sure it will, and that's good to know. My daughter is a good, soft-hearted girl, and she's just proved that,' Carmel said quietly as she pulled on her leather gloves and left the room.

'I'll see you in a while then,' Jeff said to Valerie as she followed her mother.

'OK,' she said tersely without looking at him, afraid that if she did she would burst into tears and disgrace herself completely.

Terence drove down The Headland, his hands clenched tight around the wheel of the car, jolting and jerking the gears when he had to make a gear change. He was beside himself with frustration, impotence, anger, but most of all, to his surprise, a terrible sadness. His daughter had just been made little of, in his eyes, and Carmel had colluded with Tessa Egan to make sure that that young cur would walk away from his responsibilities, while Valerie would carry a burden of childrearing from which there was no escape. Not to mention the stigma of being an unmarried mother. She had ruined her life, ruined it, he raged in despair, wiping away blurry tears from his eyes.

They had all ignored his concerns as though his views were of no importance. Well, in fairness to Lorcan he had understood where Terence was coming from. Terence now felt the way he had felt when his parents had told him he was being sent to live with his aunt and uncle, on the other side of the country, far from all he knew and was familiar with. He had protested that he didn't want to leave home but his protests were ignored. His feelings didn't count. He would do as he was told, his father had thundered.

Those old, sad, angry feelings were swirling around him, smothering him, making him feel panicky and anxious. He took a few deep breaths as he came off The Headland onto the main street. He had been belittled once again, but it was one time too many. From now on he would keep his own counsel. He had done his best for his daughter, to no avail. She had listened to Carmel and Tessa and let them persuade her to let Jeff Egan off the hook. Valerie and her mother had turned their back on him; he would turn his back on them. He would have nothing to do with that child she was carrying, and that was the end of it. A large tear and then another rolled down his cheeks and Terence swore at his weakness, crying for people who didn't give a tuppenny damn about him.

'Why, Mam? Why did you agree with Tessa about us not getting married? Now I'm going to be the talk of the village. An unmarried mother! I can't *believe* you took her side!' Valerie burst out as she drove out of the Egans' yard.

'Valerie, even I can see that young fella's not ready for marriage. He's feeling trapped. That is no foundation for marriage. I'm telling you, five years down the line the pair of you would be terribly unhappy,' Carmel said firmly. 'I know you're angry and upset, but I do have your best interests at heart, even though right now you might think I don't.'

'But Jeff does love me,' Valerie protested heatedly. 'He was prepared to get married.'

'Being prepared to get married is different from wanting to get married – I'm telling you that from experience, Valerie – and if he does love you, well then, you've nothing to worry about because he will want to marry you when the time is right. Tessa was right: let him get his exams and get himself a good job and then let him marry you. I didn't want her saying that you held him back.' Carmel's mouth was a tight line, her fingers plucking agitatedly at her handbag.

'They'll all be talking about me here,' Valerie muttered, wishing she could light up a cigarette.

'Let them talk. You walk with your head held high, Valerie, always!' Carmel reached across and patted her knee. 'We'll get through this together, and I know the Egans won't shirk their responsibilities either. Lorcan is a good man. A sound man. He won't abandon his grandchild. And you have Lizzie. You couldn't find a better friend than Lizzie,' Carmel comforted as they reached home.

Terence's car wasn't there, much to Valerie's relief. She followed her mother into the house, went to her room and packed her clothes into her weekend case. 'Would you not stay for lunch?' Carmel urged, putting on her apron and opening the oven door to check on the roast.

'No, Mam, I want to get going. I just want to get out of Rockland's,' Valerie said dispiritedly.

'Ring me when you get to Dublin then, won't you?'

'I will. See you, Mam. I won't be down for a while. I couldn't bear it.'

'I'll be up to visit you then,' Carmel said firmly, and put her arms around her daughter. They held each other tightly for a few moments before Valerie drew away and walked out of the house.

She felt sick as she sat behind the wheel and started the ignition. She was angry and hurt and bitter. If Lorcan hadn't thrown the eye at Jeff he would never have suggested driving her up to Dublin off his own bat. She wasn't going to be under an obligation to him, she decided furiously as she drove towards The Headland.

He opened the door when she knocked.

'Would you like a cup of tea or anything?' he asked awkwardly.

'No, thanks. I just came to say I can drive home myself,' she said curtly. 'I'll see you in Dublin when you're up again.'

'I do love you, Valerie,' he said miserably. 'I *do* want to mind you and be there for you and the baby. I'll be with you all the way.' Now that the noose had loosened around his neck and he didn't have to get married straight away Jeff felt reprieved and wanted to reassure his girlfriend that he hadn't turned his back on her.

But not enough to marry me, and save me from shame, Valerie thought bitterly as she walked away from the house where all her hopes and dreams lay in tatters.

CHAPTER TWENTY-THREE

'Definitely a day for the fire, a good film and plenty of chocolate,' Lizzie remarked, shaking the rain off her woolly hat as she dumped the shopping bags onto the rickety old table in the kitchen.

'Yeah, but is there anything good on?' Valerie yawned, opening the bags to see what goodies her flatmate had brought home. 'Oh, yum,' she approved when she saw the tin of Denny's steak and kidney pie and the packet of Smash.

'Our favourite dinner,' Lizzie grinned. 'If my mother knew I was eating stuff out of a tin and a packet of dried potatoes she'd go mad.'

'I know. So would mine. And I *am* eating properly most days, but Saturdays are for me. Baba gets proper grub the other six days.' Valerie took out a packet of Jacobs Mikado, another firm favourite. 'Kettle's boiled, I'll make the tea.'

'Brill, I'm dying for a cuppa. It's an horrendous day out there.' Lizzie divested herself of her coat and scarf while Valerie made a pot of tea.

'Ouch!' she exclaimed indignantly as the baby gave a vigorous kick.

'What's wrong?' Lizzie's head jerked around quicker than Regan's in *The Exorcist*. Now that her friend's due date was fast approaching her nerves were shattered. She was having nightmares about having to do an emergency delivery.

Valerie laughed. 'There's nothing wrong, I just got a good kick. I bet it's a boy and he's going to be playing football with his daddy.'

'Oh, right. I thought you'd got a labour pain thingy.'

'A contraction,' Valerie corrected, handing her a mug of tea.

'And speaking of Daddy, what time is Jeff coming today?' Lizzie asked as she busied herself putting away the rest of the groceries.

'He's not. I told him to spend the day studying and I'll see him tomorrow. So I don't have to get dressed or wash my hair. I'm staying in my dressing gown *all* day! I'm wrecked!' Valerie yawned again, shucking some biscuits onto a plate.

'You poor old petal. I don't know how you're doing it, carrying that huge bump around. At least you'll be on maternity leave the week after next.'

'I can't wait. But the sooner I have the baby the better, so I can have more leave after it's born.'

'Well, you and Junior go in and put your feet up and I'll light the fire. Mrs M told me there's a very good matinée on at twelve, so we'll bunker in and watch it. And I bought *Photoplay*, *Woman's Way* and *Company* for us to loll about and read.'

'Ooohhh, we'll have a real lazy day so.' Valerie peered out of the kitchen window at the rain sluicing down in torrents, spattering out of the gutters onto the coal bunker in the yard below. The sky was murky, a sea of black threatening clouds. The wind swirled and keened around the back garden, assaulting trees and shrubs and snatching the pink blossoms off the ancient gnarled apple tree. It was more like deepest winter than an April morning. It was a perfect day to hibernate in their comfy old-fashioned sitting room and unwind.

'Mrs M told me to tell you she'll have the baby's cardigan finished by next week, by the way.' Lizzie handed Valerie two packets of crisps, two Crunchies and a large packet of Maltesers. 'For the film.' She justified her sinful purchases.

'Mrs M is a brick!' Valerie said warmly. Her landlady had shown her nothing but kindness since hearing of her pregnancy. Valerie had been very concerned that the elderly lady would not renew their lease when she found out that Valerie was expecting a baby. She wasn't sure if her landlady would judge her for having a baby out of wedlock, or if she would want to have a crying infant in the flat upstairs.

She had said nothing about her situation until one evening just before Christmas, when Valerie had seen Mrs Maguire walking up Botanic Avenue in the rain and stopped to give her a lift.

'Ah, you're a grand girl,' the old lady puffed as she settled herself into the seat and waved away the seat belt. 'I hate them things. There's no room to move with them.'

She turned to study Valerie. 'Do you know, you're getting stout when I see you sitting there. Your belt just about fits you,' she pronounced matter-of-factly. Mrs M was nothing if not pass remarkable, Valerie thought fondly, used to her landlady's direct manner. Behind her acerbic exterior reposed a kind heart. 'Too much chocolate and sticky buns, I'd wager. You gels don't eat properly these days.'

That was rich coming from someone who existed on peanut butter and cream crackers and plenty of sherry, Valerie thought in amusement, but her passenger had given her an opening to explain her situation. She took a deep breath. 'Actually, Mrs Maguire, I've been wanting to tell you . . . em . . . I'm having a baby. It's due in April. I was hoping it will be OK to stay in the flat after I have it.'

'A baby!' The old lady was startled.

'Yeah,' sighed Valerie, waiting for the disapprobation, and even worse, to be told that she would have to look elsewhere for a home for herself and her child.

'Well now, no wonder you're looking a bit portly, and a bit peaky too, deah. It's *imperative* that you take a nap in the afternoons. When I had my children I always took a nap every afternoon when I was expecting them,' she said crisply. 'Now we'll have to get a gate put in at the top of those stairs; we don't want any accidents when the baby starts to crawl,' she added pragmatically.

'Oh!' Valerie said faintly, astonished at this unexpected reaction.

'Well, it's up to you, of course, but I think it's something to be considered,' Mrs M frowned.

'Oh, yes, yes, of course. I . . . I just wasn't sure if you'd want a baby in the house.'

'Ah-ha! Did you think I was going to evict you?' Mrs Maguire eyed her sharply.

'Well . . . I . . . I . . . wasn't sure,' Valerie stuttered as they pulled up outside the house.

'And what would I do that for? Aren't you and that other harum-scarum article the nicest pair of gels I've had up there in a long time? You're very good to me, the pair of you, doing my little bits of shopping and always there if I need you. Don't you worry, Valerie, your baby will be very welcome,' she said kindly, patting her hand. 'I presume the father is that handsome young man who comes to visit.'

'Yes, Jeff,' Valerie smiled.

'A grand lad. Didn't he put those mousetraps around my kitchen for me when I was afflicted by mice a few weeks ago? There's not many would do that now. I was impressed with him, deah. Very mannerly too. And I hope your families are being kind to the pair of you. Now I must leave you and love you. I want to watch *Coronation Street*. We'll discuss the stairs when it's time, and I must go and get some wool and start knitting a few clothes for the mite. I'll do yellows and greens and lilacs, maybe. It won't matter then whether it's a boy or a girl.'

She got out of the car and marched up the path, leaving Valerie sitting open-mouthed at the wheel.

'Fair play to the old dear,' Jeff had said delightedly when she told him the news the next day, when she met him in the college canteen after work. 'You sit down and I'll get our food,' he said solicitously, leading her to an empty table. The loud buzz of chatter, the clatter of cutlery and crockery, red plastic chairs scraping against the floors – she didn't notice any of it now, she'd got so used to meeting him several nights a week to eat dinner with him while he was cramming. It was a habit they'd got into once he'd come back to college that autumn.

That day when she had driven back from Rockland's following the family meeting had been the worst of her entire life. She was sure Jeff would do a runner and the thought terrified her. She had cried a lake of tears and without Lizzie's no-nonsense attitude and firm support she would have been lost.

'Jeff is not going to do the dirty on you. I'm telling you, Valerie, he's not that sort. He's just rattled like you are. He'll adjust to the idea that he's going to be a father,' her friend insisted.

'But he ran like a scalded cat when he got the opportunity to get out of getting married. If he loved me he would have married me.' She couldn't be pacified.

'Look, I do think if you had said you wanted to get married, he would have married you,' Lizzie countered.

'Well, we'll never know now, will we?' Valerie said bitterly, hating him with every fibre of her being.

'Stop that now, Valerie, and stop that bawling. It's not good for the baby. The poor little yoke will be all stressed and anxious if you are.'

'Do you think he loves me, though?' she persisted.

'Valerie, whoever really knows about love?' Lizzie sighed.

'But I love him,' Valerie protested heatedly.

'Well, if you love him, trust him to do the right thing in his own time then,' Lizzie said patiently.

'And if he doesn't?' Valerie sniffed.

'Just stay calm and stop anticipating stuff, will you?' Lizzie retorted. 'What's for you won't pass you by. That's what my mam always says.'

'I hope she's right,' Valerie muttered.

Waiting for Jeff's phone call had been nerve-racking. Every time the phone rang at work her stomach had tied itself up in knots. But he'd hadn't phoned her at work. He had left it until the evening when he phoned her in the flat.

'You'd think you might have been interested enough to know if I got home safely yesterday.' She launched into an attack straight away.

'I thought you were mad with me so I thought I'd let you cool down,' he explained defensively.

'Good excuse,' she snapped.

'Do you want me to come up tomorrow?'

'Do you *want* to come up?'

'Not if you're going to take the nose off me,' he said sullenly.

'Well, don't bother so,' she snapped, slammed down the phone and burst into tears.

Half an hour later the phone rang again.

'Let's not fight, Val,' Jeff said dejectedly when she answered.

'OK. Please come up tomorrow,' she said, utterly relieved that he had phoned again.

'I will. I'll come straight from the boat and take you out for dinner. We'll go to Gallagher's.'

'Maybe we should start saving,' she demurred.

'It will be our last little fling,' he said, and she knew he was smiling.

'Are you sure you want to?'

'Positive,' he assured her.

They had been edgy with each other at first. She was still smarting from what she perceived as his rejection of her and couldn't pretend that things were normal between them. He bore it stoically and put up with her volatile humours over the next couple of visits. When he came back to the city for good and got into the routine of college it got easier, and gradually the shock of her pregnancy wore off. As the days shortened and the nights lengthened into a cold, windy autumn, Valerie settled into her new circumstances and her changing relationship with Jeff. He *was* going to play his part and be a good father, she realized, the day he arrived at the flat with a sturdy little Moses basket.

'It was mine. It was in the attic at home and I freshened it up and got one of my aunts, who's brilliant at sewing, to put a new lining in. Do you like it?' he asked proudly, and she burst into tears and fell into his arms, and they made love for the first time since she'd told him that she was pregnant.

Lying in his arms afterwards, Valerie felt a sense of optimism and calm return. They were together; they would face the future and all that it held, as a couple. They would need to start making plans about where they were going to live once the baby was born and Jeff had finished his exams. Her next great fear had been that Mrs Maguire would give her her marching orders and now, happily, that hadn't happened. She could stay in her snug little nest for as long as she liked.

Standing in the kitchen, looking out at the relentless rain and the wind-battered garden, Valerie found it hard to believe that she was going to give birth soon. Her pregnancy had flown by. She had not set foot in Rockland's, not even for Christmas. Jeff had come up to be with her and it had been one of the happiest times of her life, living together while Lizzie was at home celebrating the festive season. Carmel had come up for Stephen's Day, and brought a feast of home baking and a large travel bag filled with baby clothes that she had been buying since she'd found out she was to be a grandmother. Valerie had heard nothing from Terence. If he answered the phone when she rang home, he would call Carmel and walk away from the phone. Even though she expected it from him, it still hurt. He was her father, when all was said and done.

Her colleagues and her managers at work had been supportive. She had felt sick to her stomach and full of apprehension the morning she had decided to announce her pregnancy at tea break. She'd mulled over what to say and had prepared a little speech, but in the end she'd just blurted out, 'Girls, I'm pregnant.' She could see the surprise her declaration caused but almost immediately her colleagues rallied around, congratulating her, offering second-hand cots and buggys and making her feel no different from any of her married colleagues. Once she had that ordeal over she had begun to relax, and apart from morning sickness in the early months her pregnancy had been uneventful. She was lucky, Valerie reflected, as she heard Lizzie calling her into the sitting room for the start of the film, especially when she heard some of the stories from other mothers-to-be at her prenatal clinics.

'What would I do without you? You're a great friend, Lizzie,' Valerie said appreciatively as she settled herself on the sofa and Lizzie stuck a pillow into the small of her back.

'I'd expect the same from you, never you fear, missy. I'll need you one day.' Lizzie handed her a packet of crisps.

'I'll be there, for sure,' Valerie promised fervently.

'I know that.' Lizzie tucked herself into the elderly but very comfortable armchair. 'This is the life, Valerie. How lucky are we?' she remarked as Deborah Kerr's beautiful features, framed by a nun's wimple, illuminated the screen. *Black Narcissus* was a gripping film, living up to all of Mrs M's commendation, and they immersed themselves in the lives of Kerr's troubled Sister Clodagh, as she watched her colleague Sister Ruth descend into madness, while also battling her attraction to the sexy Mr Dean, in her convent at the foot of the Himalayas.

'That was brilliant. My God, that Sister Ruth was scary when she went off her rocker, wasn't she? That mad lipstick scene was something else,' Lizzie exclaimed, throwing another couple of briquettes onto the fire when the final credits rolled.

'Mr Dean was a dish,' Valerie stretched luxuriantly. 'Lovely hairy chest.'

'Yeah, except he looked a bit daft on that donkey. His feet were nearly touching the ground,' Lizzie scoffed. 'He needed to be riding a horse to do it for me. Or riding me,' she added incorrigibly.

'You know, I think I've got a name for the baby if it's a girl,' Valerie said slowly.

'I thought you'd picked Cora if it was a girl and Ronan if it was a boy.' Her friend looked at her in surprise.

'I know, but remember when Sister Ruth asked the little lad had he given one of the nuns her glass of milk?'

'Joseph, the little fella who used to call the nuns Lemenie? Ah, he was a dote. Are you changing to Joseph?' Lizzie poked the fire, sending out a shower of sparks. 'Good God! You're not going to call her *Lemenie*, if it's a girl, are you?'

'No, you daft idiot. She asked him did he bring Sister *Briony* her milk. What do you think of the name Briony?' Valerie asked eagerly, rubbing her bump.

'It's *gorgeous*! Perfect. I *love* it,' Lizzie enthused.

'Well, then, if it's a girl Briony Harris it will be. I hope Jeff likes it.'

'You wouldn't consider calling her Briony Egan?' Lizzie arched an eyebrow.

'Only if Jeff marries me,' Valerie declared firmly.

'And rightly so,' approved her friend. 'Oh, Valerie, it's exciting, isn't it? I can't wait.'

'Me neither! I think I would like a little girl now that I've got such a lovely name. It just feels right, somehow.' Valerie's eyes were glowing as the baby gave another kick. 'See, it's kicking. I think it knows its name.'

'Say it again,' Lizzie urged, coming over to kneel in front of her and putting her hand on Valerie's bump.

'Briony. Briony. Briony,' Valerie crooned, and they laughed as her baby kicked spiritedly in her womb.

CHAPTER TWENTY-FOUR

Briony sat sipping a glass of chilled white wine and nibbling on plump green olives, as the waves washed lazily against the shore and the stars glistened in a blue-black sky. Clusters of orange lights shimmered faintly on the horizon and, in spite of her anguish, Briony wondered if people were sitting on the coast of Africa looking over to the twinkling lights of the Spanish mainland. She liked to imagine they were, although the lights were probably from ships or fishing boats. A glittering cruise liner over-flowing with glamour, glister and gaiety glided through the surging sea, towards Gibraltar. Around her the happy hum of conversation and people enjoying their evening added to her sense of sadness. If only Finn were here so she could tell him of her distress. Her husband had a calm way of dealing with life's ups and downs and she valued his advice more than anyone's. It was so frustrating to have her phone lying in her bag, the battery as dead as a dodo.

'Would you like to order, Señora?' A smiling waiter stood in front of her, pen poised on his electronic pad.

'Um . . .' she peered at the menu again. 'Yes, I'll have the whitebait, please.' She smiled back at him and handed him the menu. She hadn't planned on having something to eat, but her fast, anger-fuelled walk along the beach had left her feeling thirsty, and when she had reached a popular beachside *chiringuito* she and Valerie had eaten in several times on previous trips to Spain, she'd walked up from the beach and sat at one of the more secluded, outdoor tables at the far side of the restaurant and ordered a glass of wine. When the waiter had brought the menu she realized she was slightly peckish and perused the starters. She was in no rush home. She couldn't bear to be in the same room as Valerie. Her mother's lies had deprived her of one of the most loving and comforting relationships of her life. She probably had cousins she'd never met. A whole branch of her father's family had been lost to her. How wonderful would that have been to have an aunt and uncle and cousins? Briony had no siblings, no father and just a selfish, deceitful mother, she thought sorrowfully. She took a slug of wine. She had a good mind to get hammered. If it wasn't for Katie, she would, and then she'd take a taxi to the Don Carlos further up the coast, and book into the luxury hotel for the night and to hell with penury. For certain, first thing in the morning she was going to go to an internet café and book a flight home. She was damned if she was spending a minute more than was necessary with Valerie.

Would Tessa want to see her now? Should she just drive to Rockland's and try to find her grandparents' house from memory? She could always ask someone for directions when she got there. If only she could talk to Granny Carmel and ask her advice, but her poor grandmother was living in her own private world now and didn't even recognize her even though she made regular visits to see her.

The waiter arrived with her crispy whitebait, and placed it on the table in front of her. 'More wine, Señora?' he asked.

'Why not?' she said.

'Et iss holiday.' He smiled, giving a good-humoured shrug and went to get the wine. Some holiday, she thought wryly, spearing a piece of the fish and popping it in her mouth. It was melt-in-the-mouth tender, and the accompanying salad was crisp and tasty. To her surprise she was enjoying the excellent food, but that was typical of her, she thought irritably. She never lost her appetite because of trauma or anxiety and stress. Quite the opposite, in fact; food was her comfort and companion in times of trouble. And this was surely a time of trouble. Briony sighed. She was damned if she was going to put back on the stone she'd lost through rigorous dieting before her trip to Spain. Valerie had a lot to bloody answer for, she thought viciously as she pronged another olive, buttered her crusty bread roll and took a large bite out of it. She was tempted to order a portion of chips. She could feel a full-on binge heading her way so she took another slug of wine, finished her bread and told herself that she was full.

A quartet of women at the table in front of her, who were coming to the end of their meal, laughed heartily at something one of their party said and she envied them their merriment as they clinked glasses of champagne. Obviously on a girls' jaunt, she observed as she studied them covertly. Friends who were very comfortable with each other if the jolly slagging that was going on was anything to go by. Her waiter and a tall, elegant waitress stopped to chat and enjoy the fun, and moments later four big glasses of Baileys arrived at the table, compliments of the proprietor. Hoots of laughter rippled through the night, and Briony took another gulp of wine, wishing it would ease the knots of tension that throbbed in her temples. She finished the last of her whitebait and pushed her plate away.

'Would Señora like anything else? More wine? Coffee?' the waiter, attentive and professional, asked moments later.

'No . . . thank you, it was delicious. Could you order me a taxi and could you give me *la cuenta, por favor*?' She lapsed into her schoolgirl Spanish.

'*Sí, Señora, momento.*' He disappeared inside the glass-walled restaurant and she saw him make the phone call to the taxi rank in El Zoco. She didn't fancy walking back across the beach in the dark, especially after drinking two glasses of wine, plus the cumulative effects of her stressful day had made her feel quite weary. The taxi arrived a few minutes later and she paid her bill and sank back into the leather seat as she gave Valerie's address. She hoped her mother was in bed. She was in no mood to talk. She rummaged in her bag, hoping against hope that she had her key, otherwise she was going to have to ring the bell and an encounter with her mother would be unavoidable.

She was in luck. She found the spare key her mother had given her. She could let herself in, check on Katie and fall into bed.

The light was on in Valerie's bedroom, she noticed when the taxi pulled up outside the villa less than ten minutes later. She paid her fare and opened the front door as quietly as she could. She was glad there was a side lamp on in the sitting room to guide her way. Katie was fast asleep, her silky blond hair fanned out over the pillow, her arm around Teddy Ted, her favourite cuddly toy. Briony had to fight the impulse to lift her daughter up and smother her in kisses.

She was sure Tessa had often watched *her* sleeping, all those years ago. What pain and grief to lose a grandchild on top of losing a beloved son. What had possessed her mother? How could Valerie have been so callous, Briony wondered as she lay in her bed a while later, wide awake. Well, she was going to get a taste of her own medicine because Briony was taking Katie home and neither she nor her daughter would ever return to Spain. The bond she and Valerie had shared was irrevocably damaged. Broken. Shattered beyond repair. She couldn't wait to get the hell out of here, she fumed as she twisted and turned in her mother's luxurious Egyptian cotton sheets, desperate to fall asleep and blot out the nightmare her life had turned into, for a few hours at least.

Valerie looked at the shadowy silhouettes that weaved through the slats of her shutters. The origami shapes undulating on her bedroom walls usually delighted her, but not tonight. It was 3 a.m. The luminous green figures on her small alarm clock taunted her as the minutes ticked slowly past.

Hours ago she had heard the taxi draw up outside the villa, and she'd waited, fingers curled tightly into her palms, expecting the doorbell to ring. And then she'd heard her daughter's key in the front door and exhaled a long deep sigh, not sure if she was relieved or not that she didn't have to go out and face her. She heard Briony go into Katie's room and wondered would her daughter knock on her door and come in and talk to her now that she'd had time to cool down and reflect on their situation. Part of her hoped desperately that she would. But then she'd heard movement in the sitting room as Briony turned out the lamp, and then the closing of a door and the muffled sounds of her daughter preparing for bed.

Sudden unexpected tears of disappointment brimmed in her eyes and she had to bury her face in her pillow to muffle the sobs that followed as her heart constricted in pain. How could it all have come to this, she thought in despair as she switched off her own light. Had it not occurred to Briony that something must have caused Valerie to take the actions she did? She had been *driven* to it, Valerie thought mournfully. Tessa Egan had brought their estrangement on herself with her horrible mean-spirited words and accusations. Briony thought Tessa was the wronged one, but what about *her*? Valerie had suffered enormously at the hands of Jeff's mother. Would this night never end, she fretted, wishing sleep would give her some solace. One day Briony would know of the anguish she had endured and learn of her grandmother's behaviour because that letter had opened a Pandora's box and there was no going back. Valerie turned onto her side and burrowed her head under a pillow as unwelcome memories came back to torment her, while the breeze began to increase in strength again and the shadows danced like marionettes across her bed.

CHAPTER TWENTY-FIVE

Valerie clattered along the parquet floors of Bolton Street Tech and pushed open the heavy swing doors of the library. She walked past the queue at the librarian's desk and turned right into the study area, giving a quick scan of students engrossed in their studies. Her heart lifted when she saw Jeff with his head bent, stuck in his books and occasionally writing furiously. The library was hot and stuffy; she didn't envy any of the students swotting for their exams. She wasn't sure if she would have enjoyed going to college, she reflected. She enjoyed being a career girl and her regular pay cheque. She certainly didn't lose as much sleep over it as her father did, she thought wryly.

She made her way down between the desks, trying not to bump into anyone's table. The rows between the desks were narrow, and her mammoth bulk made her awkward and clumsy. She hit one table and almost knocked down a pile of books. 'Sorry . . .' She gave a murmured apology, feeling like an idiot.

'Hi, babe,' she whispered when she reached Jeff. 'Are you ready to go?'

'Oh! Hi, Val! How did it go at the hospital?' he whispered back, and began to gather his books together. A

skinny, cropped-haired, bespectacled girl sitting at the
desk beside him glared at them, her mouth pursed in irritation. For one moment Valerie thought she was going to
tell them to shush.

'I'll tell you when we get out,' she murmured, conscious
of Skinny Minnie's basilisk stare.

'Who's that little wagon sitting beside you, who was
glaring at us?' Valerie said crossly when Jeff had returned
his reference books and they were walking along the
corridor towards the lift. An unseasonably warm sun
shone through the massive plate windows that lined the
corridor and she felt hot and uncomfortable in her heavy
winter coat, which was stretched to bursting over her
bump. Skinny Minnie was lucky she hadn't got the two
fingers because her hormones were all over the place.
She was on a razor's edge, Valerie thought irritably.

'Spider Legs? Don't take any notice of her; she's a real little
swot with an attitude problem,' Jeff derided, yawning.

'What did you call her?' She wasn't sure she'd heard
right.

'Spider Legs – that's what one of the lads nicknamed
her.'

Valerie giggled. 'You lot are *so* pass remarkable, worse
than women,' she said, highly amused at the accuracy of
the description. Minnie *had* looked like a spider with the
dark hair and the gangly limbs.

'Good, though, isn't it? It was a Dub, of course, who
came out with that. The wit of the Dubs is legendary,' Jeff
grinned. 'She should never wear jeans, that's for sure, or
minis. Not a good look. Lift or stairs?' He cocked his head
sideways and patted her bump.

'I'll risk the lift! I wouldn't mind having spider legs

right now,' Valerie sighed, tucking her arm into his as he pressed the lift pad. 'I feel like the Michelin Man.'

'Won't be for long now, though. What did they say at the hospital? I would have gone with you, you know that.' He put his arm around her shoulder as they stepped into the ancient lift and it creaked and juddered slowly down to the ground floor.

'I know, and thanks.' She snuggled into him. 'But there was no point in you hanging around over there when you could be finishing off your thesis. If I don't go into labour by Thursday they're taking me in to induce me. Don't think I fancy that. It's supposed to make it more painful, I heard.' She made a face.

'Don't be listening to those ones in the clinic and their sob stories,' her boyfriend warned as they walked out of the side exit of the college. 'Conway's for a chicken and mushroom vol-au-vent or the Bolton Horse for soup and a sandwich? You pick and I'll pay,' he offered magnanimously.

Valerie glanced over at the pub across the road and decided she wasn't in the humour for a crowded bar full of noisy, boisterous students. 'The vol-au-vent,' she said, turning right into the welcome shade of King's Inn Street.

'You'll turn into a vol-au-vent,' Jeff teased, falling into step beside her.

'I know. I'd never tasted them until I had them in Conway's. I love them,' she confessed. 'You'd never get a vol-au-vent, eating out anywhere in Rockland's. Roast chicken breast as dry as snuff is the best you could do,' she observed as they crossed Loftus Lane.

'Yeah, they're tasty all right,' Jeff agreed. 'And I love their stew. It's like what you'd get at home. Where did you park?'

'In the car park. Look, it's there in the middle.' She pointed to a cluster of cars in the centre of the parking lot they were now walking parallel to. 'I wasn't sure how long I'd be in the hospital and I didn't want to be running in and out feeding the meter. It's so handy for us around here, isn't it? Half-way between the college and the hospital, and our favourite pub down the road?'

'Yup. That's how I planned it,' Jeff laughed.

Valerie had been able to park behind the college and waddle over to her hospital appointment in the Rotunda, before meeting up with Jeff. It seemed like ages since she'd had her breakfast. She was hungry and looking forward to their lunch together. Now that she was a lady of leisure on the second day of her maternity leave, she was enjoying the singular freedom of being off work on a weekday, knowing that she wouldn't be back at her desk for the next few months.

They were lucky to get into the popular hostelry before the lunchtime rush and Valerie opted for a table near the door. Even though she loved the smell of smoke that wafted around the pub, and longed to smoke a Dunhill, she had stayed off the cigarettes, with difficulty, for the duration of her pregnancy. Their order was taken speedily and they sat back and relaxed, waiting for their drinks to be served.

When the young waitress placed the plate of steaming food in front of Valerie, her mouth watered and she tucked into the light flaky pastry and creamy sauce with gusto, but after eating half of it she began to feel quite full.

'What's wrong?' A look of panic flashed across Jeff's face as he saw her stop eating.

'Stop panicking.' She laughed. 'There's no room in there.' She patted her bump.

'I'll eat it so; pass it over here,' Jeff instructed, scoffing down the last of his own meal and mopping up the sauce with a forkful of chips.

'Gannet,' she retorted affectionately, pushing her plate over the table to him. She felt almost happy as she watched him polish off the remains of her lunch. After their more than rocky start to her pregnancy, their bond was far deeper now, nine months later. They were a team with a common goal. She was supporting him in his studies, and had typed up the main part of his thesis, being extra careful to spell all the unfamiliar technical terms correctly. He was just completing his bibliography and the index and acknowledgements, and then it was finished. She felt as much a part of it as he did. She had even suggested the colours for the binding. Green with gold lettering would be more elegant than his original choice of red and black, she proposed, and he agreed.

He needed to get a haircut, she thought, feeling quite wife-like as she noted how his dark hair flopped into his eyes, and curled down over the collar of his shirt. She hoped against hope that he would get a decent result in his exams and then find a well paid job so they could be married. As her pregnancy had progressed she had felt less insecure about her future with Jeff. He had shown he was committed to her and their baby. All he needed to do now to make her feel secure and happy was to propose.

He had come to several of her clinic appointments, even though he hated hospitals and went a strange greenish hue when he stepped over the threshold of the building. He had assured her that he would be by her side when the baby was being born, now that the father was allowed in at the birth. Valerie was torn about this and had discussed it many times with Lizzie.

'If he's coming in, make sure he looks at your face only. I heard it puts men off sex for ages afterwards,' Lizzie warned.

'I know, at least I won't be able to actually see what it all looks like down there.' Valerie shuddered. She was dreading childbirth. She hadn't enjoyed the pre-natal classes and had been mortified on more than one occasion catching sight of Jeff's aghast expression, particularly on the talk about breast-feeding and lactating. In the end she'd told him not to come and he'd acquiesced with no argument whatsoever.

'I mean, you're lying there with your legs half a mile apart in those stirrups and your fanny in a total heap, for the world and his mother to see, and then there's the umbilical cord and the placenta to deal with. Yuckkk! They *must* have flashbacks when they start having sex with you again! I won't be having Dara at the birth if we end up married and I get pregnant!' Lizzie declared emphatically. 'And if it's me that's in there with you at the birth, I'll only be looking at your face too. I don't want to have flashbacks either,' she added.

'He feels it's the *right thing* to do and he doesn't want to let me down, and I suppose it would be nice in one way. But I don't want him in there so that he can see me *suffer* and feel guilty about it all either. Lots of the women in the clinic want their partners and husbands there so they can see what they have to go through. That's not why I'd like Jeff there. I'd like him there because he wanted to be there, to be part of it, to make us closer. But I don't want him there being petrified.'

'Me neither, if I was going to give birth. And I'd prefer to have a jolly good sex life and have Dara see me as a goddess rather than an earth mother. The feminists would shoot me if they heard me say that but it's how I feel.' Lizzie undulated sexily around the room in her decidedly ungoddess-like winceyette pyjamas and bed socks, it being a bitterly cold night. 'Feminists will probably shoot me again for saying this too, but actually I'd much prefer to have another woman there with me.'

'Goddess! I wish!' Valerie grinned as Lizzie wiggled her ass across the room *à la* Marilyn Monroe. 'There's a woman at work, Orla, who prides herself on being an "avowed feminist". She tells us morning noon and night how much of a feminist she is. She's one of these super-efficient types that are climbing up the ranks rapidly.'

'Them ones don't get enough sex,' interjected Lizzie, who was having wonderful sex with her new boyfriend, who really was 'The One', at last.

'Well, Orla's husband had an affair with some young one in their tennis club,' Valerie continued, 'and she's gutted. The creep made her feel it's all *her* fault because she was concentrating on *her* career and neglecting him and now *she's* pulling out all the stops to dress sexy and make him feel important and dancing attendance on him, and *he's* the one that had the affair!' Valerie spluttered indignantly. 'And he's enjoying it all, the horrible little toad. You should see him! A weed with a comb-over and acne. Why would she bother? I'd let him slither back under the rock he crawled out from. So much for being a "feminist",' Valerie snorted. 'She hasn't a clue really about what true feminism is.' Orla Finley was not one of her favourite people.

Orla had taken her aside when news of her pregnancy had circulated around the office, and grilled her about Jeff's attitude to her and the baby, wanting to know was he giving her financial support. 'That's not really anyone's business, except mine and Jeff's,' Valerie said politely, silently fuming at the older woman's cheek.

'Well, I just don't like to see young girls being used by men who don't take any responsibility for their actions. It happens too often and men need to be made aware that it's just not acceptable. You have rights too, you know! We're not the submissive species taking everything that's dished out to us any more. You have a voice – use it. Don't let the man walk away from his responsibilities.'

'I know that, Orla, but thanks, anyway,' Valerie said crisply, not wanting to have to endure one of the older woman's rants on feminism. She felt she had been as much to blame as Jeff for getting pregnant; feminist or not, she had to take responsibility for her part in it too. Valerie had always been of an independent nature, had always subscribed to the notion of equality between the sexes, and it annoyed her that because she wasn't strident about her views Orla should make assumptions about her.

Even all these months later the staff officer's impertinence still rankled, especially as Orla had wimped out completely on 'feminism' in her own private life, in Valerie's opinion.

'Obviously a woman with issues,' Lizzie said airily. 'Sometimes "avowed" types use whatever platform they are "avowed" about so they can run away from their own problems. Now my "problem"' – she did air quotes – 'at the moment is that there is no chocolate in the flat and I am an' – more air quotes – "avowed chocaholic". What to do?' She sashayed up to Valerie and struck a pose and Valerie burst out laughing. Lizzie's good-humoured joshing had got her through many down moments in her pregnancy.

'What are you smiling at?' Jeff asked, bringing her back to reality.

'I was just thinking about a conversation I had with Lizzie. She's a total hoot.'

'She's the best.' Jeff smiled. 'What was the conversation about?'

'Umm . . . well, part of it was about the birth. Jeff, do you want to be there or would you prefer not to?' she asked bluntly.

'Eh . . . you know me and hospitals! But I don't want you going through it on your own either. And it is a momentous occasion to see your child being born, I suppose.' He eyed her suspiciously. 'Why?'

She couldn't tell him that she was afraid he would be put off having sex and see her in another light, a less than flattering light, because then it would be in his consciousness. She wasn't sure she wanted him to see her in a primal, raw state, all defences down, emotionally naked. She hadn't lived with him, they hadn't shared the intimacy that came with that, and they still had a lot to learn about each other. Although Valerie loved Jeff, she knew at one level she was more mature than he was, and knew he would love to be free and unfettered and hanging out with his friends instead of being tied down in a relationship with the added responsibility of a child in the very near future.

It was with Lizzie that she shared all these private worries and concerns, not Jeff. And besides, with his exams coming up she was anxious to keep him reasonably focused. Tessa was not ever going to get the chance to blame her if he didn't get a good result – Valerie had been determined about that from the very start. But she couldn't say these things to her boyfriend. Some things were best left unsaid, and the remark Lizzie had made about preferring to have another woman at the birth resonated with her very strongly. No one in the world knew her as well as Lizzie. You could love a man with all your might and he could love you, but no one knew you as well as your best friend did, she figured.

'Do you not want me there?' Jeff probed.

'Well, I'd be worrying about you feeling faint and stuff. And you'd hear other women groaning and moaning. There's only a curtain at the end of each cubicle in the delivery ward.'

'I won't faint, I don't think. I'll try not to, anyway. I've seen plenty of fish guts and blood.' He made a face.

'Jeff!' she protested.

'Sorry, just teasing,' he grinned.

'Look, how about if you're there for the bits at the beginning that aren't too gruesome, and then Lizzie can take over and you can come in the minute the baby's born,' she suggested carefully.

'That's a *brilliant* idea!' he exclaimed enthusiastically. 'Are you sure, now?'

'Are *you* sure?' she demanded, not wanting to feel she was depriving him of a most precious moment.

'Very sure, very, *very* sure.' He was almost gabbling with relief. They looked at each other and burst out laughing.

'I'm a bit of a wimp, aren't I? Not a so-called "new man" at all,' he said, a bit abashed.

'No you're not,' Valerie said firmly. 'If you don't feel comfortable about being there at the birth I don't mind, honestly. And if you do decide to be there at the last minute, make sure you keep looking at me and not the . . . the . . . bits down there,' she warned.

'Ma feels I should be with you, now that it's allowed,' he confessed.

'Was your dad at any of her deliveries?' Valerie could never get used to the idea of Jeff talking to Tessa about her and about their circumstances. It irritated her, but she kept her irritation to herself. Jeff loved Tessa and he was her pet.

'God, no! Men weren't allowed into the room in those days. She had us all at home and the midwife used to come and a woman from the village who always looked after women who were giving birth, and her mam and sister, of course.'

'That sounds nice, actually,' Valerie said wistfully. 'So natural and unscary, surrounded by women who knew you, and knew what it was like to give birth. It was kind of tribal, wasn't it?'

'Times are different now, I suppose. But I *will* do feeds and nappies and all of that,' he assured her earnestly. 'And then as soon as you go back to work we'll get a place to live together.'

'That's our plan all right,' Valerie agreed, shifting uncomfortably in her seat. Her back was aching more than usual and she needed to stretch her legs. 'You should get back to the library. I'm going to go over to Roches and Arnotts to get a few last bits and pieces for the baby,' she suggested, standing up.

'Right, I'll go and pay.'

'I'll wait for you at the door,' Valerie said. She suddenly felt very hot and the ache had turned into a sharp pain. She stood outside, leaning against the wall on Moore Lane, taking deep breaths. She could see the hospital across the road.

The pain began to recede just as Jeff joined her.

'Are you OK?' He looked at her warily. 'Your face is very red.'

A sudden drenching gush whooshed down her legs.

'Jesus Almighty! What was that?' Jeff went pale. 'Are you . . . is it . . . oh, jeepers!'

'It must have been the examination earlier.' Valerie felt a rush of apprehension as her waters broke. This was it. There was no stopping it now. The dreaded unknown was upon her. 'Bring me over to the hospital and then you take the keys of the car – you saw where I parked it – and go home and get my case and ring Lizzie,' Valerie said as calmly as she could, seeing Jeff's panic-stricken expression.

'Right! Right! Are you sure you'll make it across the road? Will I ring an ambulance?' he babbled. 'I think I should ring an ambulance.' He was in a complete and utter tizzy, his eyes like a startled squirrel's.

Valerie took his hand, and started walking. 'We only have to go across the road, Jeff. Just come to the door with me and wait with me until they check me in and then go home and get my case and then ring Lizzie,' she enunciated slowly, kindly, as they waited for a gap in the traffic to cross Parnell Street. Her knickers were soaking and she was tempted to wriggle out of them and squeeze them out and shove them in her handbag, but Jeff would probably freak if she did that, she thought with some amusement.

'What are you smiling at?' he demanded. 'It's not funny. This isn't funny, Valerie!' His voice had gone a pitch higher. He was a tad hysterical.

'Stay calm, nearly there,' she soothed as they crossed to the other side of the road. Another pain hit, stronger this time and she gasped.

'Oh my God! Oh my God!' Jeff was nearly doing a jig. 'Take deep breaths. Take deep breaths,' he said frantically, earning strange looks from a man who was walking past.

'Will you shut up, Jeff!' she managed, grasping hold of the hospital railings.

'I'm going in to get someone right now.' He went to go haring off but she grabbed his arm.

'Don't. It will be over in a minute.' She glared at him. 'This will go on for hours. Do you not remember the classes?' If he was like this now what would he be like with continuous contractions at the end? Lizzie was her best option at the birth for sure.

'It's gone, it's gone,' she said eventually, starting to walk as purposefully as her sopping knickers and wet thighs would allow. Through the iron gates she squelched before entering the hallowed portals of Dublin's oldest maternity hospital.

'My girlfriend's in labour. You better see to her quick!' Jeff couldn't hide his panic or his relief at being in the reassuring safety of the hospital environs.

'Calm down, son. Nothing to get excited about. It's all normal,' the porter said calmly, having seen many versions of the same scenario re-enacted over the years.

'Her waters have burst, she's having contractions. The baby's coming,' Jeff carried on, oblivious.

'Jeff! I can speak. My vocal cords are still working. Now go home, get my case and ring Lizzie.' Valerie turned him around and gave him a gentle shove in the direction of the door they had just entered.

'Right. Right. I'll be back in a minute.'

'No. Drive CAREFULLY,' she articulated clearly as if to a child, as she rooted in her coat pocket and handed him the keys.

'I will. I will. 'Bye. I love ya.' He took off as though the hounds of hell were after him.

'Sorry about that, and sorry for dripping all over your floor,' Valerie said apologetically.

'Not to worry, love. He'll be fine and we have plenty of mops here. Now come on and let's get you seen to,' the unruffled porter said, leading her to the reception desk. A surreal calmness descended on Valerie. Carmel had told her it would. Her mother had said that all her focus would be on her child. It was a relief that Jeff was gone; she didn't have to worry about him. All she had to worry about was bringing her precious baby safely into the world.

'Oh God! Oh God!' Jeff muttered as he raced past Whacker's Pet Shop, and Peats Electric, barely even stopping to look out for traffic as he crossed Lower Dominick Street and headed for the car park. He scanned it frantically, looking for Valerie's little red Mini and then saw it in the middle of a block of cars. He was sick with nerves as he found the lever under the driver's seat and pushed the seat as far back as it could go to accommodate his long legs.

Until now the baby had been a sort of vague reality. Something to talk about and plan for, and forget about occasionally when he was studying or playing football or hanging out with his mates. By this time tomorrow, if everything went OK, he was going to be a father. And a real, live little human, who would be hungry, thirsty, clamouring for food and attention and nappies to be changed, was going to be *his* reality. He just couldn't get his head around it. This was responsibility of a type he'd never anticipated and it scared the hell out of him. If he were only ten years older and he'd had a few carefree years to experience life he wouldn't feel as confined. He had tried hard to support Valerie, and not to let her know how agitated and trapped he felt.

His mother was the only one who knew of his terrors. He could talk to Tessa about it. She was a truly understanding mother, he thought gratefully. If it weren't for her he'd have been married by now and well and truly hemmed in with nowhere to run. At least, technically, he was still a free man. A ring on the finger was the same as having a ring through the nose, one of his mates had announced recently when his girlfriend had dumped him for not 'committing'. 'I'd rather be "committed"!' he'd joked. He was in the clubs in Leeson Street every weekend since, pulling birds, lucky bugger, Jeff thought enviously. He'd love to head off to Legs some night and get hammered and score a bird.

It wasn't very loyal to Valerie having these sorts of thoughts, he reflected guiltily as he started the ignition and reversed out of the space, grinding the gears in his anxiety to get going. Just as well she hadn't heard that, he thought ruefully as he crunched over the pot-holed gravel to pay the man in the booth, and headed for Glasnevin.

The drive was a blur; he could never remember it afterwards. All he could remember was rooting frantically for coins for the pay phone in the flat and the exquisite relief of hearing Lizzie's voice as he said frantically. 'Lizzie, Lizzie, quick, it's started, can you come to the hospital, we need you?'

'Relax, Jeff.' Lizzie's comforting words floated down the line. 'I'm on my way.'

CHAPTER TWENTY-SIX

'Come on, Val, you're nearly there,' Lizzie urged, wiping her friend's forehead as she struggled in the last throes of labour.

'Sorry, Lizzie,' Valerie grunted. 'Go home if you want.'

'I'm not going home. I'm just telling you to hurry up. Think of the cup of tea you're going to get. I've a packet of chocolate rings for you in my bag. I know they're your favourite.'

'Bribery will get you anywhere,' Valerie panted as another contraction steam-rollered over her. 'Uuuuhhhhhhh!' she groaned, gripping Lizzie's hand.

In the next cubicle a woman yelled abuse at her husband. 'And ya'll never put your John Thomas in me again, do ya hear me ya mangy git? AAAAAHHHHHHHH!' She yelled. She was suffering and she wanted the world to know it. Valerie wished she'd keep it down a bit; it was very unsettling listening to her. She thought enviously of Tessa giving birth in the comfort of her own bedroom, surrounded by supportive women.

'Ya should be bleedin' castrated. AAAAAAHHHHHHHH!'

'That's telling him,' Lizzie whispered. 'She's worse than O'Connor's bull bellowing in Thirty Acre Field.'

Valerie managed a giggle. The woman next door had been screeching and roaring for the last five hours and Jeff had been horror-struck during one of his brief forays into the delivery ward when Lizzie had taken a coffee and loo break.

'Why is she making such a racket?' he asked Valerie in dismay.

'Because it's bloody painful,' she gasped as another contraction gripped her and she grabbed his hand and gave a few guttural grunts that frightened the living daylights out of him.

'Give her something. Give her that pethidine stuff,' he squawked as Valerie writhed in pain.

'Soon.' The midwife patted his back kindly. 'You're doing great, Valerie. Remember your breathing exercises.'

'Oh Holy Divinity,' Valerie groaned as one contraction seemed to roll into another and she saw her boyfriend go pale with anxiety. She didn't care what he saw or how ungoddess-like she looked, all she wanted was for the baby to be born.

'Not long now, Valerie,' the midwife said knowledge-ably as Lizzie arrived back, somewhat refreshed.

'I'll leave you to it. I don't want to get in the way.' Jeff gave her a peck on the cheek and practically ran out of the cubicle. The women smiled at each other. 'He's better off in the waiting room,' said the midwife. 'He was almost ready to keel over and we don't need that.'

'I'm ready to keel over,' Valerie moaned as the pain engulfed her again. It seemed as though an hour had passed but in reality it was ten minutes later when a doctor arrived with a brisk swishing back of the curtains and a faux jolly, 'How are we getting on here then?' just as she came to the end of the worst contraction she'd endured.

'Having a ball,' she muttered to Lizzie, as the doctor spoke to the midwife.

'Excellent, ready to go,' she heard him say after he'd examined her. 'Good girl.' He patted her knee.

'Don't girl me,' she wanted to say irritably. He was a man, he was patronizing, and he would never, ever endure the agony she was going through. Another contraction came rolling in and exhaustion smote her. How much more of this would she have to suffer, she thought in desperation as sounds she never thought she was capable of making erupted from her.

'Now, Valerie, don't push until I tell you. You're nearly there, honestly,' the midwife instructed briskly, as a different energy seemed to crackle around the cubicle, a sense of excitement and anticipation taking hold, everyone on high alert. All the sounds in the ward outside faded to the periphery of her consciousness. This was it. Her baby was coming. 'Hold, hold! Now push—'

'I can see it! Oh, Valerie, it's amazing. You should see the head of hair!' Lizzie said excitedly, forgetting her 'avowed' intention not to look at the gory bits.

'Jesus! Jesus! Jesus! Help *meeeee*!' Valerie begged in desperation, bursting into tears as she summoned up every remaining ounce of strength to propel her baby into the world.

'It's a girl! It's a girl! Oh, Valerie, you did great. I'm so proud of you,' Lizzie was bawling as she wiped snot and tears from Valerie's face.

'Is she OK? Tell Jeff, quick,' Valerie said weakly, falling back against the pillows, relieved beyond measure as she heard her baby give an indignant howl. She lay spent, in a daze as all attention turned to the baby. She'd done it. It was over. She was a mother.

'Everything's fine, a healthy eight-pound two-ounce baby girl.' The obstetrician smiled at her as the nurse wrapped the baby in a blanket and placed her daughter in her arms.

'Oohhh!' Valerie exclaimed as a pair of startling blue eyes studied her intently. 'Oohhh, she's *gorgeous*.' She felt a wave of incredible love as she looked at the downy little head of black hair, the prettiest little snub nose, a pair of rosebud lips, and those incredible eyes fanned by dark lashes. She had never seen a more beautiful baby, she thought, suffused with joy as she slipped her little finger into her daughter's hand and felt her fingers grip tightly.

'Oh, Valerie, she's beautiful,' Lizzie wept. '*Beautiful*. I'll get Jeff.'

'Thanks for everything, Lizzie. I'll never be able to repay you.'

'You have, hon. You've made me an honorary auntie and a godmother, and I didn't have to do a thing. Lucky, lucky me.' Lizzie touched the baby's cheek before going to tell Jeff that he was the father of a beautiful baby girl.

Jeff was momentarily speechless as he saw his girlfriend lying with their baby in her arms. Nothing had prepared him for this. This was a life-changing moment. He was a father. They were *parents*.

'Hold her.' Valerie smiled tearily at him.

'Oh, no, I'd better not!' He felt suddenly apprehensive.

'Hold her, she's your daughter,' Valerie urged, offering up the baby to him.

He took her gingerly and placed her in the crook of his arm. She looked up at him and he was *sure* she smiled, before her eyelids closed. 'Can you believe it? Can you believe she's ours?' Jeff gazed down at his sleeping daughter as he held her carefully in one arm and squeezed Valerie's hand with his free hand.

'She's so pretty, isn't she? She's got your eyes and your chin. Look at that determined little chin on her.' Valerie peered over his shoulder as he sat on the side of the bed. 'She's a Briony, isn't she?'

'It suits her perfectly,' Jeff agreed. 'God, Val, you look wrecked. Was the last bit horrendous?' he asked, wishing now that he hadn't chickened out of the birth.

'It was a bit tough.' Valerie lay back against the pillow, her hair limp and damp, her face as white as a sheet, black smudges under her eyes. She had been in labour for fourteen hours. He felt it was the longest day and night of his life – what must poor Valerie feel, he thought, admiration for what she had been through surging through him. 'You look a bit of a sight yourself,' she teased, rubbing his stubbly jaw.

Impulsively he bent down and kissed her. 'I love you, Valerie. Thank you for our beautiful daughter,' he said tenderly, and saw her eyes light up with happiness.

'You should take Lizzie home. She has to go to work tomorrow. They're going to take me back to the ward in a little while and bring the baby to the nursery.'

'OK,' he said, placing the baby back in her arms. 'Do you want me to ring the folks?'

'We can pop you into a wheelchair and Jeff can wheel you to the phone once we've freshened you up,' the nurse said helpfully. 'Just go outside for a few minutes and we'll have her sorted.'

His mind was in a whirl as he stood outside the delivery room waiting for Valerie. Holding his baby daughter had filled him with emotions he couldn't begin to describe. Awe, pride, terror, joy. She was so tiny, so perfect. He would do everything in his power to provide for her, to mind her, to cherish her, he vowed, as he gazed out at the dark empty streets below, the silence only broken by a beer can skittering around in the wind and a skinny stray cat yowling at the moon.

He would be as good a father as Lorcan was to him. He thought gratefully of his own dad and the steady solid support and love that Jeff had taken for granted all these years. He couldn't wait to tell Tessa and Lorcan the news. Tessa had asked him if he wanted her to come up to be with him, but he'd felt Valerie might be a bit miffed if his mother was out in the waiting room and Carmel wasn't so he'd told her to stay put.

The door opened and the nurse pushed Valerie's wheelchair towards him. 'Don't keep her too long now. I want to bring her up to her ward and get her a well-deserved cup of tea.'

'Just a quick phone call to the parents,' Jeff promised.

'Can I ring Mam first?' Valerie asked. 'I know she'll be worried sick.'

'Of course you can,' he said as they reached the phone.

He dialled her home number, dropped in the coins and handed her the phone.

'Hi, Mam, it's me,' Valerie squeaked excitedly a moment or two later, which led Jeff to believe Carmel had been sitting by the phone waiting. A lonely vigil, he imagined, thinking that Terence would not have stayed up. At least Tessa had Lorcan to support her.

'We have a baby girl, Mam. She's beautiful and I'm fine. I won't stay too long because they want to bring me up to the ward. 'Night, Mam. I can't wait to show her to you. I'll talk to you tomorrow.' She never mentioned her father, Jeff noticed, and now, being the father of a new baby daughter, he suddenly realized how complex family relationships could be. What if anything ever happened between him and Briony and they became estranged like Valerie and Terence were? He couldn't even begin to imagine how Valerie's father could have beaten her with his belt.

She was handing the phone to him and he realized she wanted him to talk to her mother.

'Hi, Mrs Harris, er . . . sorry for ringing so late but everything went very well and the baby is lovely and we can't wait for you to see her.'

'I can't wait to see her either,' Carmel said, and he knew she was smiling. 'Take care of my daughter, Jeff. Be kind to her.'

'I will, Mrs Harris,' he said sombrely. 'Don't you worry. Good night.' He replaced the handset.

'Your turn,' Valerie tried to suppress a yawn. Just like at the Harris household, the phone was answered almost immediately and his mother's voice came excitedly over the line. 'Well, how did it go?'

'A baby girl, eight pounds two ounces,' he said proudly, a beam splitting his face from ear to ear.

'That's great, Jeff! How is Valerie?' Tessa exclaimed.

'She's fine. Here, say hello.' He thrust the receiver at Valerie. 'Ma.'

'Oh!' Valerie was nonplussed but she took the phone. 'Hello, Mrs Egan.'

'Valerie, congratulations. I hope you're not too exhausted. Was it difficult?' Tessa asked warmly.

'Um . . . a bit painful, but the baby is lovely, and Jeff and Lizzie were with me,' Valerie said, disarmed by Tessa's cordiality. 'I'm just going up to the ward for a cup of tea.'

'Well, enjoy it. We'll leave it to come up and see you the day after tomorrow to give you a chance to have a rest.'

'I'll see you then. I'll hand you back to Jeff. Good night, Mrs Egan.'

'Tessa – please call me Tessa,' Jeff's mother urged.

'Good night, Tessa,' Valerie said tiredly. She felt suddenly wilted.

'Ma, I'll talk to you tomorrow. Valerie needs to get to bed,' Jeff said, seeing her pallor. 'I'll just say good night to Da.'

'A little girl,' Lorcan said delightedly when he came on the line. 'Congratulations, son, and give my very best to Valerie and take good care of her.'

'I will, Da.' Jeff felt a lump in his throat when he heard his father's deep voice.

'Get home and have a good night's sleep. It's probably the last one you'll have for a while,' Lorcan chuckled. 'Here's your mother.'

'Try and not neglect your studies, Jeff. The exams won't be long coming and it will be worth it in the end.'

'Don't worry, Ma, it's all under control,' he said reassuringly. ''Night.' He hung up the phone just as Lizzie came around the corner.

'Perfect timing,' he smiled at Valerie, pushing her back to the delivery room door. 'I'll take Lizzie home. You go and try to sleep, and I'll see you tomorrow. You did great, Valerie. Everything will work out fine.' He leaned down and kissed the top of her head.

'Here are your biscuits.' Lizzie foraged in her large bag and pulled out a packet of Chocolate Rings. 'Enjoy them. You deserve them.'

'I will,' Valerie said fervently as the nurse took hold of the wheelchair and pushed her briskly down the corridor.

'Let's get going, Pops!' Lizzie grinned at Jeff and he grinned back. His bed beckoned and his father's words were ringing in his ears.

'Get home and have a good night's sleep. It's probably the last one you'll have for a while.'

He heard a baby cry and hoped it wasn't Briony. He felt a sudden longing to see and hold his daughter again. But she'd been taken to the nursery and hopefully she was snug and warm and fast asleep in her little cot.

They were just going out the door when a young man hurried in past them saying urgently to the night porter, 'It's my wife, she's in labour, the baby's coming.'

'Been there, done that, worn the T-shirt,' Jeff said to Lizzie. 'That poor sucker's in for a long night.'

'So is his wife,' Lizzie said drily.

'Oh, yeah,' Jeff muttered. *Women! They always had to have the last word.* But he kept his observation to himself. There was another woman in his life now. He was surrounded by them, but that wasn't a bad thing. Not a bad thing at all, he thought jauntily as he strode out the doors of the Rotunda.

CHAPTER TWENTY-SEVEN

'Well?' Terence called from his bedroom as Carmel made her way back to hers.

'A baby girl. Eight pounds two ounces.' Carmel stood at his door. At least despite his bitterness over the whole affair, he'd been concerned enough to ask, she thought with relief. Since the revelation of Valerie's pregnancy and the acrimonious meeting at the Egans' house all those months ago, Terence had withdrawn into himself and their marriage had deteriorated to a new low. She knew he would never forgive her for going against him and backing Tessa. Even when she told him that Valerie had gone into labour he had just grunted and not lifted his eyes from his paper. So she was more than surprised that he had called out to her to find out what was the news.

'And there she is now, with a baby to bring up, and she could have been a doctor or a lawyer. I did my best for her, but no one would listen to me. It should have been different. He should have married her. And you should have backed me on that,' Terence said irately.

'All that matters now is that Valerie's OK and the baby's healthy,' Carmel said tiredly. 'Are you going to come up to the hospital and see her?'

'No!' Terence said brusquely.

'Shame on you that you wouldn't go and see your daughter and grandchild,' she remonstrated.

'No, Carmel. The shame isn't on me. The shame is on *her*. I told the pair of you that I was washing my hands of the whole affair and I meant it. Good night.'

Carmel felt utterly disheartened as she walked into her own room. Her husband was a bitter pill and he was going to miss out on so much in the years to come. That was his lookout and she felt sorry for him. For herself, she couldn't wait to see her daughter and her new grandchild. She was glad it was a little girl, she thought wearily as she got back into bed. It had been a long day and night, but at least Valerie had had Lizzie and Jeff to sustain her.

Carmel exhaled a long deep breath as she lay against her pillows and pulled the blanket up to her chin. She had been surrounded by strangers at Valerie's birth. Kind strangers. Efficient nurses and doctors, but strangers nevertheless. Terence had stayed for a couple of hours in the hospital waiting room but had gone home as the night progressed and there was no sign of her labour ending. In the end she'd had to have a Caesarean.

Valerie had been lucky to have two of the people she loved most by her side. That thought gave Carmel great comfort as she eventually drifted off to sleep.

'Well, thank God for that good news and that it all went well.' Tessa nestled in against Lorcan's shoulder and sipped the hot chocolate he'd made for her.

'Thank God, again,' Lorcan agreed. 'I just wish their circumstances were a bit less rocky.'

'It's not so bad. Valerie has a good job and Jeff will get a good one, and if the worst comes to the worst he

always has a job on the boat until he gets on his feet.'
She yawned.

'I know, but she's in a flat and he's in digs. He should
be with her,' Lorcan said.

'They can't afford to get a flat together at the moment,
and that's just the way it is. It's important that Jeff gets his
qualification,' she pointed out.

'We could help them out. We could pay Jeff's half of
the rent if they got a place together,' Lorcan suggested.

'Let's leave them as they are for the time being until
Jeff's exams are over,' Tessa proposed.

'We can suggest it to them and see what they say. We
can work something out, surely?' Lorcan persisted, a
frown deepening the lines chiselled in his tanned face.

'Let's not interfere too much or put pressure on them,'
Tessa said, wishing he'd drop it.

'I just feel he should be with Valerie, helping out. It's all
very new to her and she needs all the support she can get.
You know what it was like with a new baby,' Lorcan said
equably, recognizing that his wife was getting a little edgy.

'She has Lizzie,' Tessa reminded him.

'It's not up to Lizzie really.'

'Just let's see how things go. We can step in if we're
needed.' Tessa yawned again.

'OK.' Lorcan stood up and held his hand out to her.
'Come on, Grandma, I've got an early start in the morning. I won't be able to stay in bed cuddling the pillow like
you will.'

'Aahh, Lorcan, you rotter,' she groaned. 'Did you have
to say that? I'd forgotten. God, it's *so* ageing.'

'Ah, you're not a bad-looking doll for an auld wan,' he
grinned.

'I'm not being called Granny, absolutely not!' she declared emphatically as she walked up the stairs with him.

'Nana?'

'Nope!'

'Grandmamma?' he chuckled.

'What's wrong with Tessa?' she said grumpily as they reached their bedroom.

'Nothing. Tessa's perfectly lovely, but it's nice for a child to have grandparents and I'm looking forward to hearing her call me Granddad,' Lorcan revealed as he drew the curtains and shut out the night.

'Gramma, maybe. How about that? That's what I used to call my grandmother when I was young. Gramma isn't quite so elderly-sounding. That's what I'll be. Gramma Egan,' Tessa decided.

'Gramma sounds good,' Lorcan approved as he kicked off his shoes and unbuckled his belt. 'And a very sexy Gramma you are too,' he teased as she pulled her jumper over her head and unhooked her bra.

'Stop, you,' she laughed, stepping out of her jeans.

'If I wasn't so tired I'd prove it to you.' Lorcan's blue eyes glinted in amusement.

'Go to sleep. We're too old for that carry-on, we're grandparents,' Tessa retorted as she pulled her night-dress over her head, got into bed and put out the light.

'Good night, Granny.' He got in beside her and put his arms around her.

'Good night, Granddad.' She smiled in the dark. 'I love you, Lorcan.'

'I love you too,' he said sleepily and his arms tightened around her.

'*Really?* Do you, Lorcan?' she asked intently.

'Yes I do, Tessa. Please don't go down that road again and cause the two of us misery,' he sighed.

'OK.' She was subdued.

'Go to sleep and be happy. This is a good night for our family.'

'Yes, I know.'

'Tessa, please, let the past be. We've come a long way since then and everything worked out for us.'

'OK, Lorcan, go to sleep,' she murmured.

He kissed her shoulder and she relaxed a little. She was foolish to look back; her husband was right. The past was the past. But the past had the strangest way of rearing its head when least expected.

Oh, Lorcan, I wish things had been different for us all those years ago, she thought wistfully, as her husband began to snore softly and a foghorn howled a long wailing note out in the bay.

'Aah, Valerie, isn't she the little dote?' Carmel exclaimed delightedly as she cuddled her new granddaughter. 'Do you know, she's the image of you when you were born.' Carmel regarded her thoughtfully. 'And she has your nose and your long fingers.'

'I'm just glad she's safe and well,' Valerie said. After the high of giving birth and the relief that had enveloped her afterwards she felt a little down. For some reason she hadn't slept very well, even though she was exhausted. That was normal too, a nurse had assured her, as she tossed and turned and felt as though her poor nether regions would never recover. The painkiller they gave her had helped and she'd eventually dozed off just before dawn, only to be awoken by the clattering of the break-fast trolleys at an unearthly hour.

'And I'm so glad Lizzie and Jeff were with you. It's not easy,' Carmel said sympathetically, noting how weary her daughter looked. 'Would you like me to come and stay for a few days when you get home? I could sleep on the sofa, if it was all right with Lizzie?'

'Would you?' Valerie said in surprise.

'Of course I would.'

'What about Dad?'

'What about him? He's well able to look after himself. I'm not his servant,' Carmel said tartly.

'That would be great, Mam. I feel a bit nervous going home with her,' Valerie admitted.

'Right, I'll go back home after visiting hours and organize myself, and you let me know when you're getting out and I'll be straight up to you,' Carmel declared. 'Just make sure Lizzie has no objections.'

'I know she won't – she's the best in the world – but I'll say it to her, of course. Oh, Mam, thank you. I won't be half as worried going home with her now. I'm really grateful to you.' Valerie's eyes filled with tears.

'You don't have to be grateful. I'm your mother, of *course* I'd be with you. Don't cry now, there's a good girl.' Carmel kissed the top of her head. 'Your hormones are all over the place: you'll be laughing one minute and crying the next.'

Valerie blew her nose. 'I know. I'm in a heap.'

'It's normal. They'll settle too. Don't forget your body is going through big changes. It takes time to get over the birth and adjust.'

'Did Dad say anything? Valerie asked hesitantly.

'He asked me how you got on.' Carmel stroked the baby's cheek. 'He was relieved it had gone well.'

'But that's it?'

'He'll adapt. You know what he's like,' Carmel said lightly. 'Don't let it bother you. You have enough to be thinking about with this little angel.'

'He'll never accept her,' Valerie fretted.

'Well, if he doesn't, that's his enormous loss, Valerie, and I feel sorry for him,' Carmel said quietly. 'Look what he's missing,' she added as Briony opened her big eyes and gave a little gurgle.

'Yes, a little angel, that's what you are,' Carmel cooed tenderly, engrossed in her wondrous grandchild.

Valerie observed her mother as she crooned to the baby. It was a side of Carmel that she had never seen before, this gentle, happy, peaceful energy that she was sharing with her grandchild. It was very comforting and she relaxed against her pillows, content to watch them together.

'Briony is a gift in our lives, just as you were a gift in mine, Valerie. Be joyful about her,' Carmel said gently when she leaned over to kiss Valerie goodbye as the bell signalling the end of visiting hours rang throughout the hospital.

'Thanks for everything, Mam. I love you very much.' Valerie gave her a hug. 'And now Briony has brought us even closer. I hope I'll be as good a mother to her as you are to me.'

'I love you too, dear,' Carmel said, inordinately happy at her daughter's unexpected declaration. She could never remember them telling each other that they loved each other until today.

It was certainly one of the most momentous days of her life, Carmel reflected as the bus taking her back to Wicklow sped along the N11. Exuberant flashes of yellow gorse dressing the landscape in spring finery lifted her spirits even more. When she had held her grandchild it had brought back long-forgotten memories of the time Valerie had been born. It had been a happy time in her marriage too, she recalled with surprise, remembering how she and Terence had been so pleased to have become parents. They had someone other than each other to focus on. They had a mutual goal to do the best for their daughter. For a while, it seemed that they were like other couples of their acquaintance and that had been a great comfort for a couple of years. Yes, she'd forgotten that they had once had a time in their marriage where there was affection and contentment, if not love. That had been Valerie's gift to her and Terence.

If only her husband could put aside his bitterness and the baggage from his past, Briony could be a source of healing and a gift for him too, but he was too entrenched in his 'poor me' outlook on life to see what was out there for him.

When she got off the bus in Rockland's, Carmel made her way to St Anthony's, went to the shrine of Our Lady and lit some candles.

'Thank you, dear Mother, for my beautiful grandchild. Keep her and my daughter in your loving care, O Mother of Mothers. Soften my husband's heart towards them and help me be compassionate towards him,' she prayed earnestly.

Carmel was surprised at her fervour. She didn't normally go into the church to pray, except on Sunday at

Mass, but seeing that beautiful baby had touched a well-spring of love in her that she had forgotten she possessed, and as one mother to another she had felt compelled to call on Mother Mary's help.

Terence was home before her and had eaten the dinner she had left for him. How lovely it would be if he had the table laid ready for her and the casserole heated up, she thought as she set the table for herself. He hadn't even asked her how she'd got on, just turned up the sound on the TV to watch the news and immerse himself in the doom and gloom of the economy, and the troubles in the North and the political intrigues. He was very pleased that Haughey was now back in power. Carmel despised the slithery politician: a master of the political stroke, devious and egocentric. Terence admired him hugely. They were a lot alike, Carmel thought as she heard Haughey's nasally drone on the TV.

How could Terence be so unaffected by the knowledge that his only child now had a child of her own? His own flesh and blood? How could he turn his back on them so easily? If he saw the baby, would it make any difference to him? Perhaps when he saw Briony his heart would soften. When Valerie was up to it, Carmel would try to get her to come home for a few days, she decided as she sat down to eat her dinner. Once her husband laid eyes on his new grandchild he would fall in love with her, just as she had, and all the resentment and bad feeling would be a thing of the past.

'How did you sleep?'
  'Not great, how did you sleep?'
  'Not great either.'

Jeff and Valerie smiled at each other as she breast-fed Briony. The curtains were pulled around her bed and they felt cocooned in a little pink bubble despite the hustle and bustle of the ward.

'She's guzzling away, isn't she?' Jeff studied his daughter in fascination.

'Yeah, at last. It took us a while to get the hang of it. I thought I was going to have to bottle-feed. The nurses were very kind, though, and very patient, and I'm glad now that we've cracked it. But I can express milk too, and you'll get the chance to give her a bottle so you won't lose out,' Valerie said happily. She was feeling better and very relieved to have her baby contentedly suckling at her breast. Although she would only admit it to Lizzie, it wasn't that she would have felt a failure as a mother if Briony hadn't latched on, she would have been more disappointed about not being able to breast-feed because it was so *handy*. It made life much easier than fussing about with bottles, and there was the added bonus of losing weight quicker. She wouldn't be able to drink, but that wouldn't kill her.

'Ma and Da are dying to see her,' Jeff interrupted her musings.

Valerie's heart sank. In the excitement of giving birth and Carmel's earlier visit she had forgotten that her daughter had two other grandparents. She was going to have to engage with Tessa and Lorcan a lot more. She liked Lorcan – he was a kind man; she had no problem with him – but Tessa was another kettle of fish. It was because of Tessa and her interference that she and Jeff weren't yet married. She blamed her much more than her own mother. Carmel would have backed down on the marriage issue if push came to shove; Tessa never would.

Valerie looked at her boyfriend, eyes fixed intently on their now sleeping daughter, his index finger gripped tightly by her tiny fingers. Of course he would want his parents to see his daughter, just as she had been so eager for Carmel's visit. It behoved her to behave well, unfortunately.

Valerie plastered a smile on her face and said with as much sincerity as she could muster, 'It will be lovely for them to see their first grandchild. I'll try and have her fed before visiting hours. I wouldn't feel comfortable doing it in front of them.'

'Oh, yeah, right,' he agreed, taking the sleeping baby from Valerie. 'Mam wants to talk about the christening. She'd like to have a little family party at home for us afterwards. Isn't that nice?' He gave a boyish grin.

'Oh!' Valerie was dismayed. She hadn't given Briony's christening ceremony any thought. Trust Tessa to start interfering already. She wasn't even sure if she wanted to go back to Rockland's with her baby and face the neighbours.

And what about Carmel? Would she be invited? Terence definitely wouldn't set foot in the Egans' house again, Valerie could guarantee that. Why couldn't Tessa just let things be? She fretted as all these new complications took shape.

'Look, let's not make any decisions yet. Let me get the baby home to the flat and settled in. If we're going to be living in Dublin maybe we should have her christened up here. We'll talk about it when I'm out of hospital.' She fastened the buttons on her nightdress and didn't see the look of disappointment that flashed across Jeff's face.

'Oh, OK,' he agreed, sighing.

The visitors' bell rang. 'Go home and do some studying. I don't want your mother thinking we're distracting you too much,' Valerie urged. After hearing the news about the proposed christening party *chez* Tessa, she was very put out. Clearly she was going to have to keep a tight rein on Tessa Egan to keep her from sticking her nose in where it wasn't wanted. She'd have to nip her interference in the bud from the very beginning and make sure that Jeff's mother never got the chance to meddle in her life again. Valerie watched Jeff tenderly lay the baby in the small cot at her bedside and felt sick at the thought of his parents' impending visit.

CHAPTER TWENTY-EIGHT

Oh Lord, Tessa thought, her heart sinking as she saw Terence coming out of Mrs Breen's front garden with his lawnmower. She took a deep breath and fixed a smile on her face. She hadn't seen him to talk to since that fraught meeting in her sitting room the previous year.

'Terence, how are you?' she greeted him politely. 'Isn't it great news about Valerie and the baby? Thank God it all went well for her. We're going up to see them tomorrow. We're hoping to have a christening party for the baby, and you and Carmel will be most welcome to come,' she added magnanimously. She felt she had to invite him. It would be incredibly rude not to.

'Hello, Tessa,' Terence said coldly.

'Have you gone up to see them yet? Jeff said Carmel had been up earlier today.' Tessa knew she was prattling.

'No, I haven't,' he said stiffly.

'Oh!' she said. 'Well, of course, you were at work.'

'Nor do I plan to,' he added dourly. 'When I said I was washing my hands of the whole affair, I meant it. And I won't be coming to any party, thank you.'

'Oh, Terence!' Tessa exclaimed, dismayed. 'What a shame to feel like that. You have a beautiful little grandchild.'

'I'd far prefer to have a beautiful little grandchild in *wedlock*, but thanks to you, that didn't happen.' He thrust his jaw out aggressively and his eyes sparked with antagonism.

'Carmel backed me up on that, Terence,' Tessa said heatedly.

'Well, the pair of you were very misguided, if you ask me,' he said shortly, his anger evident in the thinning of his mouth and the hard glare he gave her.

'But, Terence, there's plenty of time for them to marry. They're so young. Isn't it better for them to be sure of their feelings for each other?' she protested.

'Better for him, you mean.'

'Look, Terence, I stood up for my son. I'm a mother – that's what a mother does. I didn't want to see him adding one mistake to another,' Tessa said crossly.

'And I tried to stand up for my daughter, for all the good it did me. Do none of you see that?' he said indignantly. 'How would you feel if it was *your* daughter, Tessa? In that situation you'd do the same. You'd want to see her married. Wouldn't you? Or if *you* were in Valerie's position? Ask yourself, Tessa, how would you feel if it was *you*?'

It was me! She screamed silently. *It was me!*

For one awful moment she was sure she'd spoken the words aloud.

'Ye see, you've no answer to that,' he said triumphantly.

'I'm sorry you feel like that,' she said stiffly, and walked away. She struggled to compose herself but it was no use. Tears smarted her eyes and she hurried to the safety of her car, hoping that she would get to it before she was accosted by Nellie Andrews, a sharp-eyed, nosy busy-body who ran the church committee. Nellie was bearing down fast but Tessa made it to the car and had the engine started with seconds to spare, giving the woman a wave as she drove off at speed.

Her composure faltered and a cry that came from the depths of her erupted in an animal-like howl. She drove out of the village, desperate to get away so she could be alone with her sorrow as the grief she had struggled to keep a lid on since Jeff had told her of Valerie's pregnancy would no longer be denied.

'*How would you feel if it was you?*' Terence had tormented her. Well, she knew more than anyone what it was like to be pregnant outside of marriage at a time when girls who were unfortunate enough to get into the situation were treated like the lowest of the low. She had endured that particular anguish, she thought bitterly, as she spun the wheel of the car to drive down a narrow lane that led to a small, secluded beach known only to the locals.

Valerie thought she was a bitch. Tessa knew that. She'd seen the look of horror and dismay on her face when Tessa had put her spoke in about them waiting to marry. Valerie had been gutted. She'd thought Tessa was acting out of spite. Nothing could have been further from the truth. If only the young woman could have realized that Tessa was trying to save her from an agony that she herself had endured for the whole of her marriage. The misery of not knowing if Lorcan *truly* loved her had blighted her life and her relationship with her husband as she tormented herself with wondering if things had been different would he have asked her to marry him because he *wanted* to, not because he *had* to.

Lorcan was a good man. The best. He had been a loyal, supportive husband. But she knew him, knew the cut of him. When Lorcan put his mind to something he gave it his best shot and followed it through to the best of his ability. He had iron discipline and strength of will. Once he had asked her to marry him when she'd discovered that she was pregnant with their daughter he had put his shoulder to the wheel and made the best of it. But after her encounter with Lorna Burton, his ex, she could never get over the notion that he loved her because he had to make the best of things and not because it was how he really felt.

Even though Lorcan assured her to the contrary many times, it was like a horrible black malignancy of doubt deep inside that she could never escape from. She had thought she had put it behind her and dealt with it, especially in the latter years of her marriage, which she had to admit had been a very happy one for the most part. But when Jeff had come home and told her about Valerie it had all come surging back, and the malignancy had grown and grown again until sometimes it was all she could think of.

Valerie thought it was malice that had made her act as she had, but it wasn't. It was hard, bitter experience, she thought as she pulled on her parka and got out of the car to walk along the windy beach. The sun had set and the dusk was deepening the sky, but there was another half-hour of light so she made for the shoreline where it was easier to walk.

She hadn't particularly taken to Valerie when Jeff had first brought her home, Tessa acknowledged as she made her way across the dunes and slithered down onto the beach. She'd seen a young girl with the world at her doorstep. Her own car. Money to spend on fashion and make-up. A life in the city. All the things Tessa would have loved to have experienced when she was young and beautiful herself, and eager to escape the confines of village life. All of that had passed her by, as had her youth. She was now a middle-aged woman with no opportunity to spread her wings. That was very difficult to accept. The dreaded menopause was wrapping its tentacles around her. Her body was changing, losing its elasticity, aching, reminding her that she was no longer young. Grey hair was invading what had once been her crowning glory. The lines around her mouth and eyes were deepening, so yes, she was jealous of Valerie, Tessa conceded. Not admirable. Not nice. Irrational, she knew, but honest.

Valerie had seemed so confident, so sophisticated, with her stylish clothes and her own car. She'd had a bockety old bicycle when she was young, Tessa remembered with a pang.

Oh yes, she had been horribly jealous of Jeff's girlfriend at first. Envious that Valerie would have all the things that Tessa had longed for and would have treasured. The declaration of love. The romantic proposal. The engagement and all the excitement that went with it. The white wedding and the romantic honeymoon. And eventually, a baby when the time was right.

It hadn't worked out at all like she'd dreamed of. She and Lorcan had been dating for a year and she loved him with all her heart. He was in ag college up in Dublin and she was always afraid some sophisticated city slicker would get her claws into him. They had gone to a dance one hot summer's night, and drank too much. They'd gone courting in a barn, full of sweet-smelling hay, on her father's farm on the way home, and it had been so wonderful having him in her arms, desiring her as much as she desired him, that all their hitherto caution and restrained behaviour was swept away in a tide of wanting, and she'd lost her virginity eagerly and paid the price for her recklessness for the rest of her life.

She'd fallen pregnant, been proposed to, married – in a pale blue suit – with only her parents and Lorcan's, and her sister as bridesmaid and his brother as best man, at the wedding, all within the space of three months. Her parents had been horrified, as well as furious at the shame she had brought on the family and had wanted her away from the village as soon as she could get going. The wedding had been a grim affair. They had been married at eight o'clock in the morning, the priest radiating disapproval, her mother sobbing into her handkerchief, her father stern and unyielding. There had been no wedding breakfast. No speeches and throwing of bouquets. She and Lorcan had got into his car immediately after the ceremony and driven straight to Dublin.

The honeymoon had been a weekend in Dublin in Wynn's Hotel. She had left her village, where she had been the subject of much whispered gossip, to live in Lorcan's village, Rockland's, in his elderly aunt's rambling home, until they had enough money to buy a place of their own. He had given up college to work on his father's fishing boat there and so Tessa carried the added guilt of knowing he had ended up working in the very job he had wanted to escape from.

Her husband had borne his new circumstances stoically, but she had been riven with grief and regret and an unquenchable fear that he had only married her out of duty and not love. The day she'd met Lorcan's ex, Lorna Burton, had reinforced that belief beyond a doubt.

She'd taken Lisa for a walk to settle her down after a feed one Saturday not long after she was born and had been feeling surprisingly happy as the afternoon sun warmed them. And then she'd seen Lorna Burton walking briskly in her direction and her heart plummeted. Lorna had been dating Lorcan for a year before they'd had a falling out and he had started going with Tessa. Lorna was a sexy little blonde vamp who was always flirting with men and playing them off against each other. She couldn't be more different from Tessa.

'So this is Lorcan's daughter!' Lorna forced her to come to a halt in the middle of the footpath. She cast a cursory glance into the pram at Lisa. 'Lovely baby, Tessa. Clever move, getting pregnant. Congratulations. But he would have come back to me if you hadn't, you know that, don't you?' Lorna's green eyes were icy flints as she stared at Tessa.

It took every ounce of self-control not to betray how deeply wounded she was by Lorna's cruelty.

'Lorcan was free to do whatever he wished, Lorna, I can assure you, and if he'd wanted you he'd have gone back to you, make no mistake about it,' she said coldly, manoeuvring the pram around her.

'As I say, Tessa, clever move, getting pregnant but not one I'd use to get a man,' Lorna said scornfully over her shoulder as Tessa gripped the handles of the pram tightly and tried hard not to cry.

Those cold, harsh words had ploughed a deep furrow of torment in Tessa and undermined her marriage, despite Lorcan's protestations to the contrary and reassurances that he did indeed love her. The damage had been done and Tessa could never entirely convince herself that what he said was true.

And so when Jeff, the child she loved the most of all her children, had arrived home with his new girl, she had seen in Valerie shades of the girl she was all those years ago before that first pregnancy had robbed her of all her dreams. All her old fears and regrets seemed to resurface just as she was inexorably sliding headlong into menopause and all the difficulties that entailed.

And then Jeff had come home with the news that his girlfriend was pregnant and it was like her and Lorcan's past was being replayed all over again. A pattern being repeated. But things were different now from in her day, Tessa reassured herself as the sea caressed the shore and the breeze brushed her hair from her face, and a faint thrum of a fishing boat's engine as it chugged towards harbour, broke the silence of the encroaching night. She turned to walk back towards the car. Valerie might hate her now, but the day would come when she would be grateful for the stance Tessa and Carmel had taken that had prevented her from rushing down the aisle and having to live with all the torments and doubts such a hasty trip entailed.

Perhaps Jeff would want to marry her in the future, and Tessa would be happy for them if it was what he really wanted, but for now her son had to focus on his chosen career. She would be damned if he had to give up college like his father had. His life was not going to be ruined. He had choices and she would try her utmost to make sure that he made the best ones for him, his baby and Valerie. In the meantime she would support them as best she could.

She *would* throw a lovely christening party to honour Briony, where their new grandchild would be surrounded by family and friends welcoming her into the world. So different for her own daughter's christening which had been attended only by Lorcan and herself and the godparents; a subdued, restrained affair that had to be endured rather than enjoyed, with no sense of celebration, just shame.

Briony's christening would be so different: a time of welcome and joy, with the church full of family and Jeff and Valerie's friends. She sincerely hoped Carmel would come and that Valerie would see it as an olive branch. There was nothing more she could do about Terence; she'd made her offer of peace. The arrival of a baby was a special occasion, no matter what the circumstances. Patterns could be changed, Tessa decided, feeling suddenly energized as she climbed up the dunes to get to the car. This was an opportunity for all of them to put the past behind them and start afresh. Something to celebrate and look forward to, no matter what Terence Harris thought.

Chapter Twenty-Nine

Valerie sat in her dressing gown beside her bed, rubbing Briony's back gently. Her daughter gave a small burp, and then her eyelashes fluttered down over her cheeks and she fell asleep.

'Good little girl,' Valerie crooned, placing her back in her cot and covering her with her blanket.

A nurse poked her head around her cubicle curtains. 'Valerie, I'm just going to take baby for her heel prick test.'

'Will it hurt?' Valerie winced at the thought.

'She'll be grand,' the nurse said reassuringly, pushing Briony's cot briskly down the ward. The cubicle felt strangely empty and she pulled back her curtains and smiled at the woman in the next bed.

'I think I'll just run down to the bathroom to slap on a bit of make-up. Jeff's parents are coming in this afternoon; I need to look presentable.'

'If you can run I take my hat off to you. I can hardly move,' the older woman groaned. She had given birth to her third child, a daughter, the same night as Valerie. She was a friendly, good-hearted woman and both of them had confided to each other that they were glad they weren't in the same ward as the one who had been screeching and roaring the night they were in labour.

Valerie gathered up her toilet bag and towel and made her way to the bathroom. Fortunately it was vacant and she didn't have to hang around outside. Valerie shut the door with a sigh. It was nice to have some peace and quiet. The hospital was busy and noisy. There was always activity of some sort, and the inevitable background cacophony of babies crying. She hadn't slept well and a fug of tiredness shrouded her. She was looking forward to going home at the weekend and sleeping her brains out. Lizzie had offered Carmel her bed and said she'd go to Rockland's for the weekend. She wouldn't have to worry about her friend being disturbed by a crying baby for the first two nights.

She looked wrecked, she decided, as she washed her face and applied some make-up. She felt she had aged ten years. Her boobs were sore and leaky, and her tummy looked like a pasty pudding. Far from goddess-like, she had informed Lizzie. She couldn't imagine ever looking attractive or having sex again.

'Ah, wait until you get a rub of the relic and you'll be fine,' Lizzie assured her briskly, having no clue as to what her friend was experiencing.

'I wonder, will I be much looser down there?' Valerie worried.

'Are you doing those exercises?' Lizzie demanded.

'Religiously,' Valerie assured her, tightening as she spoke.

Valerie smiled, remembering the discussion of the previous day. Lizzie had arrived in with a box of liquorice allsorts, a supply of sanitary towels, breast pads, a pretty pale green floral nightdress and two new pairs of big cotton knickers. 'Not to be seen by man nor beast,' she advised. 'But they'll cover a multitude until you get back to normal.'

Whenever that would be, if ever. Valerie grimaced as she gave her hair a brush, glad she'd got a shaggy cut again. It was so much easier to manage. She could hear people walking and talking along the corridor and knew that visiting hour had started. She squirted a spray of Apple Blossom on her neck and wrists, packed away her cosmetics, made her way back to the ward and spent a while tidying up her bits and pieces.

Briony's little face was scrunched up and teary when the nurse brought her back and Valerie took her out of the cot and cuddled her, murmuring soothing endearments until she fell asleep in her arms. She laid her back in her cot and covered her up, and felt suddenly weary.

Valerie eased herself up on the bed, wincing with pain. Piles were the pits, and extra punishment on top of the discomfort after childbirth. She flicked through a magazine but she was too agitated to read. She wished the Egans' visit was over. She was mortified that they would see her in her dressing gown, but at least she had her make-up on.

Thank you for your kind offer of a party for the christening but we haven't made a decision on where we're having it yet, she practised silently. Just be firm, she told herself, yawning. She settled back against the pillows more comfortably. The sun was shining in on her, making her feel even more lethargic than before. She'd just have a little rest until her visitors came.

'Don't wake her up,' she heard a man's voice say. Something wet was running down her chin. Valerie came to with a start to see Jeff, Lorcan and Tessa studying her as she gazed at them bleary-eyed.

'Oh, I must have fallen asleep,' she murmured, wiping her chin. She was mortified. She had a strong suspicion she had been caught snoring with her mouth open, as well as dribbling.

'God love you, are you exhausted?' Tessa said kindly, handing her a gift-wrapped parcel.

'Er . . . Thanks very much, Mrs Egan,' she said politely, hoping the other woman wouldn't kiss her.

'Tessa – please. "Mrs Egan" makes me feel so old,' Tessa protested. She didn't look old, Valerie thought. She looked so healthy and tanned and fit compared to herself. Tessa was wearing black trousers, a cream ribbed polo-neck jumper and a smart grey belted trench coat, which she removed. 'It's warm in here,' she remarked. 'Can we see the baba?' She leaned over the cot to take a peep.

'Have a hold of her,' Jeff said excitedly.

'She's *asleep*!' Valerie exclaimed, shooting Jeff a glare.

'Mam won't wake her.' Jeff shot a glare right back at her.

Tessa looked at Valerie. 'Would you prefer if I left her?' she asked. A strained silence descended as they all turned to look at her.

It would be churlish not to let Jeff's mother cuddle her new grandchild, Valerie supposed, and besides, Tessa *had* asked. At least she hadn't swooped down and lifted the baby up without a by-your-leave.

'Not at all, take her up,' she said as graciously as she could manage. Tessa needed no second urging. She drew back the blanket, lifted her grandchild out gently and studied her intently.

'She's beautiful,' she breathed, and to Valerie's surprise Tessa's eyes filled with tears.

Lorcan threw his eyes up to heaven. 'She's an awful woman for the waterworks,' he said affectionately, peering at his new grandchild over his wife's shoulder.

'This is a precious moment,' Tessa gulped. 'The first grandchild. Jeff's daughter. I'm entitled to cry.'

'See, Valerie thinks she has my chin,' Jeff pointed out.

'Thank God she hasn't your ears,' Lorcan teased, and they all laughed.

'She's a big baby, is she feeding well?' Tessa stroked Briony's cheek, sitting on the chair Jeff had acquired for her.

'Like a horse,' Jeff said proudly.

'I was asking Valerie,' Tessa said, laughing.

'She's a good little grubber, thank God,' Valerie replied, wondering was this the same woman who had been so dogmatic and determined that she and Jeff should not marry. She was much nicer today, much softer. She opened the parcel Tessa had given her and couldn't help but be delighted at the snug little lilac romper suit and matching coat and bonnet. There were two Prize Bonds in an envelope with Briony's name on it, and a lovely cotton nightdress and matching négligé for Valerie.

'These are gorgeous.' Valerie was surprised that gifts for herself were included. 'You shouldn't have gone to such trouble.'

'It's not every day you welcome a grandchild into the family,' Tessa said affably. 'And she is our first so we have to spoil her. And you can never have enough nighties when you're feeding a baby yourself, from what I remember of it.'

'Thanks, they'll get a lot of use,' Valerie acknowledged the other woman's thoughtfulness.

'And you're getting out at the weekend?' Tessa observed a while later, after some general chitchat about the hospital and the weather and other innocuous subjects. 'Are you coming down to Rockland's to stay at your mother's?'

'No, I'm going home to the flat. Mam's coming up to help me out for a few days. I don't want to be distracting Jeff from his studies.' Valerie got her little dig in.

'That's important too,' Tessa agreed, and Valerie wasn't sure if she was unaware of the barb thrown in her direction or was choosing to ignore it.

'So when do you think you might be down?' Tessa placed the baby in Lorcan's arms.

'I don't know really, to be honest,' she said slowly, knowing what was coming.

'Have you made plans for the christening?' Tessa probed. 'No.'

'Oh! It was just that I was saying to Jeff that we'd love to have a party for the christening to celebrate Briony's safe arrival. A family hooley for anyone you'd want to invite.'

'It sounds great,' Jeff interjected.

Valerie could have flattened him. He knew she wasn't happy with the idea.

'Um . . . Well, I haven't really talked to Jeff about it in detail. I'm not sure if I want to have her christened in Rockland's. And I'm not sure if I'm ready to go back there yet. Thanks for the offer, Tessa. We'll let you know, won't we, Jeff?' She looked up at her boyfriend, who was lounging over the meal trolley at the end of her bed.

'Yeah,' Jeff sighed. 'We'll let you know what Valerie decides,' he said with heavy irony.

'It's early days yet, and you've enough to be getting used to. There's plenty of time to arrange parties.' Lorcan smiled over at her and she could have hugged him for his sensitivity. She was saved from answering by the unexpected arrival of two of her colleagues from work. Perfect timing, thought Valerie as she made a flurry of introductions

'We should go, we don't want to tire Valerie out,' Lorcan said, handing the sleeping baby back to Tessa for a final cuddle.

'Do you want to put your daughter in her cot?' she asked Jeff, giving the baby a tender kiss. He took her and placed her gently in the cot while Tessa put her coat on.

'Thanks very much for coming,' Valerie said, smiling up at Lorcan. She meant it for him. With Tessa she was merely being polite.

'You take care. We'll see you when we see you, won't we, Tessa?'

'Hopefully sooner rather than later,' Tessa said, giving a last longing look into the cot. 'Look after yourself, Valerie.'

'I will. Safe home,' Valerie said, delighted that the dreaded visit was over.

'I'll see you tonight.' Jeff leaned over and gave her a peck on the cheek.

'Maybe you should stay at home and study,' she said offhandedly. She was mad with him for saying that the party sounded like a great idea and she also wanted Tessa to see that she wasn't being in any way demanding.

'I'll come in for half an hour to give the baby a good night kiss,' he said firmly.

'Fine,' she said coolly. She wasn't going to get into an argument with him in front of everyone. 'Thank you again for the gifts,' she said to Tessa and Lorcan and waved them off as her friends cooed over the baby.

'We're not going to get to see much of that baby,' Tessa said dejectedly as Lorcan drove them back to Rockland's later that afternoon.

'Don't say that,' her husband chided.

'Well, did you hear her? She doesn't know when she's coming down to Rockland's. She doesn't know if she'll hold the christening there or not, as if Jeff has no say in the matter.' Tessa fiddled with the tape deck, most put out.

'Her family circumstances aren't great, Tessa, don't forget that. You don't know what way Terence is with all of this,' Lorcan pointed out.

'Well, she can stay with us then if he doesn't want her at home,' Tessa said crossly.

'She hardly knows us.'

'She'd better *get* to know us. That baby is our grand-child,' Tessa reminded him.

'Her name is Briony Harris, not Briony Egan, Tess,' Lorcan said quietly.

'I know that. I know that very well, Lorcan. I could see her name tag on her wrist,' Tessa snapped, and didn't speak another word for the rest of the journey home.

'All Ma wanted was to have the christening in Rockland's and a party after it. Is that so awful?' Jeff was truculent that evening as he and Valerie walked along the hospital corridor to the main entrance. He was going home to study and she was glad to see the back of him because they were being snippy with each other.

'It's all right for you, Jeff; people won't point the finger at you,' Valerie said heatedly.

'Let them. Who cares?' he retorted.

'*I* care, actually.'

'Well, when are they going to get to see the baby if you won't come down to Rockland's?'

'They can come up to Dublin.' She glared at him.

'Look, Briony's their grandchild. I'm their son, I want them to play a big part in her life,' he argued.

'Is that right?' said Valerie coolly. 'Well, forgive me, Jeff, if I'm slow on the uptake because, to be honest, that wasn't the impression I got when your mother laid down the law at that meeting in your house when I was dragged up there by my da. Just to remind you, I'm not your *wife*. They're not my *in-laws*. That's the way you wanted it and that's what you've got. You can't have it every way, Jeff, and neither can Tessa,' she said bluntly as they reached the front door. 'Good night,' she said, and walked away as fast as her physical discomfort would allow, leaving him slack-jawed as the implications of her words sank in.

'. . . and then I said, "Just to remind you, I'm not your *wife*. They're not my *in-laws*. That's the way you wanted it and that's what you've got. You can't have it every way, Jeff, and neither can Tessa'," Valerie said triumphantly to Lizzie twenty minutes later. Her friend had called in for the last ten minutes of visiting and had missed Jeff by a whisker. 'Good, wasn't it?' She smirked, delighted that she had finally asserted her authority and reclaimed some control over her situation. Tessa Egan wouldn't be so quick to interfere now that Valerie had laid down her boundaries. And it was good for Jeff to realize that he didn't have quite as much a say in things as he thought he had. It would have been a different kettle of fish if they were married.

Lizzie whistled. 'You certainly didn't hold back with Jeff, and I'm sure Tessa will think twice about making plans without asking you, but as your oldest and, I hope, dearest friend can I just say something to you?'

'Go on,' Valerie said slowly, knowing Lizzie always spoke her mind. There was a reproach coming down the line. She could see it in Lizzie's serious expression. Her friend sat on the bed and looked at her. 'Don't take this the wrong way, Val, and you know I'm always on your team, but just take it a bit easy when you're laying down the law, hon. You and Jeff are in this together. You're Briony's parents. She's your child. Don't use her as a weapon.'

'Oh,' said Valerie, deflated. 'I was just trying to stand up for myself.'

'I know, but life is hard, and you and Briony are going to need all the help you can get. Don't cut yourself and her off from a family who are willing to be supportive and hands on. You don't know what's coming down the tracks in the future and it's good to have people in your camp, that's all I'm saying.'

'But it's just that now that I've had the baby they want to be involved but I wasn't good enough to be part of their family through marriage,' she said sulkily.

'Do you *really* want Tessa Egan for a mother-in-law?' Lizzie arched an eyebrow at her.

'It's going to be hard going back to Rockland's with the baby. You know what they're like down there?' Valerie scowled.

'You just tell me when you feel up to going down and I'll come with you. You'll walk down the village with your head up, missy, and I'll be beside you. Let them do their worst. Anyway, most people are very nice at home; it's not the worst place in the world,' Lizzie said gently. 'Don't be letting that bother you.'

'I know. I just feel a bit all over the place, and Tessa gets my back up,' Valerie said tearfully, her high evaporating. Lizzie's words made her feel she'd been spiteful. Deep down she knew she had behaved badly, but it had felt good after all the hurt she'd endured.

'She doesn't mean it. She has a good heart, and Lorcan's a lovely man. Try and work with them, not against them, for Briony's sake,' Lizzie urged.

'Yeah, OK,' she said dispiritedly as the visitors' bell rang.

'I'm not giving out to you, I'm just trying to help.' Lizzie stood up. 'A good godmother has to do her best for her godchild.' She bent over the cot and kissed Briony, who was gazing intently at something above her head.

'Ah, look at her, Valerie, she's playing with the angels,' Lizzie said tenderly. 'She's just gorgeous.'

'Thanks for being a good friend, Lizzie.' Valerie hauled herself off the bed and went to stand beside her.

'It will all work out fine,' Lizzie said comfortingly, giving her a hug. 'I'll see you after the weekend. There's plenty of food in the fridge – I stocked up – and there's a few treats there as well.'

'If you were a man I'd marry you,' Valerie teased as her friend buttoned up her coat.

'If I was a man I'd marry myself.' Lizzie blew her a kiss and clickity-clacked her way down the ward in her high heels.

Valerie picked her daughter up and held her close, loving the way she grabbed her finger. Lizzie had been very direct. But she was right, Valerie conceded reluctantly. Briony shouldn't be used to score points. She'd try not to use her as a 'weapon'. But she wouldn't be walked on either. Tessa and Jeff could not dictate what was going on in her life, no matter how much they might want to. The fact was, she was a single mother, and until her circumstances changed and she and Jeff were at least living together in a place of their own, Valerie would do the best she could for her and her daughter. But Lizzie was right about one thing. Family was important and it would be unfair to deprive Briony of that bond. Once Valerie was settled back in the flat and had some sort of routine going she'd turn her attention to the christening and try to work out something that would suit everyone. She could do no more than that.

Jeff studied his notes, trying to make out the scribbles in the margin that he'd written to emphasize a point. He was finding it hard to concentrate. Valerie had been pretty nasty earlier. He'd almost felt she didn't want him in her life. She'd really rubbed his nose in it and made him feel like a heel. She didn't *own* Briony, although you'd think that she did the way she was talking, he thought resentfully. And his parents had every right to suggest having a party to celebrate their grandchild's christening.

God, his life was a mess, he thought, sinking his head into his hands. He was a new parent; he had exams coming up, a cranky girlfriend, and a mother who felt she was being sidelined. He was sick of women, heartily sick of them. He wanted to go out and get hammered and go to a club with his mates and be carefree and irresponsible and pull some girl and ride her ragged and never see her again. He hadn't had sex with Valerie in weeks. And now all her attention would be given to the baby and he'd be lucky to get a look in. He'd made such a mess of his life before it had even started, he thought glumly, hearing the phone ring out in the hall.

'Jeff, it's for you,' his landlady yelled.

'Thanks,' he said, coming out into the hall to take the call. Probably his mother to let him know they were home.

'Hi, it's me. Sorry I was a bit of a bitch earlier,' Valerie said contritely.

Relief swept over him at the sound of her voice. That was one thing he loved about Valerie: she would always say sorry when she was in the wrong and she never held a grudge with him.

'It's OK, Valerie. I'm glad you rang. Let's not fight. We'll sort things out.' He leaned against the hallstand and felt some of the tension seep out of his body.

'I know we will, Jeff. I'm just all over the place at the moment. My hormones are in chaos and I just can't face the thought of going home to Rockland's, for a while anyway,' his girlfriend explained.

'That's OK, Val, we'll make some sort of arrangement about the christening,' he assured her. 'How is our daughter?'

'Our daughter's yelling her head off. I'd better go and feed her,' Valerie said, but he knew she was smiling. 'Good night, Jeff.'

'Good night, Val,' he said. 'See you tomorrow.' He put the phone back in the cradle and went back to his room. Another hurdle jumped. Another crisis averted. He'd placate his mother some way or another. For now he and Valerie were back on track until the next mini drama, though he was sure there'd be plenty of them in the months to come. He closed the door to his room and glanced at the pile of books on the table. He'd had enough of them. To hell with it, he was going out. Valerie would shortly be home from the hospital and he'd have to sit in with her and the baby; he might as well have one last night of freedom. One of his mates had phoned earlier inviting him out for a drink to wet the baby's head. He'd dithered, not being in the mood after his row with Valerie. But everything was sorted now. Whistling, he rummaged in his wardrobe for a clean shirt and a pair of boxers. You only lived once, he was beginning to realize. He might as well have what fun he could.

CHAPTER THIRTY

'Oh, no, here's Father O'Shea,' Valerie muttered to Lizzie, noticing Rockland's parish priest cross The Triangle to head in their direction. Her hands tightened on the handle of the baby stroller.

'Stay calm, he's not an ogre,' Lizzie murmured out of the side of her mouth as the priest came alongside them.

'Girls,' he said cheerily, 'I haven't seen you around together in a long time. The Folk Group isn't the same since you went up to the Big Smoke.'

'Hello, Father,' they replied simultaneously.

'And who have we got here? Is this the new arrival?' The elderly priest bent down and peered into the buggy. 'Well, isn't she the little pet!' he exclaimed. 'And how are you, Valerie?' His blue eyes were kind as he straightened up and turned to her.

'I'm well, thanks, Father,' she said, warily waiting for some sort of censure.

'Good. Are you back at work yet?'

'Yes, Father, I went back at the end of the summer.'

'I'm sure that it was hard to leave her. Well, it's great to see the pair of you looking so well. Don't be a stranger to us now. If you feel like coming to the Folk Mass tomorrow we'd love to see you. And when the little one is old enough make sure to bring her to the Children's Mass if you're down at the weekend and we'll find a part for her to play. Enjoy your walk now. I'd say the air down here makes her sleep like a baby.' Father O'Shea chuckled at his little joke and gave them a wave as he took his leave of them.

'Isn't he a champion?' Lizzie declared. 'Jesus would be proud of him. No judgement, no sermon, just kindness, acceptance and compassion. That's my kind of priest. I'd love him to marry myself and Dara.'

'Are you making plans?' Valerie looked at her in surprise as they continued their walk.

'Yeah,' Lizzie said happily. 'I wasn't going to say anything until after the party, but we're thinking of going to London.'

'London!' Valerie shrieked.

'Shush, here's Franny Powell; you know what she's like for gossip,' Lizzie hissed.

'Ah, Valerie, is this your new baby? You left it long enough to come back to Rockland's to show her off, but sure, I suppose that's to be understood considering your circumstances. I'd say Father O'Shea had something to say about that. I saw him talking to you.' Franny pursed her lips as she glanced down at the baby.

'Not a word, Franny, except to invite us to sing at the Folk Mass on Sunday, and telling Valerie to make sure to bring Briony to the Children's Mass when she's old enough. But then, of course, Father O' Shea is a *real* Christian, not like a few Altar Crawlers I know. Pharisees, I think they were called in the Bible.' Lizzie smiled sweetly.

'Is that right?' Franny said, nostrils flaring. 'I wouldn't have taken *you* for a Bible reader.'

'Don't judge a book by its cover, Franny,' Lizzie said smartly. 'Goodbye now. We're just going into the church to light a candle. We'll include you in it.'

'You're a wagon,' Valerie giggled as Lizzie took hold of Briony's buggy and turned it in the direction of St Anthony's, walking away from Franny at a fast lick.

'Smug old crone, she's got a chin like a bristle brush. I bet *she* reads the Bible every night, for all the good it does her,' said Lizzie, who had never opened the Bible in her life. She pushed the stroller into the church grounds.

'What were you saying about going to London?' Valerie demanded, hoping that she hadn't heard right.

'We're thinking of it. Dara's company wants him to move to their London office to get more experience in their Sales and Marketing department. He'll get a rent allowance and a whole load of other perks for a year. It's a great opportunity. If we get married I can claim the marriage gratuity so we're thinking seriously of going for it.' She was bubbling with excitement.

'Yikes, Lizzie, I . . . I just can't imagine my life without you in it.' Valerie's lip wobbled.

'Don't. Don't start blubbing, I'm warning you,' Lizzie cautioned sternly. 'I didn't want to say anything but it's been really hard to keep it to myself. But listen,' she said earnestly, 'it means Jeff could stop looking around for a new place and you could keep the flat. You'd be together at last!'

'I guess that would make your going a bit easier,' Valerie said slowly as she dropped some coins into the collection box and lit a handful of candles at St Anthony's shrine. 'The places we've seen that we can afford aren't a patch on Mrs M's. Most of them are so small, or filthy, or totally unsuitable for a baby, or too far from work and the crèche. I haven't seen one place that I liked. It would be fantastic if we could stay where we are.'

'Tell Jeff after the party. It will be a good night for him. Celebrating his baby daughter, getting a First in his exams – this will be the icing on the cake for him,' Lizzie said giddily.

'Do you think so? He might get a shock, feel he's going to be tied down—'

'Will you *stop* that negativity, Valerie? You've got to believe you have a future together as a couple as well as being Briony's parents. Now enough of that nonsense and enjoy tonight, do you hear me?'

'Yes, Lizzie,' Valerie said meekly.

'Right, come on. I promised Mam we'd call in with the baby. She's dying to get a hold of her.' Lizzie marched down the aisle with her goddaughter gurgling happily in front of her.

Valerie followed, thoughts in a whirl. Her best friend was moving to England. As close as a sister, Lizzie had been with her through thick and thin. She was her rock and now she was going away. And her leaving would give her, Jeff and Briony the chance to be a real family . . . if her boyfriend wanted it. But would he? Would it be a step too far for him to move into the flat with her? Tessa and Lorcan were throwing a party to celebrate Jeff's exam results and a belated christening party. Jeff was so looking forward to it and she had been determined to make the best of it, but now she felt deflated. Just when life had got on some sort of an even keel and she'd begun to adjust to having a baby in her life, a new upheaval reared its head.

An hour later, Valerie sat in the bedroom where she had spent so much of her life when she was growing up, feeding her daughter. It was her first time in Rockland's since the baby had been born almost six months ago. It was the October Bank Holiday weekend. She'd been dreading the visit: dreading meeting her father, dreading meeting the neighbours, and dreading the party Tessa and Lorcan were having for Jeff.

But so far, it had been easier than she'd expected. Terence had muttered a surly 'hello' when she'd walked into the house, carrying the baby. 'There's tea just made in the pot if you want it,' he added, tucking his paper under his arm and heading for the sitting room. He'd hardly glanced at Briony.

'At least he didn't ignore me completely,' Valerie murmured to Carmel, who had taken the baby and was cooing delightedly to her.

'Take no notice of him. I don't any more. When he didn't come to the christening, I decided enough was enough. Now I do my own thing and let him do his.' Carmel kissed Briony again. 'Look at the head of hair on her, and look how alert she is!' She was enthralled as she sat at the kitchen table while Valerie poured them each a cup of tea. It was strange being home, but surprisingly nice, she reflected, enjoying Carmel's delight in her grandchild.

Valerie had been more hurt than she'd imagined when Terence hadn't come to Dublin for the small christening ceremony they'd held for Briony a month after she was born. She had hoped that he would come because it wasn't being held in Rockland's, and there was no opportunity for village tittle-tattle to offend his sensibilities.

But he'd flatly refused when Carmel told him of the christening plans.

'When the pair of them are married I'll attend those kind of events,' he said shortly, and that was that.

Carmel, Jeff's family, and Lizzie and Dara had come to the ceremony in the local church and then gone to a nearby hotel for lunch. It had actually been enjoyable. Valerie had been on her best behaviour with Tessa, and Tessa was on her best behaviour with her. Valerie had suggested, as a concession to Tessa, that she could have her family gathering later in the year when Jeff's exams were over and the results were out, and Jeff's mother had agreed.

Jeff's brother and sister were friendly and easy company, and because they were on neutral territory in the church and hotel, Valerie was able to relax, knowing they wouldn't all come trooping back to the flat and invade her and Lizzie's privacy. Valerie had had to lay ground rules to Tessa about visiting the flat, which hadn't gone down too well, she knew. But it was Lizzie's flat too and her friend had gone beyond friendship in accommodating Valerie's huge life change.

The last six months had been a roller coaster ride and Lizzie had been by her side, especially in the scary days after Carmel had returned home to Rockland's and it had been just her and Jeff and the baby. She'd been petrified every night for those first few weeks when Briony was asleep, holding up a mirror to her mouth to make sure she was breathing. The first time Briony had developed a raging temperature Valerie had been sick with apprehension, but Lizzie had kept her calm and sponged Briony down. Then she'd gone into Temple Street Children's

Hospital with her and stayed there that long night before going straight to work. Her friend had even endured Tessa arriving unannounced one wet Saturday morning, the first weekend after Valerie had gone back to work, when both of them were still in their dressing gowns, lounging on the sofa chatting, while Valerie fed Briony.

Their doorbell had shrilled and they'd looked at each other in surprise, wondering who'd be ringing their doorbell on a Saturday morning. Lizzie had gone into the bedroom and peered out the window and caught Tessa looking up at her.

She stuck her head around the sitting-room door. 'It's Tessa. I'd better let her in.'

'Aw, crap!' cursed Valerie, looking around the untidy sitting room, with their cereal dishes and empty coffee cups on the floor, and a pile of clothes on the end of the sofa awaiting ironing. Magazines lay strewn around. An empty wine bottle sat on the hearth. Jeff and Lizzie had imbibed the previous night, while she had stuck to tonic water. Valerie shoved the bottle hastily into the coal scuttle and settled a couple of briquettes over the top of it as she heard Tessa ascend the stairs. She was mortified and raging to be caught undressed at this hour of the morning, and with the flat looking like a tip, but it was her first week back at work and she was exhausted. She had longed for this Saturday morning with all her might, to have a chance to relax and be with her baby and chat to Lizzie. How *dare* Tessa arrive unannounced, she fumed. Tessa had come up once a week every week since the baby was born, but they had been arranged visits and Valerie had made sure the place was spick and span. And it had been during her maternity leave when Lizzie was at work. Tessa could have a second think coming if she thought she was going to come up to visit every weekend and eat into her precious time off.

'I hope you don't mind me dropping in,' Jeff's mother said gaily, following Lizzie into the sitting room. 'I wanted to see how you were after your week at work, and I was dying to see the little one. I thought you'd be up. It's after eleven.' She glanced at her watch.

'I was up early. I'm just not dressed,' Valerie said defensively. 'Actually, Tessa, I'm wrecked after the first week back, it's a horrible day out, and Lizzie and I just wanted to take it easy after a busy week. Will you have tea?' she asked coolly.

'That would be lovely. Can I have a hold of her?' Tessa sat on the sofa beside her.

'I'll make the tea,' said Lizzie helpfully.

'No, Lizzie, it's your day off. You don't have to make tea for *my* visitors. I'll make it in a minute,' Valerie said pointedly. 'I'm just giving her the last of her feed,' she added as Tessa held her arms out for Briony.

'I'll just go and have a shower then,' Lizzie said, tactfully backing out of the room.

'Can I do anything for you? Will I wash up the cups? Or will I make the tea?' Tessa gazed around the room. Valerie nearly had a heart attack. The remains of last night's Chinese were still on the kitchen counter, and the dishes were lying in the sink waiting to be washed. And there was a smelly dishcloth and tea towels steeping in a bucket.

'No, no, you're fine,' she said tightly. 'I'll make the tea in a minute as soon as I wind her.' Valerie could hardly talk to the woman, she was so annoyed. Her own mother wouldn't arrive unannounced – why did Tessa Egan think it was acceptable for her to do so? She had no manners, that was her problem.

'Was Jeff home before you left?' she asked. Jeff had gone down to Rockland's early that morning to train for a match and to spend a few days of the following week fishing with Lorcan.

'He was. I cooked him breakfast. It was listening to him talking about Briony that put the longing on me. I had to go to Bray to leave my sewing machine in for repair so I decided to carry on up to Dublin. And so here I am to see the little darling.' She beamed as Valerie handed Briony over to her.

'I'll just go and make the tea.' Valerie stood up.

'Maybe I could bring her for a walk afterwards while you're getting dressed? It's stopped raining. I could bring her over to the Botanics. I'd love that and I'm in no hurry,' Tessa suggested breezily as she bounced a gurgling Briony on her knee.

'Maybe don't bounce her yet, Tessa. She's just been fed.' Valerie tried to keep her tone polite and then groaned when Briony upchucked all over her romper suit.

Stupid, idiotic woman, she thought viciously, wishing the puke had gone over Tessa's jeans and jumper.

'Oh dear!' Tessa exclaimed. 'Will I give her a bath and change, and dress her while you make the tea?'

'OK,' said Valerie, surrendering. 'When Lizzie's finished in the bathroom.'

Tessa spent four hours of Valerie's much-longed-for Saturday, hogging the baby. She took her for a walk to the Botanic Gardens while Valerie raged to Lizzie as she tidied up the flat and sorted out the kitchen.

'The absolute cheek of her, the bloody nerve of her, arriving unannounced on our day off and taking up all my precious time with Briony and invading your privacy too. It's bad enough having to leave my baby with a child-minder when I'm at work and not being able to spend time with her but now *this*. I'm not having it, Lizzie, I'm not!' Valerie burst into tears.

'Stay calm, it's probably just a one-off,' Lizzie soothed as she scraped egg fried rice into the bin.

'It had better be,' Valerie sniffled, wiping her eyes, not wanting Jeff's mother to see that she'd been crying. 'It had just better be.'

But it wasn't.

Two weeks later, on a Saturday morning, Tessa arrived again, at midday this time. Fortunately Valerie and the baby were dressed. It was a lovely sunny day and she had planned to take Briony to the nearby park for a stroll and a chance to sit and read the paper.

'I was collecting the sewing machine so I said I'd use the opportunity to see my darling grandchild,' Tessa declared airily. 'I've brought a tart and some scones. Jeff's partial to them.'

'That's kind. We were just on our way out in a little while, actually. I'm meeting a friend for lunch,' Valerie fibbed.

Tessa's face fell. 'Oh what a shame. Would you like to go for lunch and I'll mind her?' she asked eagerly.

'Oh, no, Tessa, thanks. I want to spend time with her. I've been away from her all week,' Valerie blurted. Was the woman totally insensitive? Didn't she understand Valerie's *need* to be with her child?

'Oh, yes, I suppose. It must be hard when you're work-ing,' Tessa said slowly.

'It is, *very*,' Valerie said emphatically. She would never forget that first week away from her baby when every fibre of her being longed to be with her and the days at work dragged by and all she could think about was Briony. How she would have loved to have been able to stay at home and rear her instead of leaving her in the care of a stranger, capable and nice though she was. What a gift that would have been, Valerie thought wistfully.

'It's very different from when I was on maternity leave. Look, I can stay for another twenty minutes if you want to hold her,' she offered, 'but really, Tessa, Saturday is not the best day to come visiting now that I'm back at work.' She might as well have her say and get it over with, Valerie decided. If Tessa went home and started moaning to Jeff about what she'd said and he got on to her about it, she'd let him have a piece of her mind too.

'When *is* good then? I really do want to be involved in my grandchild's life,' Tessa said, a slight edge to her voice. 'Lorcan's only seen her a few times.'

You should have thought of that when you stuck your oar in about Jeff and me and stopped us from getting married, Valerie was tempted to say, but she managed to restrain herself.

'It's hard to say, considering our living arrangements. This is Lizzie's flat too, and I'm very conscious of how good and tolerant she's been to the baby and me. I don't like imposing on her good nature either,' Valerie said bluntly.

'Can't you come down to Rockland's and stay with us at weekends? I'll sort out Jeff's room for you,' Tessa suggested.

'Look, Tessa, after a week at work I don't want to be traipsing down to Rockland's. I have to catch up on washing and ironing and all those things that have to be done, as well as spending quality time with Briony myself.' Valerie nipped that suggestion in the bud very quickly.

'So are you telling me we're never going to get to see Briony? That's not very fair now, is it?' Tessa said heatedly.

'I'm not saying that at all, Tessa.' Valerie sighed. 'When Briony's weaned fully we can come down every so often, especially on the Sundays Jeff is playing a match. My own mother would love to see more of her but she's aware of our difficulties and she tries to come up when it suits all of us.' Valerie slipped in her little gibe.

'I don't want to be intruding, of course,' Tessa said stiffly. 'I'll phone the next time and make an appointment,' she gibed back.

'Great, that's a much better idea,' Valerie said, ignoring the sarcasm as she handed Briony over to her. Her daughter beamed up at her grandmother, and Valerie felt a bit of a heel. She knew Jeff's mother was smitten with the baby and that was good, but weekends were precious and she didn't want to spend them entertaining a woman she didn't like very much. If that made her a bitch then she was one and she didn't care, she decided. It was all right for Jeff, spending half his time in Rockland's working; he was more flexible than she was with his working days and he didn't have to entertain Carmel or Terence. If he was in her shoes he might not be so accommodating either.

'Look, you'll be having the party for Jeff the October weekend – you can spend plenty of time with her then.

We'll be able to come and visit at Christmas too, so maybe Jeff could bring her to stay overnight with you. I'll have annual leave and it will be easier.' Valerie knew she had to make some sort of effort.

'Oh! That would be something to look forward to.' The older woman was slightly mollified.

'And when Jeff gets a job and if we ever end up living together, it might be less complicated too. Now I'm really sorry I have to go or I'll be late,' Valerie said firmly. She had reached her limit and she wanted Tessa gone. The day was slipping past and she wanted to make the most of the good weather and get some fresh air with her daughter. 'Safe journey home,' she said politely as she led Tessa down to the front door.

'You never told me you were meeting someone for lunch – who was it?' Jeff said that evening when he phoned her.

'It was spur-of-the-moment. One of the girls at work who lives in Marino rang me. We'd said we must get together with our babies.' Valerie felt no compunction about telling him a fib. He felt it was perfectly fine for Tessa to call whenever she wanted. He was inclined to take Lizzie's decency for granted and she just wasn't having it any more.

'Where did you go?'

'A small Italian place in Drumcondra. Why?'

'Was just wondering. Ma was very disappointed to get so little time with Briony.' There was a hint of reproach in his tone.

'I told her she should have phoned first. I told her the weekends aren't the best time now that I'm working. And to be honest, it's not fair on Lizzie. It's her flat too and she shouldn't feel bad about going around in her dressing gown on Saturday mornings if she wants.'

'Ma wouldn't make her feel bad,' Jeff said indignantly.

'That's not the point, Jeff. We've taken over the flat, more or less, and she's never said a word. There's a limit to how much she should have to put up with, and entertaining my family and yours goes beyond it. That's the way it is at the moment, whether people like it or not,' she snapped.

'OK, OK, don't take the nose off me,' Jeff growled. 'I'll ring tomorrow. 'Bye.'

''Bye,' she glowered, hanging up.

'What's up?' Lizzie asked as she flounced into the sitting room. She was getting ready to go out and she looked a million dollars in her red cords and black tailored jacket.

'I'd say Tessa was whinging to Jeff. What am I supposed to do, sit in and wait for her to come and not make plans for my Saturday off? I'm sick of that lot,' she moaned.

'Imagine if you were married to him. Maybe it's just as well you're not.' Lizzie stroked another coat of mascara onto her dark, silky lashes. Valerie looked at her with envy. How she'd love to be going out for a night on the town. She hadn't been out for months. She hadn't had a drink in months. She was a mother now, and the high life was in the past, she realized, as Lizzie blew her a kiss and drifted down the stairs in a cloud of White Linen.

Suddenly the flat seemed terribly empty. Lizzie and some of her friends from work were going to Greece on a Budget Travel holiday and they were making all sorts of plans. She and Lizzie had always planned to holiday abroad together. That was never going to happen now.

Her social life was as good as over, Valerie figured, hearing the front door close. That thought had made her cry as she sat looking at a bag of baby clothes that were waiting to be washed.

Valerie remembered that moment vividly as, looking forward to the christening party, she rubbed Briony's back and heard her burp. Her life had certainly changed. She was tied, she had responsibilities, and she could no longer put herself first. Sometimes she had a terrible hankering for her old life. Sometimes she felt restless and resentful. She had none of the perks being married brought. But she had a lovely baby, she smiled, stroking her baby's back. Briony gave another satisfying burp. She loved the way her daughter nestled sleepily into her shoulder after her feed. There *were* good things about her new life too. She was going to express her milk before she went out tonight. She was going to indulge at Jeff's party, she decided. She'd been the perfect little mother for long enough. One night wouldn't be a disaster and besides, the baby was staying the night at Tessa's. Valerie was going to enjoy herself and let herself go, and come home and have a glorious lie-in the following morning. She was looking forward to that and looking forward to seeing how Jeff got on having the baby overnight. He was very good with Briony, but he always had Valerie at his back.

Now that Lizzie was making plans to go to London, there was nothing to stop Jeff moving into the flat. She was sure Mrs Maguire wouldn't mind. The landlady was quite fond of Jeff. Otherwise, Valerie was going to have to get a new flatmate and that wouldn't be easy. Who would want to share a flat with a mother and baby? How would Jeff react when he heard Lizzie's news? And if he did decide to move in with her, she knew without a shadow of a doubt she'd be seeing a lot more of Tessa. Valerie would have no excuse not to welcome Jeff's family into their home if they were living together. Whether she liked it or not, the very outcome she wanted, to live with Jeff as a couple, would always carry one big drawback. A drawback called Tessa.

Valerie laid her sleeping daughter in her carrycot and went to have a quick shower and prepare herself for Tessa's party. It was Jeff's night, he'd been looking forward to it for so long; she'd *try* to be on her best behaviour.

CHAPTER THIRTY-ONE

Tessa placed the massive platter of prawns in the middle of the long dining-room table, between two dishes of Marie Rose dressing, and an array of salads and slices of home-made brown bread and chunky Vienna rolls. She stood back to survey her handiwork. The prawns had come in fresh from the sea that morning, as had the lobster and scallops she was also serving. She had made a big pot of chowder, Jeff's favourite, and had prepared a beef stroganoff the previous day. The sideboard was laden with various bottles of spirits and wine, and in the centre stood the decorated sponge cake she'd ordered from a woman in the village who specialized in baking and decorating cakes for special occasions. Tessa had decided on a simple 'Congratulations' in pink script. Pink for Briony, whose birth they were celebrating, as well as her daddy's exam results.

Family, friends and neighbours were coming. Carmel Harris was coming on her own with Valerie. Tessa was more than happy that Terence had decided to stay away. She had no desire to have him in her house after their run-in.

Best of all, though, was that the baby was staying the night with them. Tessa was going to have her grandchild all to herself and she couldn't wait. And because there would be a houseful of guests, she wouldn't have to spend too much time with Valerie either. Time had done little to endear Jeff's girlfriend to her. She grimaced as she hurried upstairs to shower and change. She would not forget in a hurry the day Valerie had told her that she would more or less have to make an appointment when she wanted to see her grandchild and had then bustled her out the door so that she could go and meet some friend for lunch. Tessa had been put very firmly in her place and she knew it and it still rankled.

She had been furious driving back to Rockland's that day and had cursed the day her son had ever got involved with such a gobby little madam. She was sure Carmel Harris wouldn't have got such treatment had *she* arrived unexpectedly to visit Briony. Tessa had ranted and raved to Lorcan, but he had been uncharacteristically unsympathetic and they'd had words. It was rare for Lorcan to lose his temper – he was usually very laid-back – but when she'd kept on about Valerie's impertinence his voice had taken on an edge she rarely heard.

'Will you, for God's sake, give it a break, Tessa? The girl has a point. She only has the weekend to spend time with the baby and she's sharing that flat with Lizzie; she does have to think of her too. Just phone in future and save yourself all this stress. You brought it on yourself,' he'd said irritably.

'She's our grandchild. It's only right that I'd want to spend time with her. Why can't you see that? How come you always take her side?' she said indignantly.

'Tessa, I'm sick of this, sick of it, do you hear me? What has come over you? Why are you behaving like this? Cop on to yourself and give the girl some leeway. She's in a much worse position than you were, don't forget.' He glared at her, his hands thrust into the back pocket of his jeans, his jaw jutting aggressively. They rarely argued, and Tessa knew she'd pushed him too far.

'That's uncalled for,' she protested, stung.

'No it's not. It's time it was said. I've been holding back for too long. And another thing, Tessa, for heaven's sake let Jeff go or he'll always be a mammy's boy and there's nothing worse.' She'd been spitting feathers at *that*. Lorcan was so annoyed he marched out the door, leaving his coffee and sandwiches untouched.

Tessa frowned, remembering the row. Her husband hadn't held back. She knew at some level that he was right. She was harsh with Valerie and she was overprotective of Jeff. But he was her youngest child and the child whose birth had given her the most happiness. Her daughter's conception had been a source of dismay. Her elder son had been born two years later when she was still unsure in her marriage, but Jeff had been conceived during the happiest time in her life, when she'd managed to banish her fears and anxieties, and she and Lorcan had been happy. Jeff was her gift. She'd enjoyed every minute of her pregnancy and when she'd held him in her arms, with Lorcan sitting on the bed beside her, his arm around her, a big smile creasing his face, she had been exquisitely happy.

Her contentment had impacted on their marriage. She wasn't as emotionally demanding of Lorcan. She stopped constantly looking for reassurance that he loved her. She had allowed herself to believe that they were always meant to be. And then Jeff had come home with the news that his girlfriend was pregnant, and all her old demons had surfaced. She'd turned into a she-devil, Tessa admitted. But Valerie just pushed the wrong buttons. And now she held the upper hand, and that was the most galling thing of all, Tessa thought crossly. She stepped under the shower, turning her face up to the warm jets of water and letting some of the tension she was feeling float away.

The christening had been held in Dublin at Valerie's decree. The guests had all met at the church and gone for lunch afterwards, but they had not been invited back to the flat. *That* privilege had been reserved for Carmel, who had stayed overnight. Terence hadn't come to the christening either, and Jeff had told Tessa confidentially that Valerie's father wouldn't be attending any family events connected with his grandchild until he and Valerie were married.

'Don't let that sour little ayatollah dictate to you, Jeff,' she'd said furiously when her son had told her of Terence's edict. How *dare* that dreadful man stand in judgement over her son's behaviour when his own was completely appalling? Her indignation knew no bounds and she was very tempted to go and give him a piece of her mind, but she knew Jeff and Lorcan would be vehemently opposed to her stirring up trouble.

It was hard enough having to bite back her words when she was dealing with Valerie, without having to swallow down her bile with Terence. It was a wonder she hadn't got an ulcer she was so filled with ire, Tessa sighed, rinsing the suds out of her hair, and massaging in conditioner. Tonight she was going to make an effort to enjoy her celebration for Jeff and Briony. Her granddaughter was almost six months old and it would be her first time in her grandparents' house. Valerie Harris should be ashamed of herself for that. Mind, it was her first time in Valerie's parents' home too, so at least Tessa couldn't complain that they were getting more access. She supposed she could understand the girl's reluctance to come home to Rockland's. Tessa had to admit that Lorcan was right: she'd had it easier than Valerie. She'd been able to stay at home with Lisa, having no need to go out to work, *and* she'd been married when she'd given birth. It wasn't easy having a baby out of wedlock, even now, in the eighties, no more than it had been in her day, though attitudes had changed a lot since then. The gossips had had a field day with her, she remembered bitterly. Her poor mother had been plagued with them.

Tessa banished the memories. She didn't want to think of her past. Today was about the future, she told herself firmly, wrapping a towel around her dripping body just as Lorcan came to the top of the stairs.

'The place looks great. Food looks amazing. You're some woman, Tessa,' her husband said approvingly.

'Am I?' she said, pleased at his compliment.

'Yes you are, and I'm a lucky man,' he said warmly, putting his arms around her despite her damp hair and wet shoulders. 'Now listen to me. I know it hasn't been easy for you, and there's a bit of tension with Valerie, but let's try and put all that behind us and enjoy tonight. We've a lot to celebrate and a lot to give thanks for, haven't we?'

Tessa looked into her husband's blue eyes and saw love and kindness mirrored there. She felt a rare *frisson* of happiness. Lorcan *was* so kind to her, so understanding and accepting of her and her moods and insecurities.

Why after all this time did she still doubt that he loved her? He proved it in so many ways and yet she could not accept what he gave her without constantly doubting him. She was a fool, she reproached herself, taking his face tenderly between her hands.

'Yes, we do, Lorcan, and the thing I give most thanks for is having you for a husband. I love you so much. I always have and I always will.'

'And I love you too, Tessa,' he said, bending his head to kiss her tenderly. They drew apart and smiled at each other, and she hugged this rare moment to herself. Its unexpectedness made it even more cherished.

'You'd better hurry and have your shower.' She gave him a little shove.

'Pity I wasn't here twenty minutes ago and we could have had one together,' he teased, giving her ass a pinch as he went into the bathroom.

'Mam, Dad?' she heard her daughter call up the stairs, and her heart lifted even more.

'Hi, Lisa. We're up getting ready.' She leaned over the banisters and smiled down at her eldest child.

'I've brought the cream cakes and chocolate éclairs, and a few dozen chocolate Rice Krispie cakes,' her daughter said enthusiastically. Lisa was such a good, dependable girl, always ready to help out, always ready to shoulder responsibility. Always anxious to please. Had she absorbed her mother's fears and anxieties when she was in the womb? Did she feel she was the 'fixer', the one who had to make things better? Or did all first-born children carry the 'responsibility gene'? It was a thought that bothered Tessa sometimes. Lisa was very like her in looks but not in personality. She was much more like Lorcan there, Tessa reflected, smiling down at her daughter. Tall and willowy, with a mane of auburn hair that fell in a burnished curtain to her shoulders, she had her father's blue eyes. Like two exquisite blue diamonds sparkling and vibrant, they dominated her heart-shaped face. She had Tessa's determined chin and could be stubborn when she got a notion in her head. Now, in the carefree, delightful phase of being a newly wed, she was glowing with happiness, and Tessa gave up a swift prayer that she would always be as happy and blessed.

'Stick the kettle on. I'll be down in ten minutes. I'd better lash on some make-up. All you young ones will be showing me up,' Tessa joked. She dried her hair and took extra care with her make-up, adding blusher to her cheeks and applying some eyeliner, which she usually didn't bother with. She studied the results. 'Not bad,' she approved, noting how the eyeliner emphasized her eyes and made them bigger, and the smoky grey shade she'd used was more suited to her age than the bright blue eyeliner all the girls were using now, *à la* Princess Di.

She'd had her hair cut the previous day and it was shining and well shaped, with only the random grey strands to annoy her. She was wearing the coppery, long-sleeved V-necked jersey silk dress that was Lorcan's favourite, and emphasized her curves and height. Her patent black sling-backs and a single strand of pearls finished off the look. She scrubbed up well enough when she wanted to, Tessa decided, satisfied.

A long low wolf whistle greeted her. 'Who's this gorgeous bird in my bedroom?' Lorcan stood grinning proudly at her. She laughed. He was standing with just a towel wrapped around his slim hips, and his tanned torso and broad shoulders emphasized how fit and lean he still was.

'And who's the sexy hunk?' she asked, trailing a finger along the dark line of hair that snaked down his flat belly.

'If you're not careful I'll throw you on the bed and muss everything up,' he warned, eyes glinting wickedly.

'God, I haven't been thrown on the bed in a while. Pity I'm all dressed up,' she said regretfully. Looking at him standing there, his salt-and-pepper hair cropped tight, showing off the lean plane of his face, and the firmness of his mouth that she loved so much, she felt a sudden rush of desire.

'Feck ya, anyway, Lorcan Egan, stop standing there turning me on, go and get dressed,' she admonished, turning away. He came up behind her and grabbed her, his hands cupping her breasts.

'It's your own fault for looking so sexy in that dress,' he murmured against her ear.

'Stop! Lisa's downstairs,' Tessa giggled as his towel slid off.

'Do you want a quickie?' He was laughing at her, turning her round and kissing her passionately.

'No, we've a party to deal with.' She pushed him away.

'So? Five minutes isn't going to make much of a difference.' His eyes were glinting with amusement and desire, and he kissed her again, a slow deep kiss that she couldn't help responding to.

'Is that a yes?' He drew away.

'OK, close the door,' she said, eagerly pulling off her tights and knickers. 'And mind the dress!' she murmured, pulling it up to her waist as he threw her down on the bed and she wrapped her legs around him, burying her face in his shoulder so her moans of pleasure would be muffled.

It was hot and fast and very satisfying, and she sighed happily as she held him close when it was over. Sex was surprisingly good lately. One of her friends had told her that it was one of the few pluses of rampant oestrogen hormones having a last glorious hurrah before disappearing. Whatever it was, she and Lorcan were making the most of it before decrepitude took over.

'I'd better go and fix myself up,' she said ruefully.

'You'd better. Your hair is sticking up all over the place.' He tweaked a strand and tucked it behind her ear. 'We'd give all those young lot a run for their money, Tess. They think they invented sex,' Lorcan grinned, and she kissed him hard.

'I love you, and never forget that.'

'I won't and I don't,' he said seriously, and they held each other tight for a moment before she went to freshen up, repair the damage to her make-up and sort her bedhead.

'Gosh, Mam, you look fantastic!' her daughter complimented her when Tessa walked into the kitchen looking as though butter wouldn't melt in her mouth.

'Thank you, love. Is the tea made?' she asked, giving her a kiss.

'Sure is. Is Dad having a cuppa?'

'I'd say so. He's just getting dressed. He won't be long.'

'I'm dying to see the baby again – isn't she a little doll?' Lisa bustled around the kitchen, getting cups and putting a selection of cakes on a plate.

'Is she putting the longing on you?' Tessa smiled.

'A bit,' Lisa admitted. 'But we want to have another while to ourselves to enjoy being married.'

'That's a good plan,' Tessa said. 'Once children come the relationship changes and you never have the time for each other that you would like.'

'You and Dad don't do too bad,' Lisa said.

'No, we don't do too bad at all,' Tessa agreed, wondering what her daughter would think if she'd seen them ten minutes ago. Children never thought their parents had sex, she thought with a grin. Lorcan was right, they could give the young ones a run for their money. She should stop whining about getting old, try to get along with Valerie, and make the most of what she had.

The sound of tyres crunching on gravel made Lisa look out the window. 'Here's Jeff and Valerie,' she said.

Tessa felt a little knot in her stomach. Today had been such a good day so far it would be a shame to let bad feeling ruin it. She took a deep breath and went to the back door. 'Hello and welcome,' she called.

'Hello, Tessa,' Carmel said politely. The last time she had been in this house it had been to decide her daughter's future. She wouldn't have minded if she'd never set foot in it again but she wouldn't let Valerie down. 'Are we the first to arrive?'

'I'm glad you're here before the others. That's why I said to Jeff to come a bit early. We can all have a cup of tea and a chat before the hordes descend,' Tessa said lightly, as Valerie came to the door carrying Briony. 'Good Lord, look at the size of her!' she exclaimed. 'Valerie, she looks wonderful. Isn't she growing at a great rate?' She couldn't believe the difference a few weeks had made. Briony was holding her head straight and looking around with interest, and she'd completely lost the helpless tiny baby look.

'Would you like to hold her?' Valerie offered, earning a look of approval from Jeff.

'Would I what?' Tessa held out her arms for her grandchild. 'Help yourselves. Jeff, make a pot of fresh tea, I'm busy,' she said delightedly, cooing at her grandchild. 'Isn't the time flying?' she said as Valerie and Carmel sat at the table and Lisa offered them some of the cream cakes she'd made.

'I was pregnant this time last year.' Valerie took a bite out of an éclair.

'And now look at you.' Lisa smiled at her. 'A gorgeous baby and your figure back to normal. You look terrific, Valerie,' she said admiringly. 'I love your outfit.'

'I got it in A|Wear,' Valerie said, pleased with Lisa's compliment. She liked Jeff's older sister. She was friendly and good-natured, and she loved the baby.

'Love the shoulder pads,' Lisa said admiringly. Valerie was wearing a pair of black trousers and a black silk cami top with a vibrant purple silk wrap-around jacket. It was a very glamorous look, very Princess Diana, but she was glad she'd worn it when she saw how elegant Tessa was. Jeff had told her that she looked 'a million dollars'. She wanted to look her best and she'd left Jeff minding the baby one Saturday while she and Lizzie had spent ages looking for the right outfit.

'Hello, all, and welcome.' Lorcan came into the kitchen, dressed in smart grey trousers and a black shirt opened at the neck. His face lit up when he saw Briony. 'Isn't she a little beauty?' he declared proudly, and laughed when she gurgled up at him, giving him a huge toothless grin.

'Ah-ha, that's the old Egan charm at work.' He smiled at Valerie. 'How are you, Valerie?'

'I'm fine thanks, Lorcan.'

'Settled in back at work?'

'Yeah, I suppose. It's always a bit of a wrench leaving her with the child-minder.' She made a face.

'I'm sure it is. But at least she's thriving,' he said kindly.

'She loves her grub, loves her mashed banana and her potatoes and carrot,' Jeff said proudly, delighted with the fuss that was being made of his daughter.

'Well then, she's her father's daughter.' Tessa laughed. 'You couldn't wait for your solids.'

'And I can't wait for my solids now. I see you made a pot of chowder. Thanks, Ma, you're the best.' He kissed the top of her head.

'I know it's your favourite, and this is your party, so of course I did.' Tessa gave the baby to Lisa, who was waiting patiently for her turn to hold her. 'Get a bit of practice in,' she joked light-heartedly, and they all laughed.

Tessa smiled up at Lorcan, and began to relax. She felt a moment of contentment and happiness. She caught Valerie's gaze. For once there was no hostility or defensiveness mirrored there. Jeff was handing her a cup of tea, and then he had dropped an arm around her shoulder and Tessa thought with a little pang, I think he does love her. Maybe in time they are the ones for each other. Then she remembered Lorcan's admonition . . . 'let him go'.

This was the ideal opportunity to start afresh, she knew that. It was the right thing to do. Tessa held out the olive branch. 'I hope you enjoy our little celebration, Valerie. We really want to introduce Briony to the extended family who haven't seen her yet, and, of course, celebrate

Jeff's exam results. I do know you supported him greatly in his studies so thanks to you for that.' She made her little speech as Lorcan's hand tightened on her shoulder.

'I'd second that. This evening is a joyful celebration for both our families, who are now joined together by this darling little girl, and I hope you and Carmel enjoy the party very much,' he said, smiling at Carmel.

'Enough of the speeches, I want my chowder.' Jeff lightened the moment as everyone turned to look at Valerie.

She turned bright pink. She knew Tessa had given her an unexpected opportunity for a new beginning in their relationship. She looked at her daughter being cosseted and cherished by Jeff's family and was glad of it. Lizzie's words came back to her. 'You and Jeff are in this together. You're Briony's parents. She's your child. Don't use her as a weapon . . . Life is hard, and you and Briony are going to need all the help you can get. Don't cut yourself and her off from a family who are willing to be supportive and hands on. You don't know what's coming down the tracks in the future and it's good to have people in your camp.'

It wasn't all about her any more. It never would be again, and if Tessa could make an effort so could she. She took a deep breath. 'Um . . . thanks very much, Lorcan and Tessa. Mam and I are delighted to be here with Briony. And it's lovely that you are all making such a fuss of us. Jeff and I are very grateful for all the support we've been given. Briony is a very lucky little girl.'

'To Briony,' said Jeff exuberantly.

'And to Valerie and Jeff,' said Lorcan.

Amid laughter and warbles from Briony, teacups were raised in toast to the trio, as the doorbell rang and the guests began to arrive to join in the celebrations.

CHAPTER THIRTY-TWO

Tessa and Lorcan's party *had* been a fresh start, very much so, Valerie remembered, lying in the dark unable to sleep in her bed in Spain, as the torrents of memories flooded through her. From the night of that party, up until Jeff's death four years later, she had been relatively happy, she acknowledged with surprise. It was always that way: you never realized that you were actually happy during stages of your life until you looked back.

The only real sadness had been Lizzie's leaving the following spring, a week after Briony's first birthday. *That* had been hard. Almost as painful as a bereavement.

Even to this day Valerie could still remember the wretchedness of their parting. She had left Jeff minding Briony and had driven to the airport to meet up with Lizzie and Dara and their families. They'd all gone for a drink in one of the airport lounges, after Lizzie and Dara had checked in, and laughed and chatted and kept up a façade for their sakes, but when it was time to go, she and Lizzie had held each other tightly, wordlessly, until Dara had said gently, 'We really have to go, hon.' Watching her best friend disappear through customs, in tears, had been one of the worst moments of her life and she had felt utterly bereft. Valerie had managed to leave the airport without disgracing herself but when she'd got to the privacy of her car she'd cried like a baby all the way home. She had never missed anyone in her life the way she'd missed Lizzie those first few months, all those years ago.

Valerie got out of bed and padded silently into the kitchen to make herself a cup of tea. There was no sound from Briony or Katie's rooms and she hoped her daughter was sleeping. She might feel better in the morning and have calmed down.

She took her tea and a biscuit and went back to bed. There, she picked up the photo album and flipped the pages until she came to Lizzie's wedding. Valerie smiled looking at the photo of Lizzie and herself: Lizzie radiant in a classy white satin boat-necked gown with a veil dropping from her chignon, and Valerie in an aquamarine taffeta silk bridesmaid's dress. Each smiling brightly for the camera but holding hands tightly, knowing that they were soon to be parted. They had seen each other nearly every day of their lives since they'd met and become the best of friends in primary school when they were five. There was nothing they didn't know about each other.

It had been a great wedding, Valerie remembered, flicking through the photos. She had tried her hardest not to be envious of her friend. As she watched Dara place the ring on Lizzie's finger she wondered if Jeff would ever put a wedding ring on hers. Even now, all these years later, she couldn't help wondering if he had lived whether they would have married. They had been happy living together, for the most part, and one thing that had given her great comfort and sustained her in her darkest hours was that Jeff had been a wonderful father. He loved Briony with all his heart. He was involved in every aspect of her life, and until the day he died she had been the centre of his universe.

A photo of Jeff holding Briony, with his arm around Valerie's shoulder, outside the church was one that she'd had copied and framed. Briony's new front teeth were on show in a big grin that dominated the photo. Jeff looked so handsome in his suit and tie, his brown eyes crinkling in a smile that still tugged at her heart even now as she looked at it. She had given the framed photo to Briony years ago and she wondered if her daughter still had it.

Another photo of Lizzie and herself with Mrs Maguire caught her attention. Mrs Maguire had had a ball at the wedding, thrilled to be invited, along with her daughter. She had thoroughly enjoyed herself and got quite tipsy to boot. Valerie chuckled, remembering how their landlady had said to the two of them at one stage when they were chatting, 'Could you tell me now, gels, what are these plutonic relationships between men and women that I've been hearing about?'

'Platonic, I think,' corrected Lizzie, winking at Valerie.

'No, plutonic, deah, *plu*tonic,' Mrs M insisted resolutely.

'I think it's when a man and woman are just friends and there's no . . . er, romance or stuff like that,' explained Lizzie.

'Aha . . . I see. No riding to hounds.' Mrs M nodded wisely.

'Exactly!' Lizzie agreed with a straight face, while Valerie tried not to laugh.

'Ah, yes, well, I've plenty of them, unfortunately. Wouldn't mind a bit of hound riding, though. I can safely say the pair of you aren't very plutonic with *your* chaps,' she tittered before tottering off on her spindly heels to get another G&T, her wide-brimmed pink hat with the big bow bobbing and dipping tremulously with every step.

How she and Lizzie had snorted with laughter, holding each other up. 'She's priceless. I love her dearly. I'll miss her so much.' Lizzie wiped her eyes.

'Stop. Don't talk about it,' Valerie warned as the familiar ache of dread and sadness took hold.

She had sobbed inconsolably when Lizzie had thrown her bouquet at her, and made her way with Dara through the archway formed by family and friends to the waiting car to head off to Malta on her honeymoon.

Jeff had taken her outside and put his arms around her and she had cried into his shoulder, drenching his shirt with tears. 'You still have me and Briony,' he comforted her. 'And we'll be able to go and visit them in London. *And* I'll be moving into the flat so you won't be too lonely,' he reminded her.

That was the saving grace of the upheaval. Jeff had moved in the week after Lizzie moved out, and having him there helped take the ache of loneliness away. Those early years of Briony's life were the happiest times of her own. If she had been married to Jeff it would have been perfect. But he hadn't been keen to marry until they were on a better footing financially and able to buy their own house. She could never erase the secret fear that that was his excuse to avoid marrying her and that one day he'd leave her and find someone new, even though he would always be a good father to Briony.

But that apart, when she'd told him that Lizzie was going to live in London in the next six months, he'd jumped at the idea of living in the flat with her and Briony, and that had given her great joy. They had had ups and downs, of course, settling into living together, and sometimes she had felt as though she was giving much more to their relationship than Jeff was. Being a working mother was hard, especially when Briony had begun teething and was often fretful and out of sorts. The nights of interrupted sleep took their toll. Sometimes she felt she was in a permanent state of exhaustion. Valerie sighed, remembering one particularly fraught weekend when she and Jeff had planned to go to a friend's twenty-first party. They had been so looking forward to it and she had been thrilled that she could fit into her favourite jeans again. She'd bought a new off-the-shoulder lacy top and had got her hair cut and styled. She was feeling glamorous and stylish for the first time in ages. A babysitter was lined up, one of Mrs Maguire's grandchildren, and Valerie had been fizzing with anticipation for her night out with Jeff. Briony had been grizzly, her cheeks roaring red, dribbling a river onto her bib, and Valerie's heart sank as she felt the heat radiating from her. She slipped the thermometer under her arm and saw with dismay that her daughter had a fever.

'Ah, she'll be grand. Can't you give her some of the Calpol stuff?' Jeff said in desperation, seeing his chance for his eagerly awaited night out in danger. But Briony had got more distressed and had howled in pain as the sharp edge of her new tooth pushed its way up through her gums.

The babysitter arrived as Valerie was pacing up and down trying to soothe her daughter while Jeff waited with ill-concealed impatience for her to get her coat and bag. Without warning Briony upchucked over Valerie's new top, her howls rising to a crescendo of pain and indignation.

'I can't leave her,' she had said resignedly. 'I'll have to stay put. Sorry, Maria,' she turned to her babysitter, 'I'll have to cancel.'

'No worries. I can meet up with friends in town. I hope Briony will be OK,' she said kindly. Valerie watched her go and envied Maria her freedom.

'I'll stay too.' Jeff's disappointment was palpable. He'd pulled off his leather jacket and flung it over the banisters.

'You might as well go. There's no point in the two of us missing the party.' Valerie had felt she should give him an out.

Jeff had taken it eagerly. He'd grabbed his jacket. 'Are you sure? I'll stay if you want,' he offered half-heartedly.

'No, go on, it's OK.' She took Briony into the bathroom to take off her soiled babygrow, seething with resentment as she heard Jeff say, 'Thanks, Val, I won't be too late,' before taking the stairs two at a time.

By 2 a.m. Valerie was in a state of rampant indignation lying tense in the bed, Briony dozing beside her, as she silently railed at Jeff's selfishness and lack of consideration. He was so self-centred and inconsiderate. Briony was *his* child too. He should have known she hadn't really meant it when she'd told him he could go to the party. If he had any decency in him he would have stayed with her to mind their daughter. When he arrived home after four, wafting alcohol fumes, she could have strangled him.

'You can sleep on the sofa,' she had hissed when he'd sat down heavily on the side of the bed to take his shoes off. 'I'm not listening to you snoring in a drunken stupor for the rest of the night.'

'I'm not that drunk,' he'd protested.

'I mean it,' she'd retorted grimly, and he'd taken his pillows and sloped off into the sitting room, and minutes later she'd heard him snoring his head off.

'He's a man – what do you expect?' one of the girls at work had joshed the following Monday morning at tea break when they'd been discussing their respective weekends.

'You think that's bad. My chap went on a stag night and left me with a baby with measles, and I had to entertain his parents, who were staying for the weekend, and he didn't come home until midday the following day!'

'And my husband . . .' another woman had interjected, beginning another tale of bad behaviour. Valerie felt a sense of kinship with her colleagues as their tales took the sting out of Jeff's night out. She had got over her huff, realizing that men were indeed a different species, as one of her colleagues had pointed out, and that being a mother meant she would never be able to plan a night out without factoring in some potential hiccup, for many years to come.

The novelty of living with Jeff, of having her dinner with him when he came up from Rockland's after a day's fishing, and eating breakfast with him in the mornings, had been all she'd ever dreamed off. Bathing Briony with him, and putting her to bed, and then being able to sit together and watch TV and share a bottle of wine was such a treat. Best of all was falling onto the double-sized mattress that Mrs Maguire had graciously allowed them to place on top of the divans, and making love. This all helped her make her adjustments to motherhood and cohabiting. But most of all living with Jeff soothed the pain of Lizzie's departure. She missed her friend dearly and the weekly phone calls on Sunday night were treasured by both of them.

Eight months after Jeff had moved in with her he'd got a job in an engineering firm in Arklow. It was a good job with prospects for promotion. He was lucky to have found it because of the hardships and difficulties posed by an economy in the doldrums, mass emigration, strikes, and protests. Valerie, like most of her colleagues, had taken an afternoon of precious annual leave to walk in the huge PAYE protest march through the streets of Dublin. If Jeff hadn't had his father's boat to work on he would have been one of the thousands of unemployed and could have faced the prospect of emigration.

They had spent long hours discussing this new development. Would Jeff commute to Arklow from Dublin or should they move back to Rockland's? Valerie loved living in the city. Everything was on her doorstep, every amenity she required, and most comfortably, Temple Street Children's Hospital for emergencies, even though she'd only had need of it once. It took her just twenty minutes to drive to work, so she had more valuable time to spend with her daughter every morning, making sure that she was dressed and fed before delivering her to Anna, her child-minder. If they went back to Rockland's to live, she would have to commute to the city and that would take at least an hour. But – and it was a big but – Carmel and Tessa had offered to share the child-minding between them, and both Jeff and Valerie liked the idea of their daughter being with family in familiar surroundings, with two grand-mothers who adored her. It would also save them a fortune on crèche fees, money they could put aside for a house of their own, and they'd be able to get out more often, having two willing babysitters. And the rent would be cheaper. There were a lot of pluses to moving back to Rockland's.

Jeff was keen to go home. He could still fish occasion-ally with his father to make extra money and he could train and play football with his team, much easier than when he had been living in Dublin.

'What do you think?' Valerie had asked Lizzie during one of their Sunday night phone calls.

'I'd give it a bash. With what you save, and with the extra money from Jeff's new job, you could start saving for a house of your own. If it doesn't work out and you're not happy you can always move back up to Dublin. You have a couple of years' leeway until Briony starts going to school,' Lizzie pointed out.

'I love Dublin, though,' Valerie sighed.

'Think of picnics on the beach, and picking periwin-kles, and walking into a dewy field early in the morning looking for mushrooms and then frying them for break-fast. Think of the cuckoo in Larkin's field in May, and the wind whispering through a field of barley, and the smell of new-mown hay and the shooting stars in August,' Lizzie said wistfully. 'I never appreciated all those things when I had them and now I'd give anything to be at home sometimes. I'm still *sooooo* homesick,' she confided.

'Aw, my poor petal. I wish you were here. I'd love one of our video nights,' Valerie said longingly. 'We used to have so much fun.'

'Don't let's talk about it or I'll cry. Some of the girls from school still live at home. It's not as if you wouldn't know anyone if you went back.' Lizzie changed the subject. It was making her lonely talking about the past. 'I bet Carmel would love it.'

'Yeah, she'd be thrilled and so would Tessa, needless to say, but in fairness she's a great granny, and Lorcan is so kind to us. As long as Tessa wouldn't start interfering, although she's much better than she used to be. Remember the time she caught us lolling in our pyjamas and the flat like a tip?'

'You sorted her out, though,' Lizzie laughed. 'And you don't have to live in the village. You might get a house on the outskirts. See what sort of a house you get before you decide.'

'There's one down past the railway station, a two-bed with big sash windows – I love them – and it has sea views. It's for rent. We had a look at it last weekend when Jeff was down playing a match. It's got a big garden with a swing in it, and a fireplace as well as central heating, and a small pantry, and a room that was used as a nursery with an old-fashioned rocking horse—'

'Oh, Valerie, grab it! I know the one you're talking about. It's perfect, and not on top of Tessa, or Terence, for that matter. It's just far enough away but not too far.'

'We both liked it a lot.' Valerie felt a tingle of excitement. Lizzie's descriptions of the rural beauty had brought back some very happy memories. Briony too

could have such memories if they came back to the country to live.

'Go for it then.'

'I think I will,' Valerie said slowly. Talking to Lizzie
had helped sort her head . . . as it always did.

'Poor Mrs M will be devastated, though,' Lizzie said.

'I know. She's a bit shaky lately. She went on a bit of a
binge recently and had to go into hospital. I think her
daughter wants her niece to come and live with her, so if
we were gone she could have the upstairs flat.'

'Maybe it's just as well to start thinking of moving. The
poor old dear can't go on for ever,' Lizzie reflected. 'And
I'd better move on or my beloved husband will have a fit
when the phone bill comes. I love ya, Val. Kiss my
godchild for me,' she instructed, and then she was gone,
and Valerie, as usual, couldn't believe that twenty minutes
had passed so quickly.

'So are we moving back then?' Jeff asked eagerly when
she told him about her conversation with Lizzie.

'Sure, we can give it a try and see how it works out,'
she said slowly. Jeff swung her off her feet in a bear hug
and she laughed happily and wrapped her arms around
him.

'You know my dad will be giving out because we're
living together in sin. That's what he'll say,' she said that
night as they cuddled up in bed after making love. It was
an opportunity to see whether marriage was on his
radar.

'Let's take one thing at a time, move home and settle
in,' he said sleepily, and moments later he was snoring.

The trouble was she didn't want to have to issue an
ultimatum. She didn't want him to feel he *had* to marry

her. She wanted Jeff to *want* to marry her. She wanted the romantic proposal and the engagement ring that he would want her to have. If it were to make her happy and mean anything it had to come from him without her prompting or she'd never be at ease about it. But Jeff was the sort who was happy to drift along without much forward planning. She knew him of old and knew that for the next six months at least much of his focus would be on his new job. He wouldn't want to be sidetracked by any talks of an engagement or a wedding. She might as well face it, for the foreseeable future she would not be Mrs Jeffery Harris.

Pragmatic as ever, Valerie decided she could live with that for the time being, and she would try not to get too stressed about it, otherwise she would be a basket case and their home would be far from happy. It was the only way she could deal with it.

They had moved to Rockland's just before Briony's second birthday, waved off by a tearful Mrs M, who had told Jeff that if things didn't work out he was to 'bring my gels straight back to me, deah'. Valerie had wept most of the journey home, but a couple of weeks later, when they had held Briony's birthday party and the April sun had streamed in through the big windows, and laughter and chat had echoed through the house, and Carmel had cut the fresh cream sponge she had baked, and after Briony had blown out her candles with squeals of delight, Valerie knew she had done the right thing.

Now, all those years later, remembering what a happy early childhood her daughter had had, waves of guilt washed over Valerie as she finally had to face up to the consequences of her cutting the Egans out of their lives.

'Don't think about it now,' she muttered.

She closed the photo album and switched off the light. She was terribly tired. Surely sleep would come soon. Thinking about that happy time in Rockland's made her feel even sadder. Because the worst thing that had ever happened to her had happened there. The thing that formed her for the rest of her life and made her who she was and act the way she did. The instance in her life that had caused her unbearable grief was raising its ugly head again to cause her yet more grief. Grief she didn't think she could endure. That dark, dark Sunday that had blighted her life for ever. She couldn't bear even now to think of it.

Think of something different, something nice, something good and uplifting, she urged herself in desperation, frantically searching through her memories for one that would chase the black thoughts that loomed so threateningly.

'*Sailor, stop your roaming . . .*' The words of one of Petula Clark's biggest hits drifted into her mind. A favourite song of Jeff's. On his birthday she had cooked a special meal, the one he liked best – steak, fried onions and chips – to celebrate. She'd had a Chianti bottle with a red candle lit in it in the middle of the table, and a tape of his favourite songs that she'd compiled for him.

'Dance with me,' she'd said when Petula's husky tones filled their homely kitchen, the flames of the fire throwing flickering shadows on the walls.

He'd rested his cheek against hers, and she'd caressed the back of his head, running her fingers through his springy thick hair.

Sailor, stop your roaming
Sailor, leave the sea.
Sailor, when the tide turns
Come home safe to me.

As you sail across the sea
All my love is there beside you
From Capri or Amsterdam,
Honolulu or Siam
To the harbour of my heart
I will send my love to guide you
As l call across the sea
Come home to me.

She'd sung along against his cheek and he'd held her tight. She'd felt an overpowering love for him as they'd swayed to the music in the flickering candlelight.

'I love coming home to you and Briony,' he murmured into her hair, and Valerie felt a moment of pure, exquisite happiness.

It was the last time they'd danced together. A week later, Jeff was dead.

Chapter Thirty-Three

'I'm not thinking about it. No! No! No! I don't want to. I don't want to. I don't want to,' Valerie moaned, burying her head in her pillow, muffling her sobs at the memory of the last loving special occasion she'd ever had with Jeff. Why were these recollections so real, so vivid? Had she not let them go all those years ago? It was all Tessa's fault, Tessa and that damn letter. The woman who had ruined her life once before was back haunting her with a vengeance. She would not think about that terrible day Jeff died, and the vicious row that followed. She could not go back to the days of dark despair. It would destroy her.

But like a storm that would not be halted, the crucifying memories crept inexorably back, back to that warm early September Sunday afternoon when Jeff had been playing a football match and she and Briony had been picking shells on the beach.

'Oohh, look, Mommy. Look, a merrymaid shell!' Briony exclaimed excitedly, picking up a pearly hued conch as the water swirled around their feet and the sand sucked them down into warm squelchy puddles. A faint haze tempered the sun. Seagulls glided high, dipping and diving, and a lazy lethargy permeated the air. They were the only ones on the small golden curve of strand that was just a few minutes' walk from the house, the beach on the far side of the harbour being the more popular one for tourists.

'Valerie, Valerieeee!' She looked up to the top of the sand dunes and saw her mother calling her. Why was Carmel looking for her? Had she, on impulse, brought a picnic to share with them? A sudden fear swept over Valerie as she saw her mother's agitation and the way she was waving and skittering down the dunes. Something was wrong! She could not tell how or why she knew, she just knew.

She left Briony filling her bucket with water, slipped into her espadrilles and raced to where Carmel was slogging down through the soft sand. 'What's the matter? What's wrong?' She was feeling sick with apprehension.

'Jeff took some sort of a turn when he was playing his match and an ambulance has taken him to the hospital. Your father's in the car over the dunes, ready to take you there. I'll mind Briony.' Carmel was pale and panting.

'What happened? What sort of a turn? Did he break his ankle, his arm?' Valerie was bewildered at her mother's agitation. A broken limb often came with the territory when playing football.

'No, I don't think so, I think he just collapsed.' Carmel's lip was trembling.

'Jesus, Mam, you're frightening me. Is he OK?' Valerie was faint with anxiety.

'Just go quickly with your da so you can be with him.' Carmel gave her a shove up the dunes. 'Go on,' she urged. 'Briony will be fine with me. I have your spare key.' She watched as her daughter went ghost white and took off across the beach, her hair flying behind her.

'Our Lady, Mother of Mothers, who watched your son die, comfort and protect my poor daughter through this trial of pain and grief,' Carmel prayed, tears streaming down her face as she walked towards the water's edge to her grandchild, knowing what was awaiting Valerie.

Valerie cursed as the soft sand slowed her down. What the hell was going on? Jeff must have fainted or something. He was never sick, though, and he was as fit as a fiddle. All his training and the hard physical work on the boat meant he was toned and strong and vigorous. But something bad must be going on if her da was taking her to the hospital.

She was red-faced and out of breath when she made it to where the car was parked on the small narrow lane behind the dunes.

Terence had the car door open and the engine running. 'Put your seat belt on,' was all he said as she got into the car.

'What's wrong with Jeff?' Her fingers were trembling as she tried to fix the clasp into the lock.

'He took a turn playing his match and the ambulance was called for him. Seanie Reilly said you should come. The Egans have been told too.' Terence revved the engine and the wheels spun in the dirt track before getting traction.

'But he's going to be OK, isn't he?' she demanded anxiously.

'Look, just stay calm and see what the story is when we get there,' Terence said in a kindly tone that she had not heard from him since she was a child. That more than anything frightened the living daylights out of her and she sat beside him as he sped towards the hospital, her hands clenched tightly in her lap, wondering was this all a bad dream and would she wake up from of it and feel utter relief.

She knew it was no nightmare when she saw Tessa and Lorcan's faces as they stood shell-shocked and distraught in a hospital corridor outside a room where she and Terence had been directed.

'Valerie,' Lorcan said, holding his arms out to her. She felt very frightened. Something bad had happened and she didn't want to hear about it. She grasped Lorcan's hand. 'I want to see him. I want to talk to him. What's wrong with Jeff? Where is he?' she asked on a rising note of hysteria.

'Jeff's dead,' Tessa said slowly as if she were testing out the words. 'Jeff's dead.'

'What?' Valerie couldn't comprehend what the older woman was saying.

'Jeff's dead,' repeated Tessa, dazed.

'Noooooo!' wailed Valerie in a low strangled howl. 'No! No! No!' She put her hands over her ears. This wasn't happening. If she couldn't hear the words they weren't real.

Lorcan took her hands in his and lowered them. She could see his lips moving, could hear him speak as though from some great distance.

'Valerie, do you want to see him or do you want to remember him how he was when he was alive and have those images to comfort you? You have to decide and you must do what's right for you.' His face sagged with grief.

A nurse came out of the room. 'You can go in now,' she said gently.

Valerie pulled away from Lorcan and raced past the nurse. There had to be some mistake. This wasn't real.

'Jeff, Jeff,' she called, frantically hurrying into the room and coming to a halt when she saw the pale, waxy figure lying on a bed, a crisp white sheet pulled neatly up to his shoulders.

'Jeff,' she whispered, perplexed, 'talk to me.' He lay with a half-smile on his face, as though he were asleep, his hair mussed against the pillow, but pale, so pale and white. She reached out and touched him, expecting to feel his warm skin beneath her hand. Then, and only then, when she felt the marble coldness of him, did the awful realization hit. Tessa, sobbing, came to stand at the other side of the bed.

'Jeff, my darling, darling son,' she wept. 'God, I will never forgive you for taking him from me. Oh, darling, darling, darling child, why have you left me, you who had your whole life ahead of you, who had so much living to do? Why, Jeff, why?'

'No,' cried Valerie frantically. 'Stop saying that. He's not dead. He's not. Jeff, sit up, sit up now and talk to me. Stop messing!' She grabbed him by the shoulder and tried to shake him.

'For God's sake, Valerie, stop it! Stop it!' Tessa exclaimed, horrified.

'I won't. He isn't dead,' Valerie cried hysterically, trying to lift Jeff up from the pillow.

Tessa hurried to the other side of the bed and took her by the arm. 'Come outside if you can't control yourself, shaking him like that. What are thinking of? He's not messing, you stupid girl, he's *dead*!' She bustled her out of the door.

'Let go of me,' Valerie shrieked, incensed as Tessa's fingers gripped her upper arm hard. 'You can't push me around. I have as much right to be in there as you have. I love him too, you know.'

'If you can't behave in a proper manner I'm not letting you near my son, do you hear me? ' Tessa hissed. 'Show some decorum.'

'You can't stop me going in there,' Valerie protested, weak with shock.

'I can. You're not next of kin,' Tessa retorted grimly.

Valerie stared at her. 'How can you say that?' she stuttered.

'Because it's true. So behave yourself.' Tessa was shaking with grief.

'It's all your fault. If it wasn't for you I'd be married to him and Briony would be legitimate, and now that's never going to happen. Are you satisfied now you've got your way for good, Tessa? You selfish, mean-spirited woman. Now what are we going to do?' Valerie demanded, her voice rising.

'How *dare* you speak to me like that, Valerie Harris?' Tessa's red-rimmed eyes blazed with fury. Her face was so contorted with anger Valerie took a step back. 'You listen to me, you little madam, and listen well. If Jeff had wanted to marry you he would have, but he told me he didn't love you enough and he wasn't sure, that time when you got pregnant, and *that*'s why I wouldn't have it. You only marry someone because you *want* to, not because you *have* to!' Tessa shouted. 'Don't you understand that?'

'Tessa! Stop it!' Lorcan grabbed his wife by the arm while Terence turned and glared at them.

'I'm sorry for your loss,' he said, 'but I'm even more sorry for her, who can't even call herself a widow.' He

jerked his thumb in Valerie's direction. 'And that illegitimate child, who will never now have a proper father
because you lot wouldn't do the right thing.'

'You have some nerve, Terence Harris, to talk to us like
that. Jeff was a better father than you ever were,' Tessa
raged. 'You wouldn't even go to your own grandchild's
christening, you little old weasel, you. I won't take any
lectures from the likes of *you*. Now get out of here, the
both of you, and let us grieve in peace.' She pulled away
from Lorcan, who was trying to shush them all, and went
back into the room.

'Valerie, please, Tessa's not in her right mind. Don't
let's have harsh words. Jeff wouldn't want it,' Lorcan
pleaded as she began sobbing uncontrollably.

'I'm bringing you home,' Terence said gruffly. 'Come
on.'

'Terence, I want Valerie to help make the arrangements.
It's her right. I'll be in touch,' Lorcan said agitatedly as he
went to comfort his distraught wife.

Valerie had no recollection of the journey home. She
walked into the house she'd shared with Jeff and went
upstairs to her daughter's room. Briony was asleep, her
thumb in her mouth, her hair half over her face. Valerie
gently tucked it behind her ear and felt so lonesome as she
stared down at her sleeping child. How would she explain
to Briony that she would never see her daddy again?

Carmel was sitting on the window-seat on the landing,
waiting for her to come out. 'I'll stay the night. Come
down and have some tea,' she urged.

'I just want to go to bed,' Valerie said flatly. 'I just want
to be on my own, Mam.' She went into the bedroom and
undressed, and took the T-shirt Jeff had been wearing

that morning and pulled it over her head. She could get the scent of him, the manly tang of his sweat and that faint hint of Old Spice aftershave. 'The Mark of a Man,' Lizzie used to tease him when the ad came on TV. She'd have to tell Lizzie and tell her boss that she'd be away from work for a while, but not now. Nothing now except her and Jeff.

She drew the curtains on the red-tinted dusk that was beginning to darken the sea and sky, and got into Jeff's side of the bed. She lay her head on his pillow, inhaled deep breaths and closed her eyes. He was here with her, she told herself. She could smell him, feel him. He wasn't dead; it was all a bad dream. Soon he would come into the room, full of life and vigour, shouting 'We won, we won, and I scored. You should have been there. Are you proud of me or what?'

And she would say, as she always did, 'Of course I'm proud of you. You're my hero, aren't you?' And kiss him passionately.

He'd be here soon, she knew it, she kept telling herself, but the dusk turned to indigo and then black, and Jeff never came. Then Valerie, shocked and petrified at how such a blow could be dealt to her so randomly and unanticipated, knew her life would never be the same. If Jeff could be taken from her, so too could Briony, her mother, Lizzie, anyone she held dear. Even she herself could be taken, she thought in shock.

> *Because I could not stop for Death –*
> *He kindly stopped for me –*
> *The Carriage held but just Ourselves –*
> *And Immortality.*

The Emily Dickinson poem she had studied for her Leaving Certificate came unexpectedly to her mind. Had Death been kind? Or a betrayer? His polite and courteous way just an illusion?

When Death had stopped for Jeff had he felt any pain or terror? Where was he now? What was he doing? Could he see them still? Hear them? Or was he trapped in that cold immobile body in the hospital? Was there nothing more for him?

'Jeff, where are you? Come back to me,' she called, sitting up. She strained in the dark, listening to see if he would answer, desperate for the comfort of some sign that Jeff had not abandoned her, but all she felt was the faintest breath of a breeze caressing her forehead.

It was such a hot, muggy night in London. Lizzie lay in bed in her flat in Kensal Rise with just a sheet over her, listening to her husband snoring rhythmically beside her. She had felt a strange sense of unease all day. What was wrong with her? Was it PMT? She hadn't got to call Valerie today because they had been at the afters of a wedding and it had been too late when she got home. She was going back to Rockland's for a few days soon and she couldn't wait to see everyone. She was looking forward so much to seeing family and friends.

She was especially longing to see Valerie and Briony, and she and Valerie planned to visit Mrs M, who was now in a nursing home. Lizzie would enjoy the trip to Dublin with her best friend. It would be nice seeing their old landlady who, according to Valerie, was still as spirited as ever. Drowsiness overcame her and she lay in that relaxed state between waking and sleeping as thoughts flitted in and out of her brain. Three sharp raps on the window jolted her into wakefulness.

'What in the name of God was that?' she muttered, sitting bolt upright. Beside her, Dara snored on, blithely unaware of his wife's angst. She slid out of bed, went over to the window and stared down into the empty street. Not a sinner around. Just leaves dropping stealthily onto cars and pavements as the trees slowly discarded their autumn costumes. Apprehension wrapped itself around her. Lizzie knew what the knocks on the window were; she had heard them before when both her grandparents had died. Someone close had passed. Someone was saying goodbye. If it were family her mother would have phoned. Was anyone sick or ailing that she could think of? Lizzie did a quick review of elderly relatives but couldn't think of anyone to be greatly concerned about.

Troubled, she got into bed and snuggled close to Dara. 'God Bless you, whoever you are. Safe journey home,' she whispered, dreading the phone's ring and the sorrow that would surely follow.

CHAPTER THIRTY-FOUR

'I want him home, here with us.' Tessa paced up and down the kitchen, her face drawn and pale after a sleepless night of grief and torment.

'He's Briony's father, he's Valerie's partner – she has some say, Tessa,' Lorcan argued tiredly.

'He's *my* son. I bore him, I'll bury him.' Tessa was implacable. 'We'll have the wake in the sitting room. He can look out over the sea one last time. And if *she's* coming to see him –' the word was said with the utmost disdain – 'I'm going upstairs. I want to have nothing to do with her.'

'Ah, Tessa, for the love of God—'

'Here's the Farrells. Let them in. I want to ring the undertaker.' Tessa marched out to the phone in the hall. Lorcan shook his head in despair. Tessa was like a woman possessed; there was no reasoning with her.

An hour later, Lorcan drew up outside Valerie's house. Briony and Valerie's mother were playing in the garden.

'Lorcan, I'm so sorry for your loss.' Carmel came to him and took his hand in hers.

'I know you are,' he said quietly. 'But, Carmel, I'm sure you've heard, Tessa and Valerie had words and it's very difficult. I want to talk to Valerie and see what her wishes are regarding the funeral. Tessa wants to wake him at home.'

'She's inside. She's in shock. And I know the circumstances are problematic and the reality is that because they weren't married she has no say. She's not next of kin. So whatever kindness you can offer my daughter in this regard, Lorcan, I'll be very grateful for it,' Carmel said sadly, knowing that he wasn't causing the problems. She had spent the morning explaining to Valerie that despite the fact that they were living together for the past three years and had a child, because she was not married to Jeff she had no say at all, legally, in his funeral arrangements. She was not the one asked to identify his body, or the one to whom custody of his body was given. That had been Tessa.

Valerie had been so numb with shock, Carmel wondered whether her daughter had heard any of what she'd said, but just before Carmel had taken Briony out to play, Valerie had stood looking out to sea.

'I'm not going to fight her for him. She never wanted to let him go. She was always telling him what to do. If he'd really wanted to he could have stood up to her more. But he didn't. And he never asked me to marry him. And that makes me feel bitter and angry. And I have to live with that for the rest of my life. Fighting with her in the hospital was horrible. I won't lower myself to her level again,' she said resolutely.

'She *has* lost a child,' Carmel said gently. 'Time will ease the pain for both of you although you won't think it now. I'm glad you've come to this decision. It's the best for you and Briony right now.'

'He did love me, you know. Just not enough to marry me.' Her face crumpled and she dissolved into tears.

'I know he did, Valerie. And perhaps he would have married you in time.' Carmel held her weeping daughter and silent tears slid down her own cheeks. There was nothing she could do to prevent Valerie going through this heart-wrenching sorrow. She felt utterly helpless in the face of it. She'd taken Briony out into the garden so she wouldn't see her mother's distress. She'd been surprised when Jeff's father had arrived.

Lorcan Egan was doing his best, Carmel acknowledged as she looked at his exhausted, grey-tinged face. 'I have to try and stand up for my daughter, just as Tessa feels she has to do the same for Jeff. But she's not going to fight any more. Tessa can do what she wants for the funeral.'

'I understand that, Carmel, and I'll do my best for Valerie. Try not to judge Tessa too harshly. She's demented with grief,' Lorcan said, and his eyes lit up as he saw his grandchild hurrying towards him.

'Gandad. Gandad.' Briony flung herself at him, hugging his leg tightly and he lifted her up and swung her in the air as he always did and she shrieked with delight.

'Hello, sweetheart. Who's the best little girl in the whole wide world?' he said as he always did, while she pulled his hair and his heart caught as he saw how much she resembled Jeff when she turned her head to look down at him.

'I have to talk to Mammy, chicken. I'll be back out in a minute,' he said, regretfully lowering her gently to the ground. He followed Carmel into the house. Valerie was sitting at the kitchen table staring unseeingly out of the window.

'Are you OK, Valerie?' he asked, more out of politeness and something to say. Clearly she wasn't. How could she be? 'I need to talk to you about the arrangements,' he said, sitting beside her at the table while Carmel filled the kettle. 'Is there anything you'd like to be done? Any hymns or prayers in the Mass you'd like included? Have you thought about it at all?'

'Not really, Lorcan,' Valerie said dully. 'Because he's not mine to bury, he's not mine to make arrangements for. He's Tessa's. He always was and now he always will be.'

'No.' Lorcan shook his head. 'He's as much yours as ours, and he's Briony's daddy. We must all remember that.'

'She's too young to know what's going on. She'll have no memories of this. I won't be bringing her to the funeral.'

'Bring her to the Mass, at least,' he urged. 'When she's older that will mean something to her.'

'OK,' she said reluctantly.

'Do you mind if we wake him at home?' Lorcan asked hesitantly.

Valerie looked at him, her blue eyes cloudy with grief. 'I've already said, Lorcan, he's yours. Do what you want to do.'

'Will you come and see him in the house? You can be with him by yourself, if you'd like that. Just tell me what *you* want,' Lorcan said, so earnestly that she felt sorry for him. He had always been very kind to her.

'All right, I'll come, as long as I don't have to see Tessa,' she said quietly.

'That's OK,' he said. 'I'll sort that for you, and if you think of anything for the Mass that you'd like, let me know. Ring me at any time of the night or day, Valerie, if you need me. *Any time!*' he emphasized.

Carmel placed a mug of tea in front of him. 'Did you find out what happened to Jeff?' she asked.

'They're doing the autopsy today but they think it was a heart attack.' Lorcan swallowed hard and his eyes filled with tears.

'A heart attack! But he's too young. He was never sick!' Valerie exclaimed.

Lorcan nodded, unable to speak.

'Oh, Lorcan, don't.' Valerie stood up and put her arms around him and they wept together, their tears mingling on each other's cheeks, holding each other tightly. Carmel silently left them to their grief and went out to push Briony on the swing.

'It's unbelievable.' Lorcan drew away from Valerie a while later. 'Never a day sick in his life and as strong as an ox. What will we do without him?'

'I think I'm in a dream,' she confessed.

'I know.'

'If I write him a letter can I put it in the coffin?'

'Of course you can, pet. Anything you want, just tell me.' Lorcan wiped his eyes with his sleeve.

'I'll get Briony to draw him a picture,' Valerie said. 'Yes, a letter and a picture, that's what we'll do.'

'I'll ring you when I know more about when we're getting him home, and then we'll make the funeral arrangements. Have you told Lizzie?'

'Yeah, I phoned her this morning. She heard three knocks on the window last night so she knew someone had died, but she got an awful shock when she heard it was Jeff.' Valerie's lip wobbled. Saying the words 'Jeff' and 'died' together was surreal.

'Did she hear the knocks?' Lorcan was astonished.

'I always thought that was folklore,' Valerie admitted.

'Oh, no, it's very real. It's considered a gift in my part of the country. A gift that someone would knock to say goodbye. But then she was very good to Jeff, letting him stay in the flat and everything. He always had the height of praise for her.' Lorcan took a draught of tea as she sat down beside him again.

'Lizzie's a great friend. The best,' Valerie said.

'Lean on her. Lean on everyone who offers you their shoulder and lean on me,' Lorcan said. He stood up to go. 'Things will settle down again between you and Tessa. She's a hothead and always was, but she's got a big heart, Valerie, and Jeff was her favourite although she would never let on.'

'I know, Lorcan,' Valerie nodded, but that was just to pacify him and treat him kindly because she knew she would never have any dealings with Tessa Egan again. That woman would never get to hurt her like she had in the past. Jeff's death cut any ties that bound her and his mother. Lorcan she would always care for.

'I'll ring you,' he said, giving her a hug, and then he was gone. She could hear him making Briony squeal again with another swing in the air.

Valerie sat numbly in the kitchen after he had left. It was so strange, but she still expected Jeff to barge through the door any minute with his football kit, saying, 'Any chance of a cup of coffee?' while he filled the washing machine with his mucky gear. Or to hear him say, 'I'll get the dinner today – will I make my special *coq au vin*?' Or, 'Can we get a babysitter? I want to bring my doll out for a drink.'

She'd never hear him say those things to her again. She would see him in his coffin, see that coffin buried deep in the ground and that was it. That would be her last contact with Jeff. She heard Lorcan's car drive off and went out to call Briony inside.

'Darling, come and draw a picture for Daddy. He's going up to Holy God and we won't see him until it's our turn to go up, so draw the best picture you can and pick out a nice present to give him,' she said, kissing her daughter's bouncy curls.

'But why is he going? Does Holy God want him to do some work for him?' Briony studied her intently. 'You have red eyes, Mammy, why are your eyes red?'

'Hay fever,' fibbed Valerie.

'Does Holy God want Daddy to get him some fish for his dinner?'

'*Exactly*,' agreed Valerie, loving the way her daughter's mind worked.

'I'll draw Daddy a merrymaid and he can have the merrymaid shell I collected yesterday,' Briony declared, struggling to escape from Valerie's grasp so she could begin her task immediately. She hurried to get her paper and crayons from the sideboard in the sitting room.

'I'll help you,' said Carmel when Briony came back into the kitchen with her drawing kit.

'I can do it mine own self, thank you, Granny,' Briony said determinedly, hauling herself up onto the chair to draw the most important picture of her life.

'I'm going to write Jeff a letter,' Valerie said.

'I'll leave you to it and go home and get some chores done and I'll be back later then,' Carmel said, squeezing Valerie's shoulder. Valerie placed her hand on her mother's. 'Thanks for everything, Mam.'

'I'm your mother, that's what mothers are for,' Carmel said, giving her a hug, and then she was gone and there were just the two of them. Briony, head bent, tongue sticking out at the side of her mouth, with fierce concentration was drawing furiously. Valerie stood up, went to the drawer in the dresser and rooted for a writing pad and a pen. She sat down beside her daughter and opened the pad. She wrote,

My Darling Jeff,

I want you to know that I love you with all my heart. For all the time we've been together I've always loved you. And I'll always love you. I had enough love for both of us. I just wish you had loved me as much. I wish you had loved me enough to marry me. The truth is now I feel angry and bitter and sad and resentful. It's horrible feeling angry with you, but I feel you've abandoned me and Briony. I'm in such turmoil I don't know where to turn or what to do. I hope these feelings will fade and I'll feel only the love again.

I know you felt trapped when I got pregnant and I never wanted that for you, but you stood by me and became the best father a man could be. You loved Briony with all your heart and that love made a man of you.

I'm sorry for all the times I nagged and I'm sorry for moaning about how much time you spent training. I know you loved football, but I loved you and wanted to spend time with you. We had such fun, though, didn't we? No one could make me laugh like you did . . . well, maybe Lizzie . . . I could write a book of Remembers. Remember when we did this? Remember when we did that? There were times that you made me very, very happy and I hope and pray I made you feel the same. Thank you for my darling Briony. She is our gift and will always be a symbol of our love.

I will always cherish every memory of you, my darling Jeff, but the one I cherish most, apart from the birth of our daughter, is of dancing with you in the kitchen last Saturday night.

Roam across the heavens, Beloved Sailor, but don't forget when that tide turns there is someone here who loves you with all their heart, mind, body and soul.

With all my love,
Valerie XXXXXXX

She read what she had written, knowing it was the truth, even the ugly angry bits. She *was* very angry with Jeff, so angry. But she loved him too, so much. She kissed the letter, folded it, and put it in an envelope. She went to the dresser where a stack of tapes lay in a higgledy-piggledy heap and rummaged until she found the birthday tape with the collection of songs she'd compiled for him. That tape of songs they had played and danced to. She knew she could never listen to it again. She took the letter out and added a PS.

Sing, my lovely Jeff, sing to our songs, and wait for me to come and dance with you. XXX

Tessa might have him now but she'd never have what they'd had, Valerie thought as she placed the letter and tape in an envelope, sealed it with Sellotape and wrote Jeff's name on the front.

CHAPTER THIRTY-FIVE

Tessa's heart contracted and she gave a little whimper as Lorcan, Steven, and Lisa's husband stood under Jeff's coffin with the undertakers to carry him into the house. At least her son was home, she comforted herself, as Lisa slipped a supportive arm around her waist. She would have her darling boy for the rest of today and tonight, before surrendering him to the Church for the removal and funeral.

'You just give us a few minutes now to get him settled, Tessa,' Timmy Roche, the undertaker, said to her as they stood back while the coffin was carried into the sitting room. She and Lisa had spent the morning preparing the room. It was filled with vases of multicoloured gladioli and roses from the garden. There was nothing funereal about the room. Tessa wanted it to be bright and colourful to match the vista of sparkling blue sea and the carpet of gold and emerald that dressed the fields outside. Jeff would not have wanted a sombre setting, of that she was sure. She had a Chieftains' tape playing on his old boom box.

A few minutes later Timmy came out to her. 'You can come in now, Tessa.' He led her into the room where her youngest child lay, eyes closed, that half-smile on his face, so peaceful he could just be asleep.

'Aah, darling,' she crooned, caressing his face. 'We have you home safe and sound.' Lorcan came to stand beside her and together they looked down at their son as she murmured endearments and told him how much she loved him. Lisa and Steven came and stood at the other side of the casket, and the family was once more united for those precious moments alone before extended family and friends would come to pay their respects and he would be theirs no longer.

Tessa wished they didn't have to come. She couldn't help it. She just wanted it to be the four of them spending that last day and night with Jeff before he was gone from them for good. But people were kind, and Jeff had many friends, as did they, and they wanted to support the family. And that was the way it was, especially in a small village where everyone knew everyone else and hardship and loss were a shared experience. For now, though, Jeff was theirs and they spoke to him of their love for him and their pride in him and their sorrow at his leaving.

Later in the afternoon, when many people had called and offered their sympathies, and brought cake and scones and other offerings, and after they'd all been given tea, there was a welcome lull. Lorcan turned to Tessa, who was sitting on the sofa looking beyond Jeff to the vista their big French doors afforded. 'I'm going to ring Valerie to tell her to come while it's a bit quiet.'

'If you must,' she said resignedly. 'I'll just go upstairs.'

'Could you not make your peace with her, Tess, for all our sakes, for Jeff's sake, for Briony's sake?' he urged.

'Don't! Don't! Today of all days, Lorcan, leave me be,' she snapped, and turned her head away from him.

'One other thing we have to sort,' he said gravely.

'What?' She wouldn't look at him.

'Valerie sits with the family in the church. In the front seat with us.'

'No, Lorcan! I don't want her next or near me.'

'She can sit beside me or Lisa,' he said quietly.

'No—'

'Tessa, you've got everything you wanted for Jeff's funeral. *I* want this and that's the end of it.'

She knew there was no arguing with him. When Lorcan spoke in that tone of voice, she had learned not to argue.

'Fine,' she said coldly, and turned away from him, seething that he would take Valerie's side against her. Lorcan shook his head and went out to make his phone call as Tessa sat in silent fury.

Valerie was coming here to the house, against her wishes. She was going to be sitting in the front row of the church with them, against her wishes, and because she was Briony's mother, she would be a part of Tessa's life and a thorn in her side for ever and a day. It was bad enough grieving the loss of her son without having to accommodate that spiteful, sharp-tongued little madam. Tessa sat in her sitting room and felt a great sorrow for herself. Just when she and Lorcan should be most united as a couple, they were most divided. And it was all Valerie Harris's fault.

Lorcan came out to the yard as soon as Valerie drove into it and she knew he must have been waiting for her. 'Gandad,' Briony yelled from her booster seat in the back.

'Hello, pet.' Lorcan opened the back door for her. 'And who have we got here? The best little girl in the whole wide world, is it?' Briony giggled and held her arms up to him.

'I thought you might like to see her,' Valerie said quietly. 'But I won't bring her into the sitting room.'

'Thank you, Valerie. She puts a balm on the ache,' Lorcan said, holding his grandchild tightly and kissing her curls. 'You can have as much time as you want with him. No one will disturb you.'

Her eyes welled up and she turned away so Briony wouldn't see. She followed Lorcan into the kitchen, sick to her stomach. None of the others would probably talk to her after the row with Tessa. She had never felt so alone in her life. Carmel had wanted to come with her but she had said no, this was something she had to do alone. She was afraid if Tessa went off on one of her rants, more words would be exchanged and she didn't want that. Carmel had enough of her own troubles.

'I'll take Briony up to see her gran. Take all the time you need, Valerie,' Lorcan said, leading the little girl through the kitchen and handing her a fairy cake from one of the plates piled with goodies.

'Thanks, Lorcan,' she said gratefully. Jeff's father was one of the most decent men she had ever met, she acknowledged as her daughter said happily. 'Yum, yum, Gandad.'

The kitchen looked like a bakery with all the cakes and pastries people had brought with them laid out on the table. A neighbour had brought a casserole, someone else had brought a tureen of potato soup and chunky Vienna rolls. There was enough food to feed an army. Lisa was the first person she saw. She was drying cups and putting them away in the press. Jeff's sister hurried to her side and put her arms around her, and then Valerie was sobbing into her shoulder.

'Oh Lisa, Lisa, Lisa, what am I going to do? I can't bear it,' she wept brokenly.

'I know, I know.' The older girl cried with her, stroking her back as she held her. 'Come on in and see him. He looks lovely,' Lisa said eventually, taking her hand. She followed Jeff's sister into the sitting room and one of his aunts, who was sitting there, stood up to leave. 'I'm sorry for your loss,' she said kindly, pressing Valerie's hand, and then she was gone and it was just her and Lisa. Valerie walked over to where her darling lay as though asleep.

'Please come back to me, Jeff. Please don't be dead,' she said urgently, frantically, half expecting his eyes to open at any moment and a big grin spread across his face. Seeing him like this, so motionless, but yet so himself, lying in a coffin, sent emotions rushing through her. He couldn't *really* be dead. He was too young, much too young. He was her Jeff, her healthy, vibrant sweetheart.

'Oh, Jeff, I'm scared. I can't do this without you. Please come back to us,' she pleaded.

But his eyes never opened and his smile never changed.

'You just talk to him and I'll leave you to have some privacy,' Lisa said, unable to bear it, imagining how she would feel if her young husband was lying in a coffin. She left the room and closed the door so Valerie could have Jeff to herself one last time.

As Valerie stared down at him, stunned and shocked, it finally began to sink in that he would never come back to her. 'I love you, Jeff, I always have,' she said fervently, and began to talk to him of all that he had ever meant to her. She opened her bag and took out Briony's drawing of a gleeful mermaid with a huge red crayoned grin, and slipped it and the conch into the coffin beside him. She kissed her letter before placing it on his chest. She didn't kiss his face when she said goodbye; instead she put her lips to his hair so she wouldn't have to feel the coldness of him. Her heart was thumping so loud she was sure it could be heard in the rest of the house.

A dazed numbness settled on her as she walked into the kitchen. She could not bear to think that this was the last time she'd ever see Jeff. But she could not sink into the hysteria that threatened to overwhelm her. She had a child to think of. She couldn't frighten her daughter.

'Will you get Briony for me?' she asked Lisa, who was sipping tea. 'I'll be out in the car. And thank you for making me welcome,' she said shakily.

'Valerie, you're family, you were Jeff's partner – why would I not make you welcome?'

'Thanks, Lisa. You were always very kind to me.' Valerie gave her a hug and walked out into the evening sun.

A lark was singing its heart out. The muted drone of a combine harvester gathering the last of the harvest, and the cooing notes of a pair of doves in one of Tessa's apple trees, drifted along on the breeze. Everything seemed so normal. But nothing was normal. Nothing would ever be normal again, Valerie thought, raising her face to the sun as she waited for her daughter.

'It's time to go now, darling,' Tessa said sadly, watching as Briony studied herself in the dressing table mirror. She wore two necklaces, bangles, a hat and some lipstick, and she had spent the last twenty minutes clip-clopping around in a pair of her grandmother's high heels. Lorcan and Tessa, despite their despair, had smiled at each other as she put on a show for them, thrilled with herself in her finery.

'Let me wipe that lipstick off,' Tessa said, pulling a tissue from a box on the dressing table.

'Please, Gramma, *pleeeease* can I leave it on?' Briony begged.

'Mom might not like it,' Tessa demurred.

'She won't mind. She lets me wear lipstick,' her granddaughter assured her confidently.

'I don't think Valerie will mind,' Lisa said as she removed the necklaces and hat and put Briony's little shoes back on.

Tessa held out her arms and Briony snuggled in tight. 'I love you, Gramma,' she said, wrapping her small arms around Tessa's neck.

'And I love you.' Tessa's lip quivered and Lisa, fearing her mother was about to dissolve into tears, took Briony by the hand and led her from the bedroom.

When she was gone, Tessa burst into tears. Silently Lorcan took her in his arms and she rested her head against his chest, listening to the steady beat of his heart. The doorbell rang downstairs. More people were arriving to offer condolences. 'Stay here for a while,' Lorcan said, handing her a tissue. 'I'll go down and see to the neighbours.'

'Thanks,' she gulped, wiping her eyes. She had a thumping headache. She rooted in her bedside locker and found a carton of paracetamol and shook two out in her palm. She looked at the pile of white tablets nestling in their container and for a brief, mad moment thought how easy it would be to take them all, to end this night-mare of grief and despair and join her beloved son wher-ever he was. Regretfully she put the cap back on. Life would have to be endured. She couldn't do that to Lorcan or her other children.

Tessa took a deep breath, squared her shoulders and went downstairs to meet a group of Jeff's teammates who were completely stunned and devastated, and hardly knew what to say to her. Most of the village had been through her door, she reflected. Jeff was very popular and that gave her some solace as she led his friends in to him to say their last farewells.

'Where did you get the lovely lipstick?' Valerie asked Briony when Lisa led her out to the car.

'Gramma let me put it on an' I was wearing hee hiles too,' she said proudly.

'Hee hiles, lucky you!' Valerie exclaimed, sharing an unexpected smile with Lisa. 'See you tomorrow then,' she said to Jeff's sister after she'd secured Briony in her car seat.

'Will you come for the closing of the casket?' Lisa asked.

Valerie shook her head. 'No. I don't want to see that. I'll meet up with you at the church,' she said as another car arrived at the gate. A man and woman got out and there was something familiar about them, Valerie thought as she squinted against the sun. And then she recognized Lizzie and she was running to her, calling her name. 'Lizzie! Lizzie! Lizzie!'

'It's all right, I'm here,' Lizzie said, wrapping her arms around her, holding her tightly.

'Oh, Lizzie, I'll never get through this, *ever*,' Valerie whispered.

'You will, Valerie, you will,' Lizzie said steadily, struggling not to cry. 'You have Briony. She'll get you through it, I swear to God she will. And I'll be with you for the funeral. One day at a time is all you have to deal with right now.'

'Oh, Lizzie, wait until you see him. You'd just think he was asleep but he's cold. So cold.'

'I'll go in now with Dara and pay my respects, and then I'll go home and say hello to Ma and Da, and then I'll come and stay the night. And we'll talk about him all night for as long as you want, all right?' She smiled at Valerie.

'Thank you, thank you so much, Lizzie. I'd love that,' Valerie said, utterly relieved that she was with the one person in the world who truly understood how she felt.

CHAPTER THIRTY-SIX

When Valerie stood with Lizzie by her side and watched Jeff's coffin being carried by his father, brother and male relatives and friends, into St Anthony's the following evening, it was as though she was completely detached. She couldn't understand it. It was as though someone had flicked a switch to 'off'.

She walked up the aisle behind Tessa and Lisa, wishing she could slip into a seat at the side where no one would take any notice of her, but Lorcan had driven over to her that morning to see how she was and to ask her if she would sit in the front seat with the family. 'It's what Jeff would want, Valerie, and it's what I want,' he said firmly. 'Your place is with us.'

She hesitated. 'But what about Tessa?'

'Family is family,' he said, lifting Briony into his arms for a hug and a kiss, and Valerie felt she couldn't deny him.

She never heard a word of the service. All she could think about was the bittersweet pleasure of the previous evening when she and Lizzie had sat beside the fire she had lit because the early autumn nights were chilly, and they had talked and talked and talked. She had relived all of her relationship with Jeff, and Lizzie had listened patiently and even reminded her of a few things she'd forgotten.

The sound of the Rosary being recited jolted her back to reality and she said the prayers to the Blessed Mother, thinking that she had never until now appreciated the words of the response to the Hail Mary. *Holy Mary, Mother of God, pray for us sinners, now and at the hour of our death. Amen.* How glibly she had uttered that response thousands of times in her life – *now and at the hour of our death* – and now it was *Jeff's* death that she called on the Holy Mother to pray for. Whenever she said those words again it would be Jeff she would think of.

She glanced over to the gleaming mahogany coffin that Tessa had selected, and caught the other woman's eye. Tessa, white as a sheet, her hands clutching her rosary beads, turned her head away sharply. There would be no reconciliation with Jeff's mother, no matter what Lorcan might wish, Valerie realized forlornly. At one level she didn't care. They'd never liked each other. They'd made the effort when Valerie and Jeff had come back to Rockland's but it had been superficial, just for family's sake. There was no affection between them, never had been and never would be. But she did like the rest of Jeff's family and that was where the difficulty lay.

Father O'Shea concluded the ceremony and then the congregation moved forward as hundreds of mourners lined up to shake their hand and offer murmured words of sympathy. When it was over, Tessa walked out of the seat without a backward glance towards Valerie. Lizzie, who had been sitting a few pews behind, waiting for her, hastened to her side.

'Let's get you home,' she said. She'd seen Tessa blank Valerie and was disgusted. 'Just tomorrow to go and then you can collapse in a heap and cry your eyes out and stay in bed with your head under the pillows, and I'll mind Briony.'

The thought of a day in bed, crying her eyes out with no one to worry about got Valerie through the Mass and burial the next day. 'I can go home and go to bed and cry when this is over,' she repeated to herself like a mantra.

'Look, Mommy, there's a treasure chest. Why is that there?' Briony asked, astonished, pointing to the coffin as they walked up to the front seat for the funeral Mass. It was the first time she'd ever seen one.

'Because it's treasure for Holy God,' Valerie explained, thinking how wonderful her daughter's innocence was. Jeff was treasure for his creator, she supposed, and that thought comforted her as she sat through the Mass, trying not to cry when the choir sang 'Nearer My God to Thee' and the Folk Group sang 'Here I am Lord'. Lorcan had asked if there was any hymn she wanted and she had chosen that one.

Briony, feeling bored, clambered over Lisa and Lorcan to get to Tessa to play with her pearls. 'Gramma,' she called, 'did you see the treasure chest for Holy God?'

A smile crossed her grandmother's face. 'I did, darling. Now hush, love, be a good girl and don't make a noise.'

Valerie bristled inwardly. Briony wasn't making noise. She was only a little girl, for God's sake, asking an inno-cent question. Her indignation helped get her through the rest of the Mass. Who did Tessa Egan think she was, bossing Briony around? Was this what it was always going to be like? This stress? This pull and push? Was she going to have to put up with this woman for the rest of her life? Her thoughts rampaged through her mind as Father O'Shea read the epistle and gospel.

And how was she going to manage when she went back to work? She had to leave home by seven thirty a.m. to drive to Dublin to get to work on time, and Jeff had always dressed Briony and given her breakfast, then driven her to Tessa or Carmel's, before going to work himself. She would be up at six, and Briony too, if she had to take her daughter to either of her grandmothers for minding.

And could she afford to, and did she want to stay in that house she and Jeff were renting? There were too many memories. Too many memories in Rockland's too. Everywhere she went she would see him or remember something of their past. Would she be better off making a fresh start somewhere else? She closed her eyes and listened to the strains of 'Ave Maria' float through the church as the congregation took Communion. So many questions. So many decisions.

'Mommy, why are you dripping water from your eyes?' Briony asked, tugging at her sleeve.

'Sorry, darling, I have something in my eye,' she whispered back, utterly relieved when the priest finally began the last part of the ceremony by asking the Angels to accompany Jeff to paradise.

Outside the church Jeff's teammates formed a guard of honour, and it was just as well that Carmel had taken Briony to go and get an ice cream because the sight of his friends and teammates, all strong young men, with tears streaming down their cheeks, undid Valerie and she wept onto Lizzie's shoulder with broken-hearted sorrow.

When she emerged into the sunlight she was immediately surrounded by a cluster of friends and colleagues who had travelled down from Dublin for the funeral. Their kindness and care was something she would think about often in the future. That all of them would take the trouble to be with her in her hour of need was a source of great comfort, as were the many messages, including a lovely note from Mrs Maguire, that Valerie had received since news of Jeff's death had filtered out.

As she watched Jeff's coffin being lowered into the grave, gripping Lizzie tightly by the hand, seeing Lorcan with his head bowed, craggy face creased in anguish, and Lisa and Tessa sobbing brokenly, Valerie knew she had to get away from Rockland's. There was nothing here for her now. Just pain and grief and strife. If she never came back again it would not bother her, she thought disconsolately as Tessa threw a rose onto the coffin and glared at Valerie as she did the same.

It was over and the house was strangely silent. The sitting room that had been dominated by Jeff's coffin was full of vases of slightly drooping blooms, and Tessa fetched a jug of water to revive them, glad of something to do. Lorcan had gone to take an elderly relative back to his nursing home. Lisa had gone home to her own house, but had assured Tessa she would be back to help tidy up. And Steven had gone back up to the graveyard to bring back the name cards on the wreaths so she would know who to thank when she sent out her acknowledgements and memory cards.

Tessa felt dead inside; flat and dispirited and more lonely than she had ever felt in her life. Empty and hollow couldn't even begin to describe it. She refreshed the flowers, put the jug back on the counter top and went upstairs. She walked into Jeff's bedroom, still with its teenage posters of racing cars and Farah Fawcett Majors, decorating the pale blue walls.

Her son's kitbag was on the bed. One of his friends had given it to Lorcan at the hospital, and he had taken Jeff's football boots and clothes from the nurse and packed them into it. She would never wash his shirt, ever, Tessa thought, burying her head in its mucky folds. She held it close, like treasure. She would keep this for herself. And she would keep his room the way it was so she could come in here and be with him, she decided. She took out his towel. It was still fresh because he hadn't showered after his match. She should give that to Valerie, she supposed. But then Valerie might want his football shirt. No, Tessa decided. She wasn't getting her hands on that; she had enough of Jeff's clothes. Tessa would keep the kitbag and all that was in it, his toiletries, everything. She was his mother, she deserved some small little part of him, she thought desolately. She could smell a ripe banana and she rooted around and found it in a brown paper bag, soft and black, and took it out to discard it. There was another bag tucked in a pocket at the side. She opened it and burst into tears. Her heart twisted with pain as she stood there alone, rummaging through her beloved son's belongings. She zipped up the bag, opened the wardrobe door and laid it on the bottom among old shoes and trainers. Only she would know it was there, this last and final part of him.

She took Jeff's football shirt, got under the patchwork quilt on his bed and held it tightly. Exhaustion overcame her, her eyes closed and for the first time since her son had died, Tessa slept.

'I'm not staying here,' Valerie said to Lizzie as they sat in front of the fire, sipping cocoa and eating toast.

'Don't make any hasty decisions,' advised her friend, licking melted butter off her fingers.

'I don't want to stay here. I don't want to have to endure Tessa's antipathy, and Dad's annoyance with the fact that I'm an unmarried mother for good now, and will never be free of the "stigma", as he calls it. He was nearly going to have another go at Tessa today in the graveyard, only Mam read him the riot act and told him not to disgrace us in front of the neighbours, and that got to him. You know him and his image. But I can't be listening to that kind of stuff every time I go home to Mam with Briony. And I don't want him saying things like that when she's older. I don't want her to feel she's in any way different from her friends here.'

'I know. He's the old school of thinking. London is so different. Honestly, nobody gives a hoot. It's very liberating. We are so bamboozled with guilt by the Church and society here it's very wearing on the spirit. There's a sad lacking of real Christianity.' Lizzie threw another log on the fire and they watched it spark and blaze.

Valerie yawned. Waves of fatigue had washed over her once the funeral was over. She had come straight home from the graveyard and not gone to partake of the refreshments the Egans were providing in the hotel. Tessa would not want her there and she did not want to be there.

'Why don't you go to bed?' Lizzie suggested.

'I hate being in the bed without Jeff. I hate sitting at the kitchen table looking at his empty chair. I can't stay in this house. I keep expecting him to walk through the door. It's doing my head in,' Valerie sighed. 'And anyway, with just one salary coming in now I can't afford to pay the rent for this place. It's too big for us, *and* I have to pay a fortune for petrol for that commute. And besides, having to get Briony up so early so I can get to work on time is not practical. It was different when Jeff . . . when Jeff . . .' She swallowed hard, but couldn't say 'was alive'. 'He used to get her dressed and bring her to Mam's or Tessa's because he had loads of time to get to work. I won't have that,' she amended.

'Well, I suppose if you are thinking of going back to Dublin, at least you know the city. It's not as if it was your first time living there, and Briony's the right age. She hasn't started school yet so it won't be as big a wrench,' Lizzie said slowly. 'And you've plenty of friends from work to help out. They were great the way they all travelled down for the funeral.'

'Yeah, they're a good bunch. The only big drawback to moving back is taking Briony away from all she knows, but, like you say, she's at the right age and she'll be going to school next year. She'll love that because she's very sociable.'

'And you'll be able to bring her down here for holidays,' Lizzie reminded her.

Valerie shook her head. 'I won't be coming back. Mam can come up and stay with me in Dublin whenever she wants.'

'And what about Tessa?' Lizzie enquired delicately.

'What about her?' Valerie said dismissively. 'That *lady* – and I use the term lightly – has seen the last of me.'

CHAPTER THIRTY-SEVEN

'Ring me when you're there safe and sound, won't you, Valerie?' Carmel said dejectedly as her daughter closed the boot of her Toyota Corolla and came to stand beside her.

'Just as well I changed the car last year. I'd never have fitted everything into the Mini or the Renault,' Valerie said wryly, surveying the front seat of her car, which was crammed with an assortment of plastic bags on top of a black sack. 'So you'll lock up and leave the key in Donnelly's.' She kept her back to the house so she wouldn't have to look at it.

'Granny, look at Molly!' Briony waved her new doll with the long brown hair at her. She was brushing it diligently and making pigtails, chatting away to Molly.

'She's a lovely doll, sweetie. You should be a hairdresser you're so good at doing hair. You have fun in your new house and I'll see you at the weekend. We'll go to the park and I'll push you on the swing,' Carmel said tenderly.

'Real high up into the sky, Granny?'

'Real high into the sky,' promised Carmel, smiling.

'I'll see you at the weekend, Mam, and thanks for everything. I'm going to go quickly now, otherwise I'll start crying.' Valerie gave her mother a quick hug, got into the car and started the engine. She didn't look back as she drove away from the house where she'd been so happy with Jeff. She was glad she didn't have to go through the village; that would have been hard. There were so many memories to leave behind, especially when she knew she wouldn't be coming back. She drove to the crossroads, took a left turn and pulled up a few minutes later outside the graveyard. She took from the seat beside her the bouquet of pink and yellow roses she had cut fresh from the garden that morning and got out of the car.

'Do you want to come or do you want to play with Molly?' Valerie asked her daughter, hoping she would stay in the car.

'I'll bring Molly with me,' Briony said cheerfully, trying to unhook her seat belt. 'Are we going into the garden with all the flowers again?'

'Yes, darling, just one last time,' Valerie said as her daughter slipped her hand into hers and they walked through the wrought-iron gates to the peaceful country cemetery. The fog that had rolled in off the sea earlier was lifting and a hazy sun was beginning to break through. Autumn leaves of red and gold fashioned the bracelet of oak trees that encircled the graveyard. The breeze played with them, tossing them gently as they floated down into crisp deep piles. Valerie filled a container with water from the tap by the gate and Briony let go of her hand and skipped along ahead, knowing exactly where to go. Half-way up the gravel path and to the right, a mound of loamy brown earth – with a small wooden cross adorned with a gold plaque with Jeff's name and dates of birth and death – was covered with pots of vibrant polyanthus and pansies that Tessa had made up. It would be months before the grave had settled and the headstone could be put in place. She was glad in one way not to see it. A headstone was so final. The Mass for his Month's Mind had taken place the previous week and Valerie could hardly believe that Jeff was five weeks dead.

She cleared the remnants of the roses she'd brought the last time she'd visited, filled the vase with fresh water and arranged the sweet-scented roses carefully. They looked so soft and pretty, and gave off a perfume that filled her nostrils.

'They are very, very lovely, Mommy,' Briony exclaimed, stroking a petal when Valerie held the vase out for her to smell them.

'These are for Daddy. He can see us putting them here for him while he's working for Holy God up in heaven,' Valerie explained.

'Daddy, Daddy,' Briony called, waving vigorously up to the sky. 'Tell God you have to come back down and push me on my swing,' she yelled, peering heavenward, hoping to see her daddy. 'Will he come down on a cloud just like Mary Poppins?' she asked Valerie, who was trying hard not to dissolve into tears.

'No. God needs him to do some more work for him,' Valerie said, her heart breaking as she looked into her daughter's trusting brown eyes.

'But I miss my daddy, I haven't seen him in *ages*!' she said plaintively.

'Oh, so do I, Briony,' Valerie said with heartfelt empathy. 'Now we had better go and bring Molly to our new house.' She swallowed hard and knelt down at the grave. 'Jeff, I won't be back. I leave you to your mother's care, sleep well,' she said, placing the vase in front of the cross. 'I love you.'

'Why are you talking to the garden?' Briony asked, perplexed. 'You should be talking up there.' She pointed heavenwards.

'I should indeed, Briony. What would I do without you to tell me things?' Valerie bent down and kissed her. She blessed herself and, taking her daughter's hand, walked out of the graveyard after placing the discarded roses on the neat hillock of grass cuttings at the gate. The sun emerged triumphantly through the fine grey cloak that had kept it hidden, vanquishing the last of the haze, and warming her face as they reached the car. She could smell the sea on the breeze, see the blue of the sky appearing, and hear the birds singing in the trees. She envied Jeff his resting place of peace and serenity. He had no cares or woes or grief and regrets and she was filled to bursting with them, she thought with an edge of bitterness, wishing she still didn't feel that he had abandoned them.

She secured Briony into her seat, got into the car and started the engine. This was her last stop. This was where she said goodbye. A new life waited for her. Heavy-hearted, Valerie started the engine and headed north.

Carmel gave the counter top a last run over with the dishcloth and popped it into a plastic bag containing dusters and tea towels, ready for a wash. She looked out into the garden where she had pushed her grandchild on her swing countless times. Valerie had cut the grass and weeded the flowerbeds, and Donnelly's Estate Agents would have no complaints when she handed them back the keys on her daughter's behalf.

The house was eerily empty, as if all the energy had been sucked out of it. It had once been a house of laughter, and childish cries of glee, a happy house. It would be so again when some new family took up residence. At least Valerie would have those priceless memories to look back on when she was able to. For now, Carmel understood her daughter's need to get away and start afresh where there was nothing of Jeff to remind her of what she had lost.

Valerie had made her promise that she would never tell Tessa her new address. Carmel wasn't happy about it, or the fact that the other woman had no idea that Valerie was upping sticks and moving for good.

'I don't want her in my life. She said appalling things to me when Jeff died. She wouldn't talk to me at the funeral so now she can take the consequences,' Valerie said angrily when Carmel had said Tessa had a right to see Briony.

'The flight into Egypt,' Lizzie had called it. Trust Lizzie. Carmel smiled. She was a true friend, of that there was no doubt, and she was so glad her daughter had Lizzie in her life.

Sadness filled her. She would not see her beloved daughter and grandchild every day as she had these past few years. They had filled her life with pleasure and given her something to look forward to. Now it was just her and Terence again. Carmel sighed, watching the lemon sorbet sun burst out through the filmy haze that had veiled the sky, its light diffused in delicate pastel rays that fell onto the milky sea.

Terence had given her an envelope with money in it for Valerie, and she had slipped it into her daughter's cavernous handbag for her to find when she got to Dublin. He hadn't come to say goodbye. He had made no effort to get to know his grandchild, and now she was gone from him and he would never get the chance again. Carmel, to her surprise, found herself feeling immensely sorry for him that his bitterness and stubbornness had kept him from such a gift as Briony.

'Thank you for your shelter and your comfort,' she said aloud to the house as she locked the heavy wooden blue door for the last time and walked down the path, feathered with lobelia still, and closed the garden gate behind her, leaving the place bathed in sunlight.

Terence glanced at his watch: ten thirty. Valerie would be on the road to Dublin now and he was glad she was getting out of Rockland's. It was no place for her in her single state with that fatherless child. Carmel had told him that she had found a house to rent, not too far from where she'd lived before. So she was going to familiar territory. He didn't know Dublin at all, but from what Carmel had told him it seemed a nice enough area.

Their house would be quiet without the little one. She was as bright as a button and he had often listened to her chattering to her dolls, while he pretended to be engrossed in his paper, and been entertained by her imagination.

Briony. He hadn't liked the name at all when he'd first heard it, but now he acknowledged that it suited her. Carmel would be devastated that they were gone. That little girl had brought his wife a lot of happiness. Now they would be back to living their humdrum lives, and she would get depressed and uncommunicative and he would bear the brunt of that.

And all because Valerie had done things her own way with no concern for herself and gone and got herself pregnant with a spoiled mammy's boy who wouldn't marry her. She was surely reaping what she'd sown. She could have had the widow's pension if she'd listened to him, but the few hundred quid he'd put in the envelope would pay the rent for a month or two until she was settled in and back on her feet in Dublin. She'd be nearly there by now. He should have taken the morning off work and helped her settle in. That was the kind of thing Lorcan Egan would do, he supposed. Terence frowned.

There was no point in comparing himself to another man as far as Valerie was concerned. She and he had never got on and never would, and that was the way of it. He didn't know if she would welcome his gift or toss it aside, but he had given it. It was the best he could do, considering their relationship. All he'd wanted was for her to be treated properly and to be married before that child was born. What was so awful about that? As long as he lived he would never understand why no one had listened to him. Terence shook his head. No point in crying over spilled milk. He had to get back to work. There was a new consignment of rubber mats, soaps and disinfectants and paper towels in; he wanted to help himself to a few of them.

The first thing Carmel saw when she got home was the little china tea set that she had bought for her grand-daughter to play with the previous Christmas. Briony had a selection of toys that she loved to play with. A pang twisted her heart: when would Briony be back in the house again? Never, if Valerie kept to her decision not to set foot in Rockland's again. She was sure Tessa had many toys for Briony to play with too. Carmel would not be cut off from contact with her beloved grandchild; Tessa and Lorcan and their family would.

Carmel made herself a cup of tea. She was terribly troubled. She didn't particularly like Tessa Egan but the woman had lost her son and now she was losing her granddaughter. It wasn't right. And it wasn't right that Valerie had done a flit without telling her. It would be awful for her to hear from some neighbour that Valerie had moved to Dublin. She didn't deserve that.

Carmel took a deep breath, picked up the phone and flicked through her address book. She dialled Tessa's number.

'Hello?' The other woman's voice was flat and sad.

Carmel cleared her throat. 'Tessa, it's Carmel Harris. I'm just phoning you because I don't want you to hear it from someone else. Valerie has moved out of the house and gone to live in Dublin. She says she won't be back. I felt you should know.'

'What do you mean, gone to Dublin? When will she be back? Has she taken Briony with her?' Tessa demanded.

'Yes, she's going to live in Dublin to be near her work so she'll have more time to spend with Briony.'

'Where? What's the address? Why won't she be back? How do I get to see Briony?' Tessa fired the questions at her.

'Tessa, she says she won't be back. And she doesn't want me to give out her address. I'm sorry,' Carmel said uncomfortably.

'You *must* give it to me. She can't just take Briony away from us like that.' Tessa was horrified.

'I don't agree with Valerie on this but I must do as she asks me. You were loyal to Jeff once and put my daughter in a terrible position. I must be loyal to her now. As a mother I'm sure you will understand. I'm sorry, Tessa. I just rang you as a matter of courtesy. Goodbye.' Carmel hung up the phone.

Despite their chequered history she felt the utmost sympathy for the other woman. The loss of a child and the loss of a grandchild were events she might possibly never recover from. Carmel could only pray that Valerie would change her mind at some time in the future. The path of vengeance could only take its toll on all of them.

'Oh God!' Tessa sank onto a kitchen chair. She felt weak. Not only had she lost Jeff, now it seemed that she had lost Briony. Could Valerie just whisk their grandchild, Jeff's daughter, up to Dublin and deprive them of seeing her? Surely there must be some law against it.

Carmel couldn't just refuse to give her Valerie's address, could she?

A terrible fear and doubt filled Tessa. Her granddaughter was, as Lorcan had once pointed out to her, Briony Harris. Not Briony Egan. They had no rights. Just as Valerie had had no rights when Jeff had died. Just as she had punished Valerie, Valerie was now punishing her. And Briony was caught in the middle. The innocent victim.

Valerie Harris was a hard-hearted little madam, and she'd got the better of Tessa. She wept bitter tears. She had lost everything.

'We might never see her again, Lorcan,' she cried when her husband came up for his lunch from the boat shed, where he had spent the morning repairing nets.

'All we can do is pray that time will lessen Valerie's hurt and she will come to her senses,' Lorcan said, ashen-faced at the news.

'How can God do this to us? Haven't we suffered enough?' Tessa cried.

Lorcan said nothing. A battle raged inside him. He so badly wanted to shout at her, 'God isn't doing this to us. You've caused this because of the way you treated Valerie. It's because of *you* that we have lost our grandchild. Now are you satisfied?' But he knew it would be the undoing of his wife and the end of them, and so he stayed silent.

He made a pot of tea and ate the sandwich Tessa made for him without tasting it, and when he was alone in his car on the way back to the boat, Lorcan pulled into a narrow lane that led to a field of grazing cattle and leaned his head on his arms and cried his heart out.

It was midweek and people were at work so the traffic was light. Valerie was lucky to get a clear run of lights from Deans Grange to the Merrion Gates. She drove through Sandymount, looking over across Dublin Bay to Clontarf and Howth, and promised herself that she would bring Briony to the coast at weekends to get healthy sea air. Good thing she liked Dublin. It would be a thousand times worse coming back if she hated the place.

Was it true, she wondered, driving up to the new East Link Toll Bridge, that when one door closed another one opened? Certainly she had been extremely fortunate in the house she was moving to. Two weeks after Jeff had died she had asked Carmel to babysit and had spent a day in Dublin viewing flats and houses. Some of the places she viewed she had liked very much but the rents were on the high side and she knew she'd have to share with someone, something she was reluctant to do. The less expensive dwellings were not so well maintained, and one poky flat she viewed was filthy and smelled of cats. Some of the houses had postage-stamp-sized gardens or, in some cases, no gardens at all, and Valerie was desperate for Briony, used to the big flower-filled one in Rockland's, to have a garden to play in. How she longed to be able to drive up to Mrs Maguire's and go back to live with her, she thought wistfully, driving along Botanic Avenue after her futile day's viewing.

The following week she again drove up to the city and saw a small house in Ballygall, which she liked and which was within her price range. She paid a holding deposit to the estate agent, who assured her the existing tenant would be out of the house in two weeks and she could take possession. She drove home, relieved that at least she and Briony would have somewhere to live when she moved back to Dublin.

Two days later the estate agent phoned to say that the landlady had decided to rent the house to her niece and Valerie's cheque was in the post to her. Valerie had wept despairingly for hours afterwards, convinced that her life was going from bad to worse.

Ten days later she had gone up to Dublin to collect her pay, even though Personnel would have posted it to her in Rockland's. But she was desperate to get away again and Carmel had once more offered to mind Briony. She'd bumped into some of her friends on their lunch break and they'd asked her to come with them for a bite to eat. One of the girls had asked what her plans were and she'd said that she'd been looking for a house or flat some-where near where she had lived before but had not had much luck.

'My sister is looking for a long-term tenant. I wonder, would you be interested?' Denise, one of her colleagues, said. 'She's off on a five-year contract with a hospital in Saudi and she wants to rent out the house but she's fussy about who to let it to. She hasn't found anyone yet that she likes. Would you like to meet her and have a look? It's not far from where you lived before in Glasnevin.'

'Are you serious? There are lovely parks for Briony, good schools, and the Botanic Gardens, and it's very handy for work,' Valerie said eagerly. 'I'd love to have a look, if it's OK with your sister.'

'Let me sort it,' Denise said. 'I'll phone her and see if you could see it this evening, if you like?'

'Perfect,' agreed Valerie. 'But of course, if the rent is too much I won't be able to take it on my own.'

'You can talk to her about it,' Denise said.

The house, when she saw it, was a small, neat, two-bedroom town house, in a cul-de-sac of similar houses off Mobhi Road. The bedrooms were small after what she was used to in Rockland's but she could fit two divans in Briony's room. The kitchen-dining room was L-shaped with French doors opening out onto a west-facing back garden with a patio area and well-manicured lawn and shrubs.

'I'm going to Saudi to earn enough to pay off the mort-gage,' Geraldine, Denise's sister, explained when she'd finished showing Valerie around. 'I want a long-term tenant. Not someone who's going to be gone in six months or a year. If you take it, I'll reduce the rent. It would be worth it to know someone was taking care of my home for the next five years, not some tenant who didn't give a toss about the place. If you think you'd like it, I'd like you to have it. It would be nice to know you and your little girl were making a home in my home.' She mentioned a figure that was within Valerie's reach and Valerie heard herself say without hesitation, 'I'll take it. When can I move in?'

'Two weeks OK? I'm starting work in a month but I want to go on holiday with Denise before I head off.'

'That's fine. I'll be going back to work at the beginning of November, so that will give me time to get settled in. My doctor was very kind about giving me certs,' Valerie explained.

'I hope you can move forward and settle in well here,' Geraldine said awkwardly, not knowing what to say to comfort Valerie. It was the type of response she was well used to now. People in Rockland's had crossed the street to avoid speaking to her because they felt uncomfortable on account of her bereavement.

The anonymity of the city would be such a help, Valerie reflected, driving back home that evening. She had phoned Lizzie to tell her the news. She still couldn't believe she'd finally got a house that really suited them.

'That's Jeff sorting things for you,' Lizzie had said immediately.

'Do you really believe that?' Valerie asked doubtfully, wishing it were true.

'I absolutely do, missy. You watch out. He is still by your side. He'll never leave you and Briony, Valerie. Trust me on that one. I feel my grandmother around me all the time. Just keep talking to him as if he's with you and you will find yourself doing it automatically in time, and that way they are never lost to you. That's how it works for me and Nana. And watch out for white butterflies. That's always a sign they're around.' Valerie smiled. Lizzie constantly spoke to her much-loved grandmother, who had passed away six months before they'd moved in together, so that even Valerie had felt she was still around, and had often said 'Hello, Nana' to the lovely photo Lizzie had of her on her bedside table.

'I'll try it,' she said dubiously, knowing that if she started talking too much to Jeff she'd end up giving out to him for leaving her and Briony and mucking up their lives completely. But still, the thought that Jeff had sorted out a house for them gave her some comfort in the weeks that followed as she set about sorting their belongings.

Because the house in Rockland's had been rented to them fully furnished, she had no need of a removal van. Two carloads of belongings to her new house had been sufficient. She hadn't told Briony they were moving until the day before, in case she said it inadvertently to Tessa. She had not seen the other woman until the Month's Mind Mass, and even then Tessa had coldly averted her gaze from her and had not invited her back to the house afterwards. Lorcan had visited her several times, asking if she was all right for money and wanting to know if there was anything he could do for her.

'I'm OK, Lorcan,' she assured him. 'Jeff and I had insurance policies out on each other so I'll be getting a lump sum when that's processed.'

'And you'll be getting what's in his Credit Union savings, once we have all that sorted with the solicitor,' he told her, uncomfortable with the fact that she was not Jeff's next of kin with automatic rights to all his possessions.

Lisa had called on her way home from work a few times and had asked hesitantly if she could bring Briony to see Tessa. 'Of course you can,' Valerie agreed, wanting to keep things as normal as possible. Tessa Egan, although she did not know it, should, Valerie decided, make the most of her grandchild because when Valerie left Rockland's it would be a long time before she came back, if ever. If Tessa could treat her like dirt, she could return the compliment, Valerie thought grimly that evening when she had returned from the Mass, disgusted with the way Jeff's mother had treated her. Briony would still have Carmel. Her greatest loss would be Lorcan, and he would be a big loss, Valerie acknowledged, but she couldn't see any other way forward. Briony was very young. Her memories of her grandparents would fade. It would have been much more difficult if she were older.

As she drove up Mobhi Road, Valerie felt sad thinking of Jeff's father. He had always treated her with the utmost respect and consideration and he adored Briony. Going to Dublin without saying a word was like stabbing him in the back and she felt guilty about it, but it was the only thing she could do if she wanted Tessa's toxic energy out of her life.

She would write Lorcan a letter and post it to him today. That would be the final cutting of the ties, Valerie thought, turning left into the small neat cul-de-sac, which would be hers and Briony's home for the next five years.

Dear Lorcan,

First can I say how grateful I am to you for all the kindness you have shown me and Briony over the years. You are a wonderful man, and a wonderful father and grandfather. Jeff loved you so dearly, but you know that.

Lorcan, I've moved to make a fresh start for myself and Briony. The house in Rockland's is too big and expensive to run now that we are on our own. And without Jeff to help with Briony in the mornings and evenings the commute would be too much when I go back to work, as well as being too expensive.

It is easier to be near work so I can spend as much time as possible with Briony. And, moving now is not as big a trauma for her as it would be if she had started school.

It's very hard to say this, Lorcan, but I can no longer deal with Tessa's anger towards me or mine towards her. I am making a complete break and intend never to return to Rockland's. I said my goodbyes to Jeff at the grave this morning, knowing that his grave will always be looked after by his family, of which Tessa made sure I did not become a member.

I'm sorry, Lorcan. I know all this hurts you terribly and that is the last thing I want to do. I will always be in your debt. You will never know how much your strength, kindness and compassion helped me when I got pregnant and then when Jeff died.

I love you, Lorcan, and so does Briony.

With all my love,

Valerie xxx

Valerie read the letter, which bore no address, slid it into the envelope and sealed it. She wrote Lorcan's name and address neatly, licked a stamp and stuck it on the envelope. He would be shocked receiving it, she knew that. But it was Tessa's fault. The blame lay solely with her. On the phone, Lizzie had said bluntly that she was being spiteful, moving without telling them where they were going, and that Briony would suffer. And Valerie had said equally bluntly that Lizzie could look at it like that if she wanted to, but it had been hard enough dealing with Tessa when Jeff was alive; she was damned if she was going to deal with her now that he was dead, and if Jeff didn't like it wherever he was, tough. He'd left them to their own devices. She would do what felt right for her, and she wasn't going to talk to Lizzie about it again.

She'd been huffy when she'd hung up because guilt had niggled at her. She was taking Briony from loving grandparents, but her child was young; she'd adapt. There was plenty to keep Briony occupied in the city, and in time, the Egans would be a faded memory for both of them.

'Come on, Briony,' Valerie said to her daughter, who was putting Molly to bed in her cot. 'Let's go post a letter and then I'll take you to the park for a swing. How would you like that?'

'Yippee, swings.' Her daughter jumped to her feet and Valerie laughed as she fastened Briony's padded jacket, and pulled on a fleece herself. Hand in hand, mother and daughter walked out of their new home, into the crisp autumn sunshine, as the leaves skittered gaily around their feet and a white butterfly fluttered along in front of them.

CHAPTER THIRTY-EIGHT

The first few months in Dublin were the darkest and loneliest of Valerie's life. Getting Briony settled in her crèche while she went back to work was strange and exhausting. Christmas was a nightmare. She felt she had to put up a tree and make a fuss, and pretend to be excited about Santa's much-anticipated arrival. It was Briony and the familiar routine of work that got her through. Carmel had come up to Dublin on Christmas Eve and set about ratcheting up the excitement factor for Briony, keeping her occupied while Valerie slipped upstairs to her bedroom to cry muffled sobs into her pillow. She left to drive home to Rockland's after Briony was safely tucked in bed with her stocking hanging from the bedpost and a carrot and glass of milk sitting on the fireplace for Santa and Rudolph.

Pretend it's just another day, had been Valerie's mantra that day as she cooked vol-au-vents and chips for their dinner, eschewing the traditional feast. Briony had tucked in happily, feeding her new dolly little titbits. She was ecstatically happy with her new dolls' buggy and her nurse's outfit. The sitting room had been turned into a hospital ward after lunch and Valerie lay on the sofa being attended to, with one eye on the TV, and gradually daylight dimmed to dusk and the glow of lights on the Christmas tree grew brighter, and the day that Valerie had dreaded with all her heart slipped away. It was with huge relief that she went back to work in the New Year, now that the ordeal of the first Christmas without Jeff had passed.

Three weeks later, she got a phone call at work from the crèche to say that Briony was running a temperature and could she come and take her home. She had to take three days of her precious annual leave to nurse her through an ear infection because Carmel was stricken with the flu and couldn't come up to stay.

Being a working single mother wasn't easy. Valerie lived in dread of phone calls from the crèche, or getting stuck in traffic and being late picking Briony up, but her friends in Dublin were kind, and Carmel could always be depended upon to help out in a crisis, so she muddled along. As the days began to lengthen and the winter turned to spring, although she mourned Jeff deeply, Valerie began to feel as though she had survived a violent upheaval and nothing could ever be as bad again.

In early summer she got an unexpected windfall. Back money from a wage agreement and a tax rebate came with her salary cheque and she told Lizzie about it during their Sunday night phone call.

'Why don't you come over for a few days? I'd love to see you,' Lizzie urged. 'I'm so lonely and homesick,' she wheedled.

'Chancer, you've been there nearly five years!' Valerie laughed. 'You told me you were starting to enjoy life in London.'

'I'd enjoy it even more if you came to visit. Come on and see our new flat,' Lizzie cajoled. She and Dara had moved from Kensal Rise the previous year.

'I'll think about it,' Valerie said, laughing.

'Don't do that, be spontaneous and just come,' Lizzie urged.

'We'll see.' She put the phone down and tried not to remember when she and Jeff has spent several fun-filled mini breaks in London with their friends, and Tessa had looked after Briony for them. But it would be wonderful to be with Lizzie, and she and Briony deserved some fun.

'Would you like to go on an airplane and see Auntie Lizzie?' she said to Briony the next day when she was getting her ready for the crèche.

'In the sky? Where Daddy is?'

'Yes.'

'Can I bring Molly?'

'Yes, darling, of course you can,' Valerie said, beginning to feel excited. Be spontaneous, Lizzie had said, so that lunchtime, having applied for annual leave, Valerie booked their flight to London for the following Thursday morning.

Lizzie flung her arms around them in Arrivals at Heathrow, hardly able to believe that her best friend and goddaughter were standing before her. 'We are going to have such fun!' she declared, cuddling Briony. 'We're going to fly a kite on a big hill where you can see all of London.'

'Sounds good. Where is it?' Valerie asked as her friend led the way down to the tube.

'Primrose Hill. It's quite near us; we can have a picnic. It's very posh. You might even see a film star or two,' she said jauntily, stepping onto the Heathrow Express.

'Dara's going to meet us for a quick coffee.' Lizzie was still beaming when they reached Paddington, and she led them across the street to an elegant pub, The Pride of Paddington, while Briony stared around at the red buses and big black cabs with their light on top, fascinated at this new exciting place. Dara had embraced them in a warm bear hug and they'd sat for half an hour catching up before taking the tube to Swiss Cottage, where Lizzie took them down a tree-lined road full of neat red-brick houses off the Finchley Road, and to the flat she now called home.

The smell of strange spices and aromas filled Valerie's nostrils as they climbed the stairs to Lizzie's two-bedroomed flat. 'An Egyptian couple live downstairs and they cook a lot of Arabic food. It rather perfumes the air.' Lizzie threw her eyes up to heaven as she showed them into a bright airy flat, painted in shades of cream and white. Two sofas, and a huge TV filled the room, and the sun gleamed on the wooden floors, dotted with rugs.

'We're going for the minimalist look. Rather Swedish, don't you think? Lizzie said, showing Briony her two bonsai trees.

'Poseur!' Valerie teased. 'It's lovely and so uncluttered. I'd never get away with that now. We could open our own toyshop.'

The kitchen was small and compact, with a selection of cupboards that didn't quite match. 'Dara think's he's a DIY expert. Wait until you see the wardrobes,' Lizzie grinned, leading the way into their bedroom, which was decorated in shades of off-white with the wall behind the big double bed sponge-painted with pink daubs.

'It reminds me of someone with the measles, but nothing would do him but to give it a try after seeing it being done on the TV,' Lizzie said resignedly. 'Just as well I love him.'

'Interesting, though,' Valerie said diplomatically, and they burst out laughing.

The break had been just what she needed, and she and Lizzie had sat up until the early hours, just like in the old days, talking about how their lives had changed, sometimes laughing, and sometimes crying.

Watching Dara race down Primrose Hill, a huge red kite trailing behind him, and Briony, yelling with excitement, running after him, Valerie had felt unutterably sad, wishing that Jeff had been there with them. Lizzie had seen the look on her face and wordlessly reached out, caught her hand and squeezed it.

Boarding the flight home on the Sunday, Valerie knew she would be back. This was the first of many such visits. It would be something to look forward to, something to keep her going when she was missing Jeff with all her might.

Tessa heard Lorcan's car start up, the gravel crunching under the tyres as he drove out onto the road. She listened as the sound of the engine grew fainter and reached out for the cup of tea he had left on her bedside locker.

It was pelting rain. She could hear the relentless onslaught against the windows. She sipped the hot tea, then put the cup down and snuggled back under the bedclothes, letting them fold around her. She glanced at the clock. Just after six. The house was empty and silent, the loneliness, sorrow and despair seeping through the walls. 'Jeff. Jeff. Jeff.' She called his name and convulsed into sobs, weeping unrestrainedly, knowing she could not be heard, relieved that she could grieve without upsetting the rest of her family.

She wept until she was drained and then she lay exhausted, reliving the horror of that life-changing day when her son had died. She looked at the clock again, wishing she could sleep. Seven thirty. Her heart lurched. When it was her day to mind Briony, Jeff would arrive with her at half seven and the little girl would run into the house eager to see Tessa, ready for the adventures they would have and the games they would play. Tessa missed her grandchild greatly, now more than ever. Briony was their kith and kin, their last link with Jeff. It was cruel of Valerie to disappear the way she had, taking their grandchild with her. It was abduction, no more no less, Tessa raged. She had to confront her; there was no other way around it. Christmas, the worst of their lives, had come and gone, and Carmel had refused point-blank to take the Christmas presents she had bought for Briony or to give Tessa Valerie's new address.

'Please, Tessa, stop harassing me. I have to respect my daughter's wishes. Please understand that. I feel terribly sorry for you and maybe time will heal, but for now leave me be,' Carmel said wretchedly.

Tessa had felt like murdering her. She didn't care if Carmel was upset with her – couldn't the woman understand how *desperate* she was to see her grandchild? Remembering her grief and frustration during those dark days of the festive season, Tessa came to a decision. She would have to take the matter into her own hands.

She jumped out of bed, wrapped her dressing gown around her and hurried downstairs. She took the telephone directory into the kitchen and flipped the pages until she found the large entry for Dublin Corporation. She found the address for the department Valerie worked in and wrote down the address and telephone number. She made a mug of tea and took a map of the capital out of a drawer in the dresser, poring over it until she was familiar with the route she planned to take. For the first time since Jeff died, Tessa felt a sense of purpose. She showered and dressed, and just after ten she dialled the number she had written down.

'Could I speak to Valerie Harris, please?' she said to the girl on the switchboard, hoping her voice didn't sound as shaky as she felt.

'Just a moment while I put you through,' the receptionist said pleasantly. Tessa's fingers curled around the phone cord and her heart began to thump.

'Hello, Valerie Harris,' she heard a familiar voice say briskly. Tessa hung up immediately. Valerie was at work – that was all she needed to know. She grabbed her bag and car keys, locked the door and hurried out to the car, her fingers trembling as she switched on the ignition. She had to take a chance that the passage of time would have helped Valerie to realize just how unfair her actions were to Briony, Jeff's family and Jeff's memory. Tessa spun the steering wheel, slipped into gear and began her journey to Dublin, veering from sickening deep dread to wild optimism as the miles flew by.

She could eat lunch on the run and do her grocery shopping, Valerie thought, instead of doing it after she'd collected Briony from the crèche, when they'd both be tired. She hurried down the steps of her workplace, anxious not to lose a minute of her lunch hour, and failed to notice the woman in the black trench coat take a step towards her. She was mentally going through her shopping requirements when she became aware of her name being called and she turned, still preoccupied, and felt a sickening thud in her stomach when she recognized Tessa.

Dismay was swiftly replaced by fury. 'What are you doing here?' she demanded angrily, stopping in her tracks.

'Valerie, we need to talk. It's wrong of you to keep Briony away from us, from Jeff's family. He wouldn't want it. He'd be appalled. Surely you know that. Surely you know that you are not acting in Briony's best interests, depriving her of a loving family unit. You are being thoroughly selfish.' Tessa's accusations were like a punch in the stomach.

'How *dare* you?' Valerie's lip wobbled, stunned at the other woman's onslaught.

'I dare because Briony is Jeff's daughter—'

'Briony is *my* daughter, and I will raise her in a way Jeff would be proud of, Tessa. I haven't forgotten how you treated me when he died. I'll *never* forget it or forgive it. Now get out of my way and don't *ever* come here again.' Valerie's voice shook and she brushed past Jeff's mother and didn't look back.

Tessa watched Valerie race away from her and knew she had lost her grandchild. She hadn't meant to sound accusatory – her intention had been to placate – but Valerie's evident antipathy had raised her hackles and her tone had been unintentionally strident and confrontational.

'You fool, Tessa,' she cursed herself as Valerie disappeared around the side of the building, leaving her demoralized and shaken at yet another hostile incident with Jeff's partner.

Valerie felt physically sick getting into the car. Tessa's unexpected reappearance in her life had thoroughly rattled her. Fear raced through her. If Tessa had tracked her to work did she know where she and Briony lived? Did she know what crèche Briony was in? Would she take it a step further and take her from the crèche? It was unthinkable. But not beyond the bounds of possibility. Agitated, she turned off the engine and got out of the car. She needed to ring the crèche supervisor and make absolutely sure that Briony was never to be collected by anyone unless Valerie had left specific instructions. Tessa was a loose cannon and not to be trusted.

For months after the encounter Valerie worried that Tessa would do something untoward, and she hated Tessa for the added stress she now endured. Her attitude towards Jeff's mother hardened even more and Valerie determined that Tessa would never be part of Briony's life, no matter what.

On the first anniversary of Jeff's death, Valerie flew to London again, to be with Lizzie and Dara. There had been no contact with Tessa since the confrontation outside the office, and for the first time Valerie felt Tessa was out of their lives for good. Briony had started school and seemed happy, having made a few friends, and gradually she stopped talking about her grandparents and Rockland's. It grieved Valerie that she didn't talk about Jeff as much either, but she felt it meant her daughter was adjusting to their new circumstances, and to a degree she was herself. She had got over the first year of her life without Jeff and had made a home for herself and her daughter. That could only be something to be proud of.

*

My Darling Briony,

I know today is your eighteenth birthday and I hope that you are very happy and fulfilled in your life. Now that you are of an age to make your own decisions it would give your granddad and myself so much joy to meet with you and to get to know you and talk to you about your wonderful dad. You are always in our thoughts, our hearts and our prayers. You are now and always have been very precious to us, and to your aunt and uncle.

It would be lovely if you could get to know your cousins. They are all longing to meet you and we have so many memories and photos to share with you.

Please know, darling, that our door is always open to you and we have never stopped loving you.

With all my love,
Gramma xxxxxx

Tessa reread what she had written, and added her phone number under her signature. She folded the letter neatly and slid it into the envelope.

That afternoon she drove past The Triangle and turned down the street where Carmel and Terence lived. She took a deep breath before knocking on the door.

Carmel answered and Tessa got a shock when she saw the other woman's careworn appearance. Valerie's mother had aged considerably. In fact she didn't look at all well.

'Oh, it's you. What do you want, Tessa?' Carmel asked tiredly.

Tessa swallowed hard. 'Carmel, I know it's Briony's eighteenth birthday today and I'm begging you to send her this letter. You've had the joy of her all these years – can you not find it in your heart to show Lorcan and me some compassion and send her this letter so she can at least make a choice herself whether to get in touch or not? Please, Carmel, on my bended knee I beg of you,' Tessa pleaded.

Tears sparkled in Carmel's eyes and Tessa felt a surge of hope.

'Please,' she entreated again.

'All right, Tessa, give it to me. I'll post it to Briony,' she agreed. 'I do understand how hard it is for you and Lorcan but, you know, if you had left Valerie alone to get over her grief all those years ago, I think she would have relented and got in touch. You pressurized her, Tessa, and you upset her and you lost whatever chance you had.'

'I know,' Tessa sighed. 'Believe me, I know.'

'I'll send it to Briony, Tessa, but it's up to her whether she replies or not.' Carmel looked flushed and flustered.

'Thank you, Carmel, I appreciate it. I'll always be grateful,' Tessa replied.

'Who will I say it's from?' Carmel said, her eyes suddenly cloudy and unrecognizing.

'From me – Tessa. Jeff's mam,' Tessa said, perturbed.

'Of course. Don't mind me, my memory's gone to pot,' Carmel said hastily.

'You will send it? This afternoon, if possible?'

'Certainly,' Carmel said firmly, and closed the door.

Tessa walked slowly down the path. She wondered if the other woman was unwell. She certainly looked pale and wan. But Carmel had agreed to post the letter and Tessa had no doubt that she would. In her own quiet way Carmel Harris was a woman of principle.

Please, please, Jeff, she begged silently, let Briony get the letter and let her get in touch.

Carmel wrote Briony's address on the stamped envelope and placed it on the hallstand. She was in plenty of time to catch the five o'clock post. Tessa was right: Briony should have a chance to contact her grandparents if she so chose. Valerie could argue the toss with her about it but Carmel would stick to her guns. Briony was eighteen now, old enough to vote and old enough to make her own decisions.

She felt terribly weary. This lassitude that was affecting her made her want to sleep and made her forgetful. It was disturbing. Something wasn't right with her but she couldn't figure out what it was. She'd go and lie down for a while. She'd probably feel better after a little rest.

Carmel fell into a restless doze and woke with a start an hour later. She felt muzzy. There was something she had to do, she remembered, but what was it? She got up and wandered out to the kitchen to make herself a cup of tea. She'd need to start the dinner. Terence would be in from work soon and he'd be cranky if his dinner wasn't waiting.

She cooked chops, potatoes, cabbage, but forgot to turn on the gas under the carrots. Never mind, he could eat them raw, she decided, blessing herself as the Angelus bell rang at six. It was a lovely spring evening, she thought, opening the back door. She took a chair out, sat in the sheltered warmth of the back yard and felt a tranquil peace envelop her as she raised her face to the sun's rays.

Terence opened the front door, caught the aroma of cooking and sighed with relief. Carmel was cooking his dinner; she must be having a good day. She was beginning to behave rather strangely, forgetting things, buying groceries they didn't need, on one occasion going down the village and leaving the front door wide open for any intruder to walk in and help themselves. He had a terrible fear she was going doolally.

He noticed a letter on the hallstand where his wife always left his post, and ripped it open. He read the contents, momentarily perplexed, and then his brow drew down in a frown. Tessa Egan must have persuaded Carmel to post young Briony a letter. Valerie's lassie would be better off having nothing to do with that lot. All they did was cause trouble. The cheek of Tessa, declaring undying love. If she'd loved her grandchild as she'd professed, she'd never have allowed her to be born illegitimate and remain so when that ne'er-do-well of a son of hers was alive. You had your chance, Madam Egan, all those years ago. It's too late now, he thought dismissively. He crumpled up the letter and the envelope and shoved it in his pocket. He'd burn it later, and if Carmel asked him about it he'd say he dropped it in the postbox for her.

CHAPTER THIRTY-NINE

'Mom, Miss Lala is very hungry and wants Coco Pops for breakfast.' Briony struggled to consciousness to see Katie peering into her face, with her doll in one hand and her teddy in the other.

Light streamed in through the shutters, and she blinked, suddenly remembering where she was. Briony stretched luxuriantly. She was in Spain on her holidays, no longer any need to get up and feed Katie and rush to start the day. Bliss!

And then the dull ache of recollection: finding the letter, Tessa's letter. Valerie's betrayal. Reality hit. Briony felt sick.

'Can we have our breakfast outside, Mom? Are we going to Zoco today, Mom? Mom, will you come for a swim today?' The barrage of questions was relentless.

'Let's just have breakfast first and then we'll sort ourselves.' She swung her legs out of bed and felt a rush of nausea. Great, all she needed, a dodgy tummy on top of everything. She sat on the side of the bed taking deep breaths as Katie beamed at her, her blond curls tousled, her cheeks pink. Briony held out her arms, and Katie snuggled in, smothering her in kisses. 'Morning, Mom.'

'What time is it? Briony glanced at the alarm clock. 'Katie, it's seven thirty; we're on our holidays,' she chided.

'But Miss Lala's hungry and my sleep's all gone,' Katie explained patiently.

'Well, my sleep isn't,' she said crossly. 'Come on, I'll get your breakfast and I'll open my bedroom door and you can play on the terrace and I'll get back into bed for a snooze,' she grumbled, getting off the bed.

'Now, Miss Lala, look what you did. You made Mom cross. You shouldn't wake up so early,' Katie remonstrated with her dolly.

'I'm sorry. I didn't mean to be cross.' Briony dropped to her knees and wrapped her arms around her daughter. 'Come on, let's have breakfast outside. We don't want Miss Lala to faint with hunger,' she teased.

'I love you, Mommy,' Katie said good-naturedly, and Briony's heart melted.

'I love you too,' she said, leading her out to the kitchen. Valerie's bedroom door was closed and there was no sound from within. Wasn't she lucky to be sleeping like a log, untroubled? Briony thought resentfully, exhausted after her restless night.

How was she going to explain to Katie that they were going home? If Katie was older she'd have flown home this evening, but the only flights to Dublin landed in the early hours and she wouldn't keep her up that late. She would make a huge fuss of her today and let her spend her holiday money in the toyshop, and later, before bedtime, treat her to a sparkly fruity cocktail in the Trafalgar Bar. That was a special treat. Katie loved sitting on the little balcony overlooking the street, sipping her Kiwi Loco cocktail, decorated with the pink swirly umbrellas and sparklers. And Briony rather liked their Daiquiris. Valerie would not be invited to this evening out.

She needed to check out flights and fares after breakfast. She'd walk up to El Zoco around nine, take Briony toy shopping, check out her flights, have coffee in the Olive Tree, then spend the day on the beach with Katie, and go out for early dinner and cocktails. She wouldn't have to spend *any* time with her mother and hopefully she'd be able to fly home the next day. And that would be that! Valerie could go to hell! Briony had lost all respect for her. All the love she'd felt for her mother seemed smothered, damped down. All she felt was hurt and anger, and a huge sadness. Valerie had deprived her of Tessa and Lorcan's love, and her aunt and uncle's. Lisa and Steven probably had children of their own now, cousins that she had no knowledge of, or contact with. Her memories of Rockland's were ones of happiness, of being made to feel special, of being loved. She could have had that for all her life if Valerie hadn't cut them out of their lives. She had lost so much.

As she got older, she'd learned not to question her mother about the past. Valerie clearly didn't want to revisit it, and even at that young age she realized that it made her mother sad to talk about it. Briony felt it was up to her to make Valerie happy and so she kept a lot to herself so that her mother wouldn't fret.

Those early days when they had moved to Dublin had been so strange and unsettling. She missed her daddy, her old house, her friends, and her grandparents. For the first weeks in the crèche she felt utterly bereft when her mother would lead her in, and then leave her with adults and children she didn't know. When Valerie asked her if she had made friends and did she have fun playing, she would always say yes because she knew it pleased her mother. She remembered most the aching loss for her father that she had felt as a child. No one else in her class had lost a parent. Once, when she'd been eight or nine, her teacher had told the class to write a letter to their daddy for Father's Day. 'My daddy is dead,' Briony had said.

'You can write the letter and put it on his grave,' the teacher had said kindly. Briony had written the letter but she had put it away carefully in the drawer in her desk in the bedroom. Her mom didn't like to talk about graves. There was no point in even asking to put her letter on it, she'd thought stoically. She still had it. She could never bring herself to throw it out. Perhaps now was finally the time to go to Rockland's and make her peace with the past.

Tears smarted her eyes as she poured Coco Pops into a dish for Katie, and popped two croissants into the microwave. Briony cried for the lonely little girl she had once been until she had found her feet and made friends. Gradually she had settled down and the memories of Rockland's had faded. And because, over the years, for the most part, her life was full and happy and she had plenty of friends and a loving grandmother who came laden down with treats every weekend, Briony too relegated the past to the furthest reaches of her mind. It was never an issue between her and her mother until now.

Why? Why? Why? What had happened between Valerie and her father's family to make her sever all ties?

What difference did it make now anyway? She wasn't interested in hearing her mother's explanation. It was too late. How she wished she hadn't found that letter. It was true, ignorance *was* bliss. She made herself a mug of tea, placed the croissants and cereal on a tray and carried them outside to the patio where Katie had her dolls perched on the table.

This should have been so perfect. Such an opportunity to relax and recharge her batteries and enjoy her time with her mother. Briony could hardly eat the croissant she felt so angry with Valerie, and queasy to boot. Not even the lemon blush of the early morning sun on the sea could calm her troubled spirit. She sat, tense and irritable, hoping that her mother wouldn't appear until after she had gone up to the town. But there was silence from inside and an hour and a half later she and Katie set off on their jaunt, with no appearance from Valerie, much to Briony's relief.

Valerie woke from a deep sleep and lay immobile for a few moments in that perfect state of waking when all is well until the realization hits that something has changed. A memory of that first morning after Jeff's death surfaced, of waking up, feeling normal, and then the sudden shock of comprehension that everything had changed utterly.

Now she remembered that Briony had found Tessa's letter. Now she remembered how she hadn't gone to sleep until dawn's kiss had caressed the eastern sky. Suddenly alert, she sat up, straining to hear Katie's merry chirruping, but there was nothing, only stillness and silence. Fear struck. Surely Briony wasn't gone?

Valerie threw back the sheet, jumped out of bed and hurried out of her room. She felt almost limp with relief when she saw Katie's teddy on her bed. But then she remembered Briony's declaration that she was going to get a flight home. That was probably where she'd gone:

to book a flight in one of the internet cafés. Valerie had slept so late and so soundly after her restless night, she hadn't heard a sound. She went back into her bedroom to open the shutters, heavy-hearted. Her mobile rang and she almost jumped out of her skin. Valerie saw Lizzie's number flashing up.

'Hi,' she said dispiritedly, gazing out at a profusion of pink, violet and scarlet blossoms.

'What's up?' Lizzie said crisply. 'I rang to see how things were going.'

'I think Briony's gone to book a flight home.' Valerie burst into tears.

'Oh dear,' Lizzie groaned. 'Like mother like daughter. She's *so* like you sometimes.'

'What am I going to do?'

'Stop bawling. That won't help.'

'That's easy for you to say,' sniffed Valerie crossly. 'Try and be a bit sympathetic.'

'I *am*, but, honey, this day was bound to come. You've always known it might,' Lizzie sighed.

'Why? Lizzie, *why* do I have to go through all of this again? It's unbearable,' Valerie protested. 'I hardly slept a wink last night remembering it all. God, it was so real. It was like I was living it all again – all that pain and shock and sorrow.'

'Sometimes, if we have issues to resolve and we haven't faced them, we have to deal with them. It's a last clearing for you before you can move on,' Lizzie said patiently.

'But I *have* moved on, for crying out loud. That all happened so long ago.'

'Eh . . . noooo! You ran away to Dublin, and didn't go back. You weren't honest with Briony and that has to be attended to. Life has a funny old way of catching up with us.'

'Why do you think like that? How can you say those things with such authority, Lizzie?' Valerie said irritably.

'You know why. Because that's what life has taught me. When I lost my babies I had to go deep inside and search for answers. I had to face my pain and grief and bitterness and anger. I didn't run away from it for as long as you did, although I did run away and hit the bottle for a while. You know that. You got me through it. I'm not saying this to be in any way judgemental or unkind – you know that too. And I did seek and I asked for help and it was given to me. Now you're being taught – in a difficult way too, I'll admit – that issues can't be buried deep, that issues will always come calling to be resolved. But the great thing is, we don't have to do it alone, Valerie.'

'But I don't want to revisit the past, Lizzie,' Valerie groaned.

'Well, unfortunately sometimes we have to do that to let it go. Do you think it was a coincidence that Briony discovered Tessa's letter on Jeff's anniversary?'

'Well, yes, that was a bit strange, to say the least,' she conceded.

'Not strange in the slightest. And not a coincidence either. Rather a synchronicity, deah, as our lovely Mrs M would have said.'

'What the hell are you wittering on about, Lizzie?' Valerie said, exasperated.

Lizzie laughed. 'Think outside the box, Valerie. Who would want to see Briony and Tessa and even yourself and Tessa reconciled?'

'Lorcan? But sure, how could he have planned it or organized it? I haven't seen him in years.'

'Not Lorcan. Close, though.'

'Lisa?'

'Outside the box, Valerie,' prompted her friend.

Comprehension dawned. '*Jeff!* You're saying Jeff planned it?'

'Haven't I *always* told you he's still around you? Haven't I told you about The Mothers and The Fathers who are always guiding us and wanting the best for us?'

'You're saying Dad is involved too!' Valerie exclaimed derisively. 'Now I *know* you're mad.'

'Of course he is.' Lizzie was unperturbed. 'He wants the best for you and Briony. Now that he's passed beyond the veil he knows what life is all about and why we're here. He's remembered who he is and where he came from. So now his love for you is unconditional and he would love it if you could make your peace with him too. All of this is happening for a reason, Valerie. It's for healing. You must make your peace with the past if you want peace of mind and contentment,' Lizzie said gently. 'It really is time to let go of the old hurts and sorrows. You don't need them any more. They're only holding you back. It's toxic energy – get rid of it.'

'Are you saying I should get in touch with *Tessa*?' she squawked, incredulous.

'Briony will be, I should imagine. Do you *really* want to live the rest of your life with all that baggage, and go to your grave bitter and twisted?'

'Oh, for God's sake, I'm *not* bitter and twisted, Lizzie,' she said defensively.

'Is that right?' said Lizzie drily.

'I'm not.'

'I'm just asking, do you still want to carry all that stuff, Valerie?' Lizzie said airily. 'Now I have to be off, I've got to bring Lady Gaga to school today, because it's pissing out of the heavens over here, unlike the Costa del Sol. I'll phone tonight.'

Valerie laughed in spite of herself. 'And how is the darling girl?'

'Stomping around upstairs in a huff because, and I quote, "Like, no one in this house understands me. You're, like, *ruining* my life!" American TV has so much to answer for. Every second word is "like", and don't get me going about "lol". It makes my teeth grit.'

'I don't get that one either. It's a bit daft,' Valerie agreed. 'And why's her life being ruined? Thank God all that's behind me.'

'Because she wants an iPhone and she's not getting one. She has a perfectly adequate BlackBerry. For crying out loud, I have a Nokia that came out of the Ark. Lol,' Lizzie snorted.

'It was far from iPhones and BlackBerries we were reared,' Valerie remarked.

'OMG! Valerie, how *could* you? That's the kind of thing our mothers used to say. We've officially turned into our mothers,' Lizzie exclaimed aghast. 'Soz! I'm, like, just not having it. I am *not* my mother. Lol.'

'Soz? What's *that*?'

'It means sorry. Don't you, like, know *any* cool lingo? Better go, hon. Love ya. Let me know what's happening.'

'I will. Bye, Lizzie. Thanks for ringing. You're such a pal, even if you *did* say I was bitter and twisted.'

'No probs! Think about what I said and if anything resonates go with it. In the end we all have to find what best works for us.'

'Yeah, OK,' Valerie agreed unenthusiastically.

'Trust me on this one. It's all happening for a reason, and I know that will drive you mad – it used to drive me mad when I was going through the hard stuff and my counsellor would say it – but I'm telling you, now you think it's one of the worst things that's ever happened to you, but you will look back on this and see it's just the opposite,' Lizzie said firmly. 'Talk soon.'

Was Lizzie right? How could this possibly be a good thing for any of them? Could it be even remotely true, that Jeff was making all this stuff happen, Valerie pondered, straightening the bedclothes and fluffing the pillows. But to think that her father would want to be close to her took a bit of getting used to. A sudden memory of finding the envelope in her bag with three hundred pounds in it and her name written neatly in Terence's looping script popped into her head. Judas money, she had called it at the time, but she had kept it as a little nest egg in the Post Office in case she ever needed it. And the strange thing was, she never had. Even though things had been tight, financially, she had never wanted for money. She had always managed. Lorcan had given Carmel a letter with the cheque from the insurance company and another cheque with his savings from the Credit Union and she had put that money aside for Briony's education. He had said in his letter that whenever she felt ready to come back to them there would always be a welcome and much love for her and Briony, and he hoped that day would come soon.

Valerie sighed. Poor Lorcan, she had always felt bad for him about what she had done, but she had never forgiven Tessa. They were elderly now, Tessa and Lorcan. In their seventies. It was hard to believe. Was Lizzie right? Should she make some effort to see them now that Briony had discovered the letter? Would the door be slammed in her face? It would not surprise her if it was. There was too much anger and bitterness between them. Sometimes forgiveness wasn't possible, she told herself. Some things could never be resolved.

Out of the corner of her eye she saw a flickering movement. She turned her head just as two white butterflies dipped and danced in exuberant flight in front of her. How strange! Lizzie was always telling her to look for signs and she would get them. Could it be a sign from Jeff? From her dad?

No, this was mad stuff. It might be Lizzie's way of thinking but it wasn't hers, Valerie decided. Anything could be a sign if you wanted it to be. A butterfly was a butterfly and nothing else. And then she remembered that first day in the house in Dublin all those years ago when she and Briony had gone to post the letter to Lorcan, and a white butterfly had danced ahead of them and she had felt sure that Jeff was with them.

CHAPTER FORTY

'Have you booked a flight home yet?' Lizzie's voice floated down the airways, clear as a bell.

'I'm going to as soon as Katie's spent her pocket money. She's on a spending spree that would put the Arab sheiks to shame,' Briony said, surprised. 'How did you know I was going to? I suppose Mother went running to you,' she added sarcastically.

'I've just been talking to your mother, yes,' Lizzie said calmly. '*I* phoned her, actually.'

'And did she tell you how she's lied to me all these years? Did she tell you I found a letter from my grandmother that she kept from me?'

'I know all about your grandmother, Briony,' Lizzie said gently. 'And I know all about your mother, and your dad. It's a long and complicated story. And that's why I don't want you to book a flight home. Do you want to repeat what's happened to you, with Katie? Do you want Katie coming to you in the years ahead, demanding to know why *you* stopped her from seeing her grandmother? Is that what you want?'

'You're taking her side,' Briony protested, glad the shop was empty, apart from the young Chinese girl who was serving behind the counter. No one could hear their conversation, and Katie was engrossed in her shopping. The shop was an Aladdin's cave for a little girl intent on spending. Briony moved half-way down an aisle where she could carry on her conversation and keep an eye on her daughter. 'It was unforgivable what Mom did, Lizzie. She should be ashamed of herself and you shouldn't be defending her behaviour,' she said heatedly.

'I'm not defending anything and I'm not taking anyone's side, darling. I do feel so sorry for you, and for Tessa and Lorcan, but I know why Valerie took the decisions she took. It was a very, very hard time in her life. Will you promise me one thing?'

'What?' Briony said sullenly.

'Don't book your ticket for twenty-four hours. Just give it that much. And don't get into an argument with your mother.'

'I want to go home,' Briony argued.

'I know, love, but please, just give it another day or two and let the anger dissipate. Then make a decision,' Lizzie pleaded. 'For Katie's sake.'

'Aw, Lizzie, that's not fair. It's emotional blackmail.'

'I know. But I'm your godmother, and it's my duty to try and keep you on the right track. You really don't want Katie in a situation like this in years to come, now, do you, in all honesty?'

'All right then,' Briony said ungraciously.

'You're the best godchild in the universe,' Lizzie praised, and Briony laughed in spite of herself.

'I'm not a three-year-old, I'm thirty, for goodness' sake.'

'I know that, but you're still the best godchild, darling. Ring me if you need to talk.'

'OK, I will.'

'Now go and put it all out of your head for a while and have fun with that gorgeous little sweetheart. And make the most of the sun. It's raining cats and dogs here and it's really cold. September my ass, it's more like mid-winter. Byeeee.'

Lizzie was something else, Briony thought wryly, watching Katie studying a selection of bracelets intently. She had already bought a Spanish doll, a cuddly toy and a hairband.

'Last thing, Katie,' she said. 'Let's go and have some coffee and lemonade.'

'I'm going to buy Valwee a dolaphin bracelet, Mommy, 'cos she likes bracelets, an' I'm going to buy you a star one,' her daughter declared matter-of-factly. 'An' I have to buy a present for Daddy.'

'You are the kindest little girl,' Briony said proudly, very pleased that Katie would decide to spend some of her money on gifts, without being prompted. She had a generous nature, which was a source of satisfaction to her parents. Some of the kids in Katie's crèche had been selfish little brats.

Briony put her phone back in her bag. She wanted to ring Finn and pour her heart out to him. He'd surely take her side and understand her hurt. She had to be careful, though; she didn't want Katie getting wind of any upset with the grown-ups.

Her godmother knew exactly what buttons to press to make her feel guilty. Had Lizzie tried to talk Valerie out of her decision to cut the Egans out of their lives, all those years ago, Briony wondered as she sipped strong sweet coffee outside a small restaurant in an enclosed shaded square and watched her daughter dipping her dolly's feet into a bubbling ornate fountain. El Zoco had a Moorish atmosphere, and the arches and terracotta hues were soothing to her frazzled spirit.

She trawled back through her memories again, getting flashes here and there. She remembered crying, telling her mother she missed Gramma and Gandad and Valerie telling her they lived far away now but she still had Granny Carmel, who came to see them every week.

She remembered, when she was a little older, asking why did other girls and boys have a daddy and why had her daddy not come back to them, and Valerie explaining very gently that her daddy had died.

And then, once, when she was seven or eight, asking if she could go back to Rockland's to visit Carmel and her other granny and granddad, and Valerie telling her that her other granny and granddad didn't want to see her or Valerie ever again, because they had been cross with Valerie when her daddy had died. She couldn't understand why they would be cross and wondered, was it anything *she* had done? It never occurred to her that her mother – or any adult, for that matter – would tell her a lie so she'd just accepted what she was told. All that worry and anxiety she had silently endured because her mother had lied. Briony was still in shock thinking about the trauma her mother had inflicted on her.

She took her phone out of her bag and speed dialled Finn.

'Hi, I can't talk right now; I'm just heading into a meeting. Can I call you later?' Her husband sounded harassed.

'Oh, Finn, I need to talk to you. It's not even nine a.m. at home, ' she said, exasperated.

'But you know we have back-to-back meetings on Monday mornings, starting with a breakfast one,' he reminded her. 'What's wrong? Is Katie OK?'

'Yes, Katie's fine. It's Mom and me. I found a letter from my grandmother, my dad's mother, that was written to me years ago. Mom lied to me and I just don't want to be near her. I want to come home,' she said, glad that there was no one at any of the nearby tables.

'What? You want to come home?' echoed Finn, flabbergasted.

'Mom lied to me about my dad's parents not wanting to see me. It's hideous. I can't believe she'd do something like that. I'm devastated. I'm going to book a flight home. I want to come home,' she repeated.

'Look, don't do anything hasty. I can't talk now, I have to go. I'll ring as soon as I can, OK?' he said, sounding slightly fraught. 'Sorry, Briony, I have to go.'

'What's new?' she muttered and hung up.

'I knew this day would come eventually. And now it's a right mess,' Lizzie remarked, pouring herself another cup of coffee, having given her husband the latest update on 'the Spanish Situation'.

'Why don't you go over and sort them out? Do a Kofi Annan on it?' Dara suggested, draining his coffee and finishing the last of his toast.

'You mean go over to Spain?' She wasn't sure if she'd heard him properly.

'Look, you pair are practically joined at the hip. Just as well I'm not the jealous type,' he grinned. 'You've always been there for each other. You know Valerie's past. You love Briony like a daughter. Maybe you could act as referee. Just a suggestion.'

'Oh, Dara, you are the kindest husband.' She got up, threw her arms around him and hugged him.

'I know,' he said smugly. 'Anyway, I owe you one. You let me and Killian go to the Euros and even bought me a green jersey. Going to Spain to act as referee might not be as much fun as going to a football match but if you want to go, I'll even bring you to the airport.'

'But what about Madam?' She pointed up to the ceiling where Katy Perry was getting loud airplay.

'I can take care of the frustrated teenager. Killian looks after himself anyway, more or less. Get a cheap flight over, defuse the situation and try to fit in some R & R.'

'Yeah, but what about work? It's a bit short notice.' But Lizzie was really liking his suggestion. An unexpected trip to see two of the people she loved most in the world, *and* get some sun! What a treat, even if Briony and Valerie were having the mother of all rows.

'Take today's appointments. Reschedule or get someone else to do the rest of them for you. It's only for a couple of days and anyway, this is an emergency,' he said firmly.

'Are you sure?' she said doubtfully, following him into the hall where he put on his overcoat and took the big umbrella out of the hallstand.

'Don't worry, I'll get you again. Probably the next World Cup. Ring me and let me know what time your flight is and we'll sort out the airport.' He opened the front door. 'God, it's still chucking it down. The tube will be the pits this morning,' he groaned.

'At least let me give you a lift. Come on, Rachel,' she yelled up the stairs. 'I want to give your dad a lift to the station so we have to take a detour.'

'Like I'm going to be *so* late if we do that.' Their daughter clomped down the stairs and glowered at them.

'Like deal with it,' Lizzie said briskly, the prospect of a few days in the sun away from teenage tantrums looking more inviting by the second.

'This is for you, Valwee.' Katie raced into the garden waving a small paper bag. Valerie's eyes lit up when she saw her granddaughter running over to her where she was on her knees weeding a flowerbed.

'For me?' she exclaimed. Out of the corner of her eye, she could see Briony standing at the French doors in the sitting room.

'What is it?' Her heart filled with love at the sight of Katie's eager, upturned face, blue eyes dancing with excitement. Sometimes she looked so like Jeff she thought with a pang, as Katie wrapped her arms around her neck and planted a loving kiss on her cheek.

Valerie held her tight, savouring the moment. A thought struck her like a hammer blow and this time she couldn't run away from it, or justify her behaviour to herself. Since Briony had found her grandmother's letter, Valerie had struggled to ignore the guilt that was eating her up. She had deprived Tessa and Lorcan of moments like this. And even worse, she had deprived her own daughter of an abundance of unconditional love that would have always been there for her to tap into. She had committed a terrible injustice to the person she most loved in the world. She'd never had to face up to what she'd done all those years ago until now. She'd never actually *understood* the huge repercussions of her decision to deny Briony access to her grandparents, and to deny them access to her. When her daughter had threatened never to let her see Katie again, what she had done had finally hit home. It was horrendous! She had behaved in such a mean-spirited, selfish way, and she'd never given it serious consideration. What did it say about her, what did it say about the type of person she was? How had she felt no guilt? Lizzie was right, she had become so bitter and twisted she couldn't even see the grave injustice she'd done to her own child, let alone Jeff's parents, and indeed Jeff himself. He would never have approved of her actions.

'Look, Valwee.' Katie held out the bracelet she'd bought, proud as punch. 'It's a dolaphin one.'

'Oh, darling, it's beautiful.' Valerie's voice shook as she tried to regain her composure. 'Put it on me.' She held out her hand and Katie slid the purple and silver bracelet over her wrist.

'Valwee, it's so pwetty on you. I love dolaphins.' She fingered the little charms with delight.

'I'll always treasure it,' Valerie said, swallowing hard. 'You're a very kind girl. What else did you do when you were in El Zoco?' she asked, desperate to know if Briony had booked a flight home.

'We went to the toyshop an' then we had lemonade and a cake, an' I played at the fountain, and then we came home. Can I have some tea towels to play hospital? My dolly is very sick – she has pumonia,' Katie declared matter-of-factly.

'Oh dear, pumonia! That's serious. We'd better get the tea towels and perhaps a sponge and some water to take dolly's temperature down.' She knew Katie loved anything to do with water.

'Oh, yes, an' some sweets for when she's feeling better?' She eyed her grandmother hopefully.

'Absolutely,' agreed Valerie, laughing. She stood up and took Katie by the hand. It didn't sound as though there'd been any visit to an internet café, which was a huge relief.

Briony was slouched on the sofa flicking through the latest *Hello!*, yawning her head off. She never even glanced at her mother. She looked very peaky, Valerie thought guiltily. She probably didn't get much sleep the previous night either.

'I'm just going to set up the hospital with Katie. Would you like a cuppa?' she asked lightly.

'Thanks, I had coffee in El Zoco.' Briony never raised her head from the magazine. Valerie's heart sank even further. How would her daughter ever forgive her for what she'd done?

While Katie busied herself sorting her sick dolls on her bed, Valerie procured the requested tea towels, a small Tupperware bowl of water, and a sponge.

'Maybe we should put a towel on top of the bed just in case any water gets on it,' she suggested, getting one of the fluffy bath sheets out of her hot press.

'Gwate idea, Valwee. Don't forget the sweets, an' you have to call me Nurse now, not Katie.'

'Certainly, Nurse, sweets coming up.' Valerie hid a smile.

Nurse was completely engrossed in tending to her many patients, teddy bear included, when Valerie placed a small dish of jelly babies on the bedside table.

'Thank you, Valwee. I can't talk now I'm doing a nopo-
ration.' She popped a sweet into her mouth and turned to
resume her duties. Summarily dismissed, Valerie walked
back down the hall and took a deep breath.

'Briony,' she said, coming to sit beside her daughter,
'I'm so sorry. I can't tell you how sorry I am. What I did
was unforgivable. Would you let me try and explain? I
truly never meant to hurt you, but now I have to face the
fact that I've done something really awful.' Tears blurred
her eyes, overflowing down her cheeks.

Briony looked at her. 'It's a bit late for tears now, Mom;
that's not going to bring my grandparents and my aunt
and uncle back to me,' she said coldly. She yawned again
and stood up. 'Look, I'm tired and I don't feel the best –
can we talk about this later? I'm going in to lie down for
a while.'

'OK,' Valerie said, subdued. 'I'm glad you're still here.'

'For now,' Briony said curtly, clearly in no mood for
discussions of any sort.

What the hell was going on in Spain between Valerie and
Briony, Finn worried as his mind drifted from the droning voice of the company accountant laying down a list
of cost-cutting requirements for each department.

He had never known his wife to have a row with her
mother. They got on very well, as a rule. Something
about a letter from her grandmother. He glanced at his
watch. Twenty minutes more and they should be breaking for lunch and then he could phone her. He'd felt bad
giving her the brush-off this morning. Briony could be a
bit of a hothead. He hoped by the time he spoke to her
she would have cooled down some. It really would be a

shame for them to cut short their holiday. But if she was coming home, he'd need to put manners on the kitchen and the bedroom. Even in the three days his wife had been away, standards had slipped considerably. He didn't want to get caught on the hop. Her timing was crap, he thought ruefully. He'd never been so busy at work. He didn't have time for family spats. The sooner it was sorted the better.

'I really think you should try and work it out, Briony. Listen to what Valerie has to say. At least do that much before you book a ticket home,' Finn said patiently.

'That's easy for you to say, Finn,' Briony said crossly. She'd been having a lovely snooze when her phone had rung and Finn had demanded to know what was going on.

'I know that, but you don't make a decision like that lightly. There are always two sides to every story,' he reasoned. 'She's always been a great mother to you and a wonderful grandmother to Katie, don't forget that either.'

'All right, Finn, I hear you,' Briony said grumpily. 'But it would be nice if someone could see it from my point of view too. You and Lizzie are making excuses for Mom. I think she behaved appallingly.'

'Decide when you hear what she has to say about it all, Briony, that's all I'm asking. And I know you're hurt and upset, and I wish I was there with you, and if it does get too much to bear of course come home,' he said kindly, and she burst into tears.

'Oh, Briony, please don't cry. You know I hate it when you cry,' Finn said agitatedly.

'I'm just devastated,' she sobbed.

'Just talk to Valerie and find out why. It might help,' he urged.

'OK, I will. I'll talk to you later.'

'I love you, if that's any help.'

'It is,' she assured him, wiping her eyes with the back of her hand. 'Thanks for ringing.'

'Have you stopped crying?'

'Yeah. See ya.'

'Mind yourself,' he said, and she knew he was probably relieved the phone call was over. Much as she hated to admit it, he was right: she needed to talk to her mother and get her side of the story before she could make any real judgement. She lay on her bed, watching the sunlight spill onto the terrace, and dapple her bedroom through the dipping wisteria branches. She listened to the rhythmic melody of the sea and even in her agitated state it still had the power to soothe. It dawned on her that there was no sound apart from the sea and birdsong and the murmur of the breeze through the leaves. Katie was usually singing or running around the place. She never walked. No sound of song, or little footsteps on marble tiles. She got off the bed and went out to her daughter's bedroom. The hospital patients lay neatly on the bath sheet, each covered by a tea towel. Of the nurse there was no sign. Briony went into the kitchen. A note from Valerie lay on the counter.

Gone to the beach up by McDonald's. Didn't like to wake you. Ring if you want anything from the shops, if not will be home in a couple of hours. Plenty of cheese, salami, chorizo and olives in fridge if you want lunch when you wake up. Mom XXX

Actually she did feel quite peckish, Briony thought, glad the queasy feeling was gone. She made up a platter, buttered a crusty roll, poured herself a glass of milk and carried the repast to the table on the terrace. After she had eaten it she would change into her bikini and stretch out on a lounger with her book. She might as well make the most of her few hours of peace and quiet. And tonight, after Katie was in bed, she would take her husband's advice and have a long discussion with her mother and get her side of the story before deciding on her course of action.

CHAPTER FORTY-ONE

She couldn't be more nervous, Valerie thought wryly as butterflies danced a foxtrot up and down her diaphragm. The table on the terrace was set for a light supper. The salmon was poached and the Caesar salad tossed and waiting its dressing. The wine was chilling in the fridge. It was nine forty-five and she was waiting for Briony to join her. But her daughter was fast asleep on Katie's bed; the illustrated storybook she'd been reading aloud had slipped out of her hand onto the floor. Valerie was reluctant to wake her up. Her daughter was clearly catching up on much-needed sleep. She'd clattered a few pots in the kitchen, but so far there was no sign of her waking up.

She could do with a good long sleep herself, Valerie thought glumly. But when she and Katie had come home from the beach late that afternoon, Briony had a tasty macaroni cheese and baked potatoes waiting for them and as they carried the dishes outside, she had said quietly that when Katie was in bed she would like to hear Valerie's side of the story.

Bedtime seemed to have taken for ever. Katie had had to have a bath and get her hair washed after her day on the beach. Then her hair had to be dried and a story had to be read. By then, Valerie's nerves were frayed, to say the least.

What would her daughter make of the unhappy, fraught saga of her relationship with Tessa? Would she be at all sympathetic? Would she understand how crushed she had been that Jeff had not married her? Even though her own mother had sided with Tessa, it was Tessa she blamed most for Jeff's decision to back out of marrying her. Tessa made her give up the chance to have Briony born in wedlock. Valerie could still remember to this day, Tessa staring at her saying, 'The best thing Jeff can do for you and the baby is get his qualification, and I know if you love him you won't stand in his way.'

Tessa had backed her into a corner good and proper. Briony could have been Briony Egan! And she could have been Jeff's wife. Mrs Jeffery Egan. He was the love of her life and he was the man she would have given anything to marry.

Valerie sighed; even all these years later she would still love to have been Jeff's wife. She had nearly married another man some years back. She had met Laurence Richmond at a party in Lizzie and Dara's home and there had been an instant attraction. He was a successful businessman, ten years older than she, divorced with two adult children. He lived in an elegant penthouse apartment overlooking the Thames just below Vauxhall Bridge. With Briony working and in a relationship with her husband-to-be, Valerie had felt free to begin a romance with the London businessman and it had been a happy time in her life, rediscovering the pleasure of having a companion, being desired and made to feel sexy and attractive. After wooing her for three years, Laurence had asked her to marry him. She was tempted. She got on very well with him, they had similar tastes in literature, food, the arts, and they made each other laugh. It would be nice not to have to work to support herself any more, and she would have had an affluent lifestyle, but Laurence had a roving eye. Even when she was out with him he would flirt light-heartedly with other women, and Valerie knew that fidelity would be difficult for him. And she couldn't live with him knowing that he would eventually succumb to the lure of a younger woman. No matter how discreet he was, she would not be able to hack it. His first wife had divorced him because of his adultery. Much as she cared for him and enjoyed being with him, Valerie knew he would not change. She had turned him down, and ended their relationship two months later when she'd caught him in a lusty embrace with one of his daughter's friends.

If she'd married Laurence, would she still feel as bitter towards Tessa, she mused. When Briony quizzed her tonight she would do her utmost to be fair to Jeff's mother, because it was highly likely that Briony would seek her out, and if she laid it on too thick it could rebound on her. Tessa would want her side of the story told too.

'I fell asleep. Sorry.' Briony padded out onto the terrace, bleary-eyed, startling her.

'It's OK. I often used to do the same when you were that age,' Valerie replied, standing up to go and serve their supper. She felt awkward now that they didn't have Katie to focus their attention on. It was just her and her daughter now, time for the truth to be revealed, whatever the outcome.

'Wine?' she asked lightly, carrying the salmon and salad to the table.

'Um . . . maybe I'll just have some tonic water.' Briony pulled out the two chairs.

'Maybe I'll just have tonic too then,' Valerie said, disappointed. A couple of glasses of wine might have taken the edge off the situation.

'Have a glass, Mom, if you want. I still feel slightly queasy and the tonic water might help,' Briony said, knowing that Valerie had never liked drinking alone. Her mother always enjoyed having a drink when she had company in the house in Dublin or out here in Spain.

'Maybe I will,' Valerie said, feeling the need for alcohol to get her through the ordeal ahead. She had just uncorked the bottle when the doorbell rang. It was late – 10 p.m. – who could be at her door? She knew her neighbours to say hello to, she had a few friends along the coast, but she wasn't expecting anyone to call.

She peered out through the spy hole in the door and couldn't believe her eyes. 'Lizzie!' she exclaimed joyfully, opening the door to find her best friend beaming at her, as a taxi swung around and disappeared into the night.

'What are you doing here?' She hugged her tightly as Briony came in to bring out the Marie Rose sauce that Valerie had forgotten.

'Lizzie!' she exclaimed, a smile crossing her pale face when she caught sight of her godmother. 'What are you doing here?' She echoed her mother's question.

'I'm brokering a UN ceasefire, but first I need food. I'm starving!' Lizzie grinned. 'I raced home from work and Dara drove me to the airport and I just couldn't face one of those cardboard panini they serve on the flight. Feed me anything, girls, and I wouldn't say no to a glass of something either. Here's a bottle of bubbly – stick it in the fridge to chill for when we have a cessation of hostilities. Now kiss me, godchild.' She put her arms around Briony and hugged her tightly. 'Right, I'm on three days' R & R. Let me get out of my shoes, and plonk my ass on a chair, you can dance attendance on me tonight and I'll muck in tomorrow and help out.'

Lizzie kicked her shoes off, went out onto the terrace and stood inhaling the scented night air. 'Bliss! Oh, and I'm just in time for supper,' she exclaimed seeing the table all set. 'Have you enough for an extra mouth?'

'We've plenty. I'll plate it up in a jiffy,' Valerie said excitedly. She was thrilled to see Lizzie.

'A feast,' declared Lizzie, happily.

The evening took on a whole new energy with Lizzie wisecracking and joking through their meal, and for the first time since Briony had discovered Tessa's letter, she and Valerie declared an unspoken truce.

'What did Rachel say when she heard you were coming?' Valerie grinned as she offered Lizzie some crackers and cheese after their meal.

'Couldn't believe her luck,' Lizzie said drily. 'She really is being so bolshy these days. But it's only with me. She spent the last two weeks of August in Rockland's and had a great time with Mam and Dad, and they said she was a joy to be with. I ask you.'

'Briony went through her bolshy phase too. It will pass,' Valerie assured her.

'Sadly for me I was never able to spend two weeks in Rockland's with *my* grandparents.' Briony glowered at her mother. 'Thanks to Mom, I never got to spend *any* time with them after she took me away from there.'

'Don't be like that, Briony. You don't know what it was like,' Valerie said wearily. The convivial atmosphere changed in an instant and tension crackled around the table.

'Well, what *was* it like, Mom? Just tell me and let me make up my own mind.'

'Should I leave you to it?' Lizzie stood up.

Valerie looked at Briony. 'Do you want to do this on our own or are you happy for Lizzie to stay?'

'Don't put her in an awkward position, Val. I'll go inside and channel-surf.' Lizzie refilled her glass and made to go inside but Briony caught her arm.

'Please stay, Lizzie. Just promise me you won't take sides.'

'I won't, Briony, but I lived through it all with your mom, don't forget that. It's not to say that I agreed with every decision she made, though,' Lizzie reminded her, lowering herself into the chair again and taking a slug of wine.

'So? Why *did* you and Gramma hate each other so much?' Briony turned to her mother. 'Why *did* you tell me that she didn't want to see us any more?'

Valerie dropped her hands into her lap and sat up very straight. 'Hate is a very strong word, Briony, and yes, when your father died I suppose we did hate each other, but to go back to the beginning in so far as it concerns you, I suppose it would be fair to say that Tessa and I never really liked each other from the first time we met. I felt she smothered Jeff and made a mammy's boy of him and she interfered too much in his life. And she felt I wanted to steal him from her. He was her younger son and her favourite child. Lorcan himself told me that. She saw me as a threat, and then I did the unthinkable and the unacceptable: I got pregnant and it all went downhill from there . . .'

Briony listened to her mother telling what it was like when she'd discovered that she was pregnant, and tried hard to imagine herself in her shoes.

'But how come Granddad Harris and Granddad Egan wanted you to get married and the grandmothers didn't?' she asked, surprised when Valerie described the family summit in Tessa and Lorcan's sitting room.

'You have to understand that being an unmarried mother in the early eighties carried a stigma and brought shame on families. We were judged by the Church and society.' Valerie tried not to let the old hurts take hold as she explained.

'Young women of your generation really have no conception of what it was like for us and, bad as it was then, it was a thousand times worse for your grandmothers. There was no such thing as contraception for them. The Church really interfered in women's personal lives. It was outrageous when you look back at it,' Lizzie interjected. 'And when your mom and I joined the civil service there was what was known as "the Marriage Bar". You had to give up work if you got married. I was able to claim the marriage gratuity by resigning, and that did help when Dara and I moved to London, but neither female emancipation nor women's lib was very much a part of our lives, and your generation and indeed ours, owe a great debt to some very courageous and dedicated women.'

'Yeah, remember when all the women went up to the North on the train to buy contraceptives and were in danger of being arrested when they got back to Amiens Street?' Valerie grinned. 'And women weren't allowed on jury service until 1986. Lizzie's right, you young women take so much for granted now. You've never known any different. No one bats an eyelid now when girls get pregnant outside of marriage, and you can buy contraceptives in supermarkets. Unheard of in our day.'

'Stop saying things like that,' groaned Lizzie. 'You're making me feel *so* old. Our mothers used to say "in our day"!'

'Sorry. I suppose when you think of it, Mam and Tessa were our age now when I got pregnant.'

'You make Tessa sound so formidable, but when she minded me, she was very kind to me.' Briony nibbled on a cracker, still finding it difficult to understand how Valerie could cut all ties with her father's family.

'You were the first grandchild – Jeff's child – she adored you and so did Lorcan,' Valerie admitted. 'She even used to arrive unannounced at the flat to see you. Remember, Lizzie?' She turned to her friend.

Lizzie laughed. 'Poor Tessa, she was besotted with you when you were born, but she was a bit pushy, to say the least. She was always arriving unexpectedly, catching us in our PJs once. We were fairly put out, as I remember. Living in that flat was fun, wasn't it, Val?' Lizzie smiled.

'But if Tessa loved me so much why did you leave Rockland's? Why did you stop *me* from seeing them?' Briony demanded. She wanted to get to the bottom of the matter and wasn't interested in hearing reminiscences about living in the flat.

'Tessa and I had a terrible row the day Jeff died. Both of us were in shock. Both of us said things we could never

take back. Bitter, harsh, wounding things. I hated her
then, and she hated me. We turned on each other. I told
her that it was all her fault that we weren't married and
that it was all her fault that you weren't legitimate. Tessa
wanted to lash out and she did. She told me that Jeff
never loved me enough to marry me, she said that he'd
told her that—'

'Oh!' Briony's hand flew to her mouth.

'I was gutted. Devastated. It was Lorcan who made
sure I sat with the family at the funeral. Tessa never said
a word to me. Never even looked at me. She didn't come
near me when I went to view his body in their house. She
never asked me would I have liked to have had him
waked in our house. I couldn't have really because you
were so young, but she never gave me the choice. I had
no legal rights. She was his next of kin. I wasn't even
allowed to identify him. And if she had wanted to she
could have kept me from seeing him. At least she didn't
go that far.'

'That's unbelievable,' Briony murmured, horrified.

'I basically had to give up all rights to Jeff, even though
we'd been living together as a family for more than three
and a half years.'

'But Dad *did* love you, didn't he?'

'I *think* he did. I hope he did. The week before he
died he told me that he loved coming home to us.'
Valerie swallowed the lump that had risen to her
throat. 'I'll never really know. If he'd proposed I would
have been certain of it but he never did and I didn't
force the issue because I wanted it to come from him,
not me. But one thing was for sure: he was a wonderful
father and you were the light of his life. Not even Tessa

could deny that. But she interfered too much in our lives, and knowing her I think she would have continued to interfere.'

'And that was why you moved to Dublin and never let them see me again?' Briony said sadly.

'It was partly the reason for moving to Dublin, but not all, by any manner or means. I had a lot of pros and cons to weigh up. It would have been difficult doing the commute and leaving you at Mam's or Tessa's. We would have been up at the crack of dawn and I wouldn't have seen you until half six, seven in the evenings. I wanted to spend time with you, especially because Jeff had died. I wanted to give you extra attention and I couldn't do that if we'd stayed in Rockland's.'

'But what about poor Lorcan? He was kind to you and me. I can remember him giving me swings and showing me how to fish for shrimps. Couldn't you have arranged for him to see me?'

'Lorcan was kinder to me than my own father was. It was hard leaving him,' Valerie confessed. 'But he had to be loyal to Tessa. He was her husband.'

'Oh Mom, didn't you even think about *me* when you made that decision? I've lost so much!' Briony exclaimed, twisting her table napkin agitatedly. 'It wasn't just about how *you* were feeling.'

'I know, I know. I just wanted to get away, and I did want to get my own back on Tessa, I'm ashamed to say. They were the things that drove me. I was in upheaval mentally as well as physically.' Valerie could hardly meet her daughter's accusatory gaze.

'So I was a pawn.'

Valerie stayed silent. Briony was right: she had used

her daughter as a weapon, something Lizzie had once warned her against and now she bitterly regretted it.

'Did they ever try to find me?'

'Yes. Tessa pleaded with Mam to give her our address but I'd made Mam promise never to tell her. I know I put her in a very difficult position but she was very loyal to me and even though she didn't want me to marry Jeff either, she felt Tessa had backed me into a corner by making *me* make the decision not to get married so that Jeff could complete his studies and exams. She never liked Tessa after that.

'So Gramma gave Gran the letter for me, and you never gave it to me or let on that they loved me and still wanted to see me?'

'We'd made a new life for ourselves in Dublin. You'd started school and settled in and you were happy so I just thought they'd drift out of your consciousness gradually, which they did. It was the easiest route to go,' Valerie said tiredly. 'But, in fairness to her, Tessa was nothing if not persistent; she found out where I worked and doorstepped me on one occasion. That really upset me. If she hadn't done that to me, time might have softened my feelings towards her, but I was so angry with what I saw as her harassment that day that it finished me with her for good.'

'Did you not feel guilty?' Briony probed, wondering could she have done the same thing to Katie if she was in her mother's shoes.

'I did at the beginning, of course I did, especially about Lorcan, and if Tessa had just left me alone for a few months things might have been different. Eventually I pushed them to the back of my mind and never allowed myself to think about them. I'll be honest with you,

Briony, until Katie was born I hadn't thought about Tessa in a long, long time. And then I did start to consider the impact my decision made on all of your lives. I set it aside and told myself that you'd grown up happy and well adjusted. But, especially on this visit and when I've been having such fun with Katie, I do realize what I've deprived you and Tessa and Lorcan of. If it's of any comfort I'm not proud of myself and I'm so sorry I didn't do things differently.'

'I am going to make contact with them. You know that, don't you?' Briony eyeballed her mother. 'I think what you did was mean and vengeful, but I can see why you did it. So at least I know now.'

'You do what you have to do, Briony,' Valerie said quietly. 'I'm sure it will give them great joy to be reunited with you, and they'll adore Katie.'

What an irony, she thought: Tessa would be renewing her relationship with her grandchild, and Valerie was in danger of losing Briony and Katie if her daughter couldn't forgive her. A strained silence settled on the three of them.

'I think they live in Dublin now,' Lizzie remarked casually, topping up Valerie's glass. 'Lorcan's sister died, she left him her house and they moved up to the city. Tessa found it very difficult living in Rockland's after Jeff's death. Lisa and her husband bought their house from them and she runs a crèche in it. Ma keeps me up to date on all the news. Her letters are pages long but I always feel I'm at home when I read them.'

'Oh, I loved that house,' Briony sighed. 'I can still remember it.'

'Can you?' Valerie was surprised. 'You were very young.'

'I know, but it was a magic place. I can't remember the

house we lived in at all but I remember Dad's house, and playing there and going for picnics. You know, Mom, when you told me that my grandparents were cross with you because Dad had died and they didn't want to see us I thought it because it was something *I* had done. I thought it was all *my* fault.'

'Oh my God, Briony, I'm so, so sorry.' Valerie burst into tears, devastated at the immensity of the consequences of what she'd done after Jeff's death, and only now truly realizing how much she had deprived her daughter. 'I can understand if you never forgive me,' she wept as Lizzie reached across and took her hand.

Briony's eyes welled up. 'I wish it hadn't happened, Mom. I was very unhappy at times and couldn't tell you, but I kind of understand why you did it. Don't cry, we'll get through it.' She leaned across the table and took Valerie's other hand.

'Thank you, darling, thank you. I'll never forgive myself.' Valerie wept.

'No, don't do that to yourself. We have to put it behind us and move on. We've endured enough misery,' Briony said firmly.

'Briony's right, Valerie. The past has to be healed so that you can be free to live your lives the way you want to live them,' Lizzie counselled.

'Thank you, Lizzie for always being with us in our hour of need.' Valerie wiped her eyes with her napkin.

'You're always there for me too,' Lizzie assured her.

'We can look at the photo album, if you like,' Valerie suggested, still mopping her eyes. 'There's quite a few photos of you and your dad, Briony, and some of them are taken in Rocklands. Lizzie, there are some hilarious ones of us looking like Pam and Sue Ellen in *Dallas*, with our perms and shoulder pads and blue eyeliner.'

'Don't dare ever show them to Rachel. My street cred would be, like, torn to shreds if she, like, saw photos of me looking like that,' Lizzie warned.

'That "like" thing – even Katie's at it.' Briony threw her eyes up to heaven.

'It's all ahead of you and I wish you the joys of it,' Lizzie grinned, squeezing her hand.

'Why are you not drinking?' Lizzie asked her when Valerie brought another bottle of wine to the table, and the photo album. 'OMG, have you something to tell me?' Her eyes widened.

'What do you mean?' Briony asked.

'You know . . . not drinking . . . preggers?'

Briony's jaw dropped open.

Valerie did a double take.

'Are you?' she asked, stunned.

'Um . . . I don't know.' Briony was dumbfounded. 'I actually never thought of that. I just thought I had a dodgy tummy. But now that you say it, it's a possibility. We've been trying for the past two years but no luck, and I'm not using any contraception. Oh, wow! Could I be? Is *that* what's wrong with me? It would explain the tiredness as well.' She couldn't believe it.

'Oh, I shouldn't have said that. Me and my big mouth. It's just it's not like you not to have a drink when we're together.' Lizzie was a little abashed.

'Are you saying I'm a dipso?' teased Briony.

'I've seen you hit the G&T, the Cava, the vino and the Baileys all in the one night. I could tell a tale or two,' Lizzie said smugly.

'It's just as well I didn't do that this week if I am pregnant,' Briony said ruefully.

'It could be that now you're not so stressed because you're at home instead of chasing your tail bringing Katie to the crèche and getting to work, your body is more relaxed. Often it's when you're not thinking about it that it happens.' Lizzie speared a sundried tomato and ate it with relish.

'We can get a test kit over in the pharmacy tomorrow,' Valerie said. 'Katie will be thrilled if it's true.'

'If it's a false alarm I'll be very disappointed now that you've put the notion in my head. I've wanted another child for so long I'd be ecstatic if I'm pregnant,' Briony confessed, pushing away the cheese. Now that it was a possibility she was in such a heap she couldn't eat another bite.

'I would have loved another child. If Jeff and I had been married I would have tried for another baby, but because we weren't and because I kept waiting for him to propose, I just stayed on the pill and lost my chance,' Valerie said sadly. She caught Briony's troubled gaze. 'But the daughter I have was the best thing that ever happened to me. I'm incredibly lucky. Briony, I'm so sorry you felt things were your fault. I never realized what I was doing to you. What sort of a mother am I?' She began to cry again, gutted at what she had inflicted on her beloved child.

'You had a lot going on in your life. It wasn't easy, I realize that now. Mom, I had a very good childhood, and I lacked for nothing. You did your very best for me – I know that – so let's put the past behind us. I love you.' Briony stood up and came and put her arms around her mother.

Valerie felt a burden lift from her shoulders and float

away. It was the strangest thing but somehow she just *knew* Jeff was by her side.

'Let's have a look at the photos, then,' Briony said lightly.

They sat for an hour flicking through the pages of their past, photos of the house with the sash windows, of Briony sitting on the swing with Jeff standing protectively behind her. A photo of Tessa, Lorcan, Carmel, Lisa, Steven and Valerie standing behind Briony as she blew out the candles on her cake on her third birthday. Photos that made the three of them laugh, of Lizzie and Valerie dolled up for a night out, with Afro hairdos and glittery boob tubes. Eventually tiredness caught up with them and drove them to their beds.

Valerie insisted, despite her best friend's protests, that Lizzie sleep in her bed. She changed the sheets, and gave her fresh towels and hugged her tightly. 'Thanks for coming. It made such a difference.'

'At least the worst is over and Briony knows what's what, and you can let it go.' Lizzie pulled her nightie over her head.

'Yes, it's a huge relief, to be honest. All we can do now is see where it takes us,' Valerie said. She was glad to slide into her made-up bed on the sofa. She was exhausted. But unlike the night before, when she was tormented by memories of the past, tonight all she felt was relief. She drifted into a deep sleep and never woke once until Katie leaned over her and tenderly kissed her cheek to announce the arrival of morning.

Briony lay listening to the sound of the sea, her hand on her tummy. Was she pregnant after these past years of longing for a child, a sibling for Katie? How ironic if she were to find that she was to be a mother again at a time of discovering such flaws in her own mother's parenting.

It was hard to believe that Tessa had acted the way she had. Hard to reconcile the loving grandmother she remembered with the woman whose behaviour had had such an impact on Valerie's life. She felt Valerie had given a truthful version of what had happened. Lizzie wouldn't have let her do otherwise. She was glad Lizzie was there because had she and Valerie been on their own, she would have doubted the veracity of her mother's version of events. If Valerie could lie to her once about such a profound matter that had such a huge effect on her life, Briony would have felt that she could do it again. No, tonight at least she felt her mother had been honest, even when it did not reflect well on herself.

And Tessa and Lorcan – what a torment it must have been to lose Jeff *and* their grandchild. That was a cruel punishment, no matter what reasons Valerie had. But, on the other hand, it must have been terribly hard on her mother, living her life, wondering did Jeff love her or not and waiting for him to propose. And then when he died, not knowing, ever. Tessa had been cruel to say that he hadn't loved Valerie. *That* had shocked Briony.

Valerie had not had an easy life and she'd worked very hard to make sure that Briony had a privileged childhood. She had never wanted for anything, except for her father. How different would their lives have been if Jeff had lived? But he hadn't and there was no point going there. But she *was* going to contact Tessa and Lorcan. As soon as she got home she would make it a priority, Briony thought drowsily before falling asleep, worn out after all the emotional trauma of the past few days.

CHAPTER FORTY-TWO

They were like three giddy schoolgirls in a school loo, as Valerie and Lizzie perched on the side of the bath and Briony put the loo top down with one hand and sat on it while holding the test wand with the other.

'They're so quick now compared to the old ones.' Lizzie craned her neck to get a look as she was nearest to Briony.

'What's happening?' Valerie demanded, sticking her glasses on. She was long-sighted now and it drove her mad.

Briony's hand shook as two blue lines appeared. She held it out to her mother and godmother, afraid to believe her eyes.

'Yay!' Lizzie jumped to her feet, grabbed Valerie and they both threw their arms around Briony.

'I can't believe it.' Briony shook her head. 'Oh, I wish Finn was here to share this. He'll be over the moon!

'Are you going to tell him on the phone?' Valerie asked as they untangled from each other.

Briony wrinkled her nose. 'I don't think so. I'd much rather tell him in person but it will be so hard to keep it to myself.'

'I think you're right. It's such a special moment, telling your husband that you're going to have a baby.' Lizzie was beaming from ear to ear. 'I remember when I was pregnant with Killian, I just knew after losing my two other babies that this one was going to be fine, and I had booked us a night in a gorgeous country inn in Norfolk and I told him after dinner when we were walking in the grounds, under a full moon and heavenly stars and it was wonderful. So special.'

'And I told Finn about Katie in bed on a wet and windy Saturday morning, and we never got out of bed for the rest of the day,' Briony grinned. They turned to look at Valerie and saw the expression on her face.

'Oh, Valerie, that was insensitive of me. I'm so sorry.' Lizzie's face fell.

'Don't be.' Valerie didn't want Briony's special occasion to be spoiled. 'It was different for me. My circumstances were not ideal but once we got used to the idea we were very happy and when you were born we were thrilled, remember. You were there.'

'Indeed I was, and out you popped with a little red indignant face on you,' Lizzie grinned.

'Why is you all in the toilet?' Katie opened the door and stood gazing at them. She had been playing The Lotto, one of her favourite games, with her dollies out on the terrace, using her grandmother's lettuce spinner.

'What's that?' she asked, eagle-eyed when she saw the wand.

'Aahh . . . ahh . . .' stammered Briony, glancing helplessly at the others.

'I was just taking your mom's temperature but it's not working very well so I'll have to get a new one and we'll just throw this one out.' Valerie opened the small bin and Briony dropped the wand in.

'Is you sick, Mommy? I will be the nurse and we will play hospital.' Katie took charge and led Briony from the bathroom, delighted to have a new patient.

'Are you OK? I'm sorry about that.' Lizzie put her arm around Valerie's shoulder as they stood in the kitchen waiting for the kettle to boil.

'It was so hard telling Jeff. I knew it was the last thing he'd want. Finding out I was pregnant wasn't a joyful moment for me. It was one of the worst moments of my life. And it's only listening to you and Briony that I realize how awful it was. I never had that lovely, special feeling that you and she had. I envy you both that.' Valerie looked so sad Lizzie nearly cried.

'At least you and Briony are getting back on an even keel. And it was good for her to hear that. It might knock some of the judgement out of her. She's never had to endure the kind of knocks you did. Chin up, dearest. This too will pass. Maybe that damn letter was a blessing in disguise. You can finally let go of the past and Briony can make contact with the Egans and Jeff can rest in peace.'

Valerie nodded. 'I hope so, Lizzie. It really is time to move on.'

'Don't be too harsh on your mum, Briony. It wasn't easy for her. How different was her experience of being pregnant and ours? And she had a terrible curmudgeon of a father who gave her a very hard time,' Lizzie urged her godchild as they sat sipping coffee under an awning of a pavement café in the pretty town of La Cala. It was Lizzie's last day. She was flying home that evening.

'I know. I never realized quite how difficult it was for her. She never spoke about it. I just wished it had been different. I hate to think of what Tessa and Lorcan went through too. Life certainly hasn't been easy on them either.' Briony stirred more sugar into her coffee.

'You can help ease that pain when you go home by meeting up with them. That's one good thing to come out of this,' Lizzie pointed out. 'And I think Valerie will be glad of it after all this time. It's been a hard burden to carry; it's time to let it go. And as well as your reunion with your grandparents you have your new baby to look forward to. Enjoy your life, Briony, this is the best of times for you,' Lizzie advised.

'I know that. You're right, thanks, Lizzie,' Briony said gratefully as a young Spanish man playing a mandolin came to serenade them.

It was market day and the square was heaving. Valerie had taken Katie to the Oriental Bazaar and after another shopping spree they had gone to the big playground on the beach, while Briony and Lizzie had strolled the length of the market, debating bags, pashminas, scarves and shoes. Lizzie had stocked up on spices, and on Valerie's instructions had bought strawberries, cherries, peaches and mangoes. Briony had dragged her away from the stall with the colourful hand-made crockery when she had been very tempted to buy two large hand-painted serving platters and six matching side dishes.

'Think, hand luggage. Think trying to get small case closed. Put it down and walk away. Come with me now and forget what you saw.' Briony had put the palm of her hand on Lizzie's back and given her a gentle shove away from the stall. She had still accumulated a fair amount of purchases, which were now lying in a multitude of bags under the table.

Briony's mobile rang and she saw Valerie's number flash up on the screen. 'Hi, Mom,' she said in a more friendly tone than she'd used in the past few days. 'Yes, we're finished, OK, we'll meet you at the car. See you then.'

'Time to go,' she said to Lizzie. 'You need feeding before we bring you to the airport. It's a pity it's such a short stay.'

'It was a lovely break, and hearing your news was terrific.' Lizzie signalled for the bill.

'Just as well you came. I wouldn't have copped on that I was pregnant, I don't think, and the poor child could have been awash with alcohol,' Briony said wryly, gathering up the bags pooled at their feet.

They had a jolly lunch at El Capricho, the beachside restaurant Briony had walked to on the day she had discovered her grandmother's letter. They had ordered a selection of starters, including Valerie's favourite, paper-thin slices of aubergine deep-fried and drizzled with honey. Valerie had decided on pepper steak, Briony had seared tuna, and Lizzie a prawn salad. Katie had tucked into spaghetti bolognaise.

She played happily on the beach while the three adults lingered over their coffees, enjoying the peaceful vista in front of them, and the sight of the high Atlas Mountains running along the North African coast, across the sparkling blue Mediterranean that lapped the beach below them.

'I can't believe I've to go home to wind and rain,' Lizzie moaned. 'Briony, make the most of this.'

'I will,' her godchild said, smiling at her mother.

Valerie stretched out her hand to her and Briony squeezed it.

Mission accomplished, thought Lizzie with satisfaction, raising her face to the sun. Jeff, you're playing a blinder! It's all up to Tessa now.

'Safe journey home, darlings.' Valerie hugged Katie and tried hard not to cry. She felt terribly lonely as she said goodbye to Briony and Katie before they joined the queue to pass through security in Malaga airport. She had stayed with them through check-in, wanting to spend every last second with them. Their holiday had flown by, the days slipping lazily past in a blur. It had been a time of renewal and reconciliation for Valerie and Briony. Valerie now felt closer to her daughter than she ever had before, the distress and strain of their fall-out over Tessa's letter easing as long lazy days on the beach and nights sitting out on the terrace talking, brought them back to each other. Valerie had talked about her life in Rockland's, her relationship with her father, and her sadness that Carmel had succumbed so swiftly to Alzheimer's.

Briony had shared her worries about Finn being overwhelmed by work, and having less time to spend with them, and her anxiety that her loss of salary would have a greater impact on the family if the recession worsened, now that she was expecting another baby.

Valerie made the most of every second with Katie, trying not to dwell on the increasing guilt she felt about Lorcan and Tessa.

There was a time when she would have been furious at the thought of Briony making contact with her grandparents, now she felt relief. It was progress of sorts, she supposed.

'You take care, Mom.' Briony hugged her tightly. She had tears in her eyes.

'I will, love. And . . . em . . . let me know how you get on in Rockland's, won't you, and put a pink rose on your dad's grave for me? Remember, it's half-way up the path and in to the right.'

'I'll do that and of course I'll let you know, Mom. We'll Skype you. Now please go and we won't wave or say goodbye. I'll text as soon as we land.'

'All right. I'm going now,' Valerie said, and turned and walked away so they wouldn't see the tears stream down her face. Buying the villa had a lot of pros going for it, but it was moments like these that tore the heart out of her and made her wonder if she had made the right decision. She reached the door and turned round to have a quick peek, just as she caught Briony doing the same. She smiled in spite of herself and was answered with a grin and a big wave.

Valerie blew her daughter and granddaughter a kiss before walking out into the brilliant sunshine and striding across the concourse to the train station. They had parked in Fuengirola so they could take the train as a treat for Katie. The hum of chatter on the train as it trundled through the stations helped ease the dreadful loneliness she felt. She knew the villa would be deathly quiet when she got home and she dreaded it. Having Briony, Katie and Lizzie to stay had been such an unexpected treat.

She drove home utterly lonely and let herself into the silent villa, expecting at any moment to hear the rush of small feet on the marble floor and her granddaughter's merry chatter. She dropped her keys on the hall table and wandered into the lounge. A folded pink art page lay propped against the vase of roses on the coffee table. A drawing from Katie, she thought, touched. Her grand-daughter loved drawing and painting and had spent many happy hours engaged in artistic endeavours, which were now hanging all over the villa.

Valerie opened it and started to laugh. 'Oh, Jeff, Lizzie *is* right. You are around, aren't you?' she said when she saw her granddaughter's painting of a big white butter-fly surrounded by dozens of childishly drawn kisses and 'Thank You' written in wobbly uneven letters.

Valerie held the drawing close to her heart. She knew the thing that would please her beloved Jeff most would be if she made her peace with his mother, but would Tessa want to make her peace with her? Or would that be a step too far?

CHAPTER FORTY-THREE

'I think I'd like to go and visit the grave, it's the longest I've left it without making a visit and it bothers me. I'm edgy about it, for some reason. It's a lovely day, and I'll get back before dark. Would you mind?' Tessa lays the mug of tea on the bedside locker and sits on the edge of her husband's bed. Lorcan's face is crumpled with sleep. He blinks a few times and hauls himself up into a sitting position. The maroon colour of the new pyjamas she bought him suits him. He's still a handsome man. Pain and age have not diminished that, she thinks fondly as he reaches out for the tea.

'There'll be no rest on you until you go. Bring the doggy, and let him go for a run on the beach,' he says before taking a gulp of the hot, sweet tea. 'Lovely. You can't beat a mug of tay.' He always says that, every single morning when she brings him the first cup of tea of the day. If he didn't say it she'd worry about him, Tessa thinks, amused.

'I'll take one of those Zanna Cookhouse chicken and ham pies out of the freezer for you,' she says, taking a sip from her own mug. This is their ritual now: the mug of tea and then showers before sitting down to breakfast. Through most of their marriage when he was fishing

Lorcan would be gone to catch the early tides and they rarely had breakfast together. Tessa enjoys sharing the first meal of the day if Lorcan is in good form. Her husband is always at his best in the morning. 'You can have some peas with it. They only take a minute in the microwave,' she adds.

'Grand,' says Lorcan. 'There's a lovely bit of pastry on those pies. They taste home cooked. Of course they're from Wexford. A fine county.' This is high praise. Lorcan is fussy, to say the least, about pre-cooked foods from the supermarket. He doesn't know it but Tessa sometimes buys pre-cooked turnip or carrot and parsnip mash. He likes turnips with his liver and onions but she hates peeling and slicing them. He doesn't know either that she sometimes buys ready-made pastry. The less time she has to spend cooking and baking the better. She's had enough of it. A lifetime of it. Men might retire but women never do.

How she would love to have a housekeeper, Tessa daydreams. She's lucky she can still look after her home, she supposes. She shouldn't be giving out. A few of her neighbours in Rockland's are in nursing homes. She hopes neither she nor Lorcan will ever end up in one. There is always the fear of what old age will bring. She thinks suddenly of Carmel Harris, afflicted with Alzheimer's, recognizing no one. Carmel, who had resisted her tearful pleas to give her Valerie's address. *'You were loyal to your son, Tessa, I have to be loyal to my daughter. Please don't ask me again,'* Carmel had said tetchily after Tessa had knocked on her door for the third time in six months. She wonders did Briony ever get either of the letters that she wrote to her. She'll never be able to ask Carmel now. She remembers nothing.

'You'll be seeing Lisa too, won't you?' Lorcan intrudes on her thoughts. He takes another draught of tea, relishing it.

'Yes, I'll ring her and let her know I'm coming.' Tessa stands up and glances at her watch. It's ten to nine. She could be on the road in an hour if she gets a move on. The morning rush hour and school run will be over. 'I'll go and have my shower. The porridge is made.'

'Right-oh,' he says.

She turns on the shower so that the water will be warm before she stands under it. She has mixed emotions about going home. Tessa still calls Rockland's 'home' although it's fifteen years since she and Lorcan moved up to the city. If anyone had told her that she'd end up in a semi-detached house in a small cul-de-sac off the seafront in Clontarf she would have told them they were mad. But, ten years after Jeff's death, Sally, Lorcan's eldest sister, had died and had left her house to him. She was widowed with no children, and Lorcan had always been very good to her.

Lorcan had suggested they spend part of the week up in Dublin, to renovate it, with a view to selling it. He had decided to sell the trawler and Tessa was glad of it. Fishing was a hard life and he'd done it for long enough. They had enough put by to supplement their pensions, and the sale of Sally's house would be an added nest egg.

The idea of living in Dublin part time for a little while appealed to her. Rockland's was so full of sadness for her. Passing Jeff's bedroom door every morning never failed to grieve her. The bedroom was still unchanged, despite Lisa and Lorcan's exhortations.

'We all need to move on. Jeff would want us to.'

'It's not healthy.'

She wouldn't countenance it. Her sitting room, with its panoramic views, was no longer her haven. Tessa tried hard to banish the image of Jeff's coffin resting in front of the French doors, but could not. She might go for a week or two and feel that she was returning to normal and then something would remind her of that awful time and she would have to seek refuge in his bedroom to try to heal the hollow dull ache that never left her.

Going to Dublin had been a help to her in that regard. There were no memories of Jeff in Sally's house. It was a fine house: three good-sized bedrooms, a big kitchen, two reception rooms. But it was in need of modernization and redecoration. They had undertaken much of the refurbishment themselves, finding a new focus and common goal. The large garden too had needed a lot of work, and as the weeks rolled on they even began to spend weekends in the city. Tessa had enjoyed redecorating the house. Taking the Dart into town and foraging through furniture shops and department stores, before having lunch in one of the many bistros that lined the busy streets was a treat.

When Lisa's third child was born, she had told her parents that she and Frank were going to look for a bigger house. Their small bungalow was bursting at the seams. 'We could sell them ours and stay here, and then it would always be in the family,' Tessa had suggested offhandedly, thinking her husband would never agree to it. It was a surprise and a relief when Lorcan said if it was what she wanted he would be happy to keep Sally's house and live in Dublin. It was much easier to find distractions in the capital and they were still close to the sea. Lorcan liked fishing off the South Wall and often came home with some mackerel, pollock, and even occasionally a bass, for supper.

Tessa steps under the steaming jets of water in her ensuite. She can feel the knot of tension forming in her stomach. She knows it is because of her impending visit to the grave and home. It always happens. But she'll be glad when she's seen the grave and has put new bedding in the pots. That always brings comfort. She showers quickly. Now that she's made the decision to go, Tessa is anxious to get on the road. She will buy polyanthus, pansies and cyclamen en route. Cleaning the headstone and tidying around the grave always gives her pleasure. It's something she can do for her son. She cannot understand how some graves are left untended. She knows there are sons, daughters, grandchildren who could take an hour or two every so often to come down from the village and look after the last resting place of their loved one. How can they leave the plots to go to rack and ruin? Tessa takes pride in keeping Jeff's grave looking pristine. In a strange way she enjoys spending time there. She finds peace in the graveyard. It is afterwards that the bitterness seeps back and the old memories come again to haunt her and she grieves for Briony as well as for Jeff. Her beautiful little Briony. Her first and most precious granddaughter.

'Don't think about it now,' Tessa mutters, towelling her hair dry before finishing it off with the dryer. It might be different today. She always hopes that it will and that she will find that longed-for acceptance that Lorcan seems to have found.

*   *   *

Lorcan showers in the main bathroom. Tessa never uses it. All her lotions and potions are in the ensuite. They moved into separate bedrooms a few years back when he had a particularly bad bout of arthritis. He misses having her beside him in the bed. They still cuddle and she will spend the odd night or two with him, and occasionally make love, but she has her room now and he has his, and he misses the intimacy of sharing. Old age is a bugger, he thinks glumly.

She will be in bad form when she comes back from Wicklow. She always is when she visits the grave. He has let go of Jeff a long time ago. Acceptance brings its own peace. He wishes Tessa could do the same but she has found it impossible to do so. It was one of the reasons he agreed to leave their home and move to Dublin; a sacrifice he has made for Tessa. He misses his life on the sea sometimes, and the majesty of sky, sea and rolling fields. He had hoped the move would have helped more than it did. If Briony was in Tessa's life, he thinks, she might have let go of their son and focused on her. The trip to Rockland's will bring all the trauma of losing her back too.

He doesn't like to think of Tessa driving back to Dublin on her own, sad and forlorn. He should go and support her. Since he had the cortisone injections into his shoulder two weeks ago, it has given him some relief. He's certainly fallen on his feet with his new shoulder surgeon. The best in the country, he's been told. Well, Mr Hannan Mullett has improved the quality of his life for sure. He can even raise his arm to his head to wash his hair in the shower, Lorcan realizes, pleased. Mr Mullett is going to do keyhole surgery on him after the October Bank holiday. He assures him it will make a great difference. Tessa has being begging him to get his shoulder seen to for months. He should have listened to her. He might even be able to cast his rod again. He'd love to do a bit of fishing.

It would do him good to get out of the house too, Lorcan decides, wiping away the last traces of shaving cream. He slept well the last few nights because pain has not kept him awake, tossing and turning. He feels a bit like his old self.

'Tessa, I'm coming with you,' Lorcan shouts impulsively down the stairs, looking forward now to the jaunt to Wicklow and home.

'Damn!' mutters Tessa, stroking Blackie's head. Now she'll have to watch her speed and listen to lectures about her lane discipline and Lorcan will want to go down to the boats. And then he'll get into conversation with other fishermen and they'll be there all day. She was looking forward to listening to Pat Kenny and Ronan Collins or playing Katie Melua loudly and singing along. Her granddaughters laughed at her singing in the car. It isn't something 'old ladies' generally do. The thing is, she doesn't feel old in her head. She can't believe she is in her seventies.

'My shoulder feels so much better, Tessa. I should have listened to you long ago. That young man has certainly made a difference.'

Lorcan's voice has vigour in it. Not that flat tone she's had to listen to these past few months. If he'd taken her advice about going to get himself seen to, he could have had pain relief months ago, she thinks, cantankerously pouring his porridge into a bowl.

'It's a cracker of a day. Pure autumn.' He looks out the kitchen window. The sky is cobalt. The grass is covered in a carpet of gold and russet leaves, interspersed with a few apples that have blown down in last night's wind. The last of the apples clinging to the branches are ruby, shiny, and ready for her fruit basket. The onions, and beetroot from their vegetable patch are safely harvested in their garage. Tomatoes still grow on the vine in the small glasshouse at the end of the garden. And two pumpkins are ripening for Halloween.

'We could treat Lisa to lunch.' Lorcan turns to her. Tessa wonders if she is hearing things. Her husband is actually suggesting that they eat out. The age of miracles is not yet past. 'And we could stop in Avoca Handweavers or Mount Usher, and get some of that chicken and broccoli bake they do. We could have it tomorrow and then you wouldn't have to cook. You'll be tired after the drive.' Tessa's heart lifts. Perhaps it would be nice to have her husband with her, after all. It's been a while since they had a day out together. She should make the most of this gift of wellbeing he's feeling, she thinks, her heart softening. It's the pain that makes him cranky and demanding. Now the real Lorcan is back with her, thanks to a kind young surgeon who is a credit to his profession. She kisses her husband's cheek and when he puts his hand up to caress hers, she kisses his hand too. The love is still there. She has accepted that at last. They've had their ups and downs, God knows, but today is an up day. She will enjoy it as best she can.

'Where is we going, Mom?'

'Where *are* we going?' Briony corrected Katie automatically, tucking into the inside lane on the M50 to allow a speeding car with a northern reg, who had been tailgating her, to pass.

'Idiot,' she muttered. 'It's drivers like him that cause accidents.' Despite the fact that it was mid-morning there was plenty of traffic on the motorway heading south. 'We are going to a place called Rockland's, darling. When I was a little girl about your age I used to live there.'

'Are there swings?'

'There are, and a slide,' Briony smiled, glancing at her daughter in the rear-view mirror. 'It's beside the seaside. There might be a train going past. And there's a shop that has ice-cream cones for little girls who are very, very good.'

'Is it like heaven where Holy God lives? Or is it like Spain where Valwee is?' Katie couldn't believe all these things were in the one place.

'A bit of both, sweetheart.'

'We are visiting Holy God. Be on your very best behaviour or you won't get any ice cream,' Katie instructed her dolls in her sternest voice. 'And mind your manners.'

Briony grinned in the front seat. Her daughter was like a little parrot sometimes; she even had Briony's inflection: 'Mann*ers*!'

The miles flashed by. It had taken her only twenty-five minutes from the Port Tunnel slip road to Loughlinstown, she realized with surprise, pleased with her progress. Katie had fallen asleep in her booster seat. The nap would do her good. She had been up at seven.

How would the day go? A day in her life like no other. Valerie gave her directions to the graveyard and to Tessa and Lorcan's house where her cousin Lisa now lived. She had roses in the boot of the car to place on her father's grave. It would be strange to see her dad's resting place. She wondered if she would feel anything.

It really was a gorgeous day, Briony observed, driving past the glorious spectacle of autumnal splendour in the Glen of the Downs. It was hard to believe that she was free to drive down the country mid-morning on a week-day. Being unemployed had given her such freedom. Finn was on a trade initiative to South America and so the car was hers. Much as she missed her darling husband there were plusses to his being away. Briony grinned, thinking of nights lying spread-eagled in their big bed, with no rumbling snores in her right ear.

Fifteen minutes later she turned off the motorway and the three-lane highway became a two-lane road, and then a mile or so later a single lane running parallel to the coast. Her head swivelled from right to left as she drove past the granite sign that said Rockland's in neatly carved letters, and she felt a sudden flash of memory and then recogni-tion as she came to the crossroads that led to the grave-yard. The house she had lived in as a child was just a few yards away up to the left. When she'd made her visit to the grave she would drive past it and stop, look in at it over the gate and see what memories it would bring. Briony felt a tingle of excitement. She was so glad she had put aside her reservations and finally made the trip to Rockland's.

The sun was pouring its warmth and golden light onto the fields at either side of the road that led to the white-washed stone-walled graveyard. She pulled into the wide gravelled entrance and cut the engine. There was one other car parked just in front of the gate.

Katie, who had woken up just as they came off the slip road, clambered out of her seat, having unfastened her seat belt. 'Is this heaven?' she asked, peering around with interest.

'A part of it,' Briony said, opening the boot to take out the roses.

'And where's Holy God then?' Her daughter gazed at her in anticipation.

'See these lovely roses?'

'Yes.'

'See that lovely pile of leaves?'

'Yep!'

'See that bird singing in the tree and hear the sound the breeze makes when it rustles the leaves?'

Briony nodded.

'And see you and see me? That's Holy God.'

'Oohhh! And is Holy God my dollies too?'

'Holy God is everything.' Briony smiled down at Katie and took her hand. Her heart gave a little lurch. She was finally in Rockland's once more, the place of such pain and grief for her mother. And now she was going to have her first contact of sorts with her dad, again. She had promised Valerie she would take a photo of the headstone for her. Half-way up the gravel path and to the right, she remembered her mother's directions, pushing open the wrought-iron gate. Most of the graves were neat and well tended, she noticed, as Katie skipped along beside her. Pots of colourful bedding and vases of flowers dressed the individual plots. A few looked bedraggled and uncared for, but mostly it was a very well-tended cemetery. The trees that circled the graveyard in protective embrace silently dropped their leaves in a gold and russet circle.

Birds sang a sweet lullaby and Briony felt a sense of

peace envelop her. This was a tranquil place and she had a vague memory of coming with Valerie when she was a little girl and then getting into a car that was packed with boxes and bulging black sacks. It must have been when they were leaving to come to Dublin. She *had* been here before, definitely. Briony quickened her pace. Ahead of her she could see an elderly couple working on a neatly kept grave, adorned with bright pots of bedding plants. They were weeding the edges, their heads bent close together. Who had they lost? Parents? Grandparents? They were quite elderly themselves. The man's hair was snow white; the woman's an elegant ash grey.

'Guess what, Katie?' Briony said to her daughter. 'You are going to see your granddad's grave for the very first time. A grave is a place where we remember someone who has gone to live up in heaven. And we're going to take a photo and send it to Valerie.'

'Cool,' said her daughter. 'This is just fun, Mom. Thank you for bringing me. Are we going to have a picnic?'

'Yes, we will later on. We might have a picnic on the beach, how about that?'

'This is the best day of my life,' Katie assured her, thrilled at such a multitude of treats. Briony couldn't help but laugh. Her daughter said that often and it pleased her. A happy childhood was a great blessing. Valerie had given her a loving, secure childhood despite the fact she had no father to share it.

She was glad she wasn't on her own. Katie was such a little ray of sunshine. She would take away any sadness there might be on this very special occasion.

*   *   *

Someone else is coming to visit a grave, Tessa thinks, hearing the click-clack of high heels and a childish voice speaking to an adult.

She plants the last purple pansy in the hole she's made for it and covers it with moist loamy soil. 'Now that looks lovely, they'll last until Christmas,' she remarks, satisfied, to Lorcan, who is clearing away a few weeds at the edge of the base. She sees some weeds on her side of the edging stone and pulls them out. She feels very close to her husband today as they kneel side by side, tending their son's grave, labouring contentedly together.

The voices get nearer and Tessa looks up and sees a young woman and a little girl walking in their direction, peering at headstones as though looking for a specific grave but not sure where it is.

The little girl reminds her of someone. Tessa's breath catches as they come closer and she stands up unsteadily, holding on to the headstone for support.

'Oh my Lord!' she breathes. 'Lorcan, look! Look! Am I dreaming?'

Her husband raises his head as they draw abreast of them and the young woman smiles uncertainly. Tessa's hand goes to her mouth; the resemblance is uncanny, the big melting brown eyes, the determined chin, the curly hair tumbling over her shoulders.

'I'm looking for a grave . . .' The young woman stops and studies the headstone, her eyes flickering from it to them. Comprehension dawns.

'Gramma! Is it you?' she asks hesitantly. And Tessa is weeping, unable to speak as she stares from one to the other and sees her son's unmistakable likeness in both of them.

CHAPTER FORTY-FOUR

'Why are you crying?' Katie asked, studying Tessa intently. 'Are you very, very sad?'

'Oh, my goodness! Oh, my goodness,' Tessa said, rooting for a tissue, trying to compose herself.

'Is it yourself, Briony?' Lorcan said, getting slowly to his feet.

'Yes, it's me. This is my daughter, Katie.' She felt a lump in her throat as she saw her grandmother trying hard to compose herself. Briony couldn't begin to imagine how she was feeling, meeting granddaughter and great-granddaughter so unexpectedly after all these years.

'What's *your* name?' Katie asked, gazing up at Lorcan, not showing a hint of shyness.

'My name is Lorcan. I'm your granddad's daddy.' His eyes crinkled as he smiled down at her, enjoying her childish curiosity and direct manner.

'Oh, heavens!' Tessa exclaimed, laughing and crying at the same time. 'I can't believe I'm a *great*-grandmother. That makes me feel a bit of a crone! None of my other grandchildren have children yet. They're a bit younger than you. Briony . . .' she hesitated, '. . . could I give you a hug?'

'Of course, Gramma,' Briony said as Tessa held out her arms to her and she was enveloped in a warm hug that instantly brought back memories of the many they had shared all those years ago.

'Oh, Briony! Briony! Briony!' Tessa stroked her back, holding her tight. 'I've dreamed of this moment. I've longed for it.' The moment was bittersweet. Tessa couldn't help but grieve for all the hugs that had been lost to her, all the loving experiences that could have been hers. But Briony, Jeff's beloved child, was back now in her arms where she belonged, and that brought joy.

'Can I have a hug?' Katie asked, determined not to be left out. She liked these new people.

'Of course you can, you little pet. Aren't you gorgeous? She's the image of you, Briony, when you were her age,' Tessa said, gathering Katie into her arms. She couldn't believe that she had a great-granddaughter. Life was giving her a second chance, a chance to be happy again.

'Yes, Mom often says that,' Briony laughed, and saw the shadow that flickered across her grandmother's face.

'And where's my hug?' Lorcan asked, breaking the moment of awkwardness.

'You used to say I was "the best little girl in the whole wide world", didn't you?' Briony remembered, a grin splitting her face from ear to ear as she was enveloped in her grandfather's embrace.

'Indeed I did. And so you were,' he said, hugging her tightly.

'So this is Dad's grave.' She traced her hand along the headstone a few moments later.

'Yes, we keep it as best we can,' Tessa said sadly. 'There are always fresh flowers on it.'

'It's lovely. I want to take a photo for Mom.'

'Could she not come and see it for herself? Could she not have brought you, years ago, and brought you to see us?' Tessa blurted.

'*Tessa!*' Lorcan reproached gently.

'Mom had her reasons,' Briony said uncomfortably.

'There's no good reason to keep a grandchild away from their grandparents, especially after what we went through,' Tessa said crossly. 'Did she ever give you the letters I gave to Carmel?'

'I've read one letter, I didn't know there was another,' Briony said diplomatically. She could see why Valerie might not have got on with her grandmother. Tessa was forthright, to say the least. 'And now I'm here, and how amazing that I should come on a day when you're both here. Lizzie, my godmother, told me that you had moved to Dublin. Whereabouts?'

'Clontarf,' Lorcan said easily.

'*No!* We . . . me, my husband, Finn, and Katie live off Griffith Avenue, near what used to be Whitehall Garda Station. That's only a stone's throw away,' she exclaimed.

'Well, would you believe that? We were so near to you and we didn't know it.' Tessa couldn't keep the edge out of her voice. She was a bit of a briar, Briony thought in dismay.

'Mom, do you think your daddy would like if I sang him the new song I learned in playschool?' Katie tugged at her sleeve.

Briony could have kissed her for unknowingly defusing the tension.

'Now that's a great idea, isn't it, Tessa?' Lorcan declared, flashing a stern glance at his wife.

'What are you going to sing, pet?' Tessa bent down to her.

'I'm gonna sing "Incey Wincey Spider".' Katie preened, loving the limelight.

'Wonderful!' clapped Tessa, beaming.

Lorcan gave Briony the tiniest wink, and she felt as though she'd known him all her life.

Katie stepped confidently onto her grandfather's grave and raised her face to the heavens.

'Incy Wincy spi-DER climbed up the water . . . SPOUT!
Along came the rain and washed poor Incy . . . OUT!'

She sang lustily, performing the little nursery rhyme with the hand gestures she had learned at her playschool.

'A round of applause for Miss Katie . . .?' Lorcan looked questioningly at Briony, when she had finished her spirited rendition.

'McAllister,' she supplied, amused at her daughter's precociousness but proud of her at the same time.

'A round of applause for Miss Katie McAllister!' Lorcan led the clapping and Katie beamed from ear to ear.

'Jeff would love this,' Tessa said approvingly, thinking how wonderful that the little girl had such confidence, and belief that her grandfather could see her performing for him.

'Have you been up to the village?' she asked as Katie wandered off to dance in a drift of crisp vibrant leaves that nestled under an ancient sycamore tree.

'No, I came to the grave first. I was going to drive past the house we used to live in. I know it's near here. Mom gave me directions. And then I'd planned to drive up to The Headland on the off chance that Lisa would be in and introduce myself to her.'

'We were going to have a bite of lunch with her. Could you come with us?' Tessa asked eagerly, clasping her hand.

'I'd love to,' Briony agreed. 'Although I have promised Katie I'd have a picnic on the beach with her. But a picnic to her can be a biscuit and lemonade.'

'You can go down on the beach under our house after lunch, and she can have her little picnic. We could even have a flask. I love tea out of a flask,' Tessa said, gathering up her gardening tools.

'So do I! I remember having picnics on that beach. There were wooden steps down, weren't there?' Briony helped her pack up her cleaning accoutrements.

'There were. What else do you remember, my love?' Tessa asked, delighted.

'Playing with your jewellery. Picnics on the beach. Granddad showing me how to gather periwinkles—'

'You were good at that too. Fearless. Clambering over the rocks,' Lorcan interjected.

'And you loved wearing my high heels. You used to call them "hee hiles",' Tessa chuckled.

Briony laughed. 'I remember wearing them. Katie wears mine now.'

'I have so many photographs. Maybe you would like to see them? They'll bring back memories and help us to get to know each other again,' Tessa ventured.

'That would be great. I'd enjoy that very much and it would be lovely showing Katie more pictures of me when I was young. It's one of her favourite things to do with Mom.'

'And how is Valerie?' Lorcan asked kindly. Her mother had always said Jeff's father was a kind man, and she could see why.

'She's well. She's in Spain for another few weeks. She bought a holiday villa out there.'

'Give her our regards,' Lorcan said, ignoring the look of annoyance his wife gave him. 'Don't forget to take your photograph. Why don't we leave you to spend a few minutes on your own here? We'll wait for you at the car and we'll show you where your old house is and then we'll carry on to the hotel to meet Lisa for lunch.'

'Thank you, Granddad.'

'You used to call me "Gandad". I loved the way you said it,' Lorcan reminded her, stepping past her. 'Take as long as you need here.'

'I will,' she said gratefully, touched at his thoughtfulness. A few moments on her own with Jeff would be special.

When they were gone and she was alone, Briony stood with her eyes closed, visualizing her favourite photo of her father. 'Dad,' she murmured, 'help me to deal with this situation well. Help me to be loyal to Mom and not upset her, and help me to get to know Gramma and Granddad again. And help Gramma not to be bitter.' Briony had seen the sparks of antagonism any mention of Valerie brought. It was upsetting, if understandable. She decided, standing at her father's grave, that she would not let either woman slag off the other to her. She would not be part of their feud. It was not of her making and it was up to them to deal with their own stuff. That was why she had not mentioned how she had come across Tessa's letter. She would not give her grandmother any more ammunition to fire at Valerie. It would be difficult, but she would try to keep the middle road.

She placed her roses in a vase and filled it with water she'd brought in an old milk carton. 'For you, Dad, from Mom and me and Katie.' She took her BlackBerry out of her bag and lined up the photo for Valerie. She took a few from different angles so that her mother could get a good sense of the grave and surrounds. Katie raced over to her, ready to pose the minute she saw her mother pointing the camera.

'Where is those nice people gone?' she asked, disappointed that they had not said goodbye and made a fuss of her.

'Would you like to go to lunch in a hotel with them and we can have our picnic later?'

'Yes, please. I is hungry. Can we have lemonade?' Katie did a little jig, unable to stand still for a minute.

'We'll see. Now don't ask for anything. Remember your manners, won't you?'

'Yessssss, Mommy!' her daughter said exasperatedly. 'You say that *every* time.'

'Sorry,' Briony apologized, taking her hand. 'I forgot you have lovely manners and you don't need reminding. Say goodbye to Granddad Egan.'

''Bye, Granddad Egan. The next time I will sing you "Christopher Robin", 'cos Valwee sings it to me an' I know all the words now,' she bellowed skywards. 'Do you think he heard me?' She cocked an eye at her mother.

'Absolutely. How could *you* not be heard?' Briony grinned. 'I bet he'll be looking forward to it.' She opened her bag and found a blue envelope with '*Daddy*' written in faded childish script. She opened the unsealed envelope and read the letter she had written to Jeff, at her teacher's behest, for Father's Day all those years ago.

Dear Daddy,

Happy Father's Day. I hope you are very well in heaven with Holy God. I wish you would come back to us and not be dead. I am the only girl in my class who does not have a daddy. I would like you to come back so Mom can be more happy. I wish you would come back and push me on my swing like when I was small. Me and Mom will light a candle for you. Tell God I said hello.

With all my love from Briony Harris.

She slid the letter back in the envelope, leaned down and placed it against the headstone. 'Here you go, Dad. I still wish you were here, but I hope you're happy, wherever you are,' she said softly before taking her daughter's hand and leading her down the gravel path to where her great-grandparents were waiting.

Lorcan watched them step away from the grave and head in their direction. 'Just one word of advice, Tessa, while we're on our own.'

'What's that?' She bristled, having a good idea of what was coming.

'If you want to mend fences and have a relationship with Briony and Katie, don't get on your high horse now, for goodness' sake,' he chided. 'Just don't forget that Valerie is Briony's mother and don't criticize her to her.'

'Well, God above, Lorcan, to think that Briony was only a couple of miles away from us and we didn't know it, and all because that spiteful little madam took off and never let us see her again. It's hard.' She couldn't hide her vexation. 'We've missed out on *so* much.'

'Nevertheless, if you want to keep them in our lives,

forget the past and start again with them. Remember, blood is thicker than water. Now let's show our grandchild her history, and enjoy this very unexpected gift we've been given.' His eyes were blue and unwavering, his voice strong and authoritative. She hadn't seen this old Lorcan that she'd fallen in love with for such a long time.

Tessa took a deep breath. It would be difficult. She would have to curb her life-long tendency to score points and have her say no matter what. She knew her husband was right. She didn't want to alienate Briony and lose her again. A miracle had happened today. A miracle she had prayed for, for a long, long time. Katie was like a miniature Briony, she thought with pleasure, watching her skip like a little sprite beside her mother.

Tessa tucked her hand in the crook of her husband's arm. 'I'll do what you say, Lorcan. I'll try my best,' she sighed. It wouldn't be easy but it had to be done.

'That's my girl,' her husband said, squeezing her hand. 'You won't be sorry, and Jeff would be delighted.'

There was something else she needed to do, Tessa knew. One last bit of unfinished business before her son could truly rest in peace. She would deal with it sooner rather than later. It was something that had caused niggles of guilt every so often, but for now it was time to get to know her granddaughter and great-granddaughter.

'You know something?' Katie hurried out the gate and stood in front of them. 'My mommy's going to have a new baby. It's in her tummy. Right there.' She poked Briony's slightly rounded belly. 'But it won't come out her bottom, like I saw a baby cow coming out of its mammy's bottom once on the television.'

'Katie!' exclaimed Briony, mortified.

Lorcan turned away to hide his amusement, his shoulders shaking.

'Really?' Tessa was delighted. 'When is it due?'

'In the spring.' Briony smiled, pink-cheeked. She'd have to have a talk to Katie and explain that there were some things you didn't announce to the world.

'What joy that will bring,' Tessa predicted happily. Another great-grandchild coming – who would ever have thought she would get to meet Jeff's grandchildren?

'Congratulations, Briony, that's *wonderful* news.' Lorcan turned back to her to offer his good wishes. He was as pleased for Tessa as he was for Briony. His wife's eyes were sparkling and animated. He hadn't seen that spark in her for many years.

'This day is just getting better and better,' Tessa said to Katie, giving her a cuddle. Katie snuggled in against her happily before going to get into Briony's car.

Tessa got into her own car and waited for Lorcan to fasten his seat belt. She was dying to introduce Briony to Lisa over lunch. For the first time since Jeff's passing, all those years ago, Tessa left the graveyard with a light heart, full of optimism for the future.

'Hasn't it been a wonderful day?' Tessa sat beside her husband on the sofa watching the fire crackle and dance in the grate.

'It's the best day we've had in years,' Lorcan agreed. 'And to think I wasn't going to go with you this morning. Look what I would have missed.'

'Something was telling me to go and visit the grave. I just knew I should go today. Isn't that amazing? We were meant to go, Lorcan.'

'We were indeed. You'll get no argument from me there. God was good to us.'

Tessa remained silent. She had given up on God a long time ago. She rarely went to Mass now. God had been too cruel to her – why would she want anything to do with Him? Or Her or It or whatever it was.

Once, after one of her rants about Jeff being taken from them so young, Lorcan had said to her, 'Tessa, we all have to go back to where we came from. No one escapes it. Some of us are just left longer than others. It's not something that's "done" to us. It's not the end of us. Life is just another chapter and so is death.'

'But why, Lorcan? Why did he have to go so young? Why do mother's lose their babies? Why are there wars? Why is there genocide? Why do the crooks that ruined our economy and our country get away with it? Why, why? Why?'

'Why is there goodness? Why is there self-sacrifice? Why are there many acts of love and compassion and kindness? Why do miracles happen sometimes?' he replied. 'We don't know. And the more we think we know, the less we know. But one thing I *do* know. Jeff is still around us. I know that very, very well,' he said emphatically. 'My parents are around me. They all really are only a thought away, you know.'

'I'm fed up having one-sided conversations with him. I want to *talk* to him and get answers from him,' Tessa snorted.

'One-sided!' He arched an eyebrow at her. 'Remember the year after he died and we were going to Christmas Mass and you were crying? And what song came on the radio?'

'That was a fluke!'

'"No Woman No Cry"! I don't think so. What about the day we were coming up to Dublin to move into Sally's house and you were having a weep?'

She didn't answer.

'"Always Look on the Bright Side of Life"! When I used to be out on the boat I always knew he was with me because this one lone seagull would always follow us into port, even when all the others were gone. Every single time. And sometimes when I'd be down fishing off the South Wall, a seagull would come and fly around me for a while, squawking his head off. "There's Jeff," I'd say to myself. And I can't explain it but a sort of peace would come over me. So that's how I keep going, Tessa, because I know he's there and I know I'll see him again.'

Lorcan had never railed against God but she did often, even to this day, Tessa mused as she sat in the firelight with her husband's arm around her, tired after the day's events and all the driving. Lorcan had even made them a cup of tea when they'd got home, telling her to go and sit down and he'd bring it in to her. Another minor miracle, she thought.

'Isn't Katie a right little character? She goes on just the way Briony did when she was a child,' Lorcan smiled, remembering the look of horror on Briony's face when Katie had announced that she was expecting.

'And isn't Briony beautiful? So like Jeff around the eyes. I can't wait for them to come and visit. I'm going to make an apple crumble; Briony used to love that,' Tessa yawned.

'It certainly will be something to look forward to. This is going to be a good Christmas, Tessa. The best in a long time.' Lorcan kissed her forehead. His shoulder ached a little where she was resting on it, but he didn't care. They were on an even keel again after a very long and rocky voyage, and for that he was truly grateful.

'And how did they look?' Valerie couldn't hide her curiosity.

'You were right, Mom, Gramma's very elegant. She's tall, with grey hair cut in a bob, and she was wearing black trousers and a lovely lilac jumper. She doesn't look her age at all. I can't believe she's in her mid-seventies.'

'Believe it. And Lorcan?'

'Ah, isn't he lovely? A real gentleman. He's tall, but a bit stooped, with white hair—'

'White? He used to be salt and pepper. He was a very good-looking man.'

'You can see that in him still, in a craggy sort of way. And Lisa's very like Gramma. She's lovely too, good fun.'

'And did any of them say anything about me?' Valerie *had* to know.

'Lorcan said to give you his regards,' Briony said easily. She wasn't going to tell Valerie that Tessa had been far from pleased when her husband had said that.

'But did *Tessa* say anything?' Valerie probed.

'No, Mom,' Briony said firmly. 'She kept it very general, we just talked about old times and they've invited me to visit them in Dublin. We're going to look at old photos. Did you get the photos of the grave I emailed you?' She deftly changed the subject.

'Yes, thank you, love. It's good to see the grave. I just saw it again very briefly at Dad's funeral, and then again when I left Rockland's. The headstone wasn't erected for months after the funeral to let the ground settle so I never got to see it properly,' Valerie explained. 'So when are you going to visit them?' she asked diffidently.

'Next week.'

'Enjoy it,' Valerie said, trying to keep her tone neutral.

'I will, Mom. I'd better go and put Katie to bed. She's wall falling. It was a long day but I just wanted to let you know how it all went.'

'I bet they were entranced with little Miss Moffat,' Valerie smiled, using her nickname for her grandchild.

'Ah, she's a great little trooper. She told them I had a baby in my tummy, but it wouldn't be coming out of my bottom like a baby cow! I was mortified.'

'Oh God, kids are a hoot. No inhibitions. I'm glad it turned out so well, darling. But what a coincidence that you bumped into Tessa and Lorcan at the grave.'

'I got the impression from Tessa that she visits very regularly. At least first contact has been made and that hurdle has been jumped; it can only get better from now on,' Briony said brightly. "Night, Mom.'

"Night, love. Give Katie a kiss for me.'

'I will, but sure, it won't be too long until you're home for Christmas. The year is flying by.'

'Tell me about it,' Valerie said drily.

'Talk soon, sleep well,' Briony said and hung up. She could see her daughter's head drooping. She needed to get her into her pyjamas pronto. It had been a great day for both of them. Briony had found her family again. Grandparents, aunts, uncles, cousins. How often did that happen, she thought happily, dying to get her daughter to bed so she could ring Finn and tell him her great news.

* * *

As Briony had said, 'First contact has been made.'

Imagine, after all these years, Tessa Egan was back in her life again. Briony had been bubbling with excitement when she'd phoned to say what a wonderful day she'd had and how she had met Tessa and Lorcan so unexpectedly.

It was awful to feel jealous, but Valerie did. She wasn't proud of that, she thought with a sigh. But if Briony was happy to have the Egans back in her life, she could hardly stand in her daughter's way. Jeff would have wanted it and she couldn't help but think he had helped to orchestrate this reunion. What were the odds of Briony going to visit the grave the same day and the same time as her grandparents? Lizzie would certainly say there had to be divine intervention involved, Valerie thought with wry amusement.

A thought struck her. When Briony's baby was born in the spring, would she be inviting the Egans to the christening? Her stomach lurched. Whatever about meeting Lorcan, how awful would it be to have to come face to face with Tessa? 'Oh, no,' Valerie groaned. Whether she liked it or not, it now seemed inevitable that their paths would cross once more.

CHAPTER FORTY-FIVE

'We have a present for you,' Katie said gleefully before she had even taken her coat off.

'You can't keep anything secret with this one,' Briony laughed, helping her daughter divest herself of hat and gloves. It was a cold, windy day and the easterly breeze blowing in off the seafront in Clontarf had reddened their cheeks.

'You have a present for me?' Tessa exclaimed, her eyes lighting up as Katie presented her cheek for a kiss.

'An' for Granddad Lorcan,' Katie assured her. 'Do you want them now? Can we give the presents now, Mom?'

'Just let me get my coat off, for goodness' sake,' Briony urged, shrugging out of her black woollen coat that soon would not fasten on her. She could feel it tight over her chest, her boobs having gone up a cup size, much to Finn's delight.

'I've the fire lit in the sitting room; we can sit in there later. Even though we have the central heating there's something about a fire, isn't there? Lorcan loves the fire.'

'Where is he?' Briony asked.

'He's just gone down to the Butler's Pantry for me. They do a lovely coffee cake. I always get one as a special treat for very special visitors.' She smiled at Katie.

'Is we very special visitors?' Katie was chuffed.

'Very, very special,' her great-grandmother assured her. 'And I made an apple crumble for your mammy because she used to love it when she was a little girl like you.'

'Gramma, I hope you didn't go to too much trouble now,' Briony remonstrated, following her grandmother into a light, airy, oak kitchen. 'This is a lovely house,' she remarked.

'It is,' Tessa agreed. 'Of course, there was a lot of work to do on it when we got it first. It took us over a year to get it the way we wanted it. We were going to sell it and then we decided to move up here.'

'And do you miss living in Rockland's?' Briony asked, sitting down at the kitchen table, which was set for the four of them.

'I do and I don't.' Tessa bustled around filling the kettle. 'But it is easier living here. There aren't so many memories.'

'Mom said the same about coming to live in Dublin,' Briony said matter-of-factly. She had decided she was not going to skirt around the subject of Valerie. Her mother was not going to be the elephant in the room.

'I can see that now that you say it,' Tessa conceded. It was the first time it had occurred to her. She had always considered Valerie's move to the city as an act purely to spite her, she thought, a little ashamed.

'Hello, ladies.' Lorcan appeared at the door and Katie beamed at him. He placed a large white cardboard box on the table. 'One Butler's Pantry coffee cake, as requested,' he said to his wife.

'Thank you, love. That was quick.' She smiled at him, lifting the lid, taking out the caramel-coloured cake and putting it on a cake stand.

'We've a present for you,' Katie informed Lorcan excitedly, going to stand beside him.

'A present for me?' he echoed, pulling her ponytail gently.

'Yep, for you and for Gramma Tessa. Mom, can we give them now?'

'Go on,' said Briony, knowing there'd be no peace until the presents were handed over. Katie hadn't an ounce of patience. 'Just something to say thanks for your kindness and to say how glad we are to be with you again, isn't that right, Katie?' Briony said lightly as her daughter rummaged in the gift bag.

'You shouldn't have!' Tessa exclaimed when Katie joyfully handed her the present.

'There's three things in it,' she revealed. 'They're *so* pretty. One's a—'

'Stop, Katie. It's a surprise, remember?' Briony warned.

'OOPPS!' Her daughter's hand shot to her mouth.

'And what's this?' Lorcan felt his present carefully.

'It's a book and a C— OOPPS!' Katie glanced guiltily at her mother.

'Oh, Briony! These are beautiful,' Tessa exclaimed, opening the blue box in which reposed an elegant pearl necklace.

'An' there's earrings an' a bracelet,' Katie announced, unable to contain herself.

'It's from The Princess Grace range in the Newbridge Collection. I thought they would suit you. Mom always said you were very elegant and she was right.'

'Elegant, me?' Tessa looked surprised. And was equally surprised that Valerie would pay her such a compliment.

She held the pearls up against the neck of the black jumper she wore.

'Let me fasten them,' Briony offered, and smiled with satisfaction when they were settled right. 'Very classy. A good choice, Katie,' she approved.

'I helped pick them, didn't I, Mom?'

'You did indeed,' agreed her mother.

'I like the Newbridge jewellery,' Tessa said, walking out to the mirror in the hall to view her new gifts. 'Lisa got me a beautiful diamanté bracelet one year. I'll always treasure these. But you shouldn't have.'

'And look what I got,' Lorcan said delightedly, showing his wife a copy of a book of seafaring poems and a CD of sea shanties.

'I remember you singing "Heave Away, Haul Away" when you used to push me on the swing.' Briony explained her choice of gift for him.

'Do you remember that?' he said, his blue eyes twinkling at the memory. 'Aren't you the thoughtful girl?'

'Do you have a swing?' Katie asked hopefully.

'We don't,' he said regretfully. 'But we can get one. I have a glasshouse, though. And I've got two big fat pumpkins for Halloween. Would you like to have a look at them?'

'Oh, yes, please, Granddad,' she said eagerly.

'When we've had our tea,' Tessa said firmly and for one delicious moment, Briony was transported back to Rockland's, remembering Tessa making her wait to do something until the tea was over. It was something her grandmother had said often in those happy, carefree days. She had never thought she'd hear her say it again.

'And do you miss work?' Tessa asked an hour or so later as she and Briony sat at the kitchen table chatting, while Lorcan showed Katie his pumpkins and the bird feeder and birdbath and the two ornamental herons that stood, one-legged in a flowerbed in the garden.

'Sometimes. I miss the crack and the chat and the laughs. I miss adult company and I certainly miss my pay cheque,' she said wistfully. 'But I *love* spending time with Katie. We used to have so little time together when I worked full time. Even to be able to come to visit you on a weekday afternoon is a treat. If I was working it would have been at the weekend and there was always so much to have to try to fit in on Saturday and Sunday. Mom used to find that too. Monday morning was upon you before you knew it.' Briony nibbled at a few crumbs of the delicious coffee cake that remained on her plate.

Tessa felt a little stab of guilt, remembering how Valerie had once told her that unannounced weekend visits were not a good idea. She had thought Valerie was being vindictive. She hadn't understood how precious her free time was. She *had* been a bit pushy in those days, and thoughtless, she thought contritely. She hadn't understood what it was like to be a mother working outside the home. She'd never had those issues herself when her children were young.

I have something for you,' Tessa said, going to the hallstand where her bag was. She came back in and handed Briony a hardbound notebook filled with writing. 'These are letters I wrote to you over the years. They're all about my life, about all our lives. Read them to get to know us again.' She handed Briony the notebook.

'Oh, Gramma! How lovely! Thank you so much.' Briony was very moved.

Tessa cleared her throat. 'Do you think your mother would be willing to meet me when she's home for Christmas?' she asked, busying herself clearing the table, not looking Briony in the eye.

'Eh . . .' Briony was thrown. She hadn't expected *this*. 'I can ask her,' she said, putting the cake plates in a pile.

'I've just been thinking it would be good to try and make our peace now that you and Katie are back in our lives. Jeff would like it. And so would Lorcan and the rest of the family.'

'And what about you?' Briony asked quietly.

'I need to talk to your mother. There's one little matter that has to be cleared up and set to right, and even if it's only to meet for that, I'll be glad of it,' Tessa replied frankly.

'I'll be talking to her tonight and I'll certainly say it,' Briony promised, standing up and giving her grandmother a hug. Tessa rested her head on her shoulder and Briony held her close. Her grandmother was elderly now and had endured a lot of sadness and grief. It would be such a step forward if she and Valerie could put their enmity behind them. Was her mother ready to emulate Tessa and make a conciliatory gesture? For all their sakes Briony truly hoped she was.

'She wants to meet me? She suggested it *herself*? It wasn't Lorcan pushing her?' Valerie was astounded. She had always thought that Tessa would never bend; that she herself would have to make the first move.

'That's what she said. Did I think that you would meet her when you were home at Christmas? And let me get this right,' Briony paused, trying to recollect what Tessa's exact words were. 'She said, "I need to talk to your mother. There's one little matter that has to be cleared up and set to right, and even if it's only that, I'll be glad of it." You could have knocked me down with a feather,' Briony declared.

'And what did you say?'

'I stuttered and stammered for a minute because she caught me off guard, but then I said I'd ask and now I'm asking,' Briony said. 'So, Mommy Dearest! What will I tell her? Is it a yes or is it a no? I wonder what little matter she has to clear up with you?' Briony rubbed her swelling tummy, hoping her new baby would come into a family that was finally united.

'Oh, Briony,' groaned Valerie. 'The thoughts of it will have me in a knot coming home.'

'I'll come with you, if you like,' Briony offered.

'No! Thanks for the offer, darling, but this is between Tessa and me. If I meet her I want it to be on neutral territory, though. Tell her I'll meet her in the Botanic Gardens,' Valerie said decisively. 'We can fix a time and date that suits her. And let's get it over and done with before Christmas. I don't want that hanging over my head. OK?'

'OK, Mom,' Briony agreed equably. But Valerie couldn't see her punching the air and giving a silent *Yesssssss!*

So now she was committed. Wait until Lizzie heard this news, Valerie thought, sipping a glass of red wine out on the terrace. She had a pashmina around her. The nights were cool now, much cooler than when Briony had stayed last month. The sun was setting closer to Africa than the High Sierras and it wasn't bright in the mornings until nearer to eight.

What did Tessa have to say to her, Valerie wondered. What matter did Jeff's mother want sorted? She couldn't think of anything that would be important after all this time. All Valerie knew was that the sooner the meeting was over the better. She was dreading it and she felt equally sure Tessa was in the same boat.

'Damn,' she muttered. She'd been looking forward to going home for Christmas and now this great big dark cloud loomed large on her horizon. Would it have a silver lining?

The Botanic Gardens. That was a good place to meet, Tessa approved after hanging up the phone following Briony's phone call. She would say nothing to Lorcan yet, she decided. Just in case she changed her mind and cancelled the proposed meeting with the woman who had caused her so much grief in her life. She climbed the stairs to her bedroom, slowly. Her knee always gave her gyp when the rain was coming.

She sat on the side of her bed and opened the drawer on her bedside locker. That drawer needed a good clearing out, she thought glumly, looking at the collection of miscellaneous items that greeted her. A carton of paracetamol, pens, her passport, earrings, buttons, an old Visa bill, half a packet of Polo mints, a tube of KY Jelly and an old mascara wand. What a mess!

She pulled the drawer open a little wider. It was where she knew it would be, right in at the back. She'd put it there fifteen years ago and had never looked for it since. Tessa sighed deeply. This would be one of the biggest ordeals of her life. There was no denying that, but it had to be endured. For Jeff. For Lorcan, Briony and Katie, and this new little baba that was coming. She would do it for them and she would not be found wanting. One meeting might be all there was between her and Valerie but at least she had the satisfaction of knowing that *she* had made the first move.

Her gaze dropped to a folded page beneath the Visa bill. She pulled it out in idle curiosity, noticing her name written in an elegant script in black ink.

She opened the page and felt a pang of sadness when she saw the prayer written neatly on the page. Olivia Morgan, one of her oldest and dearest friends, had written it out for her. Olivia's mother had given it to Olivia when she was dying in the hospice.

'It might help you sometime; it really helped Mam,' Olivia said as they had walked from the graveyard one Sunday afternoon when each of them had spent an hour tending their respective graves. Olivia knew all about Valerie's flit to Dublin with Briony, and all that had led up to it. Tessa had taken the prayer and put it in her handbag and shoved it into the drawer that evening, barely glancing at it. She didn't 'do' prayers any more, she'd thought resentfully.

She read it slowly. 'A Prayer for Healing'. Such strange things were happening to her lately, she mused, looking out at the wild night. That prayer was in her bedside locker for years and she had never bothered to take it out and read it and today when she had made the first move to contact Valerie it had come to her attention. And how apt it was for her situation. It was as though she'd had to wait until now for it to mean anything. The hair stood up on the back of her neck as she read.

Every hurt that has been done to me . . . heal that hurt.
Every hurt that I have ever caused to another person . . .
*   heal that hurt.*
I choose to forgive. I ask to be forgiven. Remove whatever
*   bitterness may be in my heart, Lord, and fill the empty*
*   space with Your love.*
Thank you, Jesus.

A tsunami of tears flooded down her cheeks as Tessa sat, head bowed over the prayer. 'I choose to forgive. I ask to be forgiven,' she wept, repeating it over and over again, feeling the release of an immense sorrow, and a great burden that she had carried for too long.

CHAPTER FORTY-SIX

God, she's got old. Still elegant but old, Valerie thought in shock as she stood at the door of the restaurant in the Botanic Gardens and recognized Tessa gazing over towards the Palm House, a cup of coffee in front of her. She was wearing tailored navy trousers and a red boat-neck cashmere jumper. Very on trend, Valerie thought in reluctant admiration. She took a deep breath. Her heart was flip-flopping all over the place. She tried to compose her face as she made her way between the crowded tables to get to where Tessa was sitting. The restaurant had a Christmassy feel, the windowsills decorated with vibrant scarlet poinsettias. A pale wintery lemon sun cast light through the big plate-glass windows, making the wooden décor gleam. There was a convivial buzz about the place and Valerie wondered if she had made a mistake in choosing such a public place for their showdown. Too late now, she thought apprehensively, reaching the window table.

'Hello, Tessa.' She couldn't believe how normal her voice sounded. She'd expected it to come out as a squeak.

'Valerie.' Tessa gave a start and half stood up. 'Thank you for coming.'

'Thank you for asking me,' she replied crisply.

'Can I get you some coffee? Tea? Breakfast?' Tessa asked politely.

'Not at all. I'll go up and get it. Would you like a fresh coffee?' They were outdoing each other in politeness, Valerie thought with a flicker of humour.

'Coffee would be good. This one's cold. I forgot to drink it.' She gave a half-smile.

'Would you like a scone, a cookie, cake?' Still the brittle faux politeness. How long could they keep it up? Valerie wondered a little wildly.

'No, no, nothing for me, thanks. Just coffee will be fine.'

'I'll just leave this here.' Valerie took off her black jacket and draped it over the back of the chair.

Tessa watched the younger woman take her place in the queue. Valerie hadn't changed much, viewed from a distance – still slender and stylish and well dressed. She was wearing well-cut jeans tucked into high-heeled ankle boots and a pastel mint-green cardigan over a white cami-sole that showed off her tan. A fresh look. A youthful look for a fifty-year-old woman. She could carry it off, but Tessa had seen the fine web of ageing around Valerie's eyes and a deepening of the lines around her mouth. There was an aura of sadness about her that she had not expected. The old perky, brash air of confidence had gone. Life's knocks had hit Valerie hard too, she thought in surprise.

'Well, this is strange,' Tessa said bluntly when Valerie was finally seated opposite her, sipping her black coffee.

'*Very*,' agreed Valerie emphatically, replacing the cup on the saucer and staring at her.

'And difficult,' Tessa added, a little disconcerted by the other woman's stare.

'*Very*,' Valerie agreed.

'Well, it has to be done. It's only fair on Briony and Katie and the new baby that we try and reconcile our differences.' Tessa shook a sachet of sugar into her coffee and gave it a vigorous stir.

'Funny, isn't it, how mothers so often have to try and do what's fair for everyone else and have to put their own needs and desires aside,' Valerie observed.

'And what would your need and desire be? Not to be having this conversation, I suppose?' The tart tone that Valerie remembered so well was back.

'Correct.' Valerie made no bones about it.

Tessa laughed. 'Well, at least we can be honest with each other, and that's a start. I feel exactly the same.'

'I would have been surprised if you didn't.' Valerie felt some of the tension ease. 'So, Tessa, are you finally going to tell me why you were so vehemently against Jeff and I getting married, even after Jeff got his exams? Is that the matter we have to sort out? If you hadn't stood in our way Briony would have been an Egan, you realize that, don't you?' Valerie tried to keep the edge of bitterness out of her voice.

'Yes, I realize that, Valerie, I realize it very well. I realize that if I had behaved differently I would have had the comfort of my grandchild's love all these years,' Tessa said quietly. 'But now that you have a grandchild of your own, you surely must admit that what you did, taking her away from us and never getting in touch, was the cruellest thing imaginable.'

'It didn't seem so at the time, Tessa. I was devastated. Overwhelmed with grief and shock and terror. I was on my own, Tessa, and for that I blamed you,' Valerie retorted in a low voice as her anger began to rise.

'I was pretty devastated too—'

'You had Lorcan and your other children, and a lot of family support,' Valerie cut in sharply.

'We shouldn't do the blame game, otherwise we'll be back to square one and this meeting will be pointless.' Tessa met Valerie's resentful gaze.

'I know, but it's hard, very, very hard, Tessa.' Valerie felt her composure slipping and tears threatened to spill.

'For me too, but let's try and sort it and make some sort of peace over it,' the older woman said in a kinder tone.

'Just tell me why you were so against us getting married. Was it because you looked down your nose at my family? Was that it?' Valerie's voice shook.

'Good Lord, no!' Tessa looked shocked. 'I *liked* Carmel. She was a lady. I didn't know your father too well except for when we had that family meeting, and I understood his feelings, although you might not think I did. And yes, we had words, him and me, but it wasn't anything to do with your family, really, and I'm sorry if you've felt it was all these years.'

'What was it then, apart from you thinking that Jeff was too young? Or what was it about *me* that you didn't like?' Valerie demanded agitatedly, as all around them the hum of chat and jangle of cutlery against crockery faded into the background.

'Oh, Valerie, it was complicated.' Tessa's face crumpled and she was the one to lose composure as a tear rolled slowly down her cheek. Seeing Jeff's mother cry shook Valerie more than she could have imagined. Impulsively she reached across the table and laid a hand on the other woman's forearm.

'Please don't cry, Tessa. I'm sorry if I'm brusque. I don't

mean to be. I'm just feeling overwhelmed. If you could just tell me your reasons it might help me put the matter to rest. I know now that I did you and Lorcan and Briony a terrible injustice, cutting off all contact. As you say, having a grandchild of my own has shown me just how awful what I did was. I didn't realize at the time that it would have such consequences, not that that's any excuse now,' Valerie said quietly, hardly able to believe she had said what she'd said. She certainly hadn't planned to. It must have been Tessa's tears that had triggered her admission.

'It was as bad as losing Jeff,' Tessa gulped. 'We *grieved* for that child. I drove up to Dublin many times to where the flat you and Lizzie shared was, and drove around that area hoping against hope that I would see her. I figured you would have moved back to Glasnevin. Every morning that the postman came I prayed for a letter from you, or Briony when she was older. It was a living hell.'

Valerie went pale. 'I *am* sorry, Tessa. Very, *very* sorry.' She had given so little thought to the consequences of her thoughtless cruel act and now she would have to live with the knowledge that she had added immeasurably to Tessa and Lorcan's misery. 'I was so angry with you when Jeff died I just wanted to get away from Rockland's and from you. And because I was working in Dublin it made sense to move back there. Even if we had been married I would probably have moved back because of the circumstances, but I wouldn't have stopped you seeing Briony . . .' She trailed off.

'It *was* partly because Jeff was so young,' Tessa admitted, rooting for a tissue in her bag. 'He was my youngest and he had his whole life ahead of him, and having a child tied him down like nothing else on earth. Being married, having to get a mortgage when all his friends were off enjoying life unfettered – it was so upsetting for me as a mother to see all his freedom and carefree existence go out the window. It was hard to deal with. But that was only part of the reason. I wanted both of you to be sure that you wanted to be together for life. I didn't want *you*, Valerie, to end up like me.' Tessa's voice cracked and she lowered her gaze and bent her head to take a sip of coffee.

'Like you? How do you mean? I don't understand.' Valerie was perplexed. What on earth was the woman talking about?

'No, you don't. I don't think there's many who would.' Tessa raised her head and looked her straight in the eye. 'I was the same age as you when I got pregnant out of wedlock. I knew *exactly* what you and Jeff were going through, believe me,' she said grimly.

'*Oh!*' Valerie didn't know what to say. This was the last thing she'd expected to hear.

'Oh indeed!' Tessa gave a glimmer of a smile.

'But surely then you'd have *wanted* us to get married. *You* got married,' Valerie said indignantly.

'Oh, yes, I did . . . I surely did . . . the classic shotgun wedding.' She gave a deep heartfelt sigh. 'And to this day, Valerie, to this day I wonder did Lorcan ever feel I tricked him, or would he have married me if things had been different and he hadn't been *forced* to. All my married life I've had this underlying fear and it's an awful thing, believe me. I didn't want that for Jeff and I didn't want it for you.'

'But Lorcan *loves* you!' Valerie exclaimed. 'You and he had a great relationship. Your marriage was so different from my parents'. It was a real marriage.'

'I know, and yes, I know now that Lorcan loves me, but the thing is, Valerie, he's a good man. He did the *right* thing. He did what he *had* to do. But was it what he wanted to do? Believe me, I'd far prefer to be married to someone who *wanted* to be married to me and not someone who *had* to be married to me.'

'I remember you saying that to me in the hospital—'

'Valerie, could we just forget that awful episode ever happened?' Tessa said hastily. 'I am deeply, deeply ashamed of it, and my behaviour around the time of the funeral.'

'I was pretty mean myself that day. It was like a nightmare,' Valerie said, almost weak with relief that they weren't going to relive that hideous day, with 'you said' and 'I said'. 'Let's not talk about that horrendous day. Did you ever stop to think that Lorcan might wonder would *you* have married him if you hadn't got pregnant?'

Tessa laughed. 'Ah, Valerie, Lorcan was every girl's dream where we grew up. He had his pick of them all.'

'You're a very attractive woman yourself and always were, Tessa. *He* might have been the one wondering,' Valerie said, astonished at what she was hearing coming out of her mouth. Had she just paid Tessa Egan a *compliment*?

'I don't know about that. What I do know is that I didn't want there to be any doubt in your mind or Jeff's, and that was why I was so opposed to you and him getting married. Because he wasn't ready, Valerie, he told me that himself. I shouldn't have said that he didn't love you. That was very wrong of me. He just wasn't ready. It wasn't like when Lorcan and I were young. Getting pregnant outside of marriage made you pariahs and your family the talk of the town.'

'It was still fairly taboo when I got pregnant,' Valerie interjected. 'I had a hard enough time too. Nowadays it's nearly the norm to have the child first and get married later!' she said with wry humour.

'I know. How times have changed.' Tessa nodded. 'Jeff *would* have married you straight away if Carmel and I hadn't argued against it. You know that, don't you?'

'I know,' Valerie said flatly.

'He was a good boy.'

'I know that too. So really what you're telling me is that it wasn't about us at all, it was all about you and Lorcan,' Valerie said dejectedly.

'What?' Tessa looked askance.

'It was all because of what you were feeling and your own emotions that you stopped us from getting married.'

'I . . . I . . . didn't want either of you to go through what Lorcan and I went through.'

'But Jeff and I loved each other despite what you want to think,' Valerie retorted.

'Do you think you and Jeff would have lasted as a couple if you hadn't fallen pregnant? Can you *honestly* say you would have?' Tessa responded.

'Yes. We were mad about each other.'

'And what about the arguments about his football training, or when he wanted to go out for a drink with the lads?' she asked pointedly.

'Every couple has those kind of arguments,' Valerie said hotly.

'Valerie, it wasn't out of spite that I stopped you from getting married, it was out of concern and fear that you might not be right for each other. I never thought Jeff was going to die.'

'Well, he did!' Valerie burst into tears, oblivious of the glances from two women at the table opposite.

'Oh, please, please don't cry. I'm really very sorry, Valerie. If I had my time over again I'd behave differently,' Tessa said pleadingly.

'No you wouldn't, Tessa. You were Jeff's mother and you were looking out for him, and if the same thing happened to a son of mine, if I'd had one, I'd probably do the same,' Valerie sniffed. 'That's what mothers do . . . interfere.' She gave a watery smile. 'For what it's worth, again, I'm very sorry too for allowing my bitterness to eat into me all these years and for depriving my daughter of her grandparents and aunt and uncle and cousins. If she never forgave me it would be good enough for me.'

'Don't say that,' Tessa exclaimed. 'We all made mistakes that have hurt and damaged us, but at least we can move on from it now if you want to.'

'Do you?'

'Yes I do, Valerie. Very much.'

'Me too,' Valerie said tiredly. 'Carrying anger and hate is a heavy burden; it would be good to let it go.'

'Lorcan will be pleased. He never holds on to things. That's one of the things I love about him.' Tessa smiled.

'Perhaps you should learn from him. He *does* love you, Tessa. You really should forgive yourself,' Valerie observed, wiping her eyes.

'Forgive myself!' Tessa echoed.

'You've never forgiven yourself for getting pregnant, have you? I always remember you saying to me, "It's

down to the girl! The girl can always say no!"' Valerie
reminded her.

'Oh God! I was a bitch, wasn't I? You're right, it wasn't
you I was mad at it, it was myself. When you got pregnant it brought me right back to that awful time in my
life. That wasn't directed at you at all. I shouldn't have
taken it out on you.'

'Tessa, how could you forgive me when you couldn't
forgive yourself? You need to let go of your own past.'
Valerie sighed. She felt drained at the intensity of their
discussion.

'I do, don't I? It's very hard, though.' Tessa shrugged.

'I know. It *is* hard. I've had to do a lot of thinking lately.
I had to address issues I had with my father and try to
forgive him for his behaviour towards me. Nothing is
ever black or white. There are reasons for everything,
especially for the way we behave. It's our past that forms
us, sometimes for better, sometimes for worse. When we
understand our past we can be more understanding of
ourselves.'

'That's very, very true,' Tessa agreed. 'Valerie, there's
one other thing,' she said hesitantly.

'Oh?' Valerie said warily.

'Do you think we could take a little walk? It's very
crowded here and those two women are earwigging,' she
murmured.

Valerie looked across at the two middle-aged women,
who looked away hastily.

'Sure, I think we've given them enough entertainment,'
Valerie said drily, and Tessa smiled. They put their coats
on, wrapped their scarves around their necks and negoti-
ated their way between the tables.

'They're still gawking!' Tessa said, glaring over her shoulder at the pair, who were staring unashamedly at them.

'I'd love to stick out my tongue,' Valerie said, holding the heavy swing doors open for the older woman. 'We could go over there.' She pointed to the Alpine Garden directly opposite. 'It's private enough and there's a bench to sit on, as far as I remember.'

'Perfect,' Tessa agreed. 'And it's sheltered from the cold,' she said, stepping down into the small enclave protected by a high natural stone wall. There was a small wooden bench backing onto the wall and they sat down on it together.

'So what's the other thing you want to discuss?' Valerie got straight to the point. There was no point in dragging it out.

Tessa put her hand in her coat pocket and pulled out a small gift bag. 'I think this was meant for you. I found it in Jeff's kitbag after the funeral.'

Valerie could see the name of a well-known jewellers engraved on the small square box. Her fingers shook as she opened it. 'Oh my God!' she breathed when she saw the sparkling solitaire engagement ring. Jeff was going to propose! 'He *did* love me, he did love me,' she whispered, and burst into tears. 'He must have been going to propose on my birthday. Did you know he was going to propose?' She turned to Tessa.

'No! He hadn't said anything to me.'

'And you never gave this to me. How could you do that to me, Tessa?' she said, aghast.

'You were gone to Dublin, I had no address,' Tessa reminded her.

'It didn't stop you from doorstepping me at work,' Valerie reminded her.

'I was mad with you then,' Tessa scowled.

'You knew where Mam lived. You left the letter for Briony there. You could have given it to her to give to me,' Valerie said heatedly.

'You kept something from me. I kept something from you. If we hadn't behaved so badly towards each other we would at least have had peace of mind since Jeff died,' Tessa said sadly.

'That's true,' Valerie conceded.

'We have behaved so badly some might say we got our just deserts. You know the old saying, "Before you embark on a journey of revenge, dig two graves."'

'Oh!' Valerie grimaced. 'That's rather apt, I suppose. Who said that?'

'My grandmother used to say it but I think she borrowed it from Confucius.' Tessa gave a wry smile, watching the diamond glinting where a shaft of sunlight caught it as Valerie gazed at, what was to her, a priceless jewel.

'Put it on and see if it fits,' Jeff's mother suggested kindly.

Valerie slipped the ring onto the third finger of her left hand. It fitted perfectly. A shower of pink rose petals floated down over her head and shoulders from one of the blooms of a climbing rose tree that grew high against the wall above her.

'Did you see that?' she exclaimed. 'Just when I put the ring on my finger. He is here. Jeff's still around us, Tessa. Things are always happening that you wouldn't believe.' Valerie's eyes were shining.

'Things happen to Lorcan and me too,' Tessa said eagerly. 'Wait until I tell him this.' She shook her head. 'Are we foolish, do you think, looking for signs? Are we just trying to delude ourselves and grasp at straws?'

Another petal drifted down between them.

Valerie and Tessa looked at each other and burst out laughing, and in that moment of delighted laughter, reconciliation was born and they reached out and hugged each other tightly just as the sun came out fully from behind a cloud, showering them with a multitude of sparkling sunbeams.

CHAPTER FORTY-SEVEN

Valerie kissed her mother tenderly as she prepared to leave the nursing home. Carmel sat in her chair, staring out into the garden. She was wearing a beautiful mauve silk blouse and pearls that Briony had bought for her. She looked very well cared for and content, Valerie thought. There had been no recognition when she had walked through the conservatory to where she was sitting. There had been little conversation.

'I'm just watching Terence out doing the garden,' she'd said at one stage, and then drifted off into her own little world.

'I'll see you again in a few weeks, and Briony will be down to visit,' Valerie said, taking Carmel's frail hand in hers.

'Briony?' Carmel raised her head. 'Is she well? And how is Katie?' Valerie's heart lifted. 'She's very well, Mam. The two of them are very well,' she said excitedly.

'Tell them I was asking for them.'

'I will. She had a new baby. A little boy.'

'A little boy! Terence would have liked a boy, I think.' Carmel's tired faded eyes studied Valerie intently. 'But I was so glad I had you.'

'Oh, Mam.' Tears filled Valerie's eyes. 'I love you very much.'

'I love you too, Valerie.' They held each other's hands joyfully and then, a few moments later the shadow came between them. 'I must go out and help Terence now. We're going to plant potatoes and peas and beans.'

'You do that, Mam,' Valerie said, kissing her soft cheek. 'But have a little rest first.'

'I think I will.' Carmel smiled, and Valerie laid the soft throw over her and watched as her mother's eyes closed and she nodded off to sleep.

She walked out of the nursing home swamped in a myriad of emotions: relief that her mother was so well cared for, sadness that her mind was far away in another realm, but mostly utterly grateful for that treasured moment of recognition, so rare now, when Carmel had been lucid and they could tell each other of their love.

At least she and her mother had always had that gift, Valerie reflected, driving towards the exit. It had been so different with her father. She glanced over at the pot of pansies and forget-me-nots that lay on the floor of the car. There were three more pots in the boot. Two of them for Terence. It would be the first time she had ever laid flowers on her father's grave. Valerie pressed down on the accelerator and headed south for Rockland's.

The sun was shining, having burned through the fog that had rolled in off the sea, when she got to the graveyard. The trees were leafing up, all vibrant and fresh in their spring glory. A late-blooming cherry tree bursting with pink and white blossoms was surrounded by clusters of bluebells. It was so nice to visit this place again, Valerie thought. She could understand now how Tessa found such comfort at Jeff's grave. It was very soothing to the spirit, arranging her flowers and talking to him.

He must be so pleased, she reflected a little while later, pulling a small weed that had dared to raise its head along the edging stone. Briony had given birth to the most beautiful baby boy a month ago and Lisa was having a party in Rockland's for him. Something like the party Tessa and Lorcan had hosted for Jeff and Valerie all those years ago. Tessa and Lorcan would be there when she arrived. They were travelling from Dublin today too. It was a party she was looking forward to very much. Lizzie and Dara were coming over from England. It was almost like the closing of the circle.

Valerie stood up, lifted the two remaining pots and made her way along the cemetery path. She took a left a few rows down and walked between two lines of graves until she reached Terence's plot. The original grey and white stones had been recently supplemented with two more sackloads, and the headstone was gleaming. She was glad she'd phoned the stonemason she'd bought the headstone from and got him to refresh the grave. She had let it go to rack and ruin for too long. She studied the grave critically. It was clean now and well kept, but very bare compared to most of the graves surrounding it. No colourful flowers or ornaments to indicate that its owner had someone who cared enough to place something there.

'Better late than never, Dad,' Valerie said, bending down to place the plant-filled pots on the stones. It was amazing the difference they made. They lifted the energy immediately and the plot took on a different hue, no longer forlornly barren.

'I hope you're resting in peace,' she murmured. 'And thanks for that money.' A car drove past, indicating to turn into the entrance, and she glanced over the wall and smiled. She should have known they'd be here too.

'Come to the party, Dad, if you're around,' she said, and edged her way back through the graves to the path just as Lorcan and Tessa came through the gate carrying pots of beautifully blooming spring plants.

'Let me carry it for you. I have forget-me-nots too,' she said, taking the pot from Tessa.

'Thank you, Valerie. I won't say no. They're heavy enough.' Tessa handed over her pot gratefully.

'Isn't it a cracker of a day?' Lorcan declared, limping slightly, stiff after the drive down.

'Peachy,' she agreed.

'And a happy day for us.' Tessa smiled at Valerie as she placed the pot in front of her own and took Lorcan's from him to place it on the grave.

'Put that one on the right-hand corner and move this one here,' Tessa ordered, pointing to one of Valerie's offerings.

Bossy as ever, Valerie thought fondly, but she did as she was told. In the months that had followed their reconciliation they had kept in touch and had slowly come to appreciate each other. Tessa had invited her and Briony, Finn and Katie to tea over the Christmas season, and Lorcan had opened the door, held out his arms to her and said, 'Welcome home, Valerie.' And it *was* like a homecoming she had realized, as they had listened to Katie singing 'Away in a Manger' for them after tea.

When Briony had given birth in April, they had met in the Rotunda – so different from when Valerie had given birth – and had cried together, remembering Briony's birth when Jeff had been with them.

Letting go of the past had been a relief for both of them. Tessa had told her that there were times now that she felt quite light-hearted, something she hadn't been since Jeff had died. They all adored Katie, and this new baby had drawn them all even closer. For the first time in her life Valerie felt she was part of a big, extended, loving family and it gave her a real sense of belonging.

'Did you ever think you'd see a day like this after all that's happened?' Lizzie asked, tucking into a bowl of Tessa's famous chowder, a few hours later. The sounds of children playing drifted in through the French doors. Valerie could see Katie playing Ring a Rosie with a couple of little girls, as happy as a lark, while Briony sat on a bench, chatting away with her aunt Lisa.

'It's a bit surreal, to be honest,' Valerie murmured. 'Did you ever think I'd put flowers on Da's grave?'

'Are you glad you did?' Lizzie studied her.

'Yes I am. And you'll never guess what came on the car radio when I turned on the engine.'

'What?' Lizzie grinned.

'Crystal Gayle singing "Somebody Loves You"! It was weird, but nice,' Valerie admitted.

'Tessa hasn't changed; still laying down the law,' Lizzie grinned as Jeff's mother ordered one of her grand-children to circulate with a plate of crispy cocktail sausages.

'She was telling me where to put the flower pots on the grave earlier,' Valerie chuckled. 'So I put them where I was bid.'

'The difference in you,' Lizzie smiled. 'The old Valerie would have bristled with indignation and told her where to put her pots.'

'I know. But it doesn't matter now. We really were our own worst enemies. I never thought I'd say it, but I'm glad we've made our peace.'

'YOLO,' said Lizzie.

'What?'

'YOLO! You only live once,' smirked Lizzie. 'Cool and hip, aren't I? Mind you, technically speaking, if you believe in reincarnation like I do, YOLO doesn't apply at all.'

'The next time I come back, I hope Jeff comes back with me and *stays* with me,' Valerie said, observing Lorcan deep in conversation with Finn and Dara, down by the gate that led to the beach. The rhododendrons and camellias were out and great splashes of red and pink blooms were a vibrant contrast to the dark blue sea. It was a warm May evening, and the sun was beginning to set, casting a pearly glow over the western sky. Valerie sighed. The view brought back memories.

'He's here, don't you worry,' Lizzie said kindly, knowing straight away the reason for the flicker of sadness that crossed her friend's eyes.

'I know, I just miss him,' she said, stroking the diamond in her engagement ring.

'Of course you do, why wouldn't you?' Lizzie said.

'But now, at least, I know that he *wanted* to marry me, and that means more to me than anything.'

'How is my son doing?' Briony appeared at the door and glanced over to the corner of the room where her baby boy lay gurgling happily in the Moses basket Valerie had passed on to Briony. Tessa came to join them and the four of them went over to admire the baby.

'Imagine, your granddaddy slept in that basket, and so did your mammy.' Tessa stroked her great-grandson's cheek.

The baby waved his small fists and gooed at them and they laughed.

'Are you going to be a boxer, Master Jeff?' Valerie slid her finger into his small hand and he grasped it tightly.

'No, my son is going to be an artist,' Briony declared.

'Let me take a photo of three generations of women for him to look back on,' Lizzie suggested, rooting for her new BlackBerry.

'Great idea,' exclaimed Valerie, slipping her arms around Tessa and Briony as they stood beside baby Jeff's basket.

'Smile,' Lizzie ordered and clicked.

'Aahh it's lovely,' Tessa said approvingly when Lizzie held it out for inspection. 'Perfect.'

'Wouldn't you wonder what has the baby so engrossed?' Briony said, studying her son intently, his gaze focused on something in the distance.

Tessa and Valerie looked at each other and smiled conspiratorially. They knew *exactly* who baby Jeff was looking at.

EPILOGUE

He studies the tableau in front of him. His Valerie with her arms around Tessa and Briony, laughing at one of Lizzie's witty remarks, all gathered around the baby. Lorcan watches from the garden, a smile of contentment crossing his features. Happy for his wife that she has found peace at last.

And then the joyful soul they have named after him, who has brought his loved ones such happiness, sees that he is there and greets him warmly. 'Hello. I knew you would come.'

'I wouldn't miss it. Well done you for going back. You're doing what you're meant to do already. Look at the happiness your arrival has brought. Look how you have united them. Forgiveness is a wonderful gift to bring.'

'Thank you for preparing the way for me.'

'I'll always be here if you need me.'

'I hope I won't forget.'

'Don't worry, I'll send you signs. Just look out for them and you'll remember.'

Someone else joins them. Great joy fills the air.

'Valerie invited you, how wonderful. And you have taught her what you promised and she has learned the lesson well. We all learn eventually that love and forgiveness are all that matter.'

'Better late than never.' The new guest repeats Valerie's recent words at the graveside, with a touch of humour. 'Her mother needed me and I wanted to be with her. It's a good party. All is well?'

'Yes, a great party and there'll be many more. All is very, very well. Everything is just as it should be.'

Acknowledgements

I never write a book alone and so it is with deep gratitude I thank 'my gang' for guiding this latest book. Jesus, Our Lady, Mother Meera, St Joseph, St Michael, St Anthony, White Eagle, all my Angels, Saints and Guides and my Beloved Mother who has brought me to a lovely publishing company, Simon & Schuster.

To my dear and precious Dad who takes such an interest and who makes me laugh heartily. To my sister Mary who minds me so well, and to all my family, a big thank you.

To Maureen, a wonderful godmother who has joined my mother in the heavenly realms, fly high and be happy. Thanks for everything.

To Yvonne and Breda who are always the first to read my manuscript and the first to pop a cork!

To Rachel and Maria Bellew, dear nieces, who keep me updated on toys and 'teenspeak'.

To Pam, Simon, Aidan, Murtagh, Joe, Helen and Cathy, shining beacons of Light and Inspiration who share a vision for The Field and the great adventure to come.

To Alil, always a phone call away, and to Tony and Darren, kindred spirits. To Geraldine Tynan, a wonderful, kind friend. And to Francesca Liversidge and Kevin Redmond who have always been so kind and supportive.

To Claudia, Mary Mac and all my writing friends for the phone calls, emails and cups of coffee. Always a treat to meet up and chat.

To Eileen, Carmel, Bernie and Ann in Flemings who always make us so welcome for the summer.

To Dee and Ray O'Callaghan for providing the most beautiful place in the world to write.

To my neighbours Ruth, Aengus and Naomi, and Angela, Dominic, Conor and Sophie, for all their kindness and for putting up with four months of hammering and banging while the builders were in!

Thanks to all at Gill Hess and co for their Trojan work. Helen, Simon and Dec, we're on a great new journey. Long may it last.

To all my dear Schusters, in every department, who have warmly welcomed me into their global family. It's a pleasure and a privilege to work with such an enthusiastic, committed, hard-working team. Maxine, it's been a joy working with, having fun with, and being edited by you on this book. You're very special and I'm very lucky. And to Sarah and Judith in the USA, home at last!

I'm very lucky also with my Lutyens & Rubinstein family, Sarah, Daisy, Jane, Anna, Juliet, and Felicity. It gets better and better, thanks for everything.

To Mr. Hannan Mullet and Grainne in the SSC without whom this book would not have been finished when it was. Thanks for fitting me in for the injections and for all the kindness over the years.

To Mr. Paul Moroney and Evelyn in the SSC, thank you so much for the foot op, and for all your kindness. Can't wait to get into high heels again!!!

To Mr. Paul Neale and Alison, who have dealt with a few 'dental emergencies' this year. Thanks for all your care over the years.

I couldn't let this opportunity go to pay one last tribute and say a very special thanks to Maeve Binchy whose generosity of spirit to all of us authors was a shining example and set the bar high. Rest in peace, you will always be with us in your wonderful books.

And last but never least, a big thank you to my dear readers who make it all worthwhile. I'm so glad to have met some of you on Facebook as well as at the signing sessions. And a huge thanks also to all in the book trade who have been wonderfully supportive all these years. It was great meeting some of you for that fun dinner in London. Times are hard and there is much change in our industry but onwards and upwards.

A Discussion with Patricia Scanlan

Q. **The three main characters in *With All My Love* – Briony, Valerie and Tessa – are all extremely different women. How do you feel about each of these women?**

A. Each of these women is deeply connected and has all the great attributes and human failings that we all have. They behave as many mothers and daughters behave. They're REAL and that's why I love them: flaws and all.

Q. *With All My Love* **is a very emotional novel and tackles heavy subjects such as death, betrayal and generation-long family secrets. Despite this, the novel is full of hope, love, and ultimately, redemption. Was it difficult to navigate all of this?**

A. Most of us have lived through such experiences and I was able to use memories of grief and sadness but also ones of joy, delight and forgiveness. And don't forget also this author has a VERY vivid imagination. How could I write otherwise?

Q. **Though all of the women's romantic partners play their parts, this novel is really all about the special bonds between women. Why did you decide to make this your focus?**

A. I don't mean this badly, honestly, (I love men and adore the character of Lorcan) but women are such *complex* beings with so many facets to their natures. How could I not focus on them?

Q. **What is your writing routine?**

A. My writing routine varies with the progress of the book. I start off gingerly and can be tempted away very easily, but then my characters start to take a hold of me and by the last quarter I can work for twelve hours straight. And woe betide anyone who comes near me.

Q. **Can you tell us a little bit about what you are working on next?**

A. There are many books written about great friendships but sometimes friends aren't all they seem to be and I wanted to explore that theme. The quote 'There comes a time when you have to stop crossing oceans for people who wouldn't even jump puddles for you' describes it perfectly in a nutshell. Nearly everyone has had a 'friend' who isn't really a friend. But why are some people so jealous of you that they will subtly undermine you and even betray you? I'm having a ball writing it!

Turn the page for Patricia Scanlan's
exclusive short story

'Life Begins at Forty'

'So you're absolutely sure that you don't want a surprise party for your fortieth?' Liz, my older sister, asks as we sit sipping vanilla coffee in the trendy new café on the seafront.

'I'm positive.' I grimace. 'It's bad enough being forty without having to make a song and dance about it in public.'

'Life begins at forty, honey,' she says airily, as our tuna wraps and salads arrive. 'Look at me: half a stone heavier, eyesight failing, grey hair multiplying at a rate of knots, everything going south and do I care?'

'That's because you've given up. You've gone Zen-like with all that yoga and meditation stuff you do. Well, I intend to fight ageing tooth and nail.'

'You do that, Amy,' Liz soothes, munching on a slice of cucumber.

I'm thirty-nine years, eleven months, two days and forty-five minutes old. I've a husband, Steve, and eight-year-old twin daughters, Molly and Daisy, all much loved. My work as a medical secretary in a busy consultant's clinic is varied and satisfying. Life is good. But I'm dreading forty.

'Well, we have to have some sort of a celebration now that you're joining the club. I told Steve I'd try and find out what you'd *really* like to do. Will we have a girls' night in Wicklow?' Liz asks.

'Don't you mean "ladies" or "women's" night?' I say dryly. 'Girls we ain't.'

'Oh, get over it. We all had to go through it. Wait until you're my age. If you think forty is bad, try forty-five.' My sister is unsympathetic to my trauma. Still, she's treating me to lunch and is trying to help my darling husband, who knows my feelings about turning forty, organize some sort of birthday treat. I shouldn't be so ungracious.

We finish our wraps and order more coffee and a selection of cream cakes. I promise myself it's my last fling. I've got to stop this comfort eating. I bite into a creamy éclair, pushing away the thoughts of calories and cellulite and all those other horrible, guilt-inducing words that are starting to become part of my vocabulary.

'We could go to The Romany Stone for a slap-up and stay the night in the cottage quaffing champers in front of the fire. No children and no husbands,' my sister suggests enthusiastically.

'Sounds blissful.' I agree. 'I'd love to get down to Wicklow for a few days. But do you think it would be a bit mean leaving Steve and the twins out of it?'

'Leave it to me. We'll have our girls' day and night on the Friday and Steve and the girls and Declan and my lot can come down on Saturday. We can have a barbecue if the weather is dry.'

I laugh. Only Liz could suggest a barbi at the end of February.

'The kids would love that. We can wrap up and drink hot ports on the deck. Jennie's all on for it,' Liz continues. Jennie is Liz's sister-in-law and she's a dote. She owns the holiday cottage next door to Liz, who has the one beside ours. We're like a little tribe in the small development of holiday cottages where we all decamp for weekends and holidays.

'You're on,' I say, enjoying the frisson of anticipation that my sister's plan generates. What could be nicer than a long, brisk walk on the beach and then sitting on the deck of our small beachside haven listening to the roar of the surf with family and friends, easing myself into my new decade?

'Great. That's that planned. I'd say Mum and Dad will be happy enough not to have to travel from Cork, especially if the weather's bad. We can have them to stay at Easter and have an excuse for another cake. It's so helpful of you to make organizing your birthday so simple.' Liz is clearly relieved that I've taken the hassle-free birthday route.

'Barbara won't be too happy that I'm not having a big bash.' I lick the last bit of cream off my fingers. Barbara is my sister-in-law. She's married to Steve's brother, Tom. She's a selfish, lazy cow – to put it mildly.

'And how *are* The Scroungers?' Liz queries as she pays the bill and shrugs into her coat.

I giggle. Liz shoots from the hip and always has. She's constantly telling me that I let Barbara walk all over me and that I should draw my boundaries. I know she's right. I'm just not good at that sort of thing. But it's getting beyond a joke at this stage. Scroungers is not far wrong when describing my in-laws. You know the type . . . the ones that arrive with one arm as long as the other, eat and drink you out of house and home and, half the time, buzz off without even doing the washing-up. My in-laws, Barbara, Tom, and their brats, Roger, Barry and Carla could give master classes in freeloading.

When Steve and I bought our small holiday cottage in Brittas Bay six years ago we certainly didn't envisage an invasion for two weeks every summer of the in-laws from hell. But that's what's happened. Barbara, Tom and Co. have come to see it as *their* cottage too.

They started arriving for weekends, unannounced, the first year. In the beginning it was fun. We all had young children. It was nice for the cousins to play together but it started becoming a habit. And Steve and I were doing all the shopping, cooking and housework.

Then Barbara started bringing the kids down for a couple of days during the summer holidays, and that was when I should have stepped in and nipped it in the bud. But I'm no good at being assertive. It's a huge personality flaw and I hate myself for my wimpishness.

Of course I plan all the things I'm going to say, like: *Barbara, I don't mind you coming the odd weekend with the kids, but my holidays are the only decent time I have with the girls and I want to be able to concentrate on them.*

Or: *Barbara, we really don't have the space, especially as the children are getting older*. This is not an excuse. We only have two bedrooms in the cottage and when the Keegans arrive, my pair end up on camp beds in the sitting room.

I keep saying I'm going to do something about it, but all I end up doing is moaning to Liz. I know she's sick of me. She'd have no problem putting the skids under Barbara.

Steve is ambivalent about it. He feels we're lucky to have a holiday home and should share our good fortune. I wouldn't mind so much if she pulled her weight, but honestly, Barbara is so lazy that I end up doing everything while she chills out on the deck reading and drinking wine. I feel *soooo* resentful because it's my holiday too. Her kids are allowed to run riot, and the poor twins invariably end up getting into trouble when it's Carla and the boys I should be shouting at.

It's all right for Steve to be so magnanimous. It's not his holiday that's ruined. We split our hols so that the girls can have the maximum time at the beach. Barbara invariably arrives for my two weeks. I feel my husband should back me up and speak to his brother about it, but he doesn't want to cause bad feeling.

'What about *my* bad feelings?' I ask resentfully, every summer as I prepare to go back to work after another ruined holiday. It's the one issue that causes conflict between us and I'm weary of it.

This year, I'm *definitely* putting an end to it, I decide as I emerge from the café into a howling gale that whips my hair from around my face and assaults my cheeks with its icy, stinging fingers. We don't linger. Liz has to pick up my twins and her youngest boy from school and I've to get back to work. I'm so lucky to have her. If it wasn't for Liz I'd have had second thoughts about staying at work once the girls were too old for the crèche. She's like a second mother to them. Barbara would never offer to help out if you were in a fix. She's one of life's great 'Me, Me, Me's' and that's probably why I feel so resentful.

The Keegans go on a foreign holiday every year. Barbara and her girlfriends jet off to Boston or New York for pre-Christmas shopping weekends. She's never once asked me to join them. On the rare occasions when I asked her to mind the twins when they were younger, she always had some excuse. I stopped asking but it took me a long time to realize that Steve and I were being used.

I know it's childish and silly, but part of me is glad that I'm not having a big party just so that I don't have to invite them. The Keegans press all my buttons and bring out the worst in me.

Fortunately, I'm so busy when I get back to work, I forget all about my in-laws and they remain far from my mind until I get a call from Barbara a few days before my birthday.

'Hi Amy,' she trills. My heart sinks to my boots. The only time Barbara rings is when she wants to moan or has something to boast about.

'So!' she demands. 'What are you doing for the big Four-O? Is Steve taking you away? Tom took me to Prague for mine.'

We're sick of hearing about the trip to Prague. 'No, it's going to be very low-key,' I say offhandedly. If she gets wind of the weekend in Wicklow, I wouldn't put it past her to muscle in, so I say nothing.

'Oh come on, no party, or even a meal out?' Barbara is incredulous.

'Just a cake with the kids. It's all I want, honestly. You know me, I hate fuss.'

But it's your fortieth,' she protests. 'Steve should push the boat out.'

'I didn't say he wasn't, Barbara!' I can't keep the edge of exasperation out of my voice. 'Look, I'm up to my eyes here today. I'll catch you again,' I fib.

'Oh . . . oh! Ok, I'll pop a card in the post for you then.' She's clearly disappointed.

'Lovely,' I say insincerely. 'Bye, thanks for ringing.' *'Phew!'* I think as I hang up. Then I start to worry. What if she hears of my night out with the girls in Wicklow? I resolve to warn them not to mention it to her if they see her. Bad humour wraps itself around me like a dark murky cloud. So what if I'm having a girls' night? It's none of her business. Why can't I just deal with it and say it to her straight out? Why am I such a wuss? Or am I just a thoroughly horrible person?

I try and forget about it, but it niggles and I bring up the subject with Liz that evening. 'Am I being a wagon? Should I invite her?' I grumble.

'Absolutely *not!*' Liz is emphatic. 'We are not spending our precious night listening to her wittering on about her new conservatory or her trip to New York and all the rest of it. Forget it.'

'Fine,' I capitulate happily, glad of my sister's authoritative stance. I don't feel such a heel after all.

My birthday dawns, dark and windy. I'm smothered with hugs and kisses from the girls and Steve's gift of a sapphire and diamond pendant brings gasps of appreciation from all of us.

'I thought it would match your eyes,' he says, a tad bashfully. 'You can change it if you don't like it.'

'It's gorgeous, Steve, I love it.' I'm thrilled with his thoughtful gift and kiss him soundly much to the girls' delight.

'Oohhh . . . kissy kissy!!' squeals Daisy. Steve laughs but I can tell he's pleased that I love it.

'We helped Dad pick it,' Molly assures me, slipping an arm around my neck.

'I couldn't have got a nicer present,' I tell her, basking in the joy of being so loved and cherished.

'Auntie Liz has a surprise for you, so you have to be dressed by eight o' clock,' Daisy informs me gleefully. I know Liz has something up her sleeve. She's told me to be ready to leave early. This is great, I think happily as I stand under the bracing spray of the shower while my darlings make pancakes for breakfast. Forty's not so bad after all.

'Where are we going?' I ask an hour later as Liz heads for Wicklow via the East Link.

'You'll see,' Liz replies smugly.

'You didn't take our exit,' I exclaim half an hour later, as Liz continues to speed along the N11.

'Just a while longer,' she soothes and I laugh. Whatever my sister is up to it's going to be fun. When we whiz onto the Arklow Bypass and she revs up to one hundred and twenty, comprehension dawns.

'Are we going to Amber Springs?'

'You bet we are. Happy birthday, little sis. I hope you're all prepared for a day of blissful pampering. I sure am. Jennie's meeting us there.'

A day at a luxurious health spa with the girls. What more could I want? Forty is getting better by the second.

It is the most perfect day. I'm massaged, manicured, pedicured and pampered to within an inch of my life. Then as the sun began to turn the Wicklow Hills pink and gold, we're chauffeured to dinner at a candle-lit restaurant and forced to drink gallons of champagne. Later, snuggled in warm dressing gowns in front of a blazing fire, listening to the roar of the sea, we watch the DVD of the second *Sex and the City* film, which I haven't seen, and guffaw at Samantha's menopausal rant in the souk. It's the best birthday I've ever had.

It's lovely to see the girls tumbling out of the car and

galloping across the dunes the next day. A brisk walk in the bracing, salty air, with the waves pounding against the shore, diminishes our hangovers. We adults laugh and joke as the kids investigate the treasure troves to be found among the rocks. I feel really happy and contented and look forward to our barbecue later on.

'Oh no! It's *that* gang!' Daisy scowls as recognition dawns when we see figures approaching along the beach.

I don't believe it. It was too good to last. Barbara is waving gaily and I hear Liz curse under her breath. A knot twists my gut. Not today, not them. Can't I have *one* day free of their unwelcome, intrusive presence? They're like ivy, smothering me, their grip getting tighter and tighter each year.

'Hey you guys, better late than never.' Tom declares expansively.

I look at Steve. He's not best pleased; I can see by the way a muscle gives a little jerk in his jaw and his eyes narrow.

'Steve told me you'd all gone to Amber Springs when I rang to wish you happy birthday. You had your mobile turned off. You never let on,' Barbara accuses with false gaiety, eyes like beady flints above her smile as she falls into place beside Jennie, Liz and me.

'I didn't know,' I manage weakly. I want to smack her.

'It was a birthday surprise for Amy, Barbara. My treat,' Liz informs her curtly.

'Oh! I could have joined you last night then,' she persists.

This is *too* much. Since when do I have to start telling Madam Barbara my every move?

'We were having a girls' night.' I hear myself say. 'I guess we didn't get to New York, like you and your friends. But Wicklow suits us fine. I just wanted to be with my two best friends.'

She inhales sharply and Liz flashes me an approving glance. 'Oohh I see,' she says snootily. 'Um . . . right. Well, Steve mentioned he was coming down for the weekend. We thought we'd come and give you your present.'

'That's very kind, Barbara. It's a bit of a trek up and down in the one day just to give me a present. It could have waited.' I'm feeling reckless now. She's not getting away with it this time.

'*Oh!*' She says again. She stares at me, not sure how to react. 'We brought the sleeping bags, we can doss on the floor,' she ventures.

I don't care anymore. I've had enough. I'm forty and it's time to draw a line in the sand. Literally. I draw a breath. I can sense Liz and Jennie waiting for my response. Bill is collecting periwinkles with the kids while Tom and Steve skim stones along the waves. Gulls circle and squeal. My lovely day is not going to be ruined. *Do it, do it*, a voice urges.

I swallow, hard. And then I think, *to hell with her.* She's not my friend and never has been. She's just someone I have to put up with.

'Actually, Barbara.' I come to a stop and eyeball her. 'I've been meaning to say this for a while. The cottage really is too small for all of us and I don't like putting the girls out of their beds. It's not fair.

And while we're on the subject, if you don't mind, this year and from now on, I'd like to spend my holidays alone with the girls. Our time is precious and the two weeks I have off in the summer is the only decent chunk of time I get to spend with them. There are nice, reasonably priced hotels and B&B's in the area. I'm sure you can find somewhere cheap 'n' cheerful to stay. And to be honest I'd prefer if you would give me advance notice if you were coming down, to see if it suits. It would make life easier for me in case we've made plans.' I'm on a roll. It's actually exhilarating.

Barbara lowers her gaze first. Two ruby spots stain her cheeks. 'I see,' she says tightly, thin-lipped. 'Fair enough.' She can't hide her shock.

'Great, that's sorted. Let's go and put the kettle on,' I

suggest brightly. I'm elated. I've done it. I've said my piece. I can't believe it. 'Let's head back to the cottage, I'm sure you'd like a cuppa before you head back home,' I say lightly but pointedly.

'Very kind,' Barbara says sarcastically, nostrils flaring. But I'm beyond caring. I raise my face to the sun's pale lemon light, feeling the merest hint of heat that reminds me that winter is over; the days are getting longer and we have much to look forward to.

'Well done, Amy,' Liz murmurs as we pour steaming tea into mugs ten minutes later. 'You should have done that years ago.'

'I know.' I sigh. 'I wish I had but better late than never.'

Barbara is chatting to Jennie on the deck; her brittle tones carry in on the breeze.

'She's raging, look at the face on her, it would stop a clock.' Liz chuckles as my sister-in-law flashes daggers in our direction.

I start laughing too. 'I don't care. 'She's a snooty little wagon and she's used me for the last time.'

'*Loved* the dig about New York. There was no answer to that. Forty suits you, keep it up,' my sister grins.

'When the Keegans get up to go, let them go,' I whisper to Steve in the kitchen a while later. 'I've had a word with Barbara. It's been a long time coming.'

'Fine,' he agrees. 'If that's what you want.'

'It is. My present to myself.' I smile at him. He hugs me.

They leave half an hour later. Barbara can't bring herself to give me her usual air kiss as her kids protest loudly. 'But we want to stay! You said we were staying.'

'Sorry, not this time,' Steve says firmly, seeing them to the door.

A weight lifts off my shoulders. I'm free. Roll on summer.